Under Color of Law

UNDER COLOR OF LAW

AARON PHILIP CLARK

THORNDIKE PRESS
A part of Gale, a Cengage Company

LIBRARY OF CONGRESS CIP DATA ON FILE.
CATALOGUING IN PUBLICATION FOR THIS BOOK
IS AVAILABLE FROM THE LIBRARY OF CONGRESS.

ISBN-13: 978-1-4328-9596-9 (hardcover alk. paper)

Published in 2022 by arrangement with Thomas & Mercer.

Printed in Mexico
Print Number: 01   Print Year: 2022

For my father, Michael Alan Clark
Your modest library offered me an
education I so desperately needed.
There's power in the words.
See you when I see you.

It is the mission of the Los Angeles Police Department to safeguard the lives and property of the people we serve, to reduce the incidence and fear of crime, and to enhance public safety while working with the diverse communities to improve their quality of life. Our mandate is to do so with honor and integrity, while at all times conducting ourselves with the highest ethical standards to maintain public confidence.

— LAPD Mission Statement

Whoever, under color of any law, statute, ordinance, regulation, or custom, willfully subjects any person in any State, Territory, Commonwealth, Possession, or District to the deprivation of any rights, privileges, or immunities secured or protected by the Constitution or laws of the United

States . . . shall be fined under this title or imprisoned not more than one year, or both; and if bodily injury results from the acts committed in violation of this section or if such acts include the use, attempted use, or threatened use of a dangerous weapon, explosives, or fire, shall be fined under this title or imprisoned not more than ten years, or both; and if death results from the acts committed in violation of this section or if such acts include kidnapping or an attempt to kidnap, aggravated sexual abuse, or an attempt to commit aggravated sexual abuse, or an attempt to kill, shall be fined under this title, or imprisoned for any term of years or for life, or both, or may be sentenced to death.

— US Department of Justice
Title 18, section 242
of the *United States Code*

PROLOGUE

May 31, 2010
Westchester, California

The night's air is warm, carrying hints of smoldering charcoal and mesquite. A day of grilled meats gives way to a night of cold beers and loud music. The summer energy is high, kinetic, and tends to last into the late hours. Like most of Los Angeles, Westchester has changed. The community is situated fewer than five miles from LAX. It's where commercial airline pilots and Boeing engineers used to call home. That was before white flight, when Westchester's proximity to Inglewood wasn't a problem because Inglewood was white, too, and back then, crime was nonexistent. Today, Westchester is a budding gang neighborhood, and the white residents who haven't left are refusing to let drugs and crime run them out of their homes.

The LAPD Pacific Community Division

is busy as usual. Like most divisions, Pacific isn't operating with an optimal number of officers — blocks once patrolled by three units now rely on one, and sometimes they require backup from Inglewood PD or the California Highway Patrol. A helicopter, an Airbus H125, shines its searchlight into backyards as our shop, a black-and-white patrol car, bombs down streets looking for a suspect: male, wearing a white T-shirt, jeans, and white sneakers. I ride shotgun with my field training officer — P2 Joey Garcia. Screaming sirens and chatter over the radio play like background music. I listen as best I can to the chatter, but I'm busy watching for oncoming traffic. As the patrol car approaches stale-red intersections, I have seconds to scan for incoming vehicles and determine if it's safe to enter.

"Clear," I say as we proceed through the intersection of Manchester and Sepulveda.

"Damn, I should have filled up," Garcia says.

There's one-quarter of a tank left.

We enter another intersection. Garcia slows, looks to his left for oncoming cars, and then mashes the pedal before checking for traffic on my side.

"Clear," I say, too late. If a vehicle were traveling through the intersection at high speed, we could be T-boned. Garcia is eager and tired, and he's getting careless.

"We've been driving for thirty minutes," Garcia says. "I think we fucking lost this guy."

"He's on foot. How far could he have gotten? He's probably hiding in one of these alleys."

"I'm not trying to shake these alleys tonight. We're clocking out in an hour, no matter what. I've got a thing tonight in Downey."

"What's her name?"

"It's a retirement party for an old copper."

"Oh yeah — who?"

"You wouldn't know him."

I scan the intersection: "Clear!"

"What the hell are we still at Code Three for?" Garcia pounds his palm against the steering wheel. "This guy is nowhere in sight. I'm slowing down."

"Copy."

"Get on the radio, and tell them to post up somewhere. Let air support do its job."

I call over the radio: "Downgrade. Kill the lights and sirens."

The lead patrol car's female driver responds in a distinct accent — a hefty bite of Boston. "Who says?"

"Garcia," I say.

11

The Bostonian slows the lead car and turns off its siren. We follow the unit into an alleyway.

"Of all the nights," Garcia says. "Best-case scenario is he gets hungry and peeks his head out of one of these dumpsters."

"And the worst case?" I ask.

"He dips into Inglewood proper and becomes their problem. Oh, wait, maybe that's the best case?"

Our units idle in darkness. Garcia's window is slightly down, so we can listen for anything out of the ordinary.

"Should we set a perimeter?" I ask.

"Just because you're a boot doesn't mean you have to act like one. Why the hell would we set a perimeter if we aren't sure where the suspect is? We'd just be guessing and wasting time."

"OK — sorry."

"And stop apologizing — that shit is annoying."

Garcia has a way of working my nerves, but I wouldn't dare pipe up to him. Talking back to a training officer is a sure way to get written up. Besides, Garcia is more hot air than anything else. I learned early to lock it down, rid my face of all emotion — anger, fear, and frustration. I don't let anything show: not to Garcia, and not to anyone we encounter on the streets because emotion can read as a weakness, a chink in the armor, and that can be the difference between life and death.

Garcia looks to me, checking my face for a reaction, a hint of a sting, but finds nothing. He taps his thumb against the steering wheel. I yawn. "Am I keeping you up?" he asks.

"No, sir." I keep scanning the neighborhood for our suspect as if Garcia's words matter less than a hovering gnat.

Westchester is growing ripe with crime, gang-related and otherwise, but for the most part, we try to keep criminal activity confined to Inglewood. It's the policy of the department to employ the grid tactic. We patrol heavily in the parts of Westchester where residents, mostly white, own homes. Our captain tells us to contain the zoo, so we concentrate our efforts on eight blocks. We're a wall that keeps the crime in Inglewood and property values in Westchester stable.

A call comes over the radio. A man matching our suspect's description was last seen about four blocks west of our location.

"We're on the move," Garcia says. He hits the lights and sirens and bolts ahead of the patrol car with the Bostonian and her partner, Monica Castillo.

"We're going to get this fucker tonight," Garcia says. "We're point now."

Joey Garcia is a hothead, quick with the tongue and OC spray. Other officers gave him the name Spray Can for spraying people without provocation. After Garcia sprayed a mother in front of her five-year-old son, our captain reprimanded him, and Personnel required him to attend anger management classes. His reform was short-lived, but his nickname stuck.

Garcia rounds a corner, and we get a visual of the suspect in an alleyway behind a grocery store. The man looks toward our car and then bursts into a sprint toward Lincoln Avenue, the south end of the alley. He's headed off by Boston and Castillo, who careen their patrol car down the alley and stop short of hitting him. With no place to go, the suspect circles with his hands up. Garcia shines the searchlight into his face and speaks into the bullhorn: "Hands behind your head!"

The suspect complies and looks somewhat relieved that the pursuit is over. He's sweating, struggling to catch his breath.

Garcia says, "Interlace your fingers and drop to your knees."

The suspect does as he's told and slowly

lowers to his knees.

Garcia turns to me. "I'm betting he's a banger. Look alive, Finnegan."

"Standing by, sir."

"Funny," he says. "I've never known a black guy with the last name Finnegan. What is it, Irish?"

"Yes. My father's roots, sir. Retired Sergeant Shaun Finnegan."

"LAPD?"

"Yes, sir."

"A legacy? Let me guess, you want to make chief one day?"

I nod silently.

"You legacies always want that shit. Well, first things first," Garcia says, staring at the suspect with eyes like daggers. "Let's see if we can make your daddy proud tonight."

Garcia steps out of the car. I follow. We both have our guns drawn and carefully approach the suspect.

"Lock your ankles," Garcia orders the man and then reaches for his cuffs as Boston and Castillo slowly approach with their guns trained on the suspect's chest.

"What's your name?" Garcia asks, holding his cuffs, ready to slap them on the suspect's wrists.

The suspect straightens his back and rolls his shoulders, puffing out his chest. "Fuck you," he says.

"Your name is *Fuck You*? That had to be hell on a kid growing up. What did they call you for short? Fucky or fuckhead? Maybe fucktard? Was that it? Fucktard?"

Garcia takes pleasure in antagonizing suspects; he says it's a perk of the job.

"Go to hell," the suspect says as he gathers phlegm in his throat, then spits into Garcia's face. A wad of saliva and white mucus lands on Garcia's cheek and drips down his chin. He slowly pulls a handkerchief from his pocket and wipes his face clean.

Something about Garcia seems to welcome the suspect's disrespect, and his peculiar smile makes me uneasy. When he looks to Boston, she gives him a subtle nod.

"I've got a nickname, too," Garcia says to the suspect, putting his cuffs away. "Want to know how I got it?"

Garcia wipes his face again for good measure and tucks the handkerchief into his uniform's pocket, taking his time.

"What the hell y'all waiting on? Just take me in, damn it."

Garcia pulls his OC spray from his belt's holder and sprays the suspect in the face. The man throws himself to the ground. He gags and moans.

"Name's Spray Can. Can you believe that shit? Not the most original, but I damn sure earned it."

The helicopter hovers above, shining its spotlight on the scene. Garcia waves four fingers in the air, signaling Code 4 — all clear. The helicopter drifts away, leaving us to see by the patrol cars' headlights and an amber streetlamp.

The suspect wheezes and dry coughs until his throat sounds hoarse. "I can't breathe," the suspect says.

"I guess you should have thought about that before you decided to boost cars."

Mucus collects at the base of the suspect's nose, and his eyes tear up.

Garcia continues to taunt him. "Easy now, Fucky. We don't want you to hyperventilate."

The suspect draws a deep breath and reaches out his hand. I'm unsure if he's reaching for help or trying to take hold of Garcia's ankle — either way, Garcia reacts as if it's an assault.

Garcia has a look, one I've seen before. I know what's coming. Another stream of OC spray. Garcia's face burns red; his forehead takes on a sheen. Time slows, and I find myself counting the seconds before he makes his next move.

One.

Two.

Three.

Four.

But Garcia doesn't spray the suspect. He holsters his weapon, pulls his baton, and strikes the man across the side of his face. Blood spurts and teeth jet from his mouth, scattering down the alley. The suspect is driven to the ground face-first. His skin breaks like a twisting vine above his eyebrows, and thick red flows into his eyes.

"Shit," I say loudly. Garcia's huffing, his shoulders rising up and down with each breath. I look to Boston and then to her partner; both are poised and ready — but for what? The suspect is down, bleeding. He isn't getting up.

"Go to the shop, Finnegan," Garcia says, pointing toward the patrol car.

"What — why?"

"It's a fucking order," he says. "Now go!"

"He needs a medic," I say. "Look at his face."

"Don't worry about what he needs. Just do what I'm telling you."

Garcia speaks as if conjuring a semblance of control, but his face tells another story. He's afraid — I know it — but not of the suspect. He knows he's gone too far, and it will be impossible to explain away the suspect's injuries. It's the kind of fear that sears like hot metal and sticks in the back of your throat. I can see the gears in Garcia's head grinding; he doesn't know what comes next.

Boston, a lanky white woman with alabaster skin, and Castillo, a short Latina with a boyish haircut, keep their guns drawn as if this man — semiconscious, a likely dislocated jaw — will rise to his feet and snap their necks.

"Take Finn back to division," Boston says to Castillo. "Garcia and I will take care of this."

Castillo holsters her gun. I don't move right away, still believing at some moment Garcia will come to his senses and call a medic.

"Let it go, Finnegan," Castillo says, pulling at my arm.

The suspect rallies the strength to say "Stop" and positions himself on his elbows and knees. Blood drips from his mouth to the concrete.

Boston pushes the suspect back to the ground with her boot's heel.

"It's enough," I say to Castillo. "We need to stop this." She's managed to lead me maybe four or five feet from the scene and continues to tug at my arm.

"I didn't hear him ask for a medic, did you?" Castillo speaks with assurance, and I realize this likely isn't the first time she's witnessed Boston violating someone's civil rights.

"We can't just leave," I say.

"I trust my partner. She has it under control. You should trust yours, too. Now, let's go."

"This is crazy," I say. "I'm going to call the medic." I pull my radio from my belt.

Castillo snatches it out of my hand. "You aren't going to do shit except get in that car."

"Officer Castillo, this is wrong," I say, trying to cut through the code of silence, the blue wall bullshit.

"As if you know what's right or wrong," she says dismissively. "Be smart — get in the car." She nudges me forward. "Go, Finn."

Silence falls like a shadow over us as I walk closer to the patrol car. I look back at the suspect again — his eyes are bloodied, as if burgundy dye had been poured into them.

I don't know what it is to be close to death. I don't know what it looks like on a person minutes before they succumb to it, but if it's anything like I imagine, the suspect is in its midst now.

He'll be lucky to survive the night.

CHAPTER ONE

Day 1, October 16, 2014

Her name is Tori, and we've been seeing each other for a month. It's the third night she's slept over, and I don't even know her favorite color. Last night, she held my hand in bed, the white of her skin against my brown, and said, "I like this, Finn. I think it's beautiful."

I didn't respond. I tried to be present, pretending I felt as Tori did, but she was dopey and idealistic, and I was miles away, thinking of two uncleared cases and how I needed to make time to visit my father. I don't doubt Tori believes that moment was charged. But we're strangers, and I prefer it that way.

I head to the bathroom. When I come out, I'm trailed by off-brand air freshener, and Tori's wearing panties and nothing else. She's flipping through my photo album, a tattered leather-bound archive of my past life.

"You cold?" I ask. "I can grab you a sweatshirt or something."

"No," she says, "I'm fine." She looks hungover, but it's nothing coffee can't cure.

"I've got hazelnut and breakfast blend — you interested?"

"Breakfast blend sounds nice."

"Give me a sec."

I'd say Tori is around twenty-five, but I don't trouble to ask. Her face is youthful, and when she smiles, it's brilliant white, and I'm sure she's had her teeth bleached. The face of a beer maiden — that's what I first thought when I saw her sitting in the dive bar, overdressed, glancing down at her phone. I walked in late, not the best move for a first date, even if we did connect on a dating app. Twenty-eight minutes late, to be exact, and I was surprised she hadn't left.

Deep-blue eyes, a beauty mark above her lip, smoky eye shadow, and ruby-red lipstick — she looked like LA personified. Golden blonde and smelling like spray-tan lotion. That night we kept the conversation on the surface, safe and genial. She told me of her German heritage, which was obvious by her looks and her last name, Krause, loosely derived from a phrase meaning *lover of alco-*

24

hol, which she found amusing given her affinity for stiff spirits. We talked about her growing up in Orange County and how she couldn't wait to leave and study at UCLA.

"The OC is gross," she said. "People there can be so ignorant."

Everything I know about Tori could fit on an index card, and I consider it plenty. But this morning I sense it's coming, the heart-to-heart, her desire to delve deeper.

"What's with all the pictures of buildings? What are these? Murals?" she asks.

"Street art."

"Don't tell me you painted these? They're ridiculously good."

"I did," I say, scooping fresh grounds into the coffee maker.

"You're serious?"

"That so hard to believe?"

"I had no idea you painted or were even artistic. I mean, this place is so bland."

I scoff. "Thanks."

"Why did you stop?" she asks with circumspection. "If it's like a sensitive artist thing, you don't have to answer."

Even though we've slept together, we haven't found a casual way to be in the same room unless intoxicated or in the throes of intimacy. It isn't Tori's fault. I know she tries, but I've constructed a wall that holds strong. No one gets too close.

And there is another possibility — we may not have much in common outside of sex and alcohol. "I didn't have time for it, or maybe I lost interest," I say. "I don't remember."

The coffee starts to percolate, and I pour myself some. I take a sip, making sure it doesn't taste scorched before serving it to Tori. The full-bodied brew slips down my throat, leaving warmth behind.

"This one is dated 2006. Is that the last time you did a piece?" She points to a mural of an old red streetcar carrying passengers in the 1940s, back when LA had better public transportation, families shared one car, and the air was cleaner. I painted the mural for the LA Preservation Society. I've always considered it one of my best.

"Probably."

"What was it like, you know, to paint something so big?"

"Tiring."

"Tiring? That's it?"

"I guess."

"But you made something out of nothing. Like it was something you dreamed up, and then you brought it to life," Tori says, her voice heightened with wonder.

"It was a long time ago. I really don't

remember."

"Well, you are full of surprises, Officer Finnegan." Tori's eyes are big, piercing blue crystals. "A street artist working as a cop — I can't say I've ever encountered someone like you, Finn."

I've been down this road before. The questions, the needing to know about my past. Tori sees me as a prospect of what could be. When people sleep together, it's like unwrapping a present on Christmas morning, not knowing if it's a gift they truly desire or if interest will wane. And when they find out it might be something worth their time and maybe even change their lives, they're grateful but cautious. Because no one really knows anyone — never after two weeks, and rarely after two decades, as was the case with my parents. My father kept my mother at a distance for most of their marriage, refusing to share his opus of secrets even as she lay dying.

"I don't know about that," I say.

"What do you mean?"

"Maybe it's the other way around? I was masquerading as a street artist, but I was a cop the whole time."

"You think so?"

"I've always been a cop, somewhere inside. I just needed that thing to push me onto

27

the path."

I make being a police officer sound storybook — the sanctified knight gallivanting through the countryside, facing down the dire and dark. It's some potent pantypeeler, but it couldn't be further from the truth.

"And what was that thing?" Tori asks.

I drink the last of my coffee and notice bits of grounds settled at the bottom of the mug. It's a bad look; I should invest in better filters. "Maybe another time," I say, knowing there won't be another time. "Coffee's ready."

"Wow. Are you shutting me down? OK, Mr. Officer."

"It's 'detective,' actually."

"Detective? You continue to impress." Tori flips her gilded hair, and it settles over her breasts. Her nipples peek through a few strands. She gently closes the photo album and puts it back on the bookcase next to tomes on Dadaism and the Baroque. "I take it black," she says with irreverence as she studies other books on the shelves: paperback novels, a Shakespeare anthology, and biographies on Van Gogh, Michelangelo, and other renowned artists.

I pour her coffee into my second-favorite mug and listen to her talk about her business as a dress designer. I envy her. Even when she breathes, it's trouble-free, not a tremble of worry in her voice. She's never been touched by real life, by tragedy. She's safe from the types of horrors I confront every day, the things that strip a person bare and leave them hollow. Tori moves through the world as if it were scripted in her favor. And though at times I want to, I'm not about to shatter her world with stories of the worst kinds of people and the things they do to the rest of us. For Tori and others like her, Los Angeles is an innocuous playground where bad things happen only to the lowly and unfortunate.

"You want to know something?" she says.

"What's that?"

"Don't take this wrong, but you seem too smart to be a cop."

"And what would you rather me be?"

Tori takes a long sip of coffee, and there's a few seconds of silence. I suspect she talks a lot when she's nervous, not always about anything important. "Well, I don't know. I'm just saying with the books you have and your love for art, I'd figure you for an art history professor or gallery owner."

"You got all that from my bookcase? I suppose if I had books on clowns, I'd make a good Bozo."

"Bozo?" she says with a half smile. "I'm not going to pretend I know what that is."

"He was a famous clown."

"See what I mean?" she says in a pitch that sounds like air escaping a balloon. "You would know something obscure like that. It's kind of hot."

"Thanks," I say, blushing, defenseless to flattery. "It's true, though . . ."

"What is?" She takes another sip of coffee, and I wonder if she's noticed grounds at the bottom of the mug.

"Police officers aren't geniuses," I say. "They're no smarter than most people. But the good ones pay close attention to details. They notice what most people never see."

"Is that right?" she says, looking skeptical. "So, what have you noticed about me?"

I'm sure Tori blackens her beauty mark with makeup, evocative of Marilyn Monroe, and like the tinsel starlet, her symmetrical nose might be the work of a plastic surgeon. And there's her ring finger, which bears a halo of discoloration. She said she's never been married and seems earnest. It could be the mark of an ended engagement. Bringing up Tori's romantic past can lead to a conversation I'd rather avoid, but what's most intriguing is Roxi, tattooed on her wrist. It's faded and lacks sentimentality. No cross, flowers, dates — just thin, cramped letters.

"Was Roxi a dog or cat?" I ask, pointing to her tattoo.

She looks down at her left wrist and grins like a child marveling at a magic trick. "I was a sensitive seventeen," she says, brushing her fingers over the name. "God, I loved that cat."

"You look like a cat person."

"Roxi could have been a hamster, you know?"

"I didn't get that feeling."

"A feeling told you she was a cat?"

"Gut feelings are important. Never steer me wrong."

"Uh-huh." Tori rolls her eyes. "Did you have a pet growing up?"

"No, we weren't exactly pet people." The sun breaches the clouds. The orange light pierces the window and strikes her face, revealing bags under her eyes. "But I had a goldfish for about a month. You sure you don't want a sweatshirt?"

"Nope. The coffee is keeping me warm." She brings the mug to her chest. "It lived only a month? You overfed it, didn't you?"

"We kept the fishbowl in the kitchen. One day it jumped out of its bowl and into the kitchen sink filled with hot dishwater. I think the water cooked it."

"That's too bad," Tori says. "I'm sure that bummed you out."

"I was relieved."

"Relieved? Why?" she asks, running her finger along the rim of the coffee cup.

"Goldfish don't live long. I hadn't grown fond of it yet, so I didn't have to worry about feeling like shit when it was gone."

"I see." She tilts her head, probably unsure of what to make of me.

"I've always respected that goldfish," I say, remembering its lifeless body drifting on the water's surface, encroached by sudsy bits of food. "Who the hell would want to live in a glass bowl, anyway? It was a prison."

"That's one way of looking at it."

"Is there another way?"

"Plenty of food. Clean water. Could've been a cushy life. And it beats the alternative, dying in dishwater."

I nod to appease her, knowing a fishbowl is far from a paradise.

"How long did you have Roxi?"

"Thirteen years."

"A good amount of time."

"It's never long enough when you love something," she says, her voice feathering to a soft whimper. "For a while, she was my world."

"Can't say I felt the same way about my goldfish."

"Sure, but I know you've loved something intensely. Like to the point of feeling you couldn't go on if that thing you loved weren't in your life."

I think about my mother, and Tori's eyes widen with a look of tenderness as if she could sense my thoughts have traversed to the past — a painful place. I quickly look at the analog clock hanging on the kitchen wall. "Traffic might be getting worse," I say. "A little more coffee for your drive?"

"I better not." Tori hands me the mug. "Besides, I'm sure you have better things to do on your day off."

"It's fine, really. I didn't want you to be late or anything."

"The best part of working for yourself is making your hours, but the last thing I want to be is *that* girl. I'll get out of your space."

Tori has pretty-girl problems, and I wonder what scars she's hiding. Because in a city like LA, there's a good chance she's been both someone's trophy and secret. And while we come from two different worlds, the one thing we have in common is the tenuous, marred tissue heartbreak leaves behind. I recognize the signs — the vulnerability, the trepidation, second to the insatiable need not to be lonely because a night with a willing stranger is worth a morning of awkward conversation.

"So," she says, putting on her bra, "I'm designing a dress for a client. An old friend. The wedding is next month . . ."

"OK," I say, worried about what comes next.

"She invited me, and I thought we could go together." She fastens her bra and adjusts the straps. "If you're free, of course."

"A wedding," I say, scrambling for the right words. "That's cool. I appreciate the invite, but with my job, it's hard to make plans. I'd hate to have to cancel on you."

"I get it." She walks over to a worn easy chair and gathers her clothes draped on the back. "I thought you might say that." She steps into her slinky black dress and pulls it over her shoulders. "Some other time, then."

The chasm between us is never more evident than in these quiet moments. I can't help feeling like a con man. Because, for our bullshit dalliance to be more than a twinkle, we'd have to be honest with each other.

"We good?" I ask, sensing Tori's disappointment.

"I'm getting a little old for the walk of shame," she says. There's sadness in her

34

voice as she works her foot into a glossy stiletto.

"What do you have to be ashamed of?"

"That we slept together, and I didn't even know your last name."

"You know it now."

"Yeah, I do," she says. "Things don't always go the way I see them in my head."

"We've got that in common."

"It's been a month, Finn."

"OK."

"I kind of need to know something. Are we dating, or are we just getting the poison out?"

"I — I don't know, Tori."

Tori hangs her purse's strap over her shoulder and walks toward me. "Don't you think we should figure it out?"

I rub my palms together, trying to think of a justification for why talking isn't necessary. A relationship with Tori — or any woman, for that matter — would be a disaster. But it's too early in the morning to have a conversation that will only end with Tori hating me. "All right," I say. "We can talk about it — later."

"I'll take what I can get," she says, resting her hand on my chest. "I'll call you."

"I can walk you to your car."

"It's OK."

"I prefer to see you out."

"I'm a big girl. I'll make it just fine," she says. "You worry too much."

I follow her out the door. "Looks like you've got a package," she says, pointing to a small box resting on the welcome mat.

I pick up the box and tuck it under my arm. I watch Tori walk down the hallway toward the elevator. Her heels click against the hardwood; then there's silence as she steps into the lift. She smiles at me, a trace of sadness still on her face.

I shut and lock the door, place the box on the counter, and walk to a large window where I watch Tori cross the parking lot and get into her car, a late-model Volkswagen Beetle, pearl white, with a rear spoiler. The Beetle reverses across the gravel lot and then drives down a narrow street toward the freeways.

Tori is a big girl, but LA can be a violent pill. Sooner or later, we all get a dose. If my father knew I was sleeping with Tori, or any woman sharing her skin color, he'd caution me: "If she were to go missing, you'd be the first one investigated. You being a cop wouldn't make a bit of difference. Something happens to a pretty white girl, all hell breaks loose."

My father and I both tend to see the bad

before the good, especially in people. Maybe it's a cop thing; he's retired LAPD and bitter to the bone. And me, I feel the only safe place is at home, in my loft. I've lived in this building for five years and never once had to flex on a vagrant or a prowler. Life here is uneventful. It's rent controlled, the tenants mostly artists. The units are considered live-and-work spaces, and people keep to themselves. No one in the building knows I'm an LAPD detective, and that's how I like it. One tenant, Christoph, remembers me from my street art days when I went by the name Du Sable. He thinks I freelance as a graphic designer. I learned early in my career that when people know you're a law enforcement officer, they either hate you or want you to fix their problems: a stalker ex-boyfriend, a cousin in immigration detention, the ubiquitous parking ticket. They tell you they feel safer with you around and ask to have your number, just in case they find themselves in a "situation." People always find themselves in situations, and they think cops do the job because it's a calling, a need to protect those around them — and some do. But there are those of us who need the paycheck, the medical insurance, the pension, and we only have time for other people's problems when we're getting paid to care.

I take a steak knife from the kitchen drawer, cut the tape from the sides of the box, and then run the knife through the tape in the box's center until I'm able to work it open with my hands. Inside, a tin of cookies, brownies in plastic wrap, and a note that reads:

Don't eat them all at once. Thinking about you.

Love,
Sarada

My work cell phone rings, and I know my day of leisure has come to an end. I answer; it's Mitch Beckett, my captain. We're friendly but not friends.

He tells me to get to Altadena. A body is on a popular hiking trail leading into the Angeles National Forest.

"How'd we catch it?" I ask. "Altadena is sheriff territory."

"We think the victim might be one of ours, an active recruit. We're still confirming, but from what we can tell, the kid was supposed to report to Davis Training Facility and never showed."

"On my way." I end the call, finish the pot

of lukewarm coffee, and hop in the shower.

After a quick scrub, I towel off and get dressed — a pair of jeans, a T-shirt, and hiking boots. I pack a sweatshirt in my gear bag, knowing the mountain air can get cold in the evening, and it may take until nightfall to process the scene. I put my Glock 22 into my gear bag with two additional magazines. I hook a pair of shades onto my shirt collar and walk out the door.

Outside, I open the trunk of my department-issued late-model green Mustang GT and put in my gear bag. The car was seized from a drug trafficker living in Silver Lake and had an aftermarket V-8 engine. I quickly became the envy of my unit, only adding to the disdain most officers have for me. I may be the most hated detective in the Southwest Division, and the officers at Pacific share the sentiment. It's not because I'm bad at my job or I can't close cases. I have an 87 percent clearance rate. But if you were to ask those I serve with, they would tell you I didn't earn my detective rank. They would say that I hustled my way to becoming a Detective I in the coveted Robbery-Homicide Division — that I bent the rules, forced the department's hand — and they wouldn't be lying.

See, I'm a good cop, but I fear I haven't been a good man in a long while.

It takes a little over an hour, and when I arrive in Altadena, Captain Beckett waves me down. I park next to two sheriff's SUVs and a black sedan with exempt plates. I hop out of the Mustang, open the trunk, take my weapon from my gear bag, and holster it to my belt. A few yards away, I see sheriff's deputies gathered at the trailhead. Crime scene tape is around the entrance. The deputies usher hikers and bikers through the trail's vehicle access.

"The winds are starting to kick up," Captain Beckett says, walking toward me. "They're calling for a storm later tonight. We need this scene processed and cleared out as soon as possible." He's of average stature, narrow shoulders, white, and balding. His bushy mustache hasn't completely lost its natural color and retains some of the coarse brown strands that once covered his head.

"You said the victim is a recruit?"

"We believe it's Brandon Soledad. Three months into the academy." Beckett rubs his hand against the nape of his neck and bats a fly with the other.

"Shit."

"Exactly."

The captain takes his phone from his suit pocket and displays a photo of the victim's ID. He angles the phone downward, directing it out of the sun's glare. "Got it," I say once I get a satisfying look at the picture.

"The deputy will drive us to the scene."

We walk toward the trailhead, where a sheriff's SUV is parked. "How far out did they find the body?" I ask.

"About a quarter mile down the trail."

We get into the back of the SUV. It's old, the seats worn to the springs. A young deputy climbs into the driver's seat, starts the vehicle, and drives us toward the crime scene.

The trail begins on a paved road lined by a long fence where a few cabins stand. Around the cabins are overgrown trees and brush. "We canvass the area yet?" I ask, looking out the window. "We know if people are living in these places?"

"The deputies collected statements," Captain Beckett says. "There are only about five residences with people living in them, and the rest are empty. They look to be old cabins and hunting shacks from when hunting was legal around here."

"What about the hikers' statements?"

"We're working on it. Most of those

people are pretty rattled. They have more questions than answers. There aren't many bodies that show up in this area."

Altadena is an unincorporated suburban community north of Pasadena. As a kid, I would hike the trails with my father and take in the San Gabriel Mountains' picturesque views. My father liked to say it reminded him of Northern California's rustic wine country: dirt roads leading to cottages and bungalows tucked behind trees that were older than our ages combined.

I suppose there are worse places to find a body, but there's no peace in dying alone up here.

"I think the sheriff was relieved when we showed up," Captain Beckett says.

"Why's that?"

"It's the body, Finn."

"Was it burned? Disfigured?"

"No — that's the thing. It might have been preserved."

"Preserved?"

"You'll see what I mean."

The SUV comes to a stop, and we get out. The area is densely wooded; the foliage blocks most of the sunlight. The earth is damp; moisture is in the air. A blanket of coldness surrounds me, and I feel chills. I don't know if it's the cold, wet air or the nature of the crime. The technicians move about, combing for evidence and taking photos of a set of tire tracks. The body is resting on the rocks of an embankment. A few feet away, a stream rushes below, and I wonder if it's the homicide scene or a dumping ground.

A technician taking pictures of the body is dressed in a blue LAPD polo and tan-colored cargo pants.

"Good morning," I say.

She looks at me like I don't belong and then looks to Captain Beckett for approval. "We good, Captain?" she asks. Beckett nods and returns to rubbing his neck. The technician moves away from the body so I can get a closer look.

I've learned the captain's neck rub translates in a few ways. He may be perplexed by the body's condition or where it's been found, or he can't wrap his head around the victim. For Beckett, some victims don't fit. He can look at a victim and get a glimpse of where they ought to be, maybe working retail, cooking dinner for their family, taking a swim lesson — anywhere but dead. It's not that people look like they deserve death, but some have faces that tell the kinds of stories that seem to end only one way, with them lifeless somewhere. Others

43

have faces ostensibly destined for more, and death is an unfathomable inconvenience. The faces of those victims can appear haughty, like they were thinking, *I'm too good-looking* — or too smart, too rich, too happy, too young — *to die now and like this.* But I don't concern myself with where they ought to be. I just need to know why they ended up dead.

"You're right about the body," I say. "Might have been kept on ice."

The victim's face resembles the ID picture, and he looks as if he died only hours ago, not days, but a temperature check of his internal organs will likely show otherwise. I think he was killed a day or so ago, and his body was likely dumped here once night fell. I presume a mountain lion or a wild boar would have gnawed on the remains. Though mountain lions are dwindling, wild boars still roam the woods in decent numbers.

The dead boy's head is shaved, his physique what I'd expect from a recruit. He's athletic, lean with well-defined muscle, but he's likely underweight, perhaps due to the academy's rigorous training, lack of sleep, and abundance of stress. Though he's of African descent, his skin is more grayish blue than brown, and he's nude. His genitals seem intact, and there's no visible trauma to his body. I take a closer look at his hands. There don't appear to be defensive wounds.

"Has the body been moved?" I ask.

"No one's touched him. I wanted to wait until you got here."

"Can you turn him over?" I ask the technician. She slowly turns the body over to reveal purple lesions on his upper back.

"Damn," Captain Beckett says.

"Let's order a rape kit," I say.

"What's that on his forearm?" he asks. The technician shines a UV light across the arm.

"It looks like scratches," I say.

"Looks like it," says the technician.

"Let's be sure to get close-ups of those."

"You think the suspect washed him in the stream?" Captain Beckett asks.

"He's too clean. There would likely be sediment. I'm thinking someone showered him, let him air-dry, and transported him here."

"But why here?" he asks.

"Not many streetlamps. The night makes a good cover," I say. "What about the rate of decomposition? I'd think there would be more signs."

"It's possible the body was temperature controlled, sir," the technician says. "The lesions could be caused by extreme cooling, similar to frostbite."

"Like refrigeration?"

"Or a freezer," the technician says.

"Cover him up," I say. "We'll wait for the medical examiner's findings."

"Yes, Detective."

Captain Beckett and I walk back toward the SUV. He's quiet, but I know he's thinking hard. "What is it, sir?"

"I want you to focus all your attention on solving this one — this is your priority now. I'm not saying to cut corners, but whatever you have to do to close this, I need you to do it."

"Pressure is on already?"

"When people heard he was a recruit, they got antsy. As I said, this sort of thing doesn't happen with us. Sure, recruits get into fights, maybe even get pinched for DUI, but the last one that ended up dead was almost forty years ago."

"How'd the sheriff know to call us?"

"The station received a tip. The caller said there was a body at this location, and LAPD would be interested."

"Man or woman?"

"Couldn't be sure," he says. "The voice was distorted. The caller might have been using a modulator."

"They triangulate the call?"

46

"All they know is it originated from a cellular phone. Likely a burner."

"Not much to go on, then. We'll need to get a sense of the victim's homelife . . . friends, family. Maybe someone wasn't keen on him becoming a cop."

"I'll have his personnel file faxed to you," Captain Beckett says as he works his neck again.

"Is there something else, sir?"

"He looks like a good kid," Beckett says. "He probably worked hard to get on board with us, and he goes out like this."

"I'll notify the next of kin."

"If there's anything you need, let me know. You have every resource at your disposal."

He prepares to walk back to the SUV when I say, "Captain?"

"What is it, Detective?"

"How exactly did Pacific catch this? It seems like this should be an RHD collar."

"It is. This is your new *special* assignment."

"I was under the impression I'd be headed back there next month."

"Your captain at Robbery-Homicide wants you to stay on with us. He thought this case would be a good fit for you."

"I see."

"It's a career-maker, Detective. And we know how you appreciate an opportunity to shine."

"Thank you, sir," I say, too annoyed to fake enthusiasm. I watch Captain Beckett climb into the sheriff's SUV to be driven back to his car. I prefer to walk back to the Mustang. It's about five hundred yards, and I don't feel like riding in the truck with Beckett. His smugness stifles the air.

Seeing the body resurrected memories I have to work to forget. I'd never let on in front of Beckett, but the recruit's flesh covered in flies, ants, and whatever else desires to feed on it does something to me that words can't explain. I feel sickened.

I've never doubted the brutality of this world, and I never will.

The forecast says Altadena will be a humid 80 degrees Fahrenheit today, with thunderstorms supposedly rolling in later. We haven't had rain in months. It shouldn't take long to process the scene. Hopefully, forensics will clear out before the local reporters get wind. The media has a way of sniffing out investigations like this and whipping up a frenzy, especially if they pull the race card.

The case's optics aren't great — a dead

black police recruit at a time when many black people don't trust or want anything to do with the police. If the victim's skin color has anything to do with him dying, it could turn the city upside down. It doesn't take much to remind Angelenos of past racism and injustice. For Los Angeles to flourish, people have to pretend that the city's racial discord evaporated like soot plumes from the aftermath of the 1992 uprising.

I drive the I-210 west to the 2 freeway and exit onto Ocean View Boulevard. My father lives in a condo in the Verdugo Woodlands, surrounded by the yuppies and new-money hipsters. He bought it in the late '90s, before the area was considered luxury living. McMansions and homes of faddish modern architecture surround his building. He says the new homes have ruined his view of the LA skyline. The only thing he doesn't complain about is how much his condo has appreciated.

I park on the street and enter the lobby. As usual, the door is propped open with a medium-size rock. I walk the stairs to the second floor; my father's unit is at the end of the hallway. I can hear the TV at high volume. I knock hard — the doorbell hasn't worked in years. My father asks, "Who is it?"

"It's Trevor."

"Just a second."

I can hear my father rummage around. Then he unlocks the door and opens it slowly to peek at me. He squints his good eye, then opens both wide and stares. "Pop, it's me."

"Boy, I know it's you — just trying to make sure. I can't be too careful."

He opens the door enough to let me in, then shuts and locks it behind us. "I see I didn't have to buzz you in. They used that damn rock again, didn't they?"

My father has complained to the home-owner's association about it. Like me, he gets paranoid about security. "Yes," I say.

"I'd wish they'd cut that shit out. Anybody could just come up in here," Pop says. "Dummies. Probably forget to lock their doors."

People never see a beast lurking until it's too late, but cops, we always do.

"I thought Shantelle was coming to clean this week?"

The condo is messy. Boxes that once held items purchased online are piled up near the couch. On the coffee table are stacks of books, dirty drinking glasses, and a bowl with crushed cereal flakes in milk.

"She was supposed to come today, but her son is sick," my father says, doing his best to tidy up. "I told her to come tomorrow."

He kicks a pizza box, possibly containing day-old crust and congealed cheese, at the foot of the couch. "Pizza?" I ask. "You're supposed to be watching your diet."

"You come here to lecture me on my nutrition?" Pop picks up a stack of magazines from the couch, carries them to the corner of the room, and drops them. Junk in Pop's condo moves from one location to another until Shantelle bags it and takes it to the dumpster.

"What difference does it make?" I ask, taking a seat next to him. "You don't listen, anyway."

Pop is moving slower than when I last saw him, and his vision may be getting worse. Glaucoma settled in his right eye years ago, and his cholesterol is steadily rising. If he cared a little more about what he put in his body, he'd be much better off.

"I just don't get it, Pop. You used to be —"

"I used to be what?" he asks. "Ain't nothing wrong with me. I'm doing just fine."

"Clearly."

He lifts his chin to size me up and postures

51

coolly. "Don't go letting that mouth of yours write checks your ass can't cash."

Looking at him in faded sweatpants and a filthy white tee covered in dried ketchup and grease stains that might be from the pizza, I might feel sorry for him if he weren't such a curmudgeon. And to think, when I was a kid, just him walking into a room could put a lump in my throat. He would tower over me, all five foot ten of him. But these days, Pop isn't so tall, having succumbed to an arching back, a hunch far too prominent for a man in his early sixties. He blames his frown lines around his mouth and eyes on his white father. "Black isn't supposed to wrinkle this early," he likes to say, usually after looking in the bathroom mirror. "Just another thing my father gave me that I never wanted."

Pop may blame his Irish father for his withered complexion, but I know the stress and sleepless nights is what aged him early. If my mother could see him, her tears wouldn't stop flowing.

God rest her soul.

"What brings you by, considering I hardly hear from you these days?" Pop says. "For all I know, you could be laid up somewhere shot. How shitty would that be for me to turn on the news and have to learn my son's been shot?" Pop lays his hands across his belly, probably unsure of what else to do with them.

I'll never forget the fear I had of those hands — bruised and cut from a hard day of patrolling, calloused and high-yellow. That's what older black people called our light skin, which Pop saw as a curse. Being fair was hard on us both, making me a target growing up. I was picked on daily. Kids' cruelty knows no bounds, and being tawny apparently meant I was soft. Maybe I was, but it wasn't because of my skin tone. But Pop had it much harder growing up biracial in Goldsboro, North Carolina. And it wasn't just growing up poor in the South that put a strain on life; he shared a home with a devil of a man.

"Say, Pop, you got a clean shirt?" I ask. "That one looks like it could use some bleach."

Pop looks down at the stains. "It ain't that bad."

One of my greatest fears is of Pop losing his mental soundness, becoming less anchored to reality. I convince myself if he's still doing laundry regularly, he's managing daily life, but I know clean clothes aren't an acceptable baseline for mental health.

"Well, if it bothers you so much," Pop

says, pulling off the dirty shirt and balling it in his arms, "I got a clean one in the back." Pop turns, preparing to walk the hallway to his bedroom in the rear of the condo.

Seeing Pop shirtless always puts a knot in my stomach. His back covered in scars: long, curving, jagged welts raised like wood glue dried across his shoulders, down his spine, and clustered low at his waist. Lashings from boyhood — belts, braided vine, wire coat hangers, and whatever else my grandfather happened to have in his hand. Pop told me that during one of my grandfather's drunken fits, he looked Pop in the eye and said having coons for children was the worst thing that ever happened to him. Then he whipped Pop until sunrise, finally collapsing, exhausted from the effort while his son lay bloody, unable to sleep on his back for a month. I wouldn't dare call my father a good man, but he never hit me — not to say he didn't want to plenty of times.

"Pop!" I shout. I listen as he knocks around in his room. "Can we turn this TV down? I could hear it from the hallway."

"Didn't realize it was that loud," Pop says, returning in a cleaner V-neck tee and then sitting down on the couch. He picks up the remote and presses a button until the ringing in my ears stops.

"You telling me people don't complain about the noise?"

"I don't know. If someone rings the doorbell to complain, it's hell on them because it hasn't worked for years." Pop laughs.

"I've meant to come by and see you. Things have just been hectic at work."

"More so than usual?"

"I guess."

"It's the morale, son. The tide is changing."

"The tide?"

My father slides a newspaper over to me and taps his finger over a story. "You hear about this?" he asks. "A veteran officer in Compton decides to stop responding to calls on her beat. The first couple of times she'd get the call, she'd show she was responding, arrive, and sit outside the location, just watching. After a couple of minutes, she'd drive off. The next few times, rather than respond, she takes her lunch, tacos from a stand she liked. Do you want to know what she said when they discovered she wasn't doing her sworn job?"

"What?"

"They worked it out on their own — didn't need her. Showing up to a house she'd been to twenty times before wasn't going to make a difference in those people's lives."

"It's a dereliction of duty."

"Some officers realize that all this meaningless bullshit isn't helping. We show up, we take notes, warn, scorn, arrest, and for what? Same shit happens again the next day."

"It's the job, Pop. You know that better than anyone."

"And what about this? They aren't even firing that officer for killing Eric Garner," he says, pointing to the TV accusingly, as if it, too, is culpable. A news broadcast shows cell phone video of Garner — a man of stature, dark-brown skin, fighting to keep his balance as NYPD officers mount him. An officer locks his arms around Garner's neck; he gasps for air. They force him to the ground. His last words: *I can't breathe.* Then his body goes limp. "NYPD still has the cop that choked him on paid leave. The man ought to be fired already. Every time I see Garner's daughter, I just want to get out there with her and march right up to NYPD headquarters and tell them . . ."

"Tell them what, Pop?"

"Tell them the truth, that's what. Murder is murder whether you've got a badge or not."

"What is marching going to do? It's just a bad situation — an unfortunate thing. The best thing to do is retrain the officers and penalize those in the wrong."

Pop sits up straight and turns to get a better look at me, his eyes tearful. "It's murder!" he says, his voice quivering. "LAPD had the good sense to outlaw that choke hold decades ago. And I promise you nothing will happen to that officer or the others, not a damn thing. Someone has to teach these bastards that they can't get away with killing us."

"Easy, Pop. Relax."

"Don't tell me to relax, damn it. Hell, you need to be less relaxed. Look at you, sitting there like this shit ain't all kinds of wrong."

"I know it's wrong! I'm living in this world, too."

"Oh, please. You've always been funny."

"Funny?" I say, glaring at Pop. "What's that supposed to mean?"

"You know — head in the clouds. Too busy painting and blasting all that rock music to know what was really going on. I blame that damn private school. But your mama just had to —"

"You trying to go there? Leave Mom out of it."

"I'm just saying . . . I tried to teach you.

Lord knows I did . . ."

I can't remember the last time Pop got this worked up. "Maybe I should go."

"Sometimes, I can't see how you wear that badge."

I throw my hands up like I gambled and lost my rent in poker. "There it is! I knew it was coming. Every time I come here, you make me feel like shit about my job."

"Maybe you should feel like shit sometimes."

"Man, I don't have to listen to this." I get up from the couch and prepare to leave.

"Not because you're a police officer — you're one of the best they've got," my father adds. "But maybe you aren't doing enough to change things. You're one of the youngest detectives on the force, and you've proven yourself time and time again. Now, you've got to use that position to do some good."

"You know it's not that easy," I say, nearly tripping over fast-food wrappers and a pile of junk mail as I inch my way to the door.

"I never wanted you to take the same road I did. I saw a different path for you — living a good life, doing your art, owning a gallery, or something."

"You never gave a damn about my art, Pop."

"Says you."

I take another step toward the door, kicking the trash from my path. I'm close enough to open it and walk out, but I don't. "Look, things are how they are, and I'm not interested in changing them," I say. "If being a cop was so bad, why the hell did you stick with it so long? And don't give me that you had me to take care of. I pretty much raised myself."

Pop rubs his knees like they need soothing and then brings his hands together in his lap. "Your mother was gone. I did what I had to."

"You had choices. You could have been a bus driver or worked maintenance for the city — something, anything!"

"And lose my pension? Not a chance. I turned a blind eye to a lot of shit on the job, but things are sharper than ever now. I'm going with Shantelle to one of these rallies downtown."

I return to my seat on the couch. "I don't think that's such a good idea," I say, working myself into a calmer state, thinking Pop might listen to me if I show composure.

"Last I checked, peaceful assembly is still a constitutional right."

"What if an officer recognizes you out there? You know how embarrassing that would be for you?"

"I'm retired. You mean it would be embarrassing for you," Pop says, head cocked, looking at me sideways as if my words couldn't be more foolish.

"For both of us."

"I don't care what they think of me. I'm doing what I need to do, especially since you won't."

"And since when are you and Shantelle so close? You're going to rallies together now?"

"We enjoy each other's company, and she listens to me. We're likeminded. Besides, there's nothing wrong with having a life partner."

"Pop, she's twenty-six."

Pop jockeys his head back and forth as if to shake loose any suggestion I've put forth that he doesn't agree with. "How about I don't judge who you spend your time with, and you do the same for me?"

"I'm just looking out for you."

"I prefer you looking out for yourself."

I sigh and drop my head. Our history, baggage like deadweight, stacks on my shoulders.

"What's really on your mind, son? Not that I mind you coming over, but the last time you showed up this on edge, you were circling a tricky case."

Though we bicker, Pop still knows me the best, and this dead recruit's case has me more tense than usual. "A recruit has been killed," I say. "We found the body this morning in Altadena on that old trail we used to hike."

"By the Jet Propulsion lab? That's the sheriff's jurisdiction."

"The sheriff doesn't want any part of it — the victim was LAPD, so it's our case."

"Murdered?"

"Looks like it, but we won't be sure until the autopsy results come in."

"Can't say I've ever come across a case like this one. And they have you working it solo?"

"My partner is still on FML."

"It sounds like it could be high-profile. Why aren't senior dicks in RHD working it with you?"

"Captain Beckett thinks I can handle it."

"Can you?"

"Yes, Pop. I can . . . I just don't want to miss anything."

"Keep it textbook. Start with the victim. What do you know about him?"

"Midtwenties, male, black."

My father chuckles and shakes his head disapprovingly. "Well, there it is."

"What's that mean?"

"The department isn't run by fools. A black detective working it looks a lot better than some white boy or Latino. It makes it seem like the department is more dedicated. Fully invested because the victim looks like you."

"Or maybe it's because I'm good?"

"They wouldn't have assigned it to you if you were shit. But this thing has the makings of a bad headline."

"You were never very good at this."

"At what?"

"Being supportive and encouraging, stuff fathers should be good at."

"Don't be that way. I have always told you the truth. No matter how hard it was for you to hear, I have always been straight with you. And that's more than what my father did for me," Pop says. "I'm just saying that a case like this has the potential to get messy. I can tell you what I'd do, and that's follow the evidence. I'd follow it like it's the North Star. No matter where it leads, I'd just keep grinding along until something breaks loose."

I'm transported back to my early days on the force, when my father doled out advice handily and with pride — insights on investigative techniques, street tactics, ways to contend with departmental politics. But that was before I became a detective. Once I got the "fancy gold shield," as Pop likes to say, the advice stopped flowing freely, and when it did come, it was begrudging, sheathed in resentment.

My work cell phone rings. "I have to take this. It's work." Pop nods, and I answer. "Finn."

"It's Ahn. I have information on your DB."

Grace Ahn is a good officer. She's squared away and thorough, but her matter-of-fact delivery has earned her the nickname "Friday," like Joe Friday from the TV show *Dragnet.* The only thing you can expect from Ahn is the dry-biscuit facts. "The academy faxed over the victim's personnel file," she says. "Recruit Officer Brandon Soledad — age twenty-one. He was residing in West Covina with his parents. I can text you the address we have on file."

"Sooner, the better."

"Roger that, sir. I'll do it now."

I end the call. "Have to go, Pop."

"All right."

"I don't agree with you attending the rally, but I get why you're doing it. Just be careful."

"Always, son. Always. And you watch your back out there." It's the closest we get to *I love you.*

I leave my father to the messy condo and twenty-four-hour news cycle.

Chapter Two

Before getting on the freeway, I stop at a coffee shop and buy a pastry and a cold brew. Given the hour, I anticipate the traffic on I-10 going east toward West Covina to be horrendous. Most Angelenos abhor traffic, but I've grown used to it. The price of life in the city. I use the time to think and process particulars in cases, the major questions — like what Brandon Soledad was involved in. Who did he cross? Why the hell was he nude?

I slam on my brakes to avoid rear-ending a minivan that stops short. "Damn it — idiots! Can nobody drive in this city?"

Pop was right; my dander is up. He thinks I'm out of touch and, though he'd never say it, maybe even a sellout. I recognize that Brandon Soledad looks like me. Hell, he could have been me. The lone black male in the academy. Black officers joke that they let in only one black man and one black woman per class — the raisins in the bran flakes. Most academy classes poorly reflect the demographics of the city. They are abundantly male, white, Latino . . . and conservative. And now, that one black face who weathered the scrutiny for an opportunity to make the city better is dead. So sure, my dander is up because to be a black cop in Los Angeles — or anywhere else, for that matter — requires the ability to walk a tightrope. And the moment you miss a step, stumble, or go crashing below, you become another example of why blacks don't belong in the ranks.

So, every day, I have to prove I'm worthy of wearing the gold shield, and I do so proudly. I have no shame in the badge. It means something, and sure, it gives me more confidence when driving at night or jogging in the early morning, wearing a hoodie through a white neighborhood. It can be satisfying to pull out the badge and watch the faces of those who question my presence go from authoritative sneers to hopeless confusion. The badge lets them know I belong to something stronger than their racism and prejudice, which can be hidden behind their liberal sensibilities. As my father likes to say, there are no liberals in LA, just white folk and whiter folk, and both will call the police when they see you in their neighborhoods.

It's after four p.m. when I arrive at the Soledad residence in West Covina. The house is an older, two-story bungalow in a gated community. I had no trouble getting through the gate, but the attendant looked worried when I told him where I was going. It's possible he knows the family or was a friend of Brandon's.

I step onto the porch. Two rocking chairs sit abandoned, squeaking in a gentle wind. Death has followed me from Altadena. I'm its messenger. Once I tell Brandon's family of his demise, death will reside here. It's just how it works; this will be a house of mourning until Brandon gets justice, and then death will leave, only to visit upon another hapless family.

I ring the doorbell and wait.

"Everything dies," I whisper, repeating something my drill instructor told me in the police academy. A heartless way of looking at death, but it has always stuck with me. It's how I get in the right mindset to deliver the worst news of all: a death notification. I tell myself that death is a part of life. What makes Brandon's death any different from his home's brittle brown lawn? It's dead, too, a victim of the months-long drought.

Or from the flower bed that's fallen barren? Dead rose petals, yellow and white, collect below thorny stems.

Some cops might argue nothing — just another dead man, another black body. But Brandon's death just feels different. It's more than a routine homicide; he's far from the common victim.

Things are quiet. Maybe no one is home?

I begin to look around. I move to the side of the house, where I meet a cherub angel of ashen stone fixed on a patch of rotting grass. If it weren't for the Southland's pestilent dryness, water might be pouring from the angel's palms into the basin, but the sun has cracked and beaten the basin to powder.

I go back to the front door and ring the bell again. A hand pushes a curtain back from the window. "Who is it?" a woman's voice calls.

"Police, ma'am."

The door opens slightly. "Police? May I help you?" she asks.

"Good day, ma'am. I'm with the LAPD. I'm here about Brandon Soledad. Are you his mother?"

I show her my badge. She puts on the rimless glasses that hang from her neck by a bedazzled chain and leans in for a closer look.

I repeat the question: "Is Brandon your son, ma'am?"

"Yes. I'm Brandon's mother," she says, opening the door fully and stepping onto the porch. She's a brown-skinned woman, petite and middle-aged, and she's wearing what my mother called a housecoat. I remember my mother wearing one often and, drearily, she died in hers.

"Is there something wrong, Officer?"

"It's best we speak inside, ma'am."

"Should I get my husband?"

"Yes, ma'am. I think you should."

Inside, the woman leads me from a tiled entryway to the dining room. "Earl!" she shouts. A man appears at the top of the stairs. He's somewhat heavy with a beard, dressed in a sweatshirt and jeans. He's slue-footed and takes his time coming down the stairs — each step is deliberate and sure.

"Who is this, Marla?"

"He's with LAPD, Earl."

Earl approaches me, and I quickly extend my hand. "Detective Finnegan, sir." We shake briefly, and then Earl draws his hand back.

"Earl Graves," he says. "You're a detective?"

"Yes."

"I didn't know you were a detective," Marla says. "What's this about?"

"It's best we're all sitting, ma'am."

"Let's just hear it," Earl says. "If you're going to tell me what I think you're going to tell me, it ain't going to make a difference who's sitting or standing. So, come on, out with it."

"Earl, what are you saying?" Marla asks.

"They probably kicking Brandon out of the academy. He's done something, hasn't he?"

Earl speaks the way my father would, presuming the worst. Thinking it had to have been something his son did to cause me to show up at his door. "No, sir," I say. I look to Marla, knowing the next words I say might break her. "I regret to inform you that we found your son's body this morning."

Marla takes her husband's arm to steady herself. "Oh, Lord," she says. "Lord — please, no. No!"

"What do you mean found?" Earl asks.

"His body was discovered in Altadena this morning, off a hiking trail."

Earl sits down in a tan leather recliner, leaving Marla to lean on the chair's headrest, sobbing. "Brandon wasn't a hiker,"

Earl says, his arms across his chest, hands shoved upward in his pits, shrugging his shoulders as if a cold draft has chilled him.

"We don't believe he was hiking, sir. His body may have been put there."

"You saying he was murdered?"

"It's a possibility, but we can't say for sure until the autopsy results come in."

"That can't be right," Marla says. "None of this sounds right. I think you all have the wrong person. Brandon is one of you. You're supposed to be looking after him now."

"We recognize he was a recruit, Mrs. Graves. And we're trying to understand what might have happened. Is there any reason he'd be in Altadena? Maybe around that area?"

Marla pulls a chair from the dining table and slowly lowers herself down onto the cushion. "Lord — why, Lord?"

"I couldn't tell you why he'd be in Altadena," Earl says, getting up from the recliner and shoving his hands into his pockets. "Brandon said he was going to study with a few classmates. Nothing out of the ordinary. He always studied with the other recruits."

"And when was the last time you saw him?"

"Couldn't say for sure. Maybe a day ago. We all keep strange hours around here. I work the late shift at a warehouse, and my wife is an in-home nurse."

I take out my notepad and pen and begin to write. "You notice anything strange, or did he seem unlike himself?"

"No. He said he had some things to take care of, and that he'd see me later."

"And you, ma'am?" I say, looking to Marla. "When did you see him last?"

Marla runs a finger under her eye, catching a string of tears and sweeping them away. She weeps, a sorrowful sound that only death can bring. "Same as Earl," she says in a broken voice. "A day ago. He was leaving the house as I pulled in. Didn't say much to each other besides hello. Had I known it would be the last time I'd see him, I would have . . ." Earl rubs Marla's shoulder, more of a heavy patting than a comforting caress.

"Any particular classmate he might have mentioned studying with?" I ask.

"I think it was more of a group thing, but you can look in his binder," Earl says. "He usually wrote his schedule in there."

"Thank you. Can I see Brandon's room?"

I follow Earl upstairs to Brandon's bedroom, a small space left of the staircase. The door is slightly ajar. "It might be a little messy. Brandon was never one to keep his room straight. His car, on the other hand, meticulous. That something they force them to do in the academy — keep their cars clean?"

"Yes, sir. There are random checks to make sure their vehicles are in order."

"I knew it," Earl says with the exuberance of guessing the right answer while watching a game show on TV. It's these odd moments — outbursts and exchanges — that mark the beginning of it, coming to terms with a dead loved one. A clean car? That's what this poor man is thinking about? Yes. Because it's better than thinking about Brandon taking his last breath and his body rotting in the woods.

"This may take some time," I say.

"OK," Earl says. "We'll be downstairs."

"Before you go, can I ask you another question? It might be a little personal."

"Go ahead."

"Were you and Brandon close?"

"As close as we could be, given the history. Brandon was my stepson. Marla had him from a previous relationship. We started living together when Brandon was going into high school."

"How was that transition for him?"

"It was tough, but he adjusted."

"And his biological father?"

"Marla doesn't talk much about him, but I know Brandon tried to find him once. The guy was in and out of rehab. Last I heard, he was living somewhere on Skid Row. Marla said he wasn't worth a penny with a hole in it. Of course, not knowing his daddy was hard on Brandon. And we just couldn't connect the way I'd hoped."

"You know his father's name?"

"Ishmael Soledad." Earl pauses, rubbing his head. "You all going to tell him his son is dead? That's if you can find him."

"I'll make every effort to try," I say, reaching into my pocket and taking out a business card. I wish I could offer more, like assurance I'll find who killed Brandon, but the LAPD advises against such claims because nothing is guaranteed. "Here's my card in case you can think of anything else that may be helpful." I hand Earl my business card, and he looks it over, running his finger across the raised ink.

"How cool would it have been for Brandon to have one of these? Detective Brandon Soledad. Has a nice ring to it, huh?"

I nod. "Yes, sir. It does."

Earl's eyes begin to well; he quickly turns before a tear can fall and walks downstairs. I enter Brandon's room. It's typical of a young man his age. There's a small flat-

74

screen TV with a video game console on a stand, copies of hot rod and police-related magazines, and video games stacked like a tower on his dresser. There's a bookshelf with framed photos, trophies, and plaques commemorating his achievements in football and track and field. His framed high school diploma hangs on the wall, along with posters of hip-hop artists, pop stars, and brown-skinned models clad in bikinis, stretched out on white-sand beaches.

On a desk is a laptop and books about law enforcement and LAPD history. Next to the laptop is his academy binder. I flip through. Inside is the schedule planner Earl mentioned. I turn a few pages and see the name Marlena Sanchez circled with the words *study session* written next to it. Sanchez may be a fellow recruit, but I won't be sure until I get a class list. Brandon's Smurf uniform is in the closet — a sky-blue military-pressed collared shirt and navy trousers, still wrapped in clear plastic from the dry cleaner. The Smurf is for training and helps recruits get in the habit of caring for their uniforms once they graduate and are sworn in.

My eye catches a few photos pinned to a message board above the desk. I remove a photo of a young Brandon and a man who might be his father, standing in front of a house. I look at the back of the photo. There, written in blue ink:

Westchester, CA — 1998
Me and Daddy

I look around the room a few minutes more before leaving with the binder. Downstairs, Earl is comforting Marla over tea. "You get what you need?" he asks.

"Yes. You mind if I take this?" I ask, holding up the binder.

"No, we don't mind . . . if it helps you catch the bastard that did this to our son."

"Ma'am," I say. Marla looks up, eyes seared red. "How long did you live in Westchester? I saw a photo upstairs of a house."

"Yes, I lived there for about fifteen years with Brandon's father. That was before the alcohol and drugs got the best of him, and I had to kick him out. We moved here when Earl and I got married two years ago."

"Did Brandon always want to be a police officer?"

"He talked about it. You know, the way boys sometimes do. Either it was joining the police or fire department. I guess he got serious about it around eighth grade, about the time he started playing football."

"Thank you, ma'am. I'm very sorry for your loss. You'll need to come down to the coroner's office to make an identification. They will call you to schedule a time to view the body."

"Wait," Earl says. "Y'all aren't even sure it's Brandon?"

"We're sure, sir. It's more of a formality. Someone from the department will be in touch to provide resources and information about grief services. If you need anything, please don't hesitate to contact me. You have my card. I'll see myself out."

"Detective," Marla says, "you're going to find out what happened to our son . . . no matter what, right? I know enough about police work to know these things don't always get solved, and we need him to matter to you."

"Yes, ma'am," I say with affirmation. "I will do everything I can to find out what happened to Brandon and those responsible."

Marla exhales softly to a sigh, and I consider how much faith she's putting in me.

I leave the house and get into the Mustang. My head is warm, swirling, and there's an intense pressure at the bridge of my nose and the base of my neck — a squeezing, burning pressure.

Anger like this can be blinding. I need to stay focused, keep it textbook, as Pop said. Let the evidence lead.

I drive back the way I came. It's never easy providing a death notification, no matter how many times I do it. It's the one thing I genuinely hate about the job, but it's unavoidable. Whether by homicide, car accident, suicide, or any other means, when people die, there's always some officer who has to shelve their humanity, fight the urge to cry with the loved ones, and tell them the person they loved isn't coming home, ever. It only makes sense that police officers drink to intoxication, have a slew of mistresses, or take up race car driving or amateur boxing — all those bottled-up feelings have to be worked out some kind of way.

I approach the gate to exit the subdivision. There's a small security booth. The attendant I encountered on my way in steps out and signals for me to roll down my window. I roll it down halfway, enough to hear him. "You a cop?" he asks. He's young and tall, with dreadlocks and an umber complexion.

"Why do you ask?"

"It's about Brandon, isn't it?"

"You two were friends?"

"Yeah. We went to high school together. Brandon helped me get this job. He's good people, steady looking out, you know?"

"What else can you tell me about him?"

"This some kind of background check or something? I thought he was already in the academy. You all running double and triple checks on brothers?"

"Not exactly. Brandon ever mention a Marlena Sanchez to you?"

"Ah, the shorty from the academy. That's what this is about?"

"So, he did?"

"Sure, but can't you just chat with him about it?"

"That's not possible."

"Why?"

"I can't disclose that. But I assure you, whatever you tell me is only going to help Brandon, not hurt him."

The attendant dallies and then asks, "Can I see your badge?"

"Sure," I say.

I lower the window more and hold the badge so he can see. He bends low to the car, studies it for a moment, like he's questioning its authenticity, and says, "OK. Cool."

"So, can you tell me anything?"

"I don't know if he'd want me talking behind his back."

"Brandon signed away that authority when he joined the LAPD. He'd want you to comply. I'm sure of that."

"All I can say is nothing funny is happening between him and Marlena, no matter what homegirl may have told you. Brandon said hooking up with a fellow recruit in the academy is forbidden, and he's not about to mess up his career before it even gets started. But after the academy, well, that's fair game, right?"

"Yes. That's fair game. Did Brandon say anything else about Marlena?"

"Only that she's fine as hell and makes the days go by faster."

"When was the last time you saw Brandon?"

"Maybe a few days ago. He said he was going to go meet up with some of his classmates. Haven't seen him since, though. Figured he comes and goes when I'm off the clock."

"What's your name?"

"J. D."

"Thank you, J. D."

"No problem." J. D. gives a weak-wristed, highbrow salute. "I still don't know why he signed on with you all, though."

"Why's that?" I ask.

"The way brothers is catching slugs these days by boys in blue ain't no joke."

I consider how to respond, given I'm still hot over the discussion with my father. "Maybe Brandon joined to try and make it better. Just because things are one way doesn't mean that's how they have to stay."

"Yeah," J. D. says, putting his hands in his pockets. "You right . . . if I see Brandon, should I tell him you're looking for him?"

"That won't be necessary," I say, rolling up the window before driving away.

I merge onto the 10 freeway, headed west. Traffic is moving, but slowly. I dial Ahn and wait. "Ahn," she answers.

"It's Finn. I need one more favor."

"Yes, Detective."

"See what you can dig up on an Ishmael Soledad. He's likely had some priors."

"Last known address?"

"Somewhere in Westchester. He's possibly homeless, now. Might be on Skid Row."

"Copy."

"Thanks, Ahn."

By the time I get downtown, it's after three

o'clock. My work cell rings — it's Ahn. "Go ahead," I say.

"Got a possible address for your guy, Soledad. My Brother's Keeper."

"The halfway house."

"3315 South Alvarado Street. You were right about the priors. Drug possession, misdemeanor assaults, and he got picked up twice on a Fifty-One-Fifty."

"You're the best. What did I get you for Christmas last year, Ahn?"

"Socks, sir."

"That's it?"

"Lotto tickets were inside the socks."

"You win?"

"Nope, but the socks are comfortable."

I end the call and turn onto Alvarado, one of the oldest streets in Los Angeles. It's seen better days, but the same can be said for the entire city. Businesses like El Toro Carniceria, La Flor Panaderia, and Moneda Lavanderia now contend with homeless encampments that have sprung up a few yards from their doors. Human beings live like scavengers in one of the country's richest cities. To our shame, Angelenos have accepted it as normal — people living in hovels made from nylon tarps, newspapers, and plastic garbage bags to keep out the rain. Buckets of feces next to discarded mattresses. Disparities like this have become an epidemic throughout the city. Homelessness is a part of LA's nomenclature. It's as routine as celebrity sightings, movie premieres, and police chases on TV. And the gap between those who have and those who don't only grows wider.

The inhabitants of this city are strong, resilient. And far beyond the Westside's boardwalks, beaches, and boutiques, or the vulgar garishness of Malibu and Beverly Hills, or the Valley's tract homes, galleries, and cineplexes exist neighborhoods like Jefferson Park, West Adams, Baldwin Hills, and Central Avenue — meccas of black and brown life that echo a past that risks being blotted out, redrawn, and built up by those who envision a much whiter Los Angeles.

I was ten when Pop decided to show me the city in all its beauty and squalor, what he called the real LA, and I fell in love with it. It was his day off, and we drove down El Segundo Boulevard. Pop was joncsing for brisket and smoked sausage. Our destination, a small parking lot in the rear of an old stucco church. I knew it only as the Barbecue Church, but I'd later learn it was called Holy Assembly Church of God. It was where Pop and other black officers took their Code 7 meal breaks. And as we pulled into the parking lot, I could smell mesquite and charcoal, meat searing on the grill. Patrons and officers, mostly black, were joking and laughing as they stood in line to put in their orders. A tall man with diasporic brown skin, sweating in a cap and apron, stood tending to a smoking barrel. I didn't see the officers waiting for service as cops or agents of authority. Rather, I saw them as black men who were a part of something important, comrades in truth and honor, and I felt like I was home.

"Trevor, this is what I protect every day I'm out here," Pop said as we sat in the car, watching the man flip slabs of meat and then slather them with sauce. "I don't care if these people have a million dollars in the bank or a dime in their pockets. Every life out here matters."

Pop would later tell me on the ride home, the car smelling of beef and chicken, "People of all walks make LA special. And just because they don't live in a fancy house or drive an expensive car doesn't mean they don't deserve protection and can't be treated with dignity and respect. But never forget, some people for the life of them, can't be decent. They give LA a bad reputation and have to be kept in check."

I nodded, holding the Styrofoam containers of food and thinking this was a good day with my father, a day I'd hope to remember forever. And I felt great pride and shame because, in my ignorance, I had taken to believe what I had seen on TV. I was seven when I began watching the news in defiance of my mother, who cautioned me. "Careful watching that garbage. It'll have you believing all black people do is rape, steal, and kill," she said. There were stories of gangland massacres, footage of neighborhoods overrun with drugs, LAPD officers holding black men at gunpoint. I hadn't thought of the people who called these neighborhoods home, the everyday people living their lives. It was easy to believe in the single story, narrowly drawn to evoke fear in prime-time news watchers, packaged for consumption by those afraid to leave their suburbs and venture south of the 10 freeway.

Then the lesson was over, and Pop said, "Hold that food good," never taking his eyes off the road. "You drop it, you'll be eating brisket off the floor mat."

"Yes, sir," I said, locking my arms around the containers.

Driving north on Alvarado, I merge into the turning lane and brake at a stoplight. I look out the passenger side window and see a wet dog, legs caked in mud, working to shake itself dry. A woman wearing a thread-bare blanket like a shroud emerges from a cardboard shelter and offers the dog scraps of food from her hand.

I can't remember the last time I saw a self-less act, or maybe I just stopped noticing them. But the woman's gesture makes me smile, and it takes the jarring honk from a two-door coupe behind me to realize the light has turned green.

I make a U-turn and park in front of My Brother's Keeper. The halfway house is an older clay-colored building with a stoop and a rusted fire escape that zigzags the building's front from top to bottom.

I approach a white man wearing a filthy green military-style coat with a braided beard down his chest. He's loitering in front of the building and looks nervous when my detective shield reflects the sunlight and bounces gold in his direction. "Ah, shit," the man says. "What is it now? Enough with the rousting already."

"I'm not here for you."

"Hope you got a warrant. Otherwise, you ain't getting in."

"You supervising this place?"

"I'm security."

"What's with the cup?"

The man jiggles a red plastic cup, the kind suburban kids divvy out at parties filled with beer and whatever else. "Annual donation drive," he says with a bullshit grin.

"Right. How much you got so far?"

"A few bucks and some change."

I reach into my pocket and pull out a five-dollar bill, dropping it into the cup.

"Seriously?" he asks, looking at the bill, unimpressed.

"I'm looking for someone. Ishmael Soledad. You know him?"

"Who's asking?"

"Detective Finnegan. LAPD. It's important I speak to him. I heard he lives here."

"What's he look like?"

"You either know him, or you don't."

The man slides out of the sun to seize a small square of shade. "I think I've heard the name. He's a black fella. Comes and goes."

"When did you see him last?"

The man halts, his mouth shut, and then sticks out his hand. I shake my head, annoyed, and drop another five-dollar bill into his cup. "Two months ago," he says.

"What?"

"He got kicked out, fell off the wagon."

"Two months ago? How can you be sure?"

"Because that's when I moved in. I'm the one staying in his old room," he says proudly. By giving me the runaround, he made himself an easy ten bucks.

Can anybody be trusted these days?

"You know where he is now?" The man hesitates again, waiting for me to pull another bill from my pocket. "Not a chance in hell," I say. "If I have to, I'll toss this place. I'm sure we'd find a handful of felonies."

"All right, all right. No reason to get nasty. Ishmael is probably back on the street," he says with a shrug. "Ask around Skid. Maybe you'll find him."

Fifty blocks of bleakness — that's what cops call Skid Row. They say all it takes is two days in the Row, and you're likely never to leave. The first day, you get your lay of the land, maybe keep to yourself, thinking it's temporary, just one night, and then you'll find a shelter. But the shelters are full, and by the second day, things are looking hopeless. Then someone blows meth in your face and tells you for a two-dollar hit, you can forget you don't have a pot to piss in. You figure, hell, a few hours of bliss isn't so bad. A few hours turn to days, and soon you're hooked and turning tricks or trafficking dope through the encampments just to feel that bliss again. It's an American nightmare on full display.

Walking through Skid Row's tent cities means avoiding garbage, urine, feces, and used needles scattered on the sidewalks. There's so much trash in the storm drains — cans, bottles, cardboard, and plastic — that flooding is imminent when the hard rains come, adding to the putrid conditions.

As I walk closer to the tenements, I'm met by a wretched odor of filth and maybe the faintness of death. It isn't rare for bodies baked for days to get pulled out of tents — OD victims, suicides, slayings, and those who die from medieval plagues. Last year a priest contracted a flesh-eating disease while providing free health care and meals to the Row residents. Other volunteers and even some police officers have been stricken with E. coli and staph infections.

A black woman, hair matted and clumped with dirt, sits on a curb in front of the Good Shepherd Mission. "Spare some change for an old woman?" she asks.

"Depends."

"Oh, you're looking for something," she says assuredly, pushing back her hair. "I can do that, but I should get cleaned up first."

"No — I need information."

"OK."

"Ishmael Soledad. You know him?"

"Sure, I know him. Muthufucker owes me money."

"Can you take me to him?"

"You gonna help me get my money back?"

"Dolores?" Officer Jerimiah Colton's voice is commanding but easy as he approaches from the Good Shepherd Mission. He's a tall man, plummy skin, who's no stranger to a bench press. He's been patrolling Skid Row for decades and is somewhat of a legend. "Baby, what are you doing?" Colton says in a lyrical way I've only heard black men speak.

"Helping this nice man find Ishmael."

"You eat yet?"

"I was waiting for Junior to come and get me."

"He's getting food around the corner with the missionaries. Why don't you go join him?"

"OK," Dolores says as she gets to her feet and fights to keep her balance.

Colton and I watch as Dolores bumbles down the street, jerking and rocking as if caught in a strong wind. "You must be new," Colton says. "Everyone knows to check in with me before coming down here."

"It was off the cuff. Part of a case I'm

working."

"What's your name?"

"Trevor Finnegan."

"Jerimiah Colton."

"I know who you are, sir. I'm pretty sure the whole department knows who you are."

We shake hands, and Colton looks at my badge. "Detective. Not every day we get a gold shield down here. You said you're looking for someone?"

"I am. Ishmael Soledad."

"Soledad is that way." Colton points down an alley. "He stays in the blue tent. I can make the introduction, and after that, you're on your own."

I nod, and we head toward the alley. Tents made from plastic sheeting, cardboard, garbage bags, and Styrofoam are cluttered about, leaving a small path stretching from each end of the alley for walking.

"How long you been a detective?" Colton asks.

"Not long," I say. "Two years."

"A hotshot rookie!"

"Not really. Still learning the ropes."

"Well, even veterans like me are still learning. These streets teach me something new every day," Colton says, waving to a man wrapped in a blanket, eating beans from a can.

"How long you been out here?"

"Twenty-two years and counting."

"Nearing retirement?"

"Nah. I've managed to save a few souls. If I stop now, this place gets worse overnight."

"I couldn't imagine that."

"Even in hell, there are some good days, Detective."

Stoned inhabitants move around in tents, their legs and feet sticking out from the unzipped holes, exposed to the harsh and unforgiving sun. We reach the end of the alley, and Colton stops in front of a blue tent. "Ishmael — you in there?"

"What you want?" Ishmael asks. His accent is of the Caribbean, but I can't place where.

"You got a visitor. Someone here to talk to you."

"I ain't got no money," Ishmael says. "Tell them I'll pay when I can."

"This isn't about money," I say.

"It's always about money," Ishmael says.

"Look, this can go on for a while. I have to get back. You good?" Colton asks.

"I can handle it."

"I'll be over by the mission if you need me."

Colton walks away and heads toward the other end of the alley. "He gone?" Ishmael asks. "I don't trust that man."

"Yes, he's gone."

"He smiles too much. Never trust a man that shows that many teeth."

Colton's toothy smile fits with his brand of policing — the neighborhood cop who uses compassion first to deescalate and defuse potentially dangerous situations in the encampments. I'd bet half my paycheck that it's been years since he's had to draw down on anyone. It's evident that people on Skid Row respect Colton, and respect goes a long way on the street.

Ishmael pokes his head outside the tent. His face is oil-smudged and sandy, and his lips crack white and blistered. He looks at me from toe to head and crawls out of the tent. He's a short man, gangly, in tattered clothes. "Who are you?" he asks.

"Detective Finnegan."

"You police?"

"I am."

Ishmael turns on his heel and runs in the direction of the mission.

"Stop! I just want to talk."

Ishmael doesn't stop.

I draw a deep breath and run after him. I haven't had to chase anyone in some time, and after a few seconds of sprinting, my lungs burn. Ishmael passes the mission and rounds a corner, headed toward another encampment. My step is short from not running as often as I should, but I keep him in my line of sight, only a few paces behind. Just as I close in, Dolores appears in front of him, with a younger man who's holding a slice of pizza and bottled water. Dolores grabs Ishmael and spins him like a top, adding a strong shake. She pushes him to the ground. "I want my money," Dolores says.

Ishmael staggers to his feet. "I ain't got it, like I done told you."

"Then Junior gonna fuck you up."

Junior is a large man with rosy skin and a baby face that makes me wonder if he's any older than eighteen. There's something simple about him — the way he stares every which way, unable to focus until he hears his name. "Junior," Dolores says, "put the food down."

"But I'm hungry!"

"Finish it after. You need to show this lying muthufucker what's up."

"Don't touch him," I say. "He's with me."

"I am?" Ishmael asks.

"And who the fuck is you?" Dolores asks.

I flash my badge. "Detective Trevor Finnegan. Now, back away from him."

Dolores and Junior take a few steps back and let Ishmael collect himself.

"It's about your son, Ishmael. We need to talk."

"Brandon?"

"Yes . . . Brandon."

"Another time, then, deadbeat," Dolores says before grabbing Junior by the arm and leading him back toward a food truck surrounded by missionaries wearing red T-shirts.

"Why'd you run, man?"

"You're a cop," Ishmael says like it's the only logical answer. "A cop nobody knows coming around here ain't never good."

"Someplace we can talk?" I ask.

Ishmael nods. "Follow me."

"No more running, deal?"

"Yeah, no more running."

I follow Ishmael back toward the mission, and we head down a walkway to the rear of the building. He leads me through a gate to a small courtyard with a few patio tables and benches.

"We can sit here," he says.

I glance over at the gate's entrance and see Colton standing guard. I give him a nod.

"So, what is this about my son?"

"I'm sorry, Mr. Soledad, but your son is deceased."

Ishmael stands up, placing his hands on his waist, revealing his protruding hip bones. "Dead?" he asks, beginning to pace. "My son is dead — you've come to tell me this? Yes, yes — you have. Why else would you have come? I see now — you've come to tell me he is dead."

"We found his body this morning. I'm very sorry for your loss."

"How did he die?" Ishmael asks, his body twisting, contorting in unnatural ways, perhaps seized by a spasm.

"We aren't sure, but we believe he was killed."

"I hear your words, and I know you're real," he says, waving his arms the way I've seen people in church do when they've caught the holy ghost. "I want to see his body — I want to see my son."

"It'll be some time, Mr. Soledad. After the autopsy is completed."

"Autopsy?" he asks. "I know that."

"When did you last see Brandon?"

Ishmael sighs. "Many moons ago. He was just a boy. His mother didn't want him coming around looking for me, but I managed to catch the bus to where he was playing football. I watched the entire game. He was something — so gifted."

"Brandon was a police recruit," I say. "He was a few months away from becoming a police officer."

"He was going to be one of you?" Ishmael asks, returning to the bench and taking a seat.

"Yes, sir. He was doing well. We think he would have made a fine officer."

"Was it because of me?"

I stare with confusion.

"A junkie father. That does something to a boy, and now he's dead," he says with fleeting resolve. He slides off the bench and looks to the sky. "Where I grew up, when people die, we burned a fire in their honor." He opens his eyes wide, stares into the sun.

"Mr. Soledad," I say with concern, "you don't want to do that."

He refuses to look away. I look for Colton, who is about twelve feet away from the gate and moving closer.

"Mr. Soledad, please think about what you're doing." The longer Ishmael stares, the tighter his fist balls. "Mr. Soledad — please!"

"What the hell is going on?" Colton shouts, breaking into a jog.

Ishmael finally diverts his eyes to look away. When he turns to face me, his eyes are red, and milky fluid has formed in the corners. "Shit," I say. "We need to get you some medical attention."

Colton enters the courtyard. "What the

hell did you do, Soledad?"

"It's my penance. I have to atone — I have to atone."

I follow as Colton guides Ishmael out of the courtyard and radios for a medic. He sits Ishmael on the curb and walks over to me. "What the hell did you say to him?" Colton asks.

"His son is dead. He was killed."

"You came to Skid Row to tell a man his son was killed? People don't take bad news well over here, in case you haven't noticed."

"His son was a recruit — one of us."

"I see."

"If I were in Ishmael's shoes and Brandon were my son, I'd want to know."

"Well, thank God you aren't in his shoes."

"He going to be all right?"

"I got an RA coming to check him out. Never thought he'd try to blind himself, but nothing surprises me anymore. It's a shame. That man used to be a marine."

I pull a business card from my pocket and hand it to Colton. "Let him know if he needs anything, he can find me at Pacific."

"Yeah, sure, Detective. Next time your work brings you this way, be sure to call me first," Colton says, snatching my card before walking back toward Ishmael, whose eyes are closed as he mumbles to himself.

CHAPTER THREE

By the time I arrive at the Pacific Division, it's almost nine p.m. As I drive into the secured lot, I see news vans and reporters loitering in front of the station.

Pacific is not my usual division, but my partner, Crickets, and I are on loan from the Southwest Division. Crickets graduated from the academy six months before me. Word is she earned the name "Crickets" because when she got nervous, she could never answer a question fast enough for her drill instructor, and he would shout, "All I hear is crickets, damn crickets!" Her real name is Sally Munoz, and under pressure, it still takes her forever to answer a question, which makes her awful on the stand when a defense attorney has her in the crosshairs.

Crickets has been on family medical leave for a few months now because of her new baby. Before her departure, she and I worked out of a modular office, a nice way of saying "trailer," for the past year. We've been on special assignment — we lent our expertise to the Pacific Division after a homeless man rummaging for food found two Mexican immigrants' bodies in a dumpster behind a pizza parlor. The case went cold: no witnesses or useful tips despite the $2,000 reward. The investigation is considered active, but that's more of a technical distinction — it's dead in the water. Since then, there have been other cases but nothing with the gravitas of Soledad.

I get out of the car and walk toward the building's rear. The savvy reporters know where to stand to get a look at officers coming into the station from the parking lot designated AUTHORIZED PERSONNEL ONLY.

A reporter notices me and shouts: "Is it true the body of an LAPD officer was found this morning in Altadena?"

The reporters know enough to come to the Pacific Division; they were likely tipped off by a crime scene tech or sheriff's deputy, but the details are wrong. Soledad was a recruit, not a sworn officer. Still, it's a bad sign that reporters already know what they know. For the next few hours, they'll be outside the fence, fishing for more information. The thirsty cops will pass their business cards to the vultures to exchange information for cash or perks.

"Got a couple of tickets to the game this Sunday. What do you say?" the reporter asks.

"You must be a damn fool." I wait before entering the building, staring the reporter down. "Get the hell out of here," I say.

She flips me the bird before walking away.

The only way to combat case leaks is to keep the investigation close to the vest. An officer who takes a keen interest in the case will be iced out, and since I'm not talking, the reporters won't have much to go on.

Inside, the station is old — muted concrete walls and wood paneling. There's a perpetual odor that lingers in the air, like an old damp closet or basement. Even with all the bleach used to mop and wipe down the walls, the odor never goes away.

It's an average night. Officers are booking the usual — drunks, homeless, sun-damaged prostitutes, and wannabe gangster types. I pass a shabby teenager mopping the lobby. He's wearing an orange vest with reflective yellow trim.

"A little late for community service, isn't it?" I ask Javier Perez, the desk jockey. "Isn't there something educational the kid could be doing?"

"It isn't detention, Detective, and they fit them in whenever and wherever they can."

Perez is an overweight P3 who decided the desk was the best place for him after taking two rounds in the chest during a foot pursuit. They never found the suspect, and Perez didn't have the heart to hit the streets again. Since then, he's become an even lazier officer than when he was working a beat.

"Can I have him sweep your office next? I'm sure it could use some freshening up."

"I'm good, Perez."

"By the way, Captain Beckett and two suits are looking for you. They're in the captain's office if you want to have a look-see."

"How long have they been in there?"

"Twenty minutes, tops," Perez says. "Probably has to do with the shit ton of reporters camped out in front of the station."

"Yup."

"Could be trouble, but it's nothing you can't handle, I'm sure."

"I guess we'll see."

"You'll dance around like Cassius Clay, ducking and dodging like you always do."

"His name is Muhammad Ali."

"He'll always be Cassius to me," Perez

says, smirking.

"Yeah, right."

Perez mumbles, "Asshole."

I pretend I don't hear it and walk to the station's rear to the captain's office. Two sentries in dress blues are guarding the door, and I realize top brass is inside. I show the sentries my ID and one officer, a young white man with clean-shaven freckled cheeks, knocks on the door. He waits until he's told to open it and enters the room while I stand outside with the other sentry, a dark-skinned man with his eyes trained to look past me.

The officer comes out of the room. "You can go in, Detective," he says.

I enter to find Captain Beckett and two other high-ranking officers drinking brown liquor from tumblers while one draws from an e-cigarette. I recognize an Asian American man with a square jaw and the most severe hair part I've ever seen as the deputy chief from Valley Bureau Homicide; he used to be a sergeant here in Pacific. The only woman in the room is Captain Rivera. I've seen her expressionless face pictured on numerous recruiting brochures. She is the first female captain to head the police academy; her staid deportment isn't surprising, given her rank and the shit she's likely had to put up with in the department to achieve it. "This is Captain Rivera from the Training Division, and you know Deputy Chief Wong, don't you, Finnegan?" Beckett asks.

"It's nice to meet you, Captain," I say, "and it's always good to see you, sir."

Neither Wong nor Rivera makes an effort to shake my hand.

"How about we skip the pleasantries?" Wong says. "We're here on behalf of the chief."

"I don't follow."

"The chief wanted us to speak with you to stress how important it is you don't fuck up this investigation."

"I don't plan on it, sir."

"It's a little late for that," Wong says. "Local news media got the word. Perhaps you saw them on your way in?"

"I did."

"What Wong is trying to say is that this needs to remain contained and controlled," Captain Beckett says.

Wong takes a drag from his e-cigarette and puffs the smoke in my direction.

Beckett adds: "We need you to make a statement."

"A statement? We don't know anything yet."

"Doesn't matter," Wong says. "You go out there, and you calm the fucking waters."

"He was my recruit, and I don't want anything to jeopardize solving this thing," Rivera says. "But you need to recognize how delicate this is. You've got a dead black recruit at a time when black people aren't very trusting of police officers. Could be a PR nightmare."

"It's possible Soledad was targeted because he was a recruit, not because of his race."

"You better hope that's the case," Rivera says, "because LAPD can't afford for the city to lose confidence in us. The last time that happened, fifty people died, and LA faced over a billion dollars in property damage."

"I understand."

"Do you, Finnegan?" asks Wong. "Because this case isn't just another way for you to leverage a promotion. We all know how you got here. You aren't fooling anyone."

"I'm the police, same as you. I'm only interested in justice for Brandon Soledad."

"Oh, that's where you're wrong. I earned my rank."

"Let's leave the past where it belongs, shall we?" Captain Beckett says. "I think he gets the point."

"Yes, Captain, I do. What do you want me to say?"

"We had something drafted up." Beckett hands me a typed statement.

I glance it over. "All right."

"Glad it's to your liking," Wong says. "Please tell me you have a decent shirt and some slacks in that modular of yours."

"I do."

"Good. Get dressed, meet us back here. We'll all walk out together, show some fucking solidarity if you can wrap your head around that concept."

I walk outside the main building to my temporary office. I put on a gray suit, white shirt, and black tie — it's dull but perfect for television.

I gather with my superiors in the captain's office, and we walk down the hallway and outside to the front of the station. The horde of reporters has grown, and there are additional news vans. Word of the case has spread around town, and journalists from various media outlets are champing at the bit to get a crack at the primary detective.

The whole thing feels like an ambush.

I step to the microphone, direct it at my mouth, and don't stand too close — a hot microphone is for amateurs. I can only imagine what the reporters are thinking:

Who's this nervous kid showered in sweat? He can't possibly be the lead detective.

I prepare to read the statement. It's short and pointed: "My name is Detective Trevor Finnegan. At this time, information is limited, but I can confirm that the body of a male LAPD recruit officer was found in the Angeles National Forest this morning. The recruit has been undergoing academy training for the past three months. We do not have any additional information, but we are asking the public if you have any information pertaining to this investigation, please come forward."

I await the questions. The first comes from a portly bald man in a striped polo shirt and jeans, holding a digital recorder. "Do you know how the victim was killed?" he asks.

"Not at this time. We're awaiting the medical examiner's report."

"There are rumors that the victim was found naked."

"We aren't entertaining rumors or commenting on details of the case."

"Was the victim targeted because of his affiliation with the LAPD?"

"As I said before, the victim was a Los Angeles Police recruit, and we are considering all possibilities. Next question . . ."

After answering a few softball questions from reporters firing blindly, given the lack of information released, I end the press conference and head back to the captain's office. Wong is hovering in the corner of the office wearing the scowl he was probably born with, and Rivera has taken a seat. When the brass isn't around, Captain Beckett is more relaxed, but I never underestimate him. He's by the book, and he has his sights on being the chief one day. "We want regular updates on the case, Finn," Beckett says.

"Not a problem . . . as long as Wong is comfortable with a group text."

Wong tenses up. "What the hell did you say?"

A year ago, Wong was reprimanded for texting inappropriate photos in a group thread. In the photos, Wong wore a Scottish kilt and nothing else. Tattoos covered his body, and Wong stood proudly as the photographer captured them in detail. Most of the shots were inappropriate but tolerable. It was the single photo of a tattooed dagger with its handle etched near Wong's anus that caused an uproar. In the photo, Wong had removed the kilt and posed with his front parts absorbed in shadow while his naked rear was on full display. Two female rookies who received the photo lodged a formal complaint, and Wong gained the reputation of being a creeper.

"Go to hell, Finnegan," Wong says. "If I have to, I'll lay you out."

"Finn, you'll communicate directly with me," Captain Beckett says. "Do we have an understanding?"

"Yes, sir."

"You're dismissed."

I leave the three of them in the office, change back into my civvies, and head to my car.

Once behind the wheel, I check my cell phone — three text messages, two from Tori asking if she can come by later and one from Sarada Rao. I haven't heard from her in over a month. True to her MO, the box of desserts outside my door this morning and now a text that reads:

You look good in high-def.
Been thinking about you. Hope you're OK.
Come to the shop tonight if you can.
Sarada ♥

Sarada opened Spinners Baked Goods &

Coffee a few years ago. It's a quaint shop on Melrose Avenue in West Hollywood. Five days a week, she serves gourmet coffee and pastries, and on weekends, the shop becomes a pop-up art gallery. Spinners is an ode to the late '90s and early 2000s. Framed album covers hang from the walls — rock, rap, punk, alternative, emo — along with black-and-white photos of famous actors, comedians, and musicians who saw their fame peak before 2010: comedian Dane Cook, the cast of the *American Pie* movies, and the long-running *Buffy the Vampire Slayer* series. The dessert names are inspired by hit songs and movies from the time. Chocolate Love, inspired by 2Pac's anthem "California Love," and Smells Like Tapioca, drawn from Nirvana's seminal hit "Smells Like Teen Spirit." My favorite is Bitter Sweet Sesame Cake. The Verve's "Bitter Sweet Symphony" is a guilty pleasure, and that goes for the cake, too. Sarada knows the names aren't very good, but she makes kitsch charming.

At Spinners, customers wax nostalgic because remembering one's youth can be gratifying. Parents walk their children around the shop, picking out albums on the walls with fondness, wearing big smiles as they remember the pop songs used to comprise mixtapes — the soundtracks to their adolescence. Even if I know it to be a lie, the past seems simpler, warmer, vivid. It's a past painted in bold colors, serpentine oil on canvas, thickly layered to richness like Sarada's devil's food cake. That's where I long to be: in the past, with Sarada, before the night that changed our lives.

We met at Pershing, a prestigious art academy in Santa Monica, which my parents could barely afford. If it weren't for a minor scholarship and a 20 percent discount for my father being a first responder, I never could have attended. My mother had the idea to transfer me to the art academy; she thought public school hindered my creativity. But that wasn't the only reason she wanted me to attend Pershing. She and my father worried about me being bullied. I was getting into fights, sometimes two or three a week, all stemming from students poking fun at my clothes and hair. I'd taken to wearing flannel shirts and torn jeans, as if I were in a grunge band. I painted my fingernails black and went months without haircuts in my attempt to grow dreadlocks. I made no apologies for my desire to look like rocker Lenny Kravitz. My father, standing in my bedroom doorway, his freshly dry-cleaned uniform draped over his arm, said I looked homeless, queer, and not American.

I came home from school one day, sporting a black eye and a puffed lip. My mother pretended it wasn't so bad, but I knew seeing me battered was a pin in her heart. She asked me what led to the fight as she pulled an ice pack from the freezer, wrapped it in a towel, and handed it to me.

"A few boys in my math class called me an Oreo," I said, pressing the ice pack to my face.

"A cookie?" she asked. "Why in the world would they call you that?"

"It means black on the outside, white on the inside. They're clowning me, Ma. They say I dress like a white boy and talk like one, too. They call me a freak, a wannabe."

My mother put her arm around my shoulder. "You're going to face that kind of ignorance your entire life. I wish I could tell you it will get better, but you just get used to it."

"I don't want to get used to it," I said.

My mother smiled. "Those kids are just threatened by you because you figured it out."

"Figured what out?"

"The only way to live in this world and be at peace is if you're true to yourself." She played with my unruly hair the way she did when I was a little boy. "I won't tell you it's easy, but authenticity, Trevor — living your truth — is the only thing that matters. It's what separates the strong from the weak. I raised you to be strong, didn't I?"

"Yes, Ma, you did."

"I'll get the Vaseline," she said. It had become a ritual: ice, then Vaseline, and two Tylenol for the pain.

My mother always knew what to say to lift my spirits, and I knew she was right about the kids at school being insecure, but my father questioned my identity the most. "Why the hell you listening to that shit?" he asked once after I played the Foo Fighters in my room. "Get you some James Brown, Otis Redding — some damn Hendrix. Something other than that shit you're playing. You need to start listening to real music with some heart and soul."

Pop would punk me for veering far from what he deemed black manhood. I can still see the shame on his face when he saw I had put up posters of blonde and brunette white actresses and models on my bedroom walls. "Since when did you get a taste for Betty and Veronica?" he asked. "You really trying to break your mama's heart, ain't you?"

■ ■ ■ ■

Months before transferring to Pershing, I listened from my room. The door cracked enough for me to hear my parents arguing in the kitchen. Pop proclaimed the academy was a waste of money. "You're giving him an out," he said. "That school is just an expensive escape route to protect him from having to stand up for himself. But sooner or later, he's going to learn that this world isn't kind to soft boys, especially ones who look like him."

"He does stand up for himself, and that's why he comes home looking how he does. Do you have any idea what he's going through?"

"Well, if he gets his ass kicked enough, maybe he'll learn how to throw a punch."

"Look, Trevor needs Pershing. It'll be good for him," my mother said in her trademark sweet voice. "He's going to that school. Period."

I relished her doting but firm nature. She was the opposite of my father in every way. Listening without judgment, never hesitating to say she loved me.

"You coddle him, and that's why he's the way he is —"

There was silence, and then I heard my father storm out of the house, as he often did. From my window, I watched him get into his car and back out of the driveway, off to someplace a married man shouldn't be.

My mother and I wouldn't see him again until morning, when he entered the front door smelling like beer and another woman's fragrance.

I park across the street and watch Sarada through the large shop windows; she's wiping down the bar and tables. I often wonder what our lives would have been like if we'd made different choices. But we were never in control, too feeble to harness the wind and bend it to our will. We were at the mercy of all things, victims of circumstance.

When my mother died, I was fourteen and a freshman at Pershing. Sarada, feeling a need to piece me back together as if I were a broken figurine, called me every day for six months. It didn't matter if we had just seen each other at school or had lunch under one of the pergolas the school had constructed around campus; she felt the need around seven o'clock each evening to talk. I'd listen to her speak about indie music and free concerts, photography, and her love for renowned art galleries. She said to me enthusiastically, "We should go to New York and Paris, Trevor. You need to see the paintings you love up close. It would be like meeting a friend you've only known through letters."

Sarada's kindness felt like charity at times. I didn't understand why she bothered with me, and part of me still doesn't know why or how we became best friends, but every day I'm grateful for her friendship, even though I'm far from deserving. Maybe it was because we both suffered in our youth — ridiculed for being perceived as different, failing to adhere to high school customs, rejecting the stereotypes often bestowed on black people that subjugate and imprison us.

Sarada was unlike anyone I had ever known, and so was her family. They were wealthy but never flaunted it. Her father was an Indian businessman from Calcutta who drove a late-model black two-seater Mercedes and wore suits I presumed were tailored but had a vintage quality that hearkened back to the 1980s. Her mother went by the stage name Lady Rao. She was a retired black actress, born in Chicago, who fled the States and found success in Bollywood movies overseas. She had developed a cult following in South Asia and the Middle East and appeared in over fifty films beginning at age twenty. I knew this because Sarada was a great fan of her mother and could recount much of her career, and their close relationship only made me pine for the one I'd shared with my mother.

Lady Rao was a stunning woman who had gifted Sarada with high cheekbones, honey eyes, and rich, sun-kissed mahogany skin, what my father would call "good genes." When he came home from patrol to find Sarada and me studying for an art history exam over pizza and cola, he said, "How's that mother of yours?"

"She's well, Mr. Finnegan," Sarada replied with polished politeness.

"I'll tell you what," Pop said while filling a mixing bowl with ice, "if the world ended and life had to begin again, God would be wise to use you and your mother as standard-bearers."

I looked to Sarada, rolled my eyes, and mouthed the words, *"I'm sorry."*

"That's kind of you, Mr. Finnegan," she said, looking at her watch. "It's getting late, Trevor. I should get home."

"OK," I said, knowing it was the presence of my father that made her want to leave. Sarada dialed her dad on the cordless phone and told him to come pick her up. We ate the pizza in silence at the dining table, waiting for him to arrive.

Pop sat on the couch and turned on the TV. He was out of uniform but hadn't changed out of his white tee. There was a smear of blood on the collar, and his right hand was shoved into the bowl of ice; his knuckles were purple balloons. I knew whoever was on the receiving end of his fist that day was in much worse shape.

Sarada looked uncomfortable. Pop had a way of sucking the air out of the room, and as soon as Sarada's father pulled into the driveway, I walked her out. I can still remember her rushing down the driveway to get into her dad's Mercedes.

When I went back into the house, Pop was sipping a beer and eating the few slices of pizza left in the box. Most days, my father mortified me; this day was no exception.

As I often did, I wished it were he who died and not my mother.

Sarada was my teacher, a cultural ambassador who introduced me to foods like sushi, lamb tagine, and shumai. She had traveled to many countries for her father's work and had lived in far-off places like the United Arab Emirates, Thailand, India, and

Japan. She was the only black person I knew who had a passport and had gone through customs, having to declare goods taken from one land to bring into another. But her experiences set her apart. Even at a private art academy, whose crest spoke of dedication to art and expression, she never did find her place among the white elites with their celebrity parents. She was often told, "You're pretty for a dark girl," and asked, "Are you from Africa or something?" Questions like these were a part of reality for black people at Pershing. We were a minority of a minority, and while my parents had thought an art school would be a better fit for their creative son, prone to daydreaming and self-loathing, it was where I developed a harder, more rugged exterior. My mother's death only hastened what I was already becoming — angry and disenchanted with the world around me, feelings I reflected in my art.

"I like the colors," Sarada said one day after class, her hair in a long braid down her back and fingernails painted yellow. We stood in the school's art studio, inspecting a painting that had taken me two weeks to complete. It was all she could say. The black strokes were violent and assaulted the canvas, the beige background speckled white. Suspended in the center, a small humanoid trapped in a sable cell. It was the type of painting that made people uncomfortable, which I appreciated at the time. I felt like the work encapsulated my mourning. My mother was dead, and grief was my life.

"What do you call it?" Sarada asked.

"Life Untitled," I said.

She smiled. "Fitting."

"I'll probably burn it." The painting hadn't won over Sarada, and she was my biggest fan — my only fan.

"You shouldn't," she said, "Keep it. It's a part of you." Sarada rubbed her hand against my back, and the gesture almost broke me. She whispered in my ear, "It'll be all right," and then walked off, the bottom hem of her silk kurti dallying above her knees.

I hadn't been an attentive friend, not like Sarada was to me after my mother died. I didn't fully understand what she was going through, the torment she suffered from the girls at Pershing. During our sophomore year, I began to hear rumors about Sarada floating through the hallways, and one was particularly cruel. A clique of popular girls began telling other students that she was having a relationship with our English teacher, Mr. Saybrook. I was never sure of the rumor's genesis. Sarada was fond of Saybrook, and they spent time together after class. He lent her books of poetry and essays — Gwendolyn Brooks, Claudia Rankine, Langston Hughes, Amiri Baraka, and James Baldwin. He was Pershing's resident cool guy. A comely bohemian and the first white man I'd seen with dreadlocks, he spoke of poetry slams and book clubs with the fervor and adoration one would hope to find in an English teacher.

The rumor circulated quickly. After a week, Sarada was called into the principal's office, along with Saybrook. He was married but had possibly strayed before. Word was his wife never believed he and Sarada didn't have a relationship, and it must have put a strain on an already shaky union. Saybrook's wife left him later that semester, and he soon quit teaching at Pershing. For our entire sophomore and junior years, people tried to humiliate Sarada, pelting her with degrading names: *whore, homewrecker, slut, ghetto bitch.*

"We should slash their tires at lunch tomorrow," I said to Sarada one day, watching Crystal Macon, Debbie Tan, and Katie Capelli twirl and cackle in the student parking lot. They were as carefree as the actors in a commercial for antidepressants. Ballet, modern, and jazz-trained dancers, they were "beauty in motion." That's how the dance department chair had described them once. But Sarada and I understood that they were far from elegance. Their real talent was malevolence.

Standing under our favorite pergola, a cool breeze from the Pacific carried salt in the air. We watched these detestable girls with cigarettes clasped between their fingers pile into a red Jeep Wrangler. They moved about with no regard for the damage they'd done, the confidence they'd tried to suck from Sarada like lifeblood from a tapped vein.

"Leave it, Trevor," Sarada said. "Slashing their tires won't solve anything. It'll just get you into trouble."

"Even if I got caught, it would be worth it," I said, nearly salivating at the idea. "C'mon, it'll make you feel better."

"It won't . . . and those girls have to live with themselves."

Sarada didn't deserve the bullying, and we both knew, though we'd never spoken it aloud, her being singled out had more to do with how she looked than anything else. There was an undercurrent of jealousy that fueled much of the rumors. Some teenage girls harm anything they regard as a threat. Not only was Sarada lovely, but she was also the most talented photographer I'd ever seen. She didn't just take photos. Her candid snapshots captured the essence of her subjects, and they hung in the school's lobby for all to see. Before it was a trending hashtag, Sarada was Black Girl Magic, a paragon of beauty reflecting the splendor around her.

For our entire four years, Sarada never dated anyone at Pershing. High school boys seemed beneath her. I had heard some boys desired to date her, and others just wanted to sleep with her, but after the fall of Saybrook, Sarada might as well have been a social leper.

Gym was my last class period of the day because I didn't like to use the locker room showers, preferring to shower once I got home. The gym was designed by a famed architect known for his modern style. There was a regulation basketball court, free weights, machines, treadmills, and bikes that rivaled luxury health clubs. The shellacked concrete walls felt as industrial and cold as I'd imagine prison to be, and it made me hate gym class even more. I despised the locker room most because I usually had to listen to horny boys delight about girls they'd slept with and objectify those they wanted to sleep with. I made it a point to use a locker on an empty aisle, far away from them, but I could still hear their loud bluster, filling the space.

I had lost count of the number of times I had listened to locker room chatter in which Sarada was the subject. They called her exotic, like a tropical bird or rare dog breed, deconstructing her by body parts. I was tired of it, and this day I boiled with animosity for their devil-may-care attitudes and sly arrogance that made them believe they were superior.

"That ass, though," a boy's voice said. I could feel the fury build. I left my aisle to get a look at him. I moved around the bank of the lockers until I had an unobstructed view. He straddled the bench near his locker. His blond hair was still wet from the shower. "I'm not sure I could handle an ass that big, but I'd sure as hell try," he said, pulling a pair of jeans over his waist. He dug in his locker, brought out a designer tee, and put it on. Then, as if possessed by the spirit of foolery, he began thrusting his pelvis forward while motioning his hand as if slapping an imaginary ass.

They sounded like shrilling jackals.

"That's how you do it, Chasen. Ride that big ass," one of the boys said, barely containing his laughter.

"Shut the hell up!" I said.

Chasen turned to look at me; his three friends were silent.

"What did you say, freak show?" he asked.

"Say one more thing about Sarada."

"Or what?" Chasen flexed his muscles and pushed his hair back, clearing the strands that hung over his face. It was a poor tough-guy performance; he wasn't a fighter. But I'd grown used to physical altercations. My parents had reached a compromise: at my father's behest, I had to take self-defense classes on weekends to attend Pershing. It began with American boxing and, months later, Krav Maga. Pop was convinced such classes would purge me of all softness.

"Fuck him up, Chasen," one of the boys said, standing on the sideline. Chasen advanced, and I struck him across the face — a straight punch down the middle. He dropped to his knees, smacking the concrete floor, and bleated like a wounded animal. I hadn't hit him hard, but it was enough for purple lesions to grow along his chin and cheek.

His ego had taken the brunt of the beating. He held his face as dollops of blood fell onto his expensive tee. He looked at me as if I were a savage, unbridled beast. Then he got to his feet, nearly stumbling back to the ground, and left the locker room with his friends close behind.

I sat in the locker room, rubbing my palms together, certain that my actions were justified. I felt no remorse for hitting Chasen, but I knew Sarada would be disappointed if she knew what I'd done. Unlike me, she saw justice as the return to a harmonic balance — restorative, transformative — and she didn't care how long it took. Those who spoke ill of her, who bullied her, would either evolve or face cosmic consequences, even if it took twenty years.

"It's like James Baldwin said, Trevor," she once recounted. "People pay for what they do, and still more for what they've allowed themselves to become. And they pay for it very simply: by the lives they lead."

As much as I wanted to affirm what Sarada believed, I couldn't. Justice was never assured, mystical, or spiritual — it was simple as a straight punch to a deserving jaw. I would have done anything in defense of Sarada, and while I didn't have the guts to tell her I loved her, I walked that campus as if the entire school knew I did. And after the fight with Chasen, no one dared say anything that didn't exalt Sarada Rao as the queen she was, at least not in my presence.

As graduation neared, the rumors about Sarada quelled, and we could barely contain our excitement. We'd both be headed to college in a few months. I'd be leaving my father's house. I'd be free, and for the first time, life was as close to perfect as it had ever been.

I get out of the car, walk across the street, and tap on the door to Spinners. Sarada startles and then snaps her head in my direction. Her disquieted look gives way to a gentle smile; she opens the door to let me in. She tosses the wet rag on a table and hugs me so tight that it makes me worry. The last time she embraced me like this was the day my mother died. "Wow. It's good to see you, too," I say as Sarada loosens her hold. "You a fortune-teller or something?"

"No, why?" she asks.

"That hug. Thought you might have seen how my story ends."

"Ugh. Why so morbid? I haven't seen you in weeks, and this is what you come at me with?"

"You're right. That was stupid of me to say."

Sarada picks up the rag and goes back to wiping down the tables. I can't keep my eyes off her. She has a way of breaking me down to a gawking fool. "There you go staring again," she says. "I guess some things never change."

"I don't get to see you much. I just need a moment to get used to you, that's all."

"You always did know how to flatter a girl."

"I did?"

"Sure. Your sweet words and those goo-goo eyes."

"You make me sound like a weirdo."

"No, it was innocent. Probably because you had no clue you were doing it."

"I was kind of a loser back then."

"You were not. You were sweet and well-adjusted, given the circumstances. Now, this new version of you, I can't explain."

"What? I'm still well-adjusted. I just don't have time for commitment these days."

"So, these girls you sleep with know this?"

"Plural? That's presumptuous."

"You're right . . . I apologize."

"To answer your question — sure, when I meet the right woman, things will change."

"I just hope you'll be able to recognize the right one when you see her."

The truth is, I measure every woman

against Sarada — it's a curse — and no matter how great they are, I feel like I'm settling. "Thanks for the baked goods, by the way."

"You're welcome," Sarada says. "A few are new recipes, so I'd appreciate your honest opinion."

"Of course, but you know I love whatever comes out of that oven."

"Easy to please —"

"You know it. So, why the text message out of the blue?" I ask.

"I saw you on TV tonight."

"OK. Did I have something in my teeth?"

"It was like looking into the past," she says, her playfulness washed from her countenance. "It was that same look you used to give when you were worried about a test or thought your painting wasn't good enough. It's the case, isn't it? Something isn't right."

"Maybe I'm a little stressed, but I'm fine, and the case is fine. Trust me."

"Trevor, do you have someone you can talk to?"

"What? Like a shrink?"

"Sure."

"Here you go again."

"What's the harm in trying it out?"

"But that's what I have you for," I say flippantly. "And you don't charge."

"I'm serious, Trevor."

"I see now. You asked me to come by for an interrogation."

"I'm concerned, that's all."

"I told you, I'm good."

Sarada cups my cheek. "Good, Trevor? You haven't been good since that night."

"Why do you do this?" I say, pulling away from her. "And every time like some idiot, I fall for it. You text, I come running."

"Because I hold out hope that at some point, you'll want to talk about what happened."

"What is there to talk about?"

"Trevor, you nearly killed someone."

"You make it sound like I'm the monster. The guy fucking deserved it."

"It's still inside of you, isn't it? That anger."

"And you're over what happened? Completely?"

Sarada weighs my words. "Sure, I think about it. But it doesn't define me, not anymore."

"I can't do that."

"What happened wasn't your fault."

"I need to go," I say. "I don't get why you're bringing all this up again."

"Because I'm worried about you."

"Don't be."

"Trevor, wait!" Sarada shouts, but I'm already out the door.

I get in the car and start the engine. As I drive away, Sarada's words pulse in my head — *what happened wasn't your fault.* These words can paralyze anyone when they believe they're to blame for something terrible. And I am to blame. I'm to blame for everything.

CHAPTER FOUR

It was weeks before high school graduation. Everyone kept telling us we were going to embark on a new chapter in our lives and that we should be excited. All I could think about was a gallery show I had booked with the help of Sarada's dad. It was a small, shabby gallery in Culver City, the usual white walls and checkered linoleum. I would showcase a few paintings, oiled abstracts with hard lines, geometric shapes, mono-chrome colors. They were commercial paintings that appealed to the young, wealthy Venice Beach dwellers, potential buyers who had made their fortunes in tech start-ups and video games.

I didn't particularly love any of the paintings and was eager to sell them, hoping to pocket enough money for new art supplies. Sarada agreed to stand in front of the gallery and hand out flyers advertising the show to passersby. Her beauty alone was enough to draw a crowd, and once she got to hyping my work, people listened and came inside. After a few hours, all my paintings had sold. A journalist from *LA Weekly* even bought one and promised a write-up on me in the newspaper. The recognition felt good, and in a few months, I'd be at CalArts, honing my craft as a fine arts major.

It was about nine o'clock when the crowd thinned. People had drunk all the sparkling water and had eaten two large platters of cookies. There were no more paintings on the walls. I remember looking at Sarada and thinking she was my lucky charm, that I'd be stupid to let her go. Sure, she would be at USC and I'd be in Valencia, but I knew we could make it work if I could only muster the confidence to tell her how I felt.

Sarada's dad had planned to help us clean up after the show. He bestowed on us large trash bags, a broom, and a dustpan. He also had the key to the gallery since his business friend owned it. In between joking and cleaning, Sarada's dad got a phone call. He needed to leave, something about a deal needing to close by sunrise in the East. Before Sarada's dad left, he gave me the key for safekeeping, and I promised to lock up once the cleaning was done. Sarada and

I were in the gallery alone. I thought it was a gift from God or fate or something. I brimmed with pride and confidence after the successful gallery show, and Sarada had to see how great we were together.

It was time to make my move.

That night she was wearing a pleated skirt with heels and a top that hung off her shoulders. I couldn't keep my eyes off her; she was perfect. While she was collecting plastic cups and napkins, I walked over. She smiled at me, likely unsure of why I was standing so close. Then, I leaned in to kiss her the way I had seen so often in movies. And just like in movies, where the hopeless nerd is rejected, Sarada lurched back. We both stood in silence for a moment, and I started to sweat — that adolescent, musty, nervous sweat. I could feel each pimple below the surface of my skin peak.

I'd messed up. Badly.

I ran outside and down the street with the gallery's keys in my pocket.

I wanted to disappear, to fade into nothingness. I felt like I was trying to shake loose a dagger lodged in my chest. It was a deep cut, an abysmal feeling, and I couldn't walk enough blocks to cure the ache. As I roamed in my funk, I played the moment over in my head and told myself I imagined it to be much worse than it was. Maybe twenty minutes had passed; I had strayed far from the gallery. I started back, and when I got close, I noticed the lights were off, and the door was shut. I couldn't remember if I'd shut it when I bolted. But the lights . . . I couldn't explain the lights.

Why the hell were the lights off?

The closer I got to the gallery, the more I felt something was wrong. When I entered the gallery, I turned on the lights. No sign of Sarada. I thought maybe she'd taken off after me. Maybe she was out walking, too, trying to find where I'd gone. I made my way to the rear of the gallery and went into a small office where the owner kept a filing cabinet, a desk and computer, and a leather couch where artists would sit before their showings. Sarada was on the couch, facedown. Her skirt had been torn from her waist. Blood clumped at the back of her head and ran down her thighs.

"Sarada, can you hear me?"

Nothing.

I gently angled her head away from the couch cushion. "Please, Sarada — please." My thoughts ran frenetically; I grappled to keep them straight. I knew time was precious. "I'm going to get help."

I dialed 911 from the office's line. "We

need help," I said to the operator. "My friend is hurt."

"Do you know what happened?" the operator asked.

"No — I think she was attacked. Assaulted, I mean."

"Is she breathing?"

I put my ear to her mouth. She coughed, and there was a slight gasp. "Yes," I said. "Please hurry."

"The ambulance is on its way. Stay with her."

Stay with her? I was tethered to her, bound by a love that meant I would have given my life for hers. I had no choice but to remain in that room, embraced by something so horrid that my cogent mind kept telling me to flee because seeing Sarada that way was too hard to take. But she was a part of me, and I'd sooner amputate a limb than leave her side.

I hung up the phone. "It's going to be OK, Sarada. Help is coming." I wanted to touch her, to comfort her, but it was a crime scene. I heard Pop's voice in my head telling me to mind the evidence. Her attacker might have left DNA behind.

Helplessly down I went, into a deep well chock-full of pain and heartache, unmeasurable in the moment. My best friend was shattered, and all I could do was tell her help was coming.

I'd made a grave error, broken a cardinal law. I'd failed to protect my love.

I hadn't prayed since my mother lay dying, but on my knees, I pleaded to a venerated God for Sarada to be all right as I waited for help to arrive.

The police and ambulance came and took her to a nearby hospital, where she remained for a week. Culver City police detectives interviewed everyone who came into the gallery that night. They used the mailing list we created, which included names, email addresses, and phone numbers. The gallery had no surveillance cameras, and the closest one was across the street, obscured by an overgrown tree.

Everyone's alibi checked out. After liaising with the lead detective over coffee from a deli stand, Pop told me that the rapist used a lamp to strike Sarada on the head and then had his way. He had worn a condom and was careful to avoid DNA transfer, which meant he likely had other victims and could have been a serial offender. "It's a tough break," Pop said, sitting on a wooden stool in the garage, rubbing black polish onto tactical boots. "The detectives will work it as long as they can. Rape cases aren't easy to close unless they've got DNA. Shame she can't ID him."

"She was knocked out, Pop."

"I know." He burnished the polish with the flame of his Zippo. "There's only been two perps I've wanted to put bullets in. One was a man pimping out his daughter to pay off a debt. The other a junkie who kidnapped a three-year-old and tried to sell her at the swap meet. But the piece of shit who hurt Sarada . . ." He snapped the Zippo closed and stared at me.

"Yeah, Pop?"

"I shouldn't be talking like this around you," he said, running a hard-bristled brush across a boot's toe. "Let's just hope they find who did it."

The police said the best chance at catching the rapist was to wait until he attacked again and left evidence behind or a victim could identify him. The idea of waiting for a crime to happen to solve a previous crime was reckless and idiotic, and I couldn't believe that was the detective's solution. There was no outrage, no rally for justice, only the thin veil of pity and victim-blaming.

"Did she always dress like that?" the lead detective asked as I sat in the cold police station. He was young, his hair greased slick with pomade.

"Dress like what?" I asked.

He looked up at me from his notepad. "You know. Scanty."

"What the hell is scanty?"

"Why did you leave her by herself?" His tie was loose. Cornflower blue with thin yellow stripes, as if someone set out to design the ugliest tie possible. I wondered why so many police officers, my father included, dressed so poorly.

"I needed air," I said. "I went for a walk."

"You had the key to the gallery, correct?"

"Yes."

"So, you left your girlfriend behind with no way to lock up? Doesn't seem right."

"Sarada isn't my girlfriend."

"But you wanted her to be?"

"We're best friends."

The detective mugged. "Yeah, stupid question. She's clearly out of your league." He focused on my painted nails and wild Afro in desperate need of shaping.

"So, who was she dating?"

"Nobody."

"A girl like that? She had to be seeing someone. Maybe her guy came by the gallery after you left?"

"I would have known if she was seeing someone."

The detective watched two officers escort a handcuffed redhead in a miniskirt through the station. "Right," he said, "because you two are best friends . . ."

"Yes."

"Good for you." He twirled his pencil and then shoved it behind his ear. "Personally, I don't think men and women can be just friends. Unless, of course, the man isn't into women."

Sarada was a black girl, and crimes against black girls don't mean much; they only matter when they're easy to solve. To the cops, Sarada might as well have been lying. A random man off the street? No ex-boyfriends? No trysts with older men? No, as the detectives put it, questionable sexual behavior? It had to have been someone she knew or something she did to invite the assault. For the detectives, it was the only explanation. Sarada couldn't remember much of the attack, but she offered one detail: the man smelled like a toilet — salty, of ammonia and rust.

I decided to investigate for myself after the detectives stopped calling Sarada and me. I canvassed the neighborhood, looking for anything the police might have missed. I replayed the night in my head, trying to remember what and who I saw as I walked.

Then, something stood out. It was a plumber's van; I recalled it sitting in front of the gallery, but I couldn't remember seeing anyone inside. When I went back to the gallery to find Sarada had been assaulted, the van was gone.

I walked the neighborhood daily for weeks, looking for the van. I didn't think I would find it or any evidence that would point me in the direction of Sarada's attacker. I just needed to be doing something because it kept my mind off the guilt.

One afternoon, just when I thought I had wasted time being an amateur sleuth, I saw the van parked near the gallery. I watched a white man, short, obese, wearing a cap and glasses, carry plumbing equipment into a bank. I copied the van's business name, SPIRELLI PLUMBING 24-7 EMERGENCY SERVICE, along with the vehicle's license plate and phone number, and I went home.

I should have gone to the police with what I'd found, but I'd lost faith in the Culver City detectives, and it was clear they were moving on from Sarada's case. I searched for Spirelli Plumbing online and found two locations, one in El Segundo and another in Culver City. The website was rudimentary, but it provided me a name and photo —

Claudio Spirelli. He was the plumber working out of the Culver City office and the man I saw going into the bank. I bookmarked the website in my browser, unsure of what to do next.

Tragic events have a way of revealing parts of who we are, parts we work to keep hidden. The night Sarada was raped, I couldn't hide the part of me that wanted retribution, to do draconic, terrible things. The image of her lying on the couch, bloodied, had been burned into my brain. No matter what I did, I couldn't get that night out of my head.

After Sarada was released from the hospital, I tried to see her. I went to her house in well-manicured Hancock Park. Her father answered the door. He wouldn't let me in, so I stood on the porch of their two-story bungalow. He could barely look at me, and I was grateful. It was easier to talk to him without having to make much eye contact, though I knew he reserved judgment for the boy who'd abandoned his daughter.

"I'm sorry, Mr. Rao," I said, not knowing what else to say.

It was the first time I had seen him out of a suit; he wore denim jeans, a cream cable-knit sweater, and loafers. I felt like he hadn't been to work in days. "It could have been any girl," he said. "But it was my daughter

— *my* daughter." In his voice, an amalgamation of all the feelings I'd expect from a father whose daughter had been sexually assaulted and her accounting of the rape vilified by police.

I wasn't sure it was my place to ask, but I did. "How is Sarada?"

Mr. Rao rolled his neck from side to side, looked toward the sky, and then down at his feet. "She sleeps most of the day. She isn't attending USC in September — she's deferred."

"I see," I said, trying to imagine what Sarada was going through. Attending USC had been her dream.

"I'll tell her you came by," Mr. Rao said before shutting the door.

I kept calling Sarada each week, sometimes multiple times a day, but the calls went to voice mail. Pop told me to give her space, but I couldn't bear losing my best friend. I thought if I stopped calling, then it meant I was giving up on her — on us.

It was a Saturday, late in the evening, when she answered. "Hello?" she said. I could barely hear her, and I knew it wasn't the phone's connection. She sounded weary.

"Sarada."

"Yes, Trevor." Her voice trembled.

I was nervous, afraid, but I wasn't sure of what. Maybe rejection or wrath. Both would have been merited. "How are you?" I asked.

"I'm alive," she said. "I'm thankful for that."

With every word she spoke, I felt like I was coming apart at the seams. "Can I see you?" I asked.

There was a brief silence. I anticipated the rebuff and told myself if she were to decline, then I'd have my answer. I'd know that she blamed me, and for her sake, I'd vanish from her life for good.

"All right," she said. "I'll let you know when."

I exhaled fast; unknowingly, I'd been holding my breath. "Yes, of course," I said. "Whenever you're ready."

A week later, we sat in her bedroom, walls painted purple with gold trim, watching television, reruns of a sitcom she liked. She was curled up in a lounge chair in the corner, her clothes an oversize sweat suit, far from the fashion-forward outfits she used to wear. I sat on the floor. Once in a while, Sarada would giggle, and her face would light up, if only for a moment, and hope would rise in me because I thought she was getting better.

Some afternoons, we'd walk around her neighborhood of Hancock Park; she kept her distance from me like I was a stranger, but I understood. A man had hurt her; it didn't matter that I was her best friend. I just wanted us to be like we were, but it was a selfish desire because there was no going back.

"Have you been painting?" she asked as we walked past an art gallery on Wilshire. Her hoodie was a size too large, and she kept her hands in the pockets.

"I don't think I can," I said, kicking a gravel chip down the sidewalk. "Haven't been able to focus on much lately."

"I get it."

"You been taking pictures?" I ask.

"I sold my camera."

"What — why?" I stopped walking and faced her. "You loved that camera."

"I can't shoot anymore," Sarada said. "I pick up the damn thing, and my hand, it just shakes. I can't hold it still. So, it's gone." I didn't inquire further, and we continued our walk in silence. As we turned the corner, headed back toward her house, she said, "I'm seeing a therapist."

"OK — I mean, that's good if it's helping."

"It's at a mental health clinic. I go for a

145

few hours a day. It helps a lot."

"I'm really happy to hear that," I said. I smiled so wide, my cheeks hurt, because I was oblivious. I thought that the therapist could fix her, return her to who she was before. I wanted to take her by the hand and say something meaningful, but nothing came to mind, and I just kept walking.

"My therapist asked about you."

"Me — why?"

"She wanted to know if you were seeing someone."

"Like a counselor?" I asked.

"Sure," she said. "A professional you can talk to."

"No — that shit's not for me." I was short, and Sarada didn't press. What I couldn't bring myself to tell her was that it wasn't like when my mother died. Talking to someone wasn't going to make me better. I had grown used to sleepless nights, headaches, fatigue. If I closed my eyes long enough, I found myself back in the gallery with Sarada lying helpless. To wake in the middle of the night in a cold sweat, wanting to put my fist through a wall, was nothing compared to what Sarada had gone through and its aftermath. Seething was all I had, and it tested the limits of my constitution. I contemplated joining my mother, out in the vast nowhere — floating among the stars, free from the inequities of life. But it was never a true option.

I put CalArts behind me and enrolled in Glendale Community College. I took courses in history, law, civics, an introduction to law enforcement, and police science. I had watched Pop for years leave the house to work the streets with the temperament of a rabid dog, and it was a comfort because I knew my father was too much of a bastard to let some suspect get the better of him. And like my father, I had no desire to join the fire department. Besides, I had spent my life with a cop undergoing a quiet indoctrination. I knew the job and what it could cost me, and I was fine with it. I didn't see myself getting married or having kids. I'd be free from worry, not having a family to burden with this life.

I studied crime and law at the college for three years. During that time, I didn't speak to Sarada much. She went on to attend USC as planned. We mostly communicated on social media through emojis, GIFs, Likes, and facile comments. Sometimes we'd text each other randomly with greetings and check-ins, and if she felt generous, she'd send me a photo of her smiling on campus, surrounded by other smiling faces, enjoying a life once deferred. I was relieved to know she had friends who could capture her happiness in photos. God had heard my prayers — Sarada was going to be all right — but I was languishing, convinced God had given up on me.

When I turned twenty-one years old, I applied to the LAPD. My father tried to talk me out of it, saying the force was no place to grieve. I contended that I wasn't grieving. I had read books on grief because I promised Sarada I would better understand my affliction, and I was still in the anger stage.

I needed a place to put my rage.

I'm not sure why I did, but I called Sarada to tell her I was following in my father's footsteps. Maybe I was looking for her blessing, thinking that her good thoughts and prayers could keep me safe. "Does this mean you're not going to paint anymore?" she said. "You're giving up, aren't you?"

I was defensive. "It's not like that. A painting never helped anyone not get assaulted or raped."

"Is that what this is about? You want someone to save?"

"It's a long shot, anyway," I said, groaning. "They only let in about two percent of black people who apply."

"So, what will you do if you don't get in?"

"I don't know. I'll figure something else out."

"You still haven't gone, have you?"

"I told you, I'm fine."

"It's trauma, Trevor, and we're both suffering. Talking to someone can help."

"I told you, we . . . I don't do that. I gotta go," I said before ending the call.

I had a decent chance of joining the department, but it still felt like I was inviting failure. I was far from a type A personality, which I'd read most cops were. I was pretty liberal and thought marijuana needed to be legalized. I also understood that being an officer was dangerous, and the LAPD had problems. Depending on the chief at the helm, the department either had a partnership with communities or alienated them. Chiefs Parker and Gates both had played racially divisive roles in the city's history, which was part of the department's DNA. There were countless accusations of police brutality and instances like Rodney King and the Rampart scandal — and cops charged with murder, rape, child porn possession, drug distribution, and other offenses. Then there were the good ole boys, white power miscreants who believed the

LAPD worked best as an all-white police force. Rumors swirled that gangs — skinheads, neo-Nazis, and South LA Crips and Bloods factions — had gotten some of their members on the force. Aside from the internal chaos, the department hadn't given their officers pay increases for over a decade. Morale was low. My father constantly said the environment was shit and that most officers counted the days until they could retire.

After I failed my first polygraph, I thought my attempt to become an officer was over. While the polygraph doesn't detect lies, it does monitor a person's biophysical reactions to questions, and I had reactions to multiple questions about drug use, which was likely from my marijuana use in high school. I told the truth about getting stoned once before school and occasionally with friends, but it didn't satisfy the test.

The interviewer, a runny-nosed redheaded woman in a shawl, asked, "You sure it was only in high school? Maybe you took a few hits and just can't remember. Something you puffed at a party or kicking back in the past few months?"

"No, ma'am. I don't do drugs."

"The polygraph suggests otherwise."

She wasn't a polygraph examiner; she just pretended to be. She was an investigator who left me in a cold, cramped interview room for nearly two hours, not allowed to use the restroom or get water. Once I became an officer, I learned this was a tactic, along with many others. When people are tired, irritable, and needing to piss, they crack and tell the police whatever they want to know. And while I sat shivering, the interviewer supposedly conferred with "others" about the exam results. In actuality, she observed me from a camera mounted in the room and fed to a monitor somewhere. When she returned, breath smelling of sour coffee, she asked if I had remembered anything and if I wanted to come clean. "Last chance," she said. "Get it off your chest."

"I don't do drugs," I said. "Am I free to leave?"

"You may get a call to retest. In the meantime, if you remember anything you think we should know, give us a call. It doesn't mean you can't join the force, but if you get in the academy and we find out you lied to us, you're gone. We don't care if you're a week from graduating — you're gone."

I left that day believing I didn't have a chance in hell of joining the LAPD.

I considered reapplying to CalArts the following semester. The school had accepted me once. Maybe they would again. I even thought about doing a series of paintings that dealt with sexual assault and violence against women to raise awareness, but that wouldn't cure what ailed me. Because the rage wouldn't leave, and nothing calmed it. I needed to do something. I had to find Claudio Spirelli.

I imagined him going on calls to fix clogs and leaks, surveying entry points, and determining the best way to break in and rape the female occupants. So much time had passed, and I wondered if Spirelli Plumbing was still in business. I revisited the bookmarked webpage. Nothing had changed. I wasn't sure what time Claudio worked, so I called the company's main number, aged my voice, and pretended to be a previous customer. I asked if Claudio was available to look at a slow leak under my kitchen sink. I added that he'd come out before for a clogged toilet and did a good job fixing it. The man on the phone had an irritating voice, raspy like a chainsmoker's. He told me Claudio came to work around nine a.m. and it would be best to call back.

I had nothing to lose. The academy wasn't going to have me. I was cursed to lie awake at night, knowing a life of ruin. I wanted a reckoning for Sarada, myself, and the hope we held for our lives.

The next morning, I drove my hatchback to the business, parked across the street, and waited for Claudio to arrive. When he did, it was after nine thirty, and he parked his truck on the street and went inside the building. Claudio came out at ten fifteen, smoked a cigarette, and got into the work van. I followed him as he drove into Redondo Beach and parked in the driveway of a house a few blocks from the ocean. He stamped out a cigarette in the driveway and carried his toolbox into the house. He stayed inside for three hours and came out sweating. Before getting into the van, he lit another cigarette and seemed to take delight in the ocean air.

I continued to follow him, even after he got gas and stopped at a local burger chain. He made two additional house calls, one in Playa Vista and another in Venice. When he finished his last call in Venice, the sun was beginning to set, and I was exhausted from trailing him all day. I supposed he was tired, too, and on his way back to the office. He drove in the direction of Culver City, and after an hour of traffic, Claudio parked the van outside the office and climbed into his truck. I followed him ten miles to an apartment building in Mar Vista, where he parked in a culde-sac, and I parked across the street.

I hadn't eaten for eight hours. I was lightheaded, shaky, and stiff from sitting the long stretch in the driver's seat, but I wasn't going to give up the opportunity I'd waited for the entire day. I put on a pair of latex gloves, a black baseball cap, and shades, and picked up a metal pipe from the floor of my car. Claudio was brutish, not taller than me, but twice my size.

I got out of the car, calmly walked across the street, and as Claudio stood at the rear of his truck, I struck him in the leg with the pipe. First, he was stunned, stumbling backward and looking at me openmouthed. It was as if the feeling of pain was foreign to him. I thought about Sarada and the pain she felt, and I struck him again. He hollered and cursed and tried to snatch the pipe from me. I quickly moved and shifted to his right side, where I struck his kneecap. There was a loud smack that sounded like a baseball hit a car window, and Claudio fell to the ground. I leaned over, took the pipe, and sent its end into his crotch with all the force I could gather. I repeated the action once more, imagining his genitals pummeled purple and swollen. I stood over him as he cried and shrieked, but he never called out for help. Rather, he smacked his fist against the concrete, mumbled a few words, and spat thick mucus.

I should have done it a long time ago. I was justified, as when I bloodied Chasen's mouth in the locker room. I had told myself Claudio was guilty, an undeniable truth.

"This is for Sarada. The girl you raped," I said.

He sucked in air and spat again. "I didn't rape nobody."

"Three years ago — a gallery in Culver City. It was you."

"Three years ago? You're crazy, man. I just moved here a year ago. You've got the wrong guy."

"You're a liar," I said. "You saw her, didn't you? That day outside the gallery. That's when you decided to do it."

"What fucking gallery? Do I look like a guy who hangs out at galleries?"

"Keep your fucking mouth shut."

I looked in his truck bed and found spools of nylon rope, a box of nitrile gloves — the type I've seen used in medical offices — and a small rubberized gear box. I grabbed the box and opened it. Inside was a zipped baggie of condoms, chalky white pills in a vial, and female underwear.

I felt the ground open up beneath me. My body was electric, all nerves firing at once. There was a groundswell, a flood of emotions. Wrath had already taken root, but there was fear, too, of not knowing what I was going to do next.

"Those are just gag gifts. It's not what you think," Claudio said.

These weren't gags; they were tools of his repulsive pursuit. My eye twitched violently. Tears formed as I thought of Sarada.

I couldn't speak. I was swallowed up by something carnal. I was in the jaws of it, a thing that had taken hold of my throat and ripped out my voice.

"Please, man," Claudio said, "let me go."

I stared at the rapist and thought how easy it would be to kill him, but I knew my mother didn't raise a murderer.

"Fuck, man. I told you I didn't do nothing to no girl." He was working his limbs, dragging his body away from me. The loose flesh on his arms drooped down to his elbows like overripe fruits hanging from weakened vines. I thought at any moment that the flaccid skin would overtake his elbows completely.

My head cleared, and I returned to the wrath that kept my heart beating with the ferocity of a coal-fired locomotive. I said, "I know what you are, and I'll be watching you. You touch another girl, I'll kill you."

I wasn't going to kill Claudio, but I needed him to think that I would. I walked back across the street, got into my car, and drove away.

As I drove down Sepulveda, headed toward the 10 East freeway, a series of tremors seized my body. With each one, I struggled to breathe, convinced it was a heart attack. I rolled down the window to let in the fresh air and looked in my rearview mirror, anticipating a police car not far behind. Had someone seen what I did to Claudio and called 911? I'd be arrested for assault with a deadly weapon, all hope of joining the LAPD dashed, but as I reached the on-ramp to the freeway, there were no police sirens or flashing lights.

I could breathe again. No longer feeling the heaviness in my chest, the gnawing ache that never left. I was lighter as I merged onto the freeway, and there in rush hour traffic, nestled between cars, I found solace.

That night I called Sarada and told her

what I'd done. "Are you insane?" she asked. "You can't just hurt people like that. What if it wasn't even him?"

"It was him — I saw the rope, the condoms, the gloves. I'm telling you, he's the guy."

"My god, Trevor, this isn't you. You don't do stuff like this."

"I did it for you."

"No, you don't get to say that. You did it because you wanted to. Don't dare say you did this in my name." She chastised me for another ten minutes. "You're no better than some criminal on the street. How could you do this? I don't know who you are anymore. Maybe I never did."

Her voice was full of anger, but I heard more sadness and disappointment than anything else. "And you want to be a damn cop?" she yelled. "Maybe I was wrong — it *is* the right profession for you. Now you can do what you want to whomever you want, and no one will think twice." And then she ended the call.

I didn't speak to Sarada for months.

The department would reschedule another polygraph; the results of that exam were deemed inconclusive. A month later, I entered the academy.

It would be six months of hell.

■ ■ ■ ■

My first day in the academy, my drill instructor, Omar Ochoa, a man with a back straight as a board who was afflicted with poor pronunciation and an unforgiving lisp, belted out: "What makes you think you can be a cop?" Each word collided with the next, and it took me a second too long to decipher what he asked, which resulted in fifteen push-ups.

When I finished the push-ups, he said: "Recover." I got to my feet and dusted off the cheap suit I'd bought from a department store days before; it would be months before we would wear our uniforms. Everything in the academy had to be earned through sweat and pain.

"So, who the hell told you that this was something you could do? What makes you think you've got what it takes to wear the badge?" DI Ochoa asked.

"Sir, I want to help keep my community safe and —"

"Lies. Try again."

"Sir, I want to make a positive impact —"

"Stop lying to me, Recruit!"

"Sir, I want to stop bad things from happening."

159

"What was that, Recruit?"

"Sir, I don't want innocent people to suffer — to get hurt. But if they do, I want to make it right."

"Justice seeking?" he said. "And you think wearing a badge means you can stop people from suffering? That it makes you a savior? You think you can make things right by what? Just showing up, arresting someone?"

"Yes, sir."

"I got news for you, Recruit — everything dies. Every living thing. We all feel pain; we all suffer, and death is guaranteed. It's the price of being alive. You can't stop that," he said, speaking a few inches from my face. "My job is to introduce you to suffering so that when you see it in the eyes of a victim or someone who needs your help, you will recognize it and act no matter what. You are no longer an individual. You are a part of the greatest damn police department in the country." He smiled; his mustard-stained teeth looked to have suffered years of neglect. "Class! Assume the prone push-up position."

The other recruits dropped to the blacktop, and we held our bodies planked in the push-up position until the DI saw fit for us to begin our push-ups. "Down!" he screamed.

It was the third-worst day of my life. And while I did want to help protect the innocent, what I didn't tell DI Ochoa was that I also wanted to punish the guilty, the people who caused pain and ruined lives. I wanted what happened to Sarada to never happen to anyone I loved. I wanted the power to keep people safe, and for people who looked like me to know that not every cop had it out for them. All people needed and deserved protection . . . and maybe a small part of me thought if I succeeded in the LAPD that my father might finally be proud I was his son.

The week after I graduated from the academy, I called the Culver City PD's Special Victims Unit. I spoke to a detective about Claudio Spirelli. I didn't know if he was still in the LA area. He might have left after the attack, moved on to another city where nobody knew him. But his roots seemed to lie with his family's business, so I knew there was a good chance he'd remained on the Westside. I identified myself as an LAPD officer and provided him with my name and badge number. We chatted about cop life, and then I said: "I have a tip for you."

The detective listened.

"There's a man named Claudio Spirelli,

161

runs Spirelli Plumbing with his family. We have reason to believe he may be a serial rapist."

The detective was quiet for a moment and then, with a sigh, said, "You shitting me?"

"No."

"Spirelli was sentenced a month ago. Funny story — he came to us as a battery victim after checking himself into the hospital. Someone beat him up real bad, but he wouldn't say who. He was evasive, wouldn't answer questions. Claimed to have no idea why someone would take a club to his private parts. We thought it was a sex crime. The guy needed a catheter just to piss. Something about the whole thing seemed off, so we collected some DNA and ran it in CODIS against our unsolved cases. We got a hit. Guy ends up confessing to a rape going back a few years."

"Damn," I said.

"Exactly," the detective said, chewing in my ear.

It wasn't likely that the beating from a stranger, a man Claudio had never laid eyes on, spurred a conscience in him. But the idea of being attacked out of the blue by a man whose color, for many, signified a courtship with violence could have driven a palpable fear into his heart. Perhaps he wondered who I was, where I came from. Maybe he was amazed by how I beat him and pondered if and when I would return. Was it the unknown that haunted him? To know someone was roaming the city willing and capable of maiming and castrating him might have caused him to crack. Or maybe he conjured me up — his boogeyman, the demon living in his mind.

It didn't matter. What mattered was Claudio was off the streets. "Can you say which rape he confessed to?" I asked.

"We traced his DNA back to one victim — a student at West LA College. He had cut himself sneaking out the woman's apartment window."

"This guy was a serial. There's no way he only did it once."

"Sure, we know that. But it's not about what you know; it's what you can prove. Prosecutor said it was a slam dunk — didn't see any reason to press him for more confessions when we didn't have evidence to connect him. No bargaining. Clean. Open and shut."

"How much time did he get?"

"Sentenced for fifteen, if I recall. He'll probably do eight if he doesn't fuck up in there."

"That's it?"

"Sorry, Officer. It's how it goes. Just remember, that piece of shit still has hell to look forward to."

I couldn't tell Sarada about Claudio going to prison. My instincts had led me to him, but he'd still evaded punishment for assaulting her. I hadn't done enough. I should have demanded he confess to raping Sarada. I should have made him remember, and if he didn't, I should have broken his legs.

"I'm glad to know Spirelli was on someone's radar," the detective said before hanging up.

That night I called Sarada. "Trevor?" She sounded spry, like her old self. "This is a surprise."

"How are you?" I asked.

"Happy to hear your voice."

"I thought about texting — wasn't sure you'd answer."

"I'm glad you didn't. You sound good," she said. "How are you?"

"I'm well," I said. I wasn't well, but I was functioning. "I'm working out of Pacific Division."

"So, you made it through — you're a real cop now?"

"I am," I spoke with loftiness. "Almost got kicked out of the academy once, but yeah, I made it."

"Sounds like a good story."

"Maybe you can hear it sometime?" I tried to rekindle the temper and easiness of our past conversations.

"I'm proud of you, Trevor."

"You are?"

"You set out to do something, and you did it. I may not agree with why you joined the LAPD, but I know you're going to be a great officer."

"That . . . that means a lot, Sarada."

"I don't like how we left things," she said. "I miss you. It doesn't feel right when we're apart like this."

"No, it doesn't."

"You're my best friend, Trevor, and that will never change."

"Figured I'd be replaced by some guy who loves Baldwin. I hear colleges are full of them."

"Please. You know you're not replaceable. And the whole college thing — well, let's just say it was interesting."

"A good interesting?" I asked.

"For the most part. I'm sure I'll miss it one day, just not anytime soon. If that makes sense?"

"I can say the same about the academy."

"I should get some sleep." She yawned. "I've got a meeting in the morning."

"Sounds important."

"I'm buying a food truck."

"You for real?"

"Yes."

"What will you sell?"

"I got pretty good at pound and Bundt cakes. I guess they're my thing."

"So, when did you become a master baker?"

"Started after my assault at the suggestion of my therapist," she said. "Once I got into it, I couldn't stop. Figured I'd turn my passion into profit. It's the Trojan way."

I held the phone away from my ear and took a moment, remembering all we'd been through. Sarada had transcended tragedy, but tragedy was all I had.

"I'm glad you called, Trevor. We'll get together soon. All right?" she said before hanging up.

I didn't deserve it, but it was a second chance to be a better friend. I hadn't slept well for years, but that night a crying baby wouldn't have woken me.

I arrive at my loft. Tori's white Beetle is parked next to my usual spot. I get out of the car with my gear bag and start thinking of excuses for not calling or texting her, but work is usually the only excuse I need.

Walking toward the building, I see her standing in front of the security door wearing a fitted red dress. Her hair is up. She's carrying an extra-large purse, or what she dubs her hobo bag.

"Shit," I say. "Did we have plans?"

"No — just wanted to see you. You feel like talking?"

"Honestly — no."

Tori pulls a bottle of wine from her bag. "We don't have to talk," she says, "unless you're too tired?"

"What else you got in that bag?"

"Let's just say something you'd have fun peeling off me."

Usually, seeing Tori at my loft with the promise of a good time would excite me, but I can't stop thinking about Sarada. I keep walking out on her, just like I left her alone that night in Culver City. Sometimes it's hard not to hate me.

I unlock the door, and Tori and I go inside the building. She's wearing her customary high heels, and her recently tanned skin smells of an ambrosial perfume. There's bourbon on her breath. We get in the elevator, my hands planted on her hips. She kisses my neck as we ride to my floor and go into my loft. Tori begins to undress, removing her clothes slowly down to her black lace bra and panties. Seduction is something she's practiced. She pushes me onto the bed, pours me a glass of wine, and tells me to relax. I do as Tori says; rain taps against the window. She massages my neck, I drink my wine, and I realize I still don't know her favorite color.

CHAPTER FIVE

Day 2, October 17, 2014

My work cell phone rings at six a.m. I answer. It's the medical examiner's office. Brandon's autopsy is complete. Tori must feel the morning's chill; she pulls the sheet over her shoulder. I don't remember much about last night, but we're both naked, and there's an empty bottle of pinot noir on the nightstand. I throw my legs over the side of the bed and slowly get to my feet. The room is at full tilt, and my stomach is churning. I immediately regret drinking in the middle of a major case. I'm slipping, and I need to get a handle on things. Maybe having Tori around is throwing me off my game? We need some time apart until I make headway in the case, maybe a week or two.

I manage to stand, walk into the kitchen, and pour a glass of water. I drink it fast, and my stomach begins to ease. I open the pantry door and slam it shut. It's enough to wake Tori.

"Coffee and bagel?" I ask.

She yawns. "I'll grab something before work."

I go to the closet and take out a starched white shirt, striped blue-and-gray tie, and blue suit. I lay the clothes at the foot of the bed. "A suit?" Tori asks. "Must be a big day."

"I have to get to the county morgue. Sorry, not much time to talk."

"It's fine. I totally get it," she says as she begins to dress. "I'll get out of your way so that you can do your thing. Sucks I don't get to see you all sexy in your suit, though."

"Maybe another time."

"I prefer your birthday suit anyway."

I watch as she finishes getting dressed, pass her the hobo bag, and usher her toward the door. "Call me," she says.

"You know how crazy things can get," I say. "I'll try."

"Well, OK . . . I guess that works."

"Be safe," I say.

"Be safe? Really?"

"You know what I mean. Just watch yourself out there."

"You're acting weird."

"I don't mean to be."

"OK — whatever. Bye."

Tori walks out the door. I shut and lock it

behind her. I don't watch her from my window; instead, I head into the bathroom to shower. I get dressed in my suit, grab my gear bag, and leave. Outside, I put my gear bag in the trunk, get into the car, and drive toward the freeway.

When I arrive at the morgue, the chief medical examiner, Dr. Richard Miles, is most likely on his second cup of Earl Grey. "Morning, Detective," he says.

"How are things, Miles?" He hands me a medical mask, and I put it over my mouth.

"Busy as always. Every season is homicide season around here," Dr. Miles says, sipping his tea from a paper cup. "It's a hell of a thing about your recruit. I'm not sure I've ever seen anything like it."

"That's not encouraging." I follow him down a dingy hallway until we reach the morgue.

"Hate to tell you this, but you've got yourself a weird one."

Dr. Miles is a shabby white man with thick black-framed glasses, the type the government issues soldiers with poor vision. I've never seen him without a lime-green tie, and his clothes are usually stained by liquid that I dare not inquire about. Today is no exception. Brown goop is smeared across the front of his pants as if he rubbed against something dead and oily.

Inside the morgue, covered bodies lie on slabs. Dr. Miles walks me over to Brandon Soledad's body. His skin is gray, a Y incision carved into his chest. His organs have been removed and rest on a tray next to his body.

"There was no evidence of a sexual assault. He was likely knocked unconscious," Dr. Miles says, resting his tea on what looks like an operating table. "There was trauma to his face and the back of his head."

"Enough to kill him?"

"No, that was to incapacitate him. What killed him was the cold."

"The cold?"

"That's right."

"Like hypothermia? The mountain cold did this?"

"No. To have this level of tissue damage, he likely was alive when the freezing first began. Once frozen, he expired and then thawed postmortem." Dr. Miles pokes at Brandon's waxy flesh. "I'm guessing he was knocked unconscious, stripped naked, put into the cold environment where he died, cleaned up, possibly hosed down, and then driven to the crime scene and dumped."

"Sounds like a lot of work." I tuck my tie

172

into my shirt before leaning over Brandon's corpse. "Someone went through a lot of trouble to kill him this way."

"The strange skin coloring that forensics noted is due to the warmer outdoor temperature, which sped up the thawing. Similar to defrosting a frozen steak in the microwave."

"And what about those lines scratched into his arm?"

"He did that to himself. He would have had about thirty minutes before the colder air began impacting his lung tissue."

"What do you think he used?"

"We found traces of his blood under the fingernail on his right thumb." Dr. Miles lowers the magnifying lamp over Brandon's arm. I'm able to see what looks to be the letter *C* followed by the numbers *4, 1,* and *1.* "Consider his fingernail's sharp edge and a seriously firm press, and you'd get these jagged scratches."

"Anything else?" I ask as I take pictures with my cell phone camera. "Stimulants — uppers, downers?"

"Nothing in his system, not even alcohol. The kid was clean."

I slip my phone into my suit pocket and take in Brandon's body one last time. Dr.

Miles notices. "You all right, Detective?"

"I'll be in touch, Doctor."

I leave the medical examiner's office and head to Ahmanson Recruit Training Center in Westchester. Since the Elysian Park location is being remodeled, Ahmanson is the LAPD's current central training facility. I phone ahead and let Captain Rivera know I'm coming. On the phone, she's curt; it's hard to tell if she's just busy or if hearing my voice pisses her off. It takes me an hour to arrive at the Ahmanson facility. The 10 freeway was congested, and if it weren't for the express lane, it would have taken longer.

I scan my badge to enter the rear parking lot. I park and walk to the front of the building. It's old, like many of the department's training centers. A large statue sits in front of the building, a rather haunting memorial to fallen officers. It's carved from green-stone, and at its base, ghostly faces swirl about, giving form to a giant hand hollowed in the middle. It's by far one of the most grotesque sculptures I've ever seen, but the LAPD isn't known for its artistic sensibilities.

When I enter the building's lobby, an older black officer greets me. He's pudgy and looks near retirement age, likely finishing out his time as the academy's doorman. "Good morning," he says, his chin angled upward. "Can I help you?"

"I'm Detective Finnegan. I was hoping to speak to Captain Rivera. It's pertaining to a case." He waves me forward. I show him my badge. Lips pursed, he examines the badge with discernment. "OK," he says, not quite smiling at me. The skin around his mouth seems to relax. "She knows you're coming?"

"I called ahead."

"NYPD is here today, so the captain is holding all her meetings. Is this something urgent?"

"It's concerning Brandon Soledad."

"You're working that case?"

"That's right."

"Alone?"

"Is that a problem?"

"Of course not — it's nice to see a brother working it, that's all."

"What brings NYPD out?" I ask.

"It's about Garner, that man they choked to death over the summer." The officer sounds sapped, like thinking of Garner's doom is taxing on his soul. "They're here to get some ideas on how to retrain their people and hopefully get them to stop choking suspects."

"And they're coming to us? They're worse off than I thought."

"Can you imagine that? I mean, we stopped choking boys to death years ago."

"Small victories, I guess."

"Victories or progress, my brother?"

"Only time will tell."

The officer looks at his watch. "If you don't mind, the drill instructors are available now. You'll want to talk to Simmons. I think he'll be the most helpful. You can head on up."

"All right." I give him an appreciative nod and walk through the lobby, which resembles a museum. Black-and-white photos of graduated academy classes dating back decades and a pictorial of the *Adam-12* cast working alongside officers on the show's set fill glass display cases, along with academy buttons, pins, patches, and challenge coins.

I take the elevator to the second floor.

Upstairs, I knock hard on the door to the drill instructors' office, then enter. It's a large room with a long rectangular table in the middle. Desks are positioned along the walls, facing outward so drill instructors can see who enters the room. Officers rarely sit with their backs to doors; it puts them at a tactical disadvantage.

"Good afternoon," I say as I approach a

man who looks to be a drill instructor.

"Good afternoon. Can I help you?" the man asks.

"I'm Detective Finnegan. I'm looking for DI Simmons."

"I'm DI Simmons." He stands up, revealing his height. He's about six foot two, bald, white, with a beach tan and broad shoulders. He looks to be in his late fifties, maybe older. "At your service," he says, extending his hand.

I let his hand linger in the air for a moment before shaking it. It makes him uncomfortable, but that's the play. An old detective tactic, helps break convention. I liken it to what Peter Falk did as Columbo. It was one of the only TV shows my father watched. I must have seen every episode on rerun. Whatever a person expected, Columbo did the opposite, always one step ahead. I'm no Columbo, but I need to establish a clear power dynamic with Simmons — he needs to know I have the upper hand.

"Were you Brandon Soledad's DI?" I ask.

"Yes, I was. The whole class is pretty torn up about it."

"What about you?"

"I don't follow."

"I heard he was doing well and would

have made a fine officer. Do you agree with that assessment?"

"Sure," he says. "He was one of our best."

"Did Brandon have any trouble with his classmates? Arguments, spats you know about?"

"No, everyone liked the guy, and that's what makes it even tougher," he says with misgauged wryness. "This is new territory for us. We offered recruits time with a grief counselor, but they all chose to go about business as usual. I think they felt that was the best way to honor Soledad's memory."

"You told the other recruits what happened to him?"

"What is there to tell? I mean, they know he's dead, if that's what you're asking."

"He was murdered."

"I didn't have that information at the time. Even if I did, we wouldn't tell the recruits one of their classmates was a homicide victim."

"They watch the news."

"We recommend they avoid TV and social media while in the academy, but if they happen to learn of his tragic demise, we will address it."

"I'm going to need to interview all the recruits and your training staff. You have a room I can use?"

"That'll take days."

"Maybe."

"I'm sure we can find someplace. I prefer to have one of my instructors present during these interviews," he says as he comes from behind his desk.

"Why is that?"

"Just looking out for my recruits. It's about support, Detective. They don't have union reps since they aren't sworn, and it's important they know their rights."

"You think that's necessary? We're on the same team."

"We are, so it shouldn't be a problem."

"No, you're right. It isn't a problem."

I follow DI Simmons outside to the rear of the building. The recruits are in formation standing on the blacktop. Thirteen of them — the class probably began with twenty or so, but some washed out. There are ten men and three women. I quickly spot who I figure is Marlena Sanchez. She's pretty, like Brandon's friend, J. D., suggested. A petite, brown-skinned woman with jet-black hair in a tight bun. I'll need a reasonable amount of time to question her, but not with one of the training staff hovering over my shoulder. I'll need to ask her some sensitive questions about her and Brandon's relationship. If they were intimate, it could mean automatic dismissal from the academy, and I need Sanchez to trust that I'm not out to sink her. If she feels comfortable enough, she'll tell me the truth without worrying she's pissing her career away before it even gets started.

DI Simmons addresses the class with the same grit I remember from DI Ochoa in my recruit days. "Class! Attention! About-face!" The recruits spin on their boot heels in unison and face Simmons. "You will now go to Training Room Six. You will line up outside the room. You will be called one at a time into the room, where Detective Finnegan will ask you questions regarding Brandon Soledad." Simmons turns to me and says, "I suggest you get set up. I'll deliver them to you in five minutes."

I head back into the building and make my way to Training Room Six. I enter the room to find my old training officer. "Joey Garcia," I say. "Figures." I tense up at the sight of him, and my first inclination is to go for his throat. How could I have forgotten this waste of space was now training recruits as a physical training officer, which means his attire is blue shorts, a T-shirt, and sneakers? A far cry from his days in uniform.

"Look who it is — good old Finn," he says. "So, it's true. You're working the Soledad case."

"Don't tell me Simmons elected you to chaperone."

"Well, he knows I can be trusted . . . unlike some people."

"Then he doesn't know you at all."

After the incident four years ago and a string of citizen complaints, I heard Garcia had staved off being fired. I guess this is how he did it, by joining the Physical Training Division at the academy.

"Don't think for a minute you're better than me," he says. "You and I both know what you are — a rat extortionist with a badge."

"What I am is a detective. You know what that means, don't you? It means I outrank your ass. So, check your tone."

As it's commonly called, the PT Division is where poor-performing or problematic officers are placed or, rather, relegated as punishment. If an officer makes a bad call on the street or racks up citizen complaints, they can enjoy a year of push-ups and three-mile runs. It's seen as a cooling-off period, a place where officers can consider their careers and still keep their pensions. These officers take pleasure in ordering recruits to kiss the concrete while they berate them, the perfect job for Garcia.

"Whatever, Finn. Lose the badge and rank, and I'd wipe the floor with you." Garcia has gone maximum meathead, putting on a few extra pounds of muscle since I last saw him. And his nose looks crooked, like it's been broken at least once, maybe twice, and didn't heal straight. He's still the same goon he was four years ago.

"You have this glorified gym teacher act down," I say. "Careful, or you'll be pissing protein shake."

Garcia takes a step closer to square up. "You want to say that again? Didn't quite hear you the first time."

"Back up, Joey," I say, staring him down intensely. "Or your shitty ears are going to be the least of your problems."

The truth has a way of getting under most people's skin, and Garcia isn't immune. He's near the bottom of the department's pecking order, and he knows it. After a year of instructing recruits in the academy, most officers return to the street, but I'm thinking that Garcia has been in the PT Division for two or more. That means the department has lost faith in him, that it's safer for the city to keep him in exercise clothes running a track than in a uniform interacting with the public.

"You just wait until I'm back in the

department's good graces."

"Were you ever in their good graces? You were always a bit of a scab."

"Keep talking, and we'll end up the same way we left things, with my hands around your throat."

"I seem to recall you taking a hook to the flank."

"Then I owe you one," Garcia says. "You just tell me when and where."

Bored with the dick-swinging, I take a seat at an empty table. "Go on, Garcia, do your job. I hear the recruits lining up, and I'd like to get to work if you don't mind. So, go on, now, fetch me the first one."

Garcia snickers and leaves the room. He returns with the first recruit, a young white boy, no older than twenty-five, so nervous he's shaking.

"Have a seat," I say to the recruit. The boy sits down and squirms a bit before settling. "What's your name?"

"Recruit Officer Howell."

"You know why you're here, Howell?"

"No, sir."

"Brandon Soledad was your fellow recruit, correct?"

"Yes."

"You look nervous. Anything you want to talk about?" Howell looks down toward his lap. "Is there an answer down there?"

Howell quickly lifts his head. "I made a mistake, sir. It'll never happen again. Please, don't kick me out."

"Come again," I say, taking out my notepad. "What are you talking about?"

"I parked illegally last week, and the traffic officer gave me a fine."

"A ticket?"

"Yes, sir. It was in the amount of eighty dollars. I paid it that day."

"So, you parked in the red zone?"

"Yes, just for ten minutes. I was picking up my cat from the vet and —"

"I don't need to hear about your cat, Recruit. And I'm not here about any parking citations. I just want to know about Brandon Soledad." Howell looks perplexed, and I realize these recruits know nothing. "How close were you to Recruit Officer Soledad?" I ask.

"Not close at all, sir."

"You didn't like him?"

"It wasn't that, sir. We just didn't interact much."

"Do you know whom he was close to?"

"I couldn't be certain, sir. Maybe Recruit Officer Sanchez and Recruit Officer Gorman?"

"Gorman," I repeat as I write the name

184

on my notepad. "Thank you for your time, Howell. You're dismissed."

After Howell leaves, I turn to Garcia, who's standing by the door, gloating. "It's going to be a long afternoon," he says.

"Just bring in the next one."

Recruit Officer Gorman enters. He's a large man, Latino, older than the other recruits, maybe in his midforties. "Good afternoon, sir."

"Gorman, take a seat," I say. Gorman sits and makes a subtle adjustment, shifting his weight backward and pulling his chair forward. "You comfortable?"

"Yes, sir." He gives good eye contact, but his face dawns a grimace. It's the type of face weight lifters make before a heavy lift, like they're scared of blowing a gasket.

"They say you and Soledad were close?"

"We were, sir."

"Would you say you were friends?"

"Yes, we were friends, sir."

"How about we give the *sir* stuff a break. Plain talk is fine."

"OK." Gorman loses the grimace and takes a deep breath.

"Now, you two were friends, correct?"

"Correct."

"Did you talk on the phone or hang out outside the academy?"

"We did. We studied together and tried our best to support each other."

"When did you last see Brandon outside of the academy?"

"Last weekend. We got pizza and studied for our exam."

Garcia snickers. "One pizza too many for you, Gorman."

I cut my eyes at Garcia and continue with my questioning. "How did Brandon seem to you, his behavior? Was he worried? Did he express that he was afraid someone might want to hurt him?"

"No. He was himself. Happy, in good spirits, just glad to be in the academy."

"You and Brandon ever argue?"

"No."

"You ever see him arguing with other recruits or anyone else for that matter?"

"No."

"Did Soledad ever identify as a recruit officer or having any affiliation with the LAPD outside of the academy?"

"Not to my knowledge."

"Did he ever talk to you about his home-life?"

"He said he and his stepfather didn't always see eye to eye, but nothing more than that. I told him I was a stepdad and that it wasn't easy to assume the father's role.

Sometimes I wish I could have done more for Brandon, treated him more like a son. He was a good kid. He was by the book, upbeat — he encouraged us."

"Us?"

"Yes, me and Sanchez."

"Marlena Sanchez?"

"That's correct. Our classmate."

"You three were friends?"

"We were becoming good friends. We spent a lot of time together. Carpooled sometimes, studied, aired out how we were feeling." A tear threatens to fall from his eye; he blinks hard and wipes the moisture from his face with a handkerchief. "At the end of this, we might have been lifelong friends had he not died."

"That's a nice thought, Gorman."

"Can I ask a question, sir?"

"Go ahead."

"Is it true that he was killed?"

I deliberate for a moment and then answer: "Yes. He was."

Garcia clenches his jaw and frowns like he's sucking on something sour. He mutters under his breath, probably something vulgar directed at me.

"Did you have a career before this?" I ask Gorman. "You seem like you have some years on you."

187

"I was a finance manager in my past life."

"You have a nickname yet?"

Gorman shrugs. "They call me Lazarus."

"That's all, Gorman. Thank you for your time. You can go," I say.

As soon as Gorman leaves the room, Garcia lays into me. "What the hell are you doing?" he asks.

"My job."

"Get the fuck off your high horse. You're going to mess up their heads."

"They want to be police officers. They need to know that we die."

"Brandon wasn't a fucking cop. He was a kid, and kids make mistakes."

"You saying Soledad made a mistake? He did something to get himself killed?"

"Maybe — hell, it happens all the time. Recruits get to feeling themselves and think they're above it all. Maybe he got into an altercation with someone and said he was a cop. And as you know, people fucking hate us."

"He didn't seem the type."

"You never really know anybody, do you?"

"Look, Garcia, if I want your opinion, I'll ask for it. Otherwise, you're a silent observer. Got it?"

"Whatever."

"Who's next?"

I talk to ten other recruits who offer nothing more than that their fellow recruit was smart, good at push-ups, and seemed to be a nice guy. As I thought, Brandon was the only black recruit. Since the late 1990s, blacks and Asians at the academy have been usually few and far between. The Middle Eastern recruits were almost nonexistent, the terrorist attacks of September 11, 2001, only making it harder for them to join. To say the department has a diversity problem is an understatement, but what police department doesn't?

Sanchez enters the room with deliberate slowness, each step measured. When she reaches the chair, she slowly pulls it out and sits, pulling it forward and closer to the edge of the table. "Good afternoon, sir. Before we begin, can I ask you something?"

"That's not how this works, Sanchez," I say.

"Yes, sir. I understand," she says somberly.

"Go ahead."

Sanchez twists her mouth and says, "How was he killed?"

"You watch the news?"

"I don't make it a habit, sir. But yes, I saw a broadcast."

"I can't get into that at this time. The investigation is ongoing."

"Yes, sir. But what they're saying on TV — it's sickening to think of Brandon that way. He suffered, didn't he?" Sanchez looks away for a moment. Maybe she's conjuring Brandon in her mind.

"I really couldn't say."

"I understand, sir."

"I take it that you two were close?"

"Yes."

"Gorman indicated you three spent quite a bit of time together?"

"We were study buddies."

"And where did most of this studying take place?"

"Sometimes at my place. Other times we'd meet up at Gorman's."

"You ever study at Brandon's house?"

"Brandon never suggested it, and we never asked. I always felt like he preferred to be out of his house."

"Did he ever discuss his family situation with you?"

"Sometimes."

"What did he say?"

"He couldn't wait to get his own place. Brandon didn't have much support at home. No one in his family wanted him to join the LAPD."

"Did he ever speak about his stepfather?"

"Yes." She stops. "There was friction, I think."

"To your knowledge, did it ever get physical?"

"Brandon mentioned a few altercations they had when he was younger, but nothing recently."

"Altercations?"

"He said when he was younger . . . high school, maybe, he pushed Brandon during an argument."

Out of all the recruits I've interviewed, Sanchez is the most at ease. There's something about her that feels vulnerable but guarded. Before she speaks, she pauses, as if to summon the right words, and then once she speaks those words, she waits — studies my reaction and then considers her next move. Perhaps she's being careful to conceal her mourning, not wanting to let on about her and Brandon's relationship? But I can see why Brandon told her so much about his life at home. Sanchez is disarming, a natural beauty with a calm demeanor and a voice like butter melting down a hot knife.

"Sounds like he confided a lot in you?"

"As I said, we were friends," she says. Her brown eyes draw me in. I imagine her outside the training walls — hair down, wielding a look that could make a man want to tell his deepest, darkest secrets, and I begin to understand why Garcia can't stop staring at her. Since the moment she's sat down, he hasn't gone more than five seconds without scanning her from top to bottom.

"You asked me earlier if I thought he suffered," I say. Sanchez is quiet, and her face begins to flush. "I think he died miserably — not quick, not in the way you'd like to think so you can rest easy. He died probably in one of the worst ways I could imagine, and he was alone."

Tears build in Sanchez's eyes, trying to break free and slip down her cheeks.

"I'm sorry to tell you this," I say, "but the person or persons who killed your friend did so with the kind of anger, the kind of malice that I rarely see. It was personal. Makes me wonder who the hell he pissed off. Who hated him that much?"

"Detective Finnegan," Garcia says with despisement in his voice, "what are you doing?"

Sanchez is crying now, tears staining her uniform. I look at Garcia. "Get her some tissues and a cup of water." Garcia doesn't move. I've disrespected him in front of a recruit. "Do I need to get the DI in here? Get her some damn tissues and a cup of water, now!"

Garcia walks out of the room in a huff. I figure he'll head to the closest water fountain on the west end of the building. That should buy me enough time. "It's just you and me now, OK?"

Sanchez nods.

"You want to tell me what happened between you and Brandon?"

"What do you mean?"

"Were you intimate?"

"No! God, no."

"Did he want to be?"

"Soledad wouldn't have done anything to get kicked out of the academy. It was too important to him."

"And you?"

"What about me?"

"Were you happy with being friends?"

"Soledad was a rule follower. He knew the handbook front to back — every rule, every regulation, every terminable offense. I mean, we all drink the Kool-Aid here, enough to get through, but Soledad believed in this place. He never made mistakes, not even when it was so easy to."

"Tell me what happened between you two. It won't leave this room. I have no interest in you getting booted from the academy. I just need some answers."

Sanchez loses her bearings, raises her voice. "It was me!" she shouts, nearly breaking down.

"Remember where you are," I say, almost whispering. "Calm down."

She moves her hands from her knees, places them on the table, and washes the emotion from her voice. "I crossed the line." Sanchez looks to the door. I surmise she's looking for Garcia, who should be returning at any moment.

"You? How so?"

"We were studying at my place, and Gorman had already gone home. I had a glass of wine, and Brandon had water like usual." She wipes the tears from her face. "I don't know. I guess I read the moment wrong? I kissed him, and for a moment, I'm pretty sure he was kissing me back. Then he stopped."

"That's it?"

"Yes. If anyone were to find out, it would have been both of our asses. So, we kept the kiss between us. I guess I thought once we graduated, we'd have a chance to talk about it."

"I'm not going to say anything."

"I'm not a bad person, Detective, and it doesn't mean I can't exercise control. It just happened — maybe it was the stress of this place."

"You're a human being. We've all been there."

"I just wish he were still here, so I could talk to him one more time."

"I'm going to find out what happened to your friend."

She wipes the last bit of tears from her face. "It's like no one around here cares."

"I care. You just concentrate on getting through this hellhole."

Sanchez laughs. "I've only heard recruits call it that."

Garcia enters with a box of tissues and a cup of water. "I couldn't find any tissues in the main office. I had to get them from storage," he says, like he completed an arduous task.

"It's appreciated," I say as a way for him to save face in front of the recruit.

Garcia hands Sanchez the tissues and puts the water on the table. She takes a sip. "I hope you get whoever did this," she says.

"I will," I say, then turn to Garcia. "That's enough interviewing for today. I'll follow up as needed. I'll let DI Simmons know when I'm coming."

"So, you're done with Sanchez?" Garcia asks.

"She can go."

Garcia takes Sanchez out of the room, briefly putting his hand on her shoulder to console her, and then lets his arm fall to his side. It's a blatant conduct violation, but Garcia doesn't seem to recognize his error.

The gesture seems natural, like something he's done before.

I head up to the DI's office. Simmons is completing paperwork. He looks bothered when he sees me. "You get what you needed?" he asks.

"Yes."

"Good. I don't suspect we'll be seeing much of you anymore."

"I go where the investigation takes me."

"Sure you do, Detective. I did some digging of my own. I asked around about you. You have quite a reputation."

"Then you've heard I still hold the academy's record for the most pull-ups during a PFQ."

DI Simmons sulks, then says, "That and the most fifteen-sevens for unsatisfactory performance issued in one day. What was the offense?"

"I spoke out of turn. I was told I needed to learn my place. But you already know that."

"I suspect you still haven't learned that lesson, have you? It's amazing that you've lasted this long in this department."

"Per the handbook, the hazing of a recruit, whether by fellow recruits or training officers, is strictly prohibited. I spoke up, said what I had to say, and accepted the consequences."

"They should have kicked you out for insubordination."

"Maybe," I say, "but here I am. By the way, I'll need Marlena Sanchez's personnel file before I go."

"What do you want with that?"

"All due respect, sir, it is a homicide investigation. Some things are need to know."

I wait fifteen minutes for him to make copies of Sanchez's file. As I leave the office, DI Simmons stares at me with a familiar distaste. DI Ochoa used to look at me the same way. I go downstairs, exit the building, and head toward the parking lot.

I can't shake the way Garcia cozied up to Sanchez without a second thought. They're too familiar. It isn't a substantial lead, but it's a thread worth pulling on. I'm not sure what I'll find in Sanchez's file, but I'm mostly interested in her personal statement. Each recruit provides a personal statement during the first week in the academy — the first homework assignment. In their statements, recruits discuss why they want to be police officers. They highlight their support system, who has their back, and who doesn't. They include potential hindrances to their success in the academy, like childcare, unsupportive spouses, or caring for aging parents. At first glance, Sanchez's file is impressive: a resident of Eagle Rock, she's fluent in Spanish and Tagalog, and she completed two years at Occidental College before leaving to join the LAPD. I can see why the academy accepted her — bilingual, college-educated, and not as much as a traffic ticket on her record.

My work cell phone rings. I answer, and after a few minutes, I realize I'm in store for severe embarrassment, the type that could send my career down the shitter faster than this case.

CHAPTER SIX

"Finnegan — you better talk to him," Captain Devaughn Wilson says, standing in the lobby of the Central Community Police Division. Wilson is one of the only black police captains in the department and an old friend of my father's, though as of today, that friendship may be on life support.

"Captain Wilson," I say. "How are you, sir?"

"I've been better. I've got your father in lockup. It's not his finest hour." Captain Wilson is what most black officers aspire to be — a cop with a spotless record and a pristine uniform that fits him like a glove. He's in good shape, with the kind of vitality my father once had. Considering they're about the same age, it's even more depressing that my father not only let his career go but also his health.

"What happened?" I ask.

"Patrol officers picked him up during a

rally near City Hall. Your father and others caused a traffic jam with their protest. He was going on about police brutality, mostly. I believe he cited other offenses systematic of the police state."

"Ah, shit."

"Word is he's the ringleader in all this." Wilson shakes his head, disappointed. "We also picked up a woman with him."

"Shantelle?"

"Yeah, that's the one. A real piece of work. We booked them both on disorderly conduct. Thought it best to call you."

"Thank you, Captain." My father is intent on destroying any memory of him being the type of cop other cops looked up to. People respected my father. He could have easily been in Captain Wilson's shoes.

"What the hell is he thinking?" Wilson asks. "I get he's trying to make things better. But I mean, is this the best way to go about it?"

"I don't know, sir. I'm sure he'd tell you he's doing what he thinks is right."

Like most black officers who outrank me, Wilson is usually quick to offer some tough love.

"Well, maybe you can talk to him?" Wilson asks. "The mayor is putting together a commission on police reform. That's where your father's voice should be heard. Not shouting in the streets."

"I'll let him know, sir," I say, knowing how my father will respond. He'll curse Wilson good and say, *I'll march wherever I damn well please.* Which is why there's no point in telling him.

"I don't like arresting him like this, but hell, he's making it easy." Wilson's lips curl in a frown. "Doesn't he know it's a bad look for you? For all of us."

I don't know if the collective *us* means black people or just black cops.

"I know you're doing the best you can." Wilson eases up; it's probably my face, the downtrodden stare that begs to ask, *Can this day get any worse?* "How about you pull around back, and I'll have some officers bring him out?"

"Thank you, sir."

"What about the woman? We have no reason to hold her much longer. We've had her for about two hours already, and she's made one phone call to a lawyer. You want her released to you as well?"

"No, hold her for as long as you want."

I park at the rear of the station. Two older, seasoned officers, likely P3s, exit from a gray, unmarked door with my father and walk toward my car, each holding one of his arms. Pop is making a fuss, but the officers shine him on.

I get out of the car and listen as my father, once a decorated officer, berates his fellow boys in blue. "You assholes — let go of me!" he yells. "Y'all are spineless. You know that? Brainwashed oppressors."

My embarrassment quickly turns to anger. "Cool it, Pop!"

"We're releasing him to you, Detective," an officer says.

"Thank you."

"Don't mention it." The officers walk away, laughing to themselves. Without a doubt, word of my father's arrest at the rally is going to spread through the department like gossip from a loose-lipped badge bunny.

"Since when did they give you a Mustang?" my father asks. "It's nice."

"Just get in the car," I say.

"That's no way to speak to your father."

"Fine. Would you please get in the car so we can get the hell out of here?"

Watching as my father gets into the passenger's seat, I notice some bruising around his cheek. I want to ask him about it, but I'm not sure I want the answer. I get into the car, throw the seat belt across me, and start the engine.

"I know you're angry, Trevor, but I figured it would just be a peaceful march."

I head toward the 110 freeway. From a distance, I see traffic forming on the on-ramp ahead. "Pop, I didn't have time for this today. Now I've got to fight traffic to get you home."

"Well, I didn't ask you to come. What you call yourself doing, rescuing me? I could have gotten out fine by myself. Shantelle has a good lawyer."

"I don't want to hear about Shantelle or her lawyer — this is about you. I don't know how you can even stomach it. All the cop-hating bullshit people like Shantelle are ped-dling out here, and you're just eating it up. After what you went through on the force to get an ounce of respect, to be treated with a bit of dignity. And you throw it away for some chick who is supposed to be cleaning your house, which by the way, is a mess. I mean, is she even working for you any-more?"

"I told her to work when she can. Her son has some autoimmune disease. Stays sick a lot."

"C'mon, Pop, this is ridiculous. She's fill-ing your head with nonsense, and she can't even keep your house from smelling like a dump. And if that's not enough, she's helping you piss away your legacy."

"Boy, would you listen to yourself? I'm not pissing away anything. I woke up — that's what I did. And I'm praying every day you'll wake up, too. Because the shit that's going on is poison, son, and if you're not careful, it is going to destroy you," he says, pointing his finger at me like I'm eight. "And my house is fine, by the way. I'm a grown man, and I can clean up after myself if I want. It was your idea to get a housekeeper in the first place. I said it was a damn waste of money."

"I regret that, too."

"Well, don't. Shantelle is the best thing that's happened to me since your mother."

"Pop, she's using you to add validity to her cause. You just don't see it. Maybe it's because you're —"

"I'm what?"

"Nothing."

"Say it, boy. Don't hold back now. You're getting stuff off your chest, so let's hear it. You think I'm losing my mind, don't you? You think I'm slipping?"

"I didn't say that."

"You didn't have to. I know what you're thinking, and you're wrong. Ain't shit wrong with my head."

After five minutes on the on-ramp, I accelerate to merge onto 110 North.

"Put yourself in my shoes or Captain Wilson's. You're looking like you're losing it."

"Oh, hell! I'm sharper than I've ever been," Pop says. "I'm crazy now because I'm calling out this country's hypocrisy and oppression? The real power lies with the people, son. Never forget that."

"Is that what happened to your face? Because it looks like someone showed you real power, Pop."

"It's nothing."

"Someone hit you."

"It might have been worse if one of the boys hadn't recognized me."

"You should get a doctor to look at that."

"I'll survive. I've had worse."

"You get the officer's name and badge number?"

"Does it even matter? What are you going to do about it?"

"You can file a complaint with IAB, have it investigated."

"I think you're the one who needs his head examined if you believe that would make a difference."

"There are procedures and proper channels for this type of thing. We have to use them. Otherwise, they're obsolete."

"Yeah, right — you keep on believing that,

and see where it gets you."

My work cell phone rings. I pull the phone from my pocket and put it to my ear. "Finn — go ahead." It's Captain Beckett. He sounds tired as usual, but his voice is elevated. I can't call it excitement, but maybe a touch of hopefulness?

"We found the recruit's car," he says. "It's at Paradise Lost in Downey."

"The strip joint?" I ask.

"That's the one."

"Copy. I'll head there now."

I end the call and drop the phone into the catchall tray of the center console. "I can't take you home yet," I say.

"Why not?"

"They found my victim's car. I need to get to Downey. As much as I'd like, I don't have time to drop you at home."

"Don't sound so annoyed. Maybe I could be of some help? Twenty-five years of experience should count for something."

"Pop, the best thing for you to do is stay in the car. OK? If you haven't noticed, this is the most important case of my life, and I can't risk any mistakes."

"Bringing your father to a crime scene is pretty unorthodox. It looks like you're already stepping out on a fine line."

"Please, Pop, don't make me regret springing you from lockup."

"Is this the Trevor Finnegan charm I've heard so much about? You must be a joy to work with. Don't worry, I'm not going to dirty up your crime scene."

I merge onto 5 South. It should take me about forty-five minutes to get to Downey, granted the traffic cooperates. My father is quiet for the rest of the car ride, which gives me time to think. Paradise Lost isn't just a strip club; it's a retreat for officers. It's been the location for birthdays, retirements, and bachelor parties, even a few clean kill celebrations for when an officer takes a bad guy off the streets for good — justifiable homicide in the line of duty, or what some officers call God's work. The owner likes to turn off the security cameras and turns the VIP section into an exclusive playground for boys with badges.

So, why was Brandon's car parked outside one of LAPD's dirty secrets?

I pull into the parking lot of Paradise Lost. Unmarked sedans and the Field Investigation Unit van are parked on the street across from a late-model Nissan Altima. A neon sign displays PARADISE LOST high above the club, casting a pink glow over the figures moving below. Officers have set up work lamps and yellow police tape around the Nissan.

I park and turn to my father, who seems to watch longingly as the officers work the scene. Maybe there's a part of him that misses the action? Perhaps he sees more than the department's flaws and still values what it offers — the surge of adrenaline, the challenge of solving puzzles, the chance to right wrongs and work for justice. Or maybe he just misses carrying the gun and badge, coffee brewed to motor-oil thickness, and a department that turned a blind eye to officers using suspects as punching bags. There was a time when a cop could work out his demons with a suspect in an interrogation room and not face reprisal. But who am I kidding? Pop has never been one for nostalgia.

"Sit tight. I'll check on you in a bit," I say.

My father grumbles. "I'm not a poodle. I'll be fine. Do what you have to do."

It wouldn't take the department shrink to figure out what's going on with my father. Guilt is a powerful thing, and we all manage it differently. For him, he's turned into a crusader — he's bought into a narrative espoused by the media and politicians looking to court minority voters. It's a narrative that says all cops are racists, crooked, worthless, and liars. But inside, I know, if he truly believed that, he wouldn't have stayed with the department for so long. My father was of the old guard, when the aroma of booze and cigarettes stayed on detectives' breath and confessions came after ten long hours, hearkened by threats against suspects, both legal and physical. The streets were a zoo — and a good cop always knew *who was who in the zoo*: the pushers, pimps, prostitutes, hustlers, junkies, and bangers. Cops like these had heads full of information they could flip through like a Rolodex. They knew everyone on their beat, every person's parents, siblings, lovers, where they went to grade school, how they liked their coffee and cognac. In my father's case, he knew the streets better than his home. Better than his wife and son.

Walking toward Brandon's car, I see a familiar face, one that hasn't aged well. The department has worked her dry but not to the bone . . . not yet. "Look who decided to show up," Amanda "Boston" Walsh says. "The man of the hour."

She's still the same brash cop from four years ago — more miles and running — only now, instead of a uniform, she's wearing a suit that hangs from her body the way it probably hung from the rack in the department store. Sloppily, without care.

"Boston," I say. "Been a while."

"It's Sergeant Walsh now."

"Sorry — Sergeant." Boston was recently made a detective sergeant with the Field Investigation Unit. It garnered a nice write-up in the LAPD bulletin. According to the article, her special focus is computer forensics, but she's well-versed in all manners of forensic investigation.

"They say this is your first solo murder case. That true?" Boston asks.

"It is. What does it matter?"

"Nothing. Just nice to see you finally wetting your whistle. Beckett and the brass must have faith in you."

"I have every intention of solving this."

"Spoken like a true detective. But let me give you some advice. Sometimes cases just don't want to be solved, and you need to know when to walk away. Otherwise, you'll lose it."

"That's terrible advice."

"Do you want to know how I made sergeant?" Boston doesn't wait for me to answer. "It's about the track record. Focus on cases that you can solve. Simple as that."

"Well, this has been very enlightening, Walsh . . ."

"Suit yourself," she says. "I'm just telling

you what I know, and that's don't be a hero. People aren't interested."

Boston can be a bitter cynic, not unlike other cops nearing twenty years, but it hasn't stopped her from getting ahead in the department. She gnashes her teeth and digs her boot heels into the dirt as if to say, "I dare you to move me." An arrogance that many officers can't stand. Sure, I know I can be a pain to work with, but Boston can be a nightmare.

"You're not jaded at all," I say with an abundance of sarcasm.

"Some cases go on for decades. Some are solved in a few days. Each case has its own story, like a thread in LA's tapestry of horrors. Of course, the dead are fortunate if they have someone who remembers them because they're just numbers to us."

"Thanks. You can table your advice for now. I'm good."

"Sure you are. Just remember that working a case alone means all the accolades when it's successful, but when it's not, you're the only one who gets shit on."

"You speaking from experience?"

"Not exactly," Boston says, coming off her soapbox. "I'm just trying to give you some perspective."

"I'd like to look at the vehicle now."

I follow Boston toward Brandon's Nissan, surrounded by work lights and crime scene technicians. "The car was open when we located it," she says.

"Who found it?"

"The club's owner."

"Isn't that guy supposed to be a reserve officer?"

"That's him."

"I didn't realize he was still playing a weekend cop."

"His expertise has come in handy on a few vice cases. I figure the department keeps him around for that."

"Strip club owner five days a week and cop twice a month. How the hell does that even happen?" I say, putting on a pair of latex gloves.

"There are other benefits to having him in the department, like no cover charge for officers. And I hear a few of his girls give decent tug jobs." Boston cups her hand and makes an obscene stroking motion.

"Why am I even surprised by that? Did he agree to turn over his security footage?"

"He was eager to help. It's with forensics now."

"Good."

I nod to a few of the technicians that I recognize. As we approach the car, a brunette wearing the department-issued windbreaker takes photos of the interior of the Altima's trunk.

"They find anything useful yet?" I ask.

"The car looks pretty clean," Boston says. "It might have been wiped down."

"When does the flatbed arrive?"

"Hopefully, in the next thirty minutes or so."

"This is a priority, Walsh. Once you get the car to the lab, I want a full workup."

"Of course. Your captain already briefed us. We have it covered."

"That's what I like to hear."

"You look tired, Finn. Maybe you should get some rest?"

For Boston to be concerned, I must look like shit. "Maybe you're right," I say. "A few hours of shut-eye would do me good."

"You're not much for the homelife, are you?"

"We getting personal now?"

"Here's a nugget —"

"Great. More unsolicited advice."

"Find someone who'll make you want to go home. It's a good feeling walking into a house where someone you love is waiting for you. Besides, married people live longer."

"I'm pretty sure that doesn't apply to

213

cops. Last I heard, the divorce rate doubled for us."

"I wouldn't know about that. Cynthia and I have been together for six years without as much as a speed bump."

"Good for you," I say, ambivalent.

"She's got her gym business, and it's doing quite well. I'll be taking PTO to help her run it as I ease into retirement."

"Early retirement? I wouldn't have guessed that from you. Always thought you'd be a lifer."

"Hell no! Being a cop isn't a forever job. You work it too long, you'll come out looking like days-old lunch meat. Anyway, I get more joy out of personal training. No long hours and no bureaucratic bullshit getting in the way of me doing my job."

"Can't argue with that."

"Remember, sooner or later, the department is going to fuck you. Nobody avoids getting their shit pushed in by this city's long, hard phallus."

"This gym got a name?" I ask.

"Fitopia." Boston seems hesitant, then pulls a card out of her pocket and hands it to me. "It's a coupon. Good for a free session or zero sign-up fees."

"That's generous."

"It's an LAPD deal."

I turn the card over to see the address. "Sherman Oaks? Expensive part of town."

"It takes money to make money. Cynthia says it's a good location to attract celebrities."

I put the card in my wallet. "Maybe I'll stop by." I can see the flatbed truck heading down a service road and my father walking toward me in the distance. "Damn it," I say.

Boston looks to my father advancing a few yards away, frowns, and then asks, "Who the hell is that?"

I sigh. "My father."

"You're bringing your dad to crime scenes now? Is it a ride-along or something?"

"Or something . . . let me know when the car's workup is done," I say as I walk quickly to intercept him. When I get closer, I can't tell if he's agitated or excited; he's gesturing and pointing toward the strip club's sign. "Pop, I thought we agreed you'd stay in the car?"

"I know this place."

"Paradise Lost?"

"I sure do. It's been years, but this is an old LAPD hangout. We had my captain's retirement party here. Talk about a wild night."

"You mean when you should have been home with your family?"

"I was working, son. These were police-related functions."

"Right."

"You're missing the point. I'm trying to say if your vic's car is here, it's a good chance he knew that this was an LAPD hangout."

"But what recruit would know about this place?" I ask. "I didn't learn about it until I was out of my rookie boots."

"Maybe he didn't find his way over here on his own?" Pop looks around suspiciously. "Maybe he was lured here?"

"Pop, I don't need this right now."

"Hear me out," he says. "What if he was meeting someone here, or he followed some-body?"

"Followed someone? Like who — a cop? Is that what you're suggesting?"

"All I'm saying is that you better look at all angles. You've got a strip club that's a known hotspot for LAPD. You've got a dead recruit's car parked out front. I'm guessing you've got no signs of a struggle, and the car is spotless."

"For all I know, the car was driven here by whoever killed him."

Pop rubs his brow like he's watching a game show, and his favorite contestant has answered wrong. "Not an ideal place to dump a car, son. It's not remote enough, and with all the cameras from the strip club and trucks coming and going from the industrial park, it would be an unmitigated risk for a perp."

"Criminals don't always think things through."

"Dumb ones, sure. But I don't think that's what you're dealing with here."

"I'm taking you home."

"I'm just trying to help."

"Yes, I know, but I need to follow the facts and not get bogged down by skewed conjecture." I start walking back to the Mustang, forcing my father to catch up double-time.

We get in, and I start the car. I take a few deep breaths and consider what my father said. The possibility of police involvement makes my shoulders tighten and the vein that runs across my temple pulse. As much as I don't want to admit it, my father is right. Nothing can be ruled out . . . nothing.

After dropping him off, I order a cheeseburger, fries, and a vanilla milkshake from a trendy burger stand in Glendale. The traffic heading downtown is light, and I'm grateful. It shouldn't take me long to get home. I'm so tired, I can barely see clearly. My eyes are heavy and ache from straining to stay open. I put the driver and passenger-side windows down, tune the radio to the Top 40 station, and crank it loud. It's one of those pop songs by a singer who couldn't hit a high note if her life depended on it. It's dreadful garbage, murder on my ears, but I'll try anything to keep from falling asleep. Nights like these make me think Boston is right: this isn't a forever job.

CHAPTER SEVEN

June 1, 2010
Pacific Division

I sit outside Sergeant Wong's office, waiting to be called in and sweating in every crevice. As a rookie, I'm still required to wear long sleeves, and the polyester uniform is chafing my elbow in the creases, which only adds to the daily shittiness. Sergeant Wong likes to remind us rookies that he wears long sleeves daily because of his tatted arms, and he once ran a four-block foot pursuit during a heat wave with long sleeves and never complained.

The door to Wong's office swings open, and Garcia and Boston walk out. Boston pays me no attention as they head down the hallway, but Garcia looks at me — a devil-may-care simper on his face and a carefree strut. I despise both of them, but if Garcia were on fire, I wouldn't spit on him to put him out.

"Finnegan, get in here," Wong says. I enter his office. The space consists of cream-colored walls, an American flag draped behind his chair, a desk, and a large, dusty file cabinet. A small oscillating fan sits on his desk; it buzzes as it works to move the stale, hot air. Wong is already short-tempered, but he seems exceptionally prickly with the air-conditioning being down for two days. "You care to explain this?" Wong flips through my report quickly for effect and then drops the pages on his desk.

"Sir?"

"What seems to be your problem, Finnegan?"

"I don't follow, sir."

"Your report differs from Garcia's and two other officers'."

"It's what I witnessed, sir."

"My understanding is you left the scene."

"I was told to leave by Officer Garcia."

"You indicate the suspect was injured before fleeing the scene. But your fellow officers say that isn't correct."

"I can't attest to the suspect fleeing the scene, sir. Only that the suspect was injured when I left with Officer Castillo."

My foot seems possessed, tapping against the linoleum to a rhythm only I can hear in my head.

Tap. Tap.

Pause.

Tap. Tap.

Pause.

"OK, Finnegan," Wong says, dabbing sweat from his brow with a handkerchief. "What precisely did you see?"

"The suspect was bleeding from the face after being struck by Officer Garcia."

"Struck?"

"Yes, sir."

"With the side-handle baton?"

"Correct."

A side-handle baton rests in the corner of Wong's office, next to a duffel bag. He picks it up and holds it firmly. "What strike did you witness Garcia give the suspect?"

"It was a power stroke, sir."

The side-handle baton weighs twenty-seven ounces. Its overall length is twenty-four inches. Wong exhibits the stroke, sending the baton through the air with a slick whistle. "A man taking that kind of strike would likely be incapacitated, wouldn't you agree?"

"Yes."

"That means he probably wouldn't have been able to get up and run, correct?"

"I don't know, sir."

"You don't know?"

My mouth is dry, not sure if it's the nerves or the heat. "I don't believe the suspect could have run," I say defensively.

"Is it possible you saw Garcia pull his baton and then execute a front punch maneuver?" Wong thrusts the baton forward. It's a short, choppy strike without much power. Enough to stun a person but not knock their teeth out.

"Sir, that's not what I saw."

"You were more than six feet away from the suspect at the time, correct?"

"I don't remember . . . maybe."

"Do you agree the lighting was poor?"

"Yes."

"So, you couldn't be one hundred percent sure which strike you saw, or if the baton even connected with the suspect."

"I'm telling you —"

"I think you should get your vision checked, Finnegan. Garcia seems to think your night eyes may be failing you. It's common with rookies who aren't used to working long hours at night. Our eyes can play tricks on us sometimes."

I look around Wong's office. Medals and patches are on display. Numerous commendations and training certificates. How does a man like this become a sergeant? The department has rewarded Wong when everything about him is foul, and I can't see past his insufferable condescension. "Consider your future, Finnegan," he says. "You sure you want to go down this road?"

"Am I dismissed, sir?"

Wong nods and lays the baton down on his desk. I turn and head toward the door. "So, that's it?" Wong says. "I thought you were smart."

I'm smarter than Wong, that's for sure. But I don't know the play. What's my best move? I could go to IAB and tell them what I saw. But it would be my word against three seasoned officers' — veterans with strong records and Wong to back them up. Nothing good would come of it, nothing but the end of my career. But it's Wong's slick tongue that lets me know what I'm dealing with.

He adjusts his desk fan so it blows air only in his direction. "Your father could have been something in this department from what I hear," he says. "It's a shame things never shaped up for him. Guess the apple doesn't fall far from the tree."

I turn to face Wong, biting back the urge to curse him. The burden of knowledge is crushing. It can break even a good man — seeing behind the curtain, knowing that everything feared is true. There's a price to pay for doing the right thing. But what if the right thing means allowing more injustice and more people getting hurt? I can walk out of Wong's office right now. I can go back to school, get a part-time job somewhere painting houses or flipping burgers. I could return to the humdrum of civilian life, but I'd always know the sting of it. Quitting. Letting Wong win.

"My father served with distinction," I say.

"Of course he did, and I'm sure you'll be happy to have a career just like his. After all, the only limits are the ones we set for ourselves." He leans back, away from the fan's cool air. "Unless . . ."

"Unless what, sir?"

"You'd like to have a future. I mean a real future with this department. Who knows, I could be calling you chief one day."

It's been this way my whole life. Having to contend with people like Wong holding all the cards, exerting their power over others. There is no room for error here — this wall is made of crystal, and what I see on the other side is an opportunity that not even my father was given. I've come to the crossroads, and until now, I've dreaded having to face a choice like this. But Wong's query is a reaffirmation that joining the

LAPD isn't a labor in futility. This is my chance to bring about change, to help end the practices that have harmed the city's image and communities and tarnished the department for decades.

"Well, Finnegan — sometime today?"

"I understand," I say.

"What's that?"

"I understand, and I'd like to discuss my future." No sooner do I utter these words than I feel myself disappearing into the machine, the vast system of bodies in blue, men and women who have sworn to protect a city that often shuns and vilifies them. This was the true LAPD, where careers were made over the phone by officers of high rank and power.

"I'll make the call," Wong says.

"Thank you, sir."

"For what?" he says, angling the fan so air moves in my direction. Wong walks from behind his desk and positions himself in front of me. "Sit down, then." I take a seat, and he dials a number on the office phone and hands it to me.

"Sir?" I ask as Wong moves to leave.

"You've got it from here, Finnegan."

Wong walks out of the room, and I know my place in the department, and my life as an officer, won't be the same.

CHAPTER EIGHT

Day 2, October 17, 2014

When I arrive at my loft, night has fallen. I park crookedly, grab my gear bag from the trunk, and toss it over my shoulder. I carry a bag of fast food like it's as valuable as the queen's purse — the smell of the cheeseburger makes my mouth water. All I can do is envision eating and collapsing on my pillow-top mattress.

The rustling I hear isn't loud, but it's enough to make me turn around. When I do, a person in black clothing — hooded sweatshirt and pants — is aiming what looks to be a shotgun at me.

Time slows.

I think of Sarada and her love of James Baldwin — his warning to the thoughtless and cruel that their actions have consequences and will bring about a life of suffering. Is that what I've done? Glimpses of past deeds and harm I've inflicted on people stream through my mind — Chasen, Claudio Spirelli, so many faces of suspects and witnesses I lied to so that I could corroborate statements, deliver confessions, and close cases. Lovers I conned and charmed with no intention of honoring their feelings. I thought myself decent, not good but decent enough. And it isn't until facing the business end of a shotgun that I realize I may be deserving of what comes next.

The moonlight dances along the black barrel, and I throw my bag of fast food at the figure and attempt to run. The only thing deadly about a burger and fries is that it's packed with cholesterol, but somewhere in my scattered, sleep-deprived brain, I thought it would be enough to distract the shooter from landing a perfect shot to my chest. I'm not sure if it worked or if the person has poor aim, but I'm struck once on the right side of my body and drop immediately.

I should be dead or close to it, but I'm not. It isn't a slug or buckshot that strikes me; it's a beanbag. The pain is familiar — the last time I was shot with a beanbag was during a training at the academy in Elysian Park. The department had issued new rounds, and Garcia and I needed a certification update. It was a four-hour training, and in the end, in true Garcia form, he volunteered me to be shot from five feet while wearing my Kevlar. It was like getting hit by a softball in the chest. This time the range is closer. I'm not wearing a vest, and it feels like someone swung a nine iron into my ribs.

My assailant presses a foot against my back and forces my face into the gravel. Then, a garbled voice says, "Next time, it'll be the real thing." My ears are ringing, and a sharp pain radiates from my side down to the balls of my feet. As much as I don't want it to be so, I'm pretty sure I've pissed myself.

I'm dizzy. I want to throw up.

I try to lift myself from the ground enough to turn and look at the shooter, but the shooter's boot weighs heavily.

I hear a woman's scream.

The shooter's boot lets up from my back, and I can lift my head some. When I do, I see Tori standing in the distance, her cries nearly drowning out the sound of crushed stone grinding under boots and kicking up with each footstep as the shooter runs away.

Tori rushes to me, takes my hand. "Just breathe, Finn. I'm here. Just breathe," she says. Her voice has found a new octave, a fear-laden shrill that's a departure from her normal vocal fry. With each breath, I can feel my rib shift — it's a new kind of pain, like the first time breaking a limb or pissing a bladder stone.

"An officer has been shot," Tori says into her phone. She's skittish and speaking fast. "He needs help."

"Tell them Code Three. They'll come faster."

"It's a Code Three," Tori repeats. "Yes, hurry."

Tori ends the call. "Finn, there's no blood," she says.

"It was a beanbag round."

"Who would do that?"

"The ambulance will be here soon. Take my keys and lock my gear bag in the trunk."

"OK." Tori snatches the keys from the ground, throws my gear bag in the Mustang's trunk, locks it, and returns to my side.

"Stay calm. You're doing great," I say before shutting my eyes.

"Finn? Finn . . ."

The paramedics wheel me into the hospital's emergency room. I'm cold as I lie on the stretcher. An oxygen mask is helping me breathe, but the pain is intensifying. Tori says, "Everything is going to be OK." I know she's close, but her voice sounds distant, like she's at the end of a tunnel.

A man in blue scrubs wearing a surgeon's

mask leans over me. Tori declares, "He's a police officer."

My profession shouldn't matter, but I know why Tori says it, even if she doesn't. There isn't an abundance of sympathy for an injured black man on a stretcher; it doesn't elicit deep concern or set off alarms unless he's bleeding and near death. Tori needs the doctor to know that I'm somebody, that I matter to enough people, and if I die or somehow leave this hospital worse off than when I came in, it means questions and important people nosing around.

"Don't worry," the surgeon says. "We're going to take care of him. Your husband is in good hands."

Tori doesn't correct him. I hear her last consoling words: "I'm not going anywhere, Finn. I'll be right here . . . waiting," she says. I raise my head enough to see her standing barefoot in luminescence, mascara running, high heels in hand, as I'm wheeled down another hallway.

A nurse injects me with a syringe of clear liquid. It must be something potent because I immediately get drowsy. Everything feels warm, heavy, and is becoming numb.

What would it be like to be someone's husband?

Stop being a fool, the voice in my head

calls. Men like me court loneliness. We aren't husbands. No, we find contentment in our work. To be married would mean becoming my father — absent even when physically there, nothing more than a shadow going through the motions of life at home. People say when you meet the right person, you just know — you feel *complete.* I don't think I've ever felt anything but fragmented. The closest I've ever come to feeling whole has been with Sarada, but it would take a miracle for her to love me.

"Let's get him prepped for surgery," the surgeon says to the blurry figures I believe to be nurses, moving alongside the stretcher. "There's pressure on your lung," he says, looking down at me. "We'll need to alleviate it."

I want to tell him, *Just fix it, do what you have to do. I need to get back to work.* All I can think of is returning to the field. I wonder if the crime scene technicians have finished analyzing the surveillance tapes from the strip club. Did they find anything in Brandon's car that could help the case?

I want to sleep . . . I need to sleep.

I know I'm far from death because when death comes calling, everything will become silent and black, and my mind will drift to some other place. My soul will slip from my body the way a crab sheds its shell, and maybe, if it's fated, I'll hear my mother's voice guiding me. At least, that's what I'd like to think. I have no idea — I only know, this isn't it.

My thoughts are getting fuzzy. It's hard to focus.

There's no fighting it anymore. I close my eyes.

Waking from perpetual darkness is like being pushed into a cold pool; it's an assault on the senses, and all I can think is, *The dark wasn't so bad.* As my eyes acclimate to the softly lit hospital room, I see Tori sitting in the corner. I stir, and she rises from the chair. Tori takes a few steps and then sits on the edge of the bed.

"The surgeon said it's a small incision, but it'll hurt like hell for a while," she says, taking my hand.

I cringe. "It's not so bad."

"I called your dad," Tori says, pulling my cell phone from her purse and setting it on the table next to the bed. "His number was the only emergency contact on your phone."

I must have made Pop an emergency contact when I worked the streets. I thought if I were to catch a bullet or worse on patrol, Pop would be the only person who could claim me, or whatever was left of me.

"That's great." I pretend to be eager for Pop's visit, foreseeing the rousting he'll surely deliver. "My dad has a way of making things worse."

"I didn't know what else to do," she says, her voice skittish. "I mean, what if you'd died in surgery?"

"I could finally get some sleep."

Tori sulks. "Not funny."

"It's OK, Tori. You did what I would have done."

"So, you aren't mad?"

"No."

"Good," she says, pleased. "I know you can't talk about it — in detail, anyway — but what the hell is going on? Who would shoot you with a beanbag? I didn't even know that was a thing."

"I don't know, but once I get out of here, I'm going to find out."

Tori strokes my forehead. "Finn, I thought you were dead."

"Guess I'm tougher than I look."

"You'd like to think so."

"It's the case I'm working. I'm close to something, and the person who shot me knows it."

"Aren't you scared? They know where you live."

"They won't be back."

"How can you be sure?"

"Because whoever shot me sent their message."

"What makes you think they won't send you another?"

I take a deep breath and clear my throat with a husky cough. "We shouldn't meet up at the loft anymore."

"When will I see you?"

I try to ignore a sharp pain on the right side of my body and look at my torso, bandaged tightly with gauze and tape. "When things cool down," I say. "I'm not safe to be around right now."

"You aren't going back to work, are you? Shouldn't you be put on leave or something?"

"Please," I say dismissively, "this is nothing." I take hold of a small button with a cord leading to a pumping device attached to the IV stand.

"The doctor said it's for pain," Tori says. "Are you hurting?"

I press the button repeatedly. I suppose the pain is on par with getting kicked by a mule, or how I imagine that experience to be.

"It's on a timer," she says. "The nurse said you could have a dose every ten minutes."

The painkiller hits my vein, and I heave a sigh of relief.

"I can see if they can change it or something," she says. "Seeing people in pain is a trigger for me. I volunteered at the children's hospital in high school. Cancer ward."

"That sounds depressing," I say, resting my eyes as the drug works its way through my body. "So, why were you at my place tonight?"

"I was waiting for you. I thought we could talk."

"My phone works, Tori."

"If only you'd answer it. I've called you five times. I got tired of leaving voice mails."

"It's the life of a detective."

"I realize that, but it feels like you're dodging me."

"I'm not," I say. It isn't the truth, but it's not a lie, either. "What was so pressing you needed to see me in the middle of the night?"

"I was in the neighborhood. Thought I'd see if you were home. And it's good I did, or who knows what state you'd be in right now? But I'm not feeling very appreciated."

"You're right." I grab Tori's hand tightly. "Thank you for helping me. You saved my ass."

"You're welcome," she says with satisfaction. "I was motivated — it's a nice ass. I'm fond of it."

"So, did you happen to see the person who shot me?"

"Not his face. He was covered up pretty good."

"So, it was a man."

"I think so — at least, the person moved like a man."

"What do you mean?"

"It was how they stood. It was wider than how a woman would stand, and they held the shotgun like this." Tori pretends to hold a shotgun level with her chest, tucked into the crease of her arm and breast. She squares her hips, opens her legs, and settles into a wide stance, and then she pulls the imaginary trigger. The way Tori pretends to hold the shotgun emulates the way a cop would, which confirms my suspicions — the shooter might be a cop or had law enforcement training.

"Then what happened?"

"After he shot you, he pinned you down," she says, "and then he picked something up."

I consider what she's told me; it must have been the round's casing. "Did you see what the shooter drove?"

236

"A pickup truck."

"Color?"

"Something blue or black — or maybe gray. It's hard to say."

"Make and model?"

"I'm not a truck girl, Finn. But it had lots of chrome at the front. I tried to get the plate number, but your building's parking lot has terrible lighting. Doesn't your place have surveillance cameras or something?"

"They're artist lofts. The residents aren't into cameras documenting their comings and goings or recreational drug use."

"The truck had black wheels. What do you call them?"

"Rims."

"Yes, the rims."

"Aftermarket."

"Yeah, I guess."

"I owe you, Tori."

"You don't owe me anything. I'm just asking for a little time. I know this case has hijacked your life, but when things settle, I expect a call."

Speaking is taking a toll. Between wheezing and sporadically gasping for air, I try to swallow with enough gusto to keep my throat from drying.

"You need water?" Tori gets up and heads toward the door. "I'll get the nurse."

"Wait."

She stops and faces me. "Yes?"

"Forget the water."

"You sure?"

"Yes — Tori, I know I've been a jerk, and I'm sorry. Just know, I'm working on my shit."

Tori returns to my bedside. "Damn you, Finn," she says and then kisses me.

The moment is interrupted when my father, along with Sarada, opens the door to the room. When Sarada sees Tori at my bedside, she gently draws my father back by the arm, so he's not able to walk in. I give Sarada an agreeable nod as Tori stands and adjusts her purse strap over her shoulder. "Looks like you have company," she says. "Is that your family?"

"My father and a friend."

"Oh, OK," Tori says. "I should get going." Tori heads to the door and opens it to reveal my father and Sarada, standing uncomfortably silent.

"Hello." Pop and Sarada enter the room. "I'm Tori. Trevor's . . ." Tori looks to me before adding, "Friend." Tori shakes Sarada's hand.

"I'm Sarada."

"Sarada?" Tori says. "Such a pretty name."

"Thank you." I can tell Sarada is delighted

by Tori. She's overly smiley. "Trevor and I went to high school together," she adds, volunteering more information.

"Wow — that's something. I guess you really know him, don't you?" Tori says before shaking my father's hand.

"Shaun Finnegan," Pop says. "Trevor's father."

"It's nice to meet you both." Tori is so sweet, it's saccharine, which is customary when first meeting the parent of the man you're screwing.

"You're the one who called me?" Pop asks Tori.

"I am," she says, flashing her porcelain-white teeth.

"Thank you for helping him."

"Of course," she says, glancing back at me. "I'm glad I was there." My father walks to my bedside.

"Feel better, Finn," Tori says before leaving the room while her perfume lags.

Sarada waits a moment before sitting in Tori's empty seat. Pop stands over me with his hands on his hips, grunting disapprovingly, inspecting the IV machine. "So, you got yourself shot," he says, acting unbothered by my condition.

"Looks that way, Pop."

"Thank God it wasn't buckshot. Why

didn't you return fire?"

"My piece was in my gear bag."

"That was a fine place for it."

"I was caught off guard. It won't happen again."

"You better hope it doesn't. Any idea who did it?"

"Yes."

"And?"

"You don't want to know."

"Why not?"

"I was shot with a beanbag round."

"Are you saying —"

"I don't know what I'm saying."

"You think another officer did this?"

"Maybe, or maybe some punk got his mugs on a shotgun that fires beanbag rounds."

"Bullshit. It's damn near impossible to get a beanbag shotgun on the street."

He's right. It does sound like bullshit. What criminal would go through the trouble of lifting a beanbag shotgun off a cop when guns that fire real bullets are plentiful and easy to get?

"When the detectives come, you tell them you've got no idea what hit you. All you know is it was a projectile," Pop says.

"Why would I lie? Tori said the guy picked

up something. I know it was the spent round."

"If you don't lie, you're an idiot. And don't mention the girl — keep her out of it. You ought to break it off with Barbie, anyway. She's just going to get hurt."

"Why are you telling me this?"

"You go around saying you were shot with a standard-issue beanbag round by someone you suspect to be a police officer, you won't like where it leads. You're lucky. You don't have any real enemies on the force, just people who think you're an asshole. And trust me, you want to keep it that way. Because if you go saying another officer might have done this, people won't take kindly to it. You won't be able to investigate a dead dog —"

I hit the pain button again. "I thought you wanted me to shout from the heavens how dirty LAPD is? If it turns out it was a cop, it confirms everything you've said about them."

"I don't need validation. I lived it," Pop says through a tight jaw, something that happens when he gets worked up. "You talk that dirty cop conspiracy shit, the department will eat you alive."

"Since when are cops shooting each other with beanbags?" Sarada asks. She's lovely as ever — fitted jeans, a tee with her bakery's name embroidered on it, and a cropped leather jacket. Looking at her kills the pain better than the IV push.

"It's the case I'm working. I've rustled someone's feathers, and they were sending me a message."

"You think?" Pop says snidely. "You've got to tread lightly, son. You don't know what these bastards are capable of." Pop shoves his hands into the pockets of his black hoodie. The front of the sweatshirt lists five high-profile killings of black men by the police — Dontre Hamilton, Eric Garner, John Crawford III, Michael Brown Jr., and Ezell Ford.

"Relax, Pop. If someone wanted me dead, I would be. They wanted to slow me down, and I need to figure out why."

"Do you even have a read on these people? I mean, who are you looking at?"

"Nothing definitive. It's just a gut feeling."

"A gut feeling?"

"Yeah, instinct."

"Oh, you've got instincts now?"

"Give me a break, Pop. What I've got are cracked ribs and very little patience."

"Fine. I'm going to get some air."

"You do that. Maybe take a walk around

the block a few dozen times."

Pop relents and leaves.

"So, that's what that looks like," Sarada says, sliding her chair next to my bedside.

"What's that?"

"A parent's worry. My parents were always so stoic. Remember my dad's perpetual poker face?"

"It still haunts me," I say. "Did he ever smile, or look remotely pissed-off for that matter?"

"Nope. Good ole Dad had a way of drifting off to some other place when reality got too much. Sounds like your dad has good reason to worry."

"It's nothing I can't handle."

"Says the guy in the hospital with broken ribs."

"Minor setback."

"If you say so, but I know how things can rattle up there," Sarada says, placing her finger to my temple. "You have more than a gut instinct about who shot you, and that means you might be on your way to doing something disastrous." Sarada lets her hand drift to my cheek. "But I need you to remember one thing . . ."

"What's that?"

"It's just a job, Trevor. As much as you've worked it up in your head to be a mission, you shouldn't get yourself killed over it."

"I won't. You'd miss me too much, anyway."

"Sure. What good would you be dead? Besides, you promised me a trip to Art Basel."

"I'm sure you could find someone."

"I don't want to go with just anybody," she says. "It's our thing. We've been planning it since homeroom."

Getting shot with a beanbag can give a man some perspective, and the only thing on my mind right now is telling Sarada the truth. "I'm not in love with her," I say.

"Pardon?" Sarada plays coy.

"Tori is a friend — that's all."

"I hadn't given it much thought. But from what I saw, I'd say she feels differently."

I sigh. "It's because she doesn't know me."

"Maybe you should change that," Sarada says. "She's kind of a knockout."

"I just don't know if I feel the same way she does."

"Might I add, it sounds like had she not been there tonight, things would have been worse?"

"I know."

"It's OK to open yourself up, Trevor. Take a chance."

"You're right . . ."

"So, what's the problem?"

"It's you, Sarada — it's always been you."

Sarada stands up and backs away from me. "We've talked about this," she says. "I've always been clear."

"Trust me. I've tried my best to maintain this friend thing, and I can't. The whole time I was lying there with my ribs busted, all I could think about was how if I were about to die, what I'd want to say to you."

Sarada brings her hand to her mouth like my words are a noxious gas filling the air. "You should stop, Trevor."

"You asked me why being a detective matters so much and why I would choose to join something that has only brought my family pain."

"I shouldn't have said that. I know being a cop is —"

"No, you were right. What happened to you changed me. It's why I first joined LAPD, but that isn't why I've kept at the job." I cough hard. A wheeze sets in. "Being a detective means I can alter the circumstances. I can right wrongs. It gives me a purpose."

Sarada looks confused. "Trevor, you don't owe me an explanation . . ."

"But I do." I take a resounding breath that tolls my lungs. "Being a cop means I can prove I'm more than the shitty things I've done."

"Prove to whom?"

"Me. There's still good in me, Sarada."

"I know that, Trevor."

"Every time I close a case, a family gets justice." I cough hard again and then hit my pain button. "They can start to heal, and part of me heals, too. And while I may never be the man you deserve, I keep trying to be better."

"I only want you to be happy, Trevor." Sarada leans her back against the wall. To get any farther from me, she'd have to walk out the door.

"I'd much rather suffer in rejection and regret than pretend that I'm anything more than yours."

She steps forward and throws her hands up with frustration. "What am I supposed to say to that?"

"Sarada, if you don't know by now . . . I'd do anything in this world for you."

Sarada is quiet. She studies me with intense calculation, perhaps trying to find the right words to say to alleviate the thick emotion in the room. The moment ends with the vibration of my work cell phone. Captain Beckett. I answer. My voice is thin: "Finnegan."

"Detective, what the hell is going on?" he asks. "Someone shot you?"

"Yes, sir. Some kind of projectile. I have a few broken ribs — nothing serious."

"I'm headed there now."

"No need, sir. I'm on my way to being discharged."

Sarada frets, shaking her head and mouthing: *"No."*

"You are?" Beckett asks.

"As I said, it's nothing major. I'll be back in the field tonight."

"It's your call, Finnegan," he says. "The techs finished analyzing the surveillance video from the strip club. I'm with them now — it's something you should see. You'll need to get down here and view it as soon as you can."

"Roger," I say before ending the call.

"You don't look like you should be discharged," Sarada says.

"Good observation," I say, trying to suppress my wheeze.

"Then why did you lie?"

"Because I'm wasting time in this bed. My victim's killer is out there. This case is rotten, and if I stop now, the chances of me catching whoever killed my victim get slimmer."

"Why can't someone else take it over?"

247

"I don't trust anyone else."

"What happened to your partner? What's her name — Sally?"

"She's out," I say. I struggle to sit up in the bed. "I'm going to need your help getting downstairs."

"You don't even know if you can stand."

"There's only one way to find out." I try again to sit up in the bed. After two tries, I'm successful. I lower the bed guard and swing my legs over the side. "A couple of pain pills and a coffee, I'm good to go."

"Will you listen to yourself, Trevor? You're doing what I warned you about. You can't investigate anything in this condition."

I take my wallet, badge, keys, and watch from a plastic bag sitting on the table next to my bed. The nurses had placed all my things there before my surgery. I look at my watch — it's late. "I need to go, Sarada. You in or out?"

"I'm going to get your dad," she says.

"No — don't! You have to trust me," I say. "I just need to get out of here. Please, will you help me?"

I remove the pulse monitor from my finger. It beeps once before I yank the cord from the wall. I pull out the IV drip from my arm and press my thumb to the bleeding hole left by the needle.

"Trevor," Sarada says, a spectral look in her eyes, "please, stop this. You're not thinking clearly."

"I'm leaving whether you help me or not."

The IV machine sounds a constant beep. I quickly press random buttons on the machine until it silences. I'd overheard a nurse say the hospital is short-staffed tonight, which means I have a few minutes to get out of the room before someone comes to check on me. When I stand, I nearly topple over. Sarada braces me up with her shoulder and begins to help put on my clothes, which are poorly folded at the foot of the bed.

"What hospital is this, anyway?"

"Memorial — East Hollywood."

"What floor are we on?"

"The fifth."

"I can take the stairs," I say as Sarada helps me slide on my pants. "I'll be less noticeable."

"You'll still have to pass the nurse's station. Someone might see you."

"Can you distract them?"

"How am I supposed to manage that long enough for you to walk out, and that's supposing they don't hear you limping down the hallway?"

"Just be your charming self. Tell them

about your famous German chocolate cake."

"Excuse me — there's more to me than baked goods!"

"I know that. I'm just saying, improvise."

Sarada sighs. "OK. And what do I tell your dad?"

"Tell him I got called away on the case. He'll understand."

She reaches into her purse and pulls out a few business cards and coupons for free desserts. "No one can turn down complimentary cupcakes," she says slyly.

We finish putting on my clothes. I slide into my shoes and lace them up. Sarada leaves the room and heads toward the nurse's station. I wait a moment, then look through the small observation window to see her chatting with the staff. When Sarada smiles and produces the coupons for cupcakes, I know she has them on the hook.

I walk out of the room.

Outside, I see two doctors rush down the hallway and a nurse performing an inventory of a medical cart. As I suspect, it's a skeleton crew, and the doctors and nurses are tending to more dire situations than my broken ribs. I wait until a janitor appears with a large rolling hamper filled with soiled linens. The janitor, a man with shuffling feet, tries his best to get the attention of a skinny nurse with hot-pink fingernails and a cheery face. When he does, they exchange a few Spanish words, and the janitor starts on what looks to be a long conversation.

Sarada continues to entertain the nurses at the desk, an older no-nonsense Asian woman, who looks like she's been a fixture on the floor for decades, and a younger black woman with elaborately thick-braided hair and a smile dazzling with life. She shows the nurses pictures of desserts on her cell phone. It's the best opportunity I have to leave. I hobble across the floor, open the door to the stairwell, and manage as best I can down the steps. When I get to the third floor, I catch my breath, working up a slight pant. I realize I never got the water I needed, and my mouth feels like I've been chewing sandpaper. I hold on to the railing and work my way down the next two flights while trying to ignore the persistent throbbing of my ribs. When I make it to the bottom of the stairs, I can taste blood in the back of my throat. I draw the blood forward with a cough and spit it onto the floor — it's rust-colored, chunky. If it were bright red, I would be alarmed, but it looks old, like it came from lung tissue scratched during surgery.

I push against the long metal bar that opens the door, and I walk out into the autumn night.

CHAPTER NINE

Once outside the hospital, I struggle to walk a block to a mini-mart. Inside, the store clerk has the TV tuned to the local news. The anchor, a young Asian woman with a conservative haircut two generations older than she, is delivering a story. I wait to pay behind a man who looks to be a vagrant buying beef jerky and a teenager holding a bag of chips and a soft drink.

The anchor says: "I'm Mary Ling with Action 7 News. We have breaking news this evening. Photographs of recently deceased LAPD Recruit Officer Brandon Soledad have appeared on the website StormWatch. Soledad, who police suspect was murdered, was found in the Angeles National Forest yesterday morning. While the case is ongoing, LAPD says they will be investigating the presence of the crime scene photos on what appears to be a pro–law enforcement blog with links to extreme right-wing and white supremacist organizations."

The clerk takes a remote from a drawer and turns up the volume on the TV.

"We warn you — many of the comments found on the website are disturbing. Some commenters mocked Brandon Soledad's death and suggested it was only a matter of time before the young police recruit would embarrass the department. Others suggested the new diversity initiatives designed to improve the racial makeup of the department are backfiring and leaving the door open to what one commenter wrote as 'hood drama.' "

"Bullshit," the clerk says. "The department leaked those pictures. Everybody knows it, too. They were sending a message. Not welcome!"

"Sources say officers in the LAPD and LA County Sheriff's Department actively post on the site, some posts appearing even after the photos of Soledad's body surfaced. An LAPD representative says the issue is under investigation, and any officer who was aware of the photos online and did not report them may face punitive action."

"Fucking cops," the clerk says. "Can't ever trust them." He's a large man with russet-colored skin and a long black beard; he finishes with the vagrant and quickly rings up the teenager's items. The boy pays and leaves. I approach the clerk and place the aspirin and water on the counter for him to ring up.

"Evening," I say, feeling compelled to be kind. Sure, he doesn't know I'm a cop, but sometimes I find myself wanting to show people we aren't all maniacs.

"Can you believe that?" the clerk asks. "I mean, that poor kid's family has to deal with this shit now, and they don't even know who killed him."

I stay quiet.

"It's just a shame — a real shame," he says. "I hope whoever killed him gets what's coming."

I can't help but cosign. "Me, too."

"Six bucks," he says. I dig around in my pocket, produce a ten-dollar bill, and hand it to him.

Maybe my father was right. There's no redeeming the LAPD. What type of person plasters pictures of a naked dead kid on the internet? They hate Brandon and didn't even know him. All he wanted to do was join something that mattered and leave a legacy of honor and pride. Instead, what does he get? Murdered. Then ridiculed online by people he'd hoped to call family.

"Take it easy, brother," the clerk says,

passing me my change. I exit through the sliding doors.

A silver C-Class Mercedes is parked with its headlights on outside the store. The driver's side window rolls down as I begin to walk past. When I'm able to see the driver, I recognize Sarada. "This was your plan — a pit stop at a corner store?" she asks.

"Needed some aspirin."

"What now?"

"I have to get back home. I was going to call a taxi."

"You do know there are apps for that?"

"I guess I'm old school."

"Are you sure going home is a good idea? Won't cops be there?"

"I need my wheels. Besides, the crime scene techs should already have wrapped up by now."

"Get in."

"Are you sure? I've asked enough from you tonight."

"Just get in, Trevor."

I get in the car and settle into the passenger seat. I drop a handful of aspirin into my mouth and swallow them with water. "You look terrible," Sarada says.

"Thanks."

"I'm serious. You need to rest."

"No time for that. I need to get some-place."

Sarada sighs and begins to drive east on Sunset toward Echo Park.

"How did you find me, anyway?" I ask.

"I waited for you near the exit door. It took you forever to get out of the building. I thought you got caught or collapsed or something. Then I saw you making your way down Sunset."

"About what I said before in the room — I shouldn't have. It was probably all the pain medicine I'm on."

"Don't do that," Sarada says. "Don't make an excuse. You said it, so own it. Do you think it's easy for me? Sometimes when I look at you, all I see is that night. There are still days I don't even want to get out of bed."

"So, why continue seeing me if I only remind you of that night?"

"I said sometimes you're a reminder of that night. Other times, I remember the fun we had and our long conversations. We used to have the best conversations, didn't we?" Sarada pauses, giving me enough time to nod, before adding, "We had the whole world in front of us. It was hard when that went away."

"It didn't have to, Sarada."

Our relationship is complicated, but it's honest. When I'm with Sarada, I'm me — not Finn, the pissed-off detective, siphoning from a reserve of rage, burning a little at a time to get through each case. I'm just the art-loving kid Sarada remembers, and maybe I miss being that person more than she realizes.

"We both changed so much," I say. "I didn't know how to make it like it was."

"I know, Trevor. I think we're more alike than I wanted to admit."

We drive ten minutes more until we reach my loft. As I predicted, all the officers have cleared out, but the yellow police tape that borders where my assault happened remains.

Sarada shifts the car into park. I realize we'd been holding hands for most of the drive. "So, what's next?" Sarada asks.

"This is where we part."

"Really? I was getting the whole buddy cop vibe. Thought this is where you ask me to team up."

"Cute."

"I could make a good wheelman — woman, I mean."

"I have no doubt. I remember how you drove in high school. How many speeding tickets did you rack up in our senior year?"

"I lost count."

"Thanks for the offer, but I'll pass."

"Your loss," she says. It takes me a moment to get out of the car. I'm careful not to jam my ribs. I shut the car door, and Sarada lowers the passenger side window. "Be careful."

"Do me a favor?" I ask.

"Yes."

"Check in on Pop for me? I won't have time over the next few days."

"I can do that."

"Thanks."

Sarada nods, and I begin to head toward the entrance to my building. I look back and see her watching me. She smiles uneasily, and I wave for her to drive away. She gases her car and drives in the direction of the freeway.

My apartment reeks of garbage. The trash hasn't gone out in days. I tie the garbage bag, but I can't lift it out of the can. After three tries, I give up and take a seat on my bed. I sit for maybe five minutes, looking around the loft, stunned by the amount of dust that's collected due to my neglect, and then I gather the strength to shower.

In the bathroom, I slowly begin to remove the gauze around my torso to reveal purple bruising and a small dressing over the surgeon's incision. I keep the wound covered, and once the gauze is completely removed, I can breathe with less effort.

It takes me thirty minutes to put on clean clothes — slacks, a collared shirt, and a jacket — after showering. I brush my teeth and give myself a quick shave. I receive a text from Captain Beckett inquiring about my ETA.

I text back: Be there in 10 min.

Captain Beckett had the video footage from the Paradise Lost's surveillance cameras sent to our downtown headquarters. It's only a few blocks from my loft. I should get there in less than five minutes at this hour, but I'm moving slower than normal, so I give myself a little more time.

I lock up my loft and take the lift to the lobby. Outside, as I walk to the Mustang, I replay the shooting in my head. The balls someone has to shoot me at my home. It means the shooter knows me. The question is, how well? It had to be someone with access to employee records to get my address. Or was I tailed?

I can think of a few people who hate me enough to want to shoot me, but only one dumb enough to act on it.

When I arrive at LAPD headquarters, I see a small group of people lining First Street. They carry signs supporting Brandon Soledad and shout demands for justice. By now, the news broadcast exposing StormWatch has gone viral, and I know it's only a matter of time before more protests and marches span the city.

I park in the garage and walk the transit bridge to the main building's lobby. There, I'm badged in by a young black officer with a lousy military pressed uniform. "Your shirt lines are wrong," I say.

"New cleaners, sir."

"Fire them. If your superior sees you like that, it won't be good. You're out here on display, for God's sake."

"Yes — thank you, sir. It won't happen again."

I take the elevator to the basement that houses the crime lab. When the elevator door opens, I see Captain Beckett conversing with the forensic technicians, surrounded by computer screens. As I approach, the captain spins in his chair to address me. "Nice to see you're alive and well. You want to tell me what happened?"

"I'm not exactly sure. I took a blow to the ribs. It might have been an air cannon."

"An air cannon?"

"Yes, sir. Like the ones that fire T-shirts into the stands at Dodger games."

"I know what an air cannon is. I want to know why someone would shoot you with one."

"Maybe some punks in the building figured out I'm law enforcement."

"You need to move out of that damn hippie commune. Face it, liberals and police are like oil and water. Next time it might be worse. It's not like the old days — people respected the badge," Beckett says, pushing his coat back to reveal his shield clipped on his belt. "We rarely had to pull our weapons, and if we did, it was for a good reason. None of this *I felt threatened* bullshit. When we were on the beat, people knew not to cross us."

"Not all cops agree there is a war on police, sir."

"You know, you should listen to Limbaugh. He gets it — we're under attack. We can't even do our jobs effectively. There is always someone there to scrutinize with a damn camera phone in their hand, but they wouldn't last a day in our shoes."

These days, in ethics training, we're

cautioned to be careful that someone with a camera might be watching, like the citizen with a camera is a criminal. The camera takes precedence over the importance of doing our jobs without violating people's constitutional rights.

"All I'm saying is, I don't want to sentence someone who doesn't deserve it," I say. "We need to work with the community."

"Save the 'Kumbaya' shit for your neighbors, Finnegan. People see one thing, and that's the badge." Beckett stands up, puts his hands on his hips, and leans back slightly. "For these people, police are the enemy, plain and simple. Out there in the streets, we're united, and all we can do is watch each other's backs. I suggest you remember that."

"Yes, sir," I say. Moments like these, I can't help but wonder if I'd be happier painting canvases.

"Bad news first. Soledad's car was clean. Nothing out of the ordinary, which will make sense when you see the video. The techs have it up over here," Beckett says as I follow him toward another bay of monitors. "Mind you, it's black-and-white and grainy as hell, but it's something."

Two large monitors display surveillance from the strip club.

"The footage wasn't the best. The owner's cameras are about fifteen years old," says the forensic technician, a petite blonde with her hair pulled into a ponytail. She rewinds the video to the beginning. "You can see the victim parks and walks across the street to the club's entrance. We pulled this footage from the secondary camera." The technician points to another monitor that shows Brandon standing at the entrance to Paradise Lost. He's speaking to a door attendant — shows his ID, pays the cover charge, receives a hand stamp, and enters the club.

"That's it?" I ask. "Where's the footage from inside the club?"

"There wasn't any," she says. "The owner said the system wasn't working that night."

"It was a private party. Some beat cop's birthday," Beckett says.

"So, the owner turns the cameras off. Perfect."

"Hey, these guys have wives." Beckett winks, and I'm unsure if it's at the technician or me.

"Twenty-seven minutes after our victim entered the club, he was walking back to his car. Then he stops and looks back toward the club," the technician says. "But we're out of luck there. No angle on what he was looking at."

"He seems upset," I say as I struggle to read his expression. Brandon pauses like he's hesitant; then he crosses the street and disappears out of frame.

"I know this isn't much," the technician says, "but maybe there's something you can use."

A few moments after Brandon disappears from view, what could be a black pickup truck pulls out of the strip club's parking lot. It moves fast across the screen, but I can make out shiny dark rims — I'm betting it's the truck Tori described from my attack. "Were you able to see that truck parked in the lot?" I ask.

"No. It was possibly parked out of the camera's range, but it got me curious, so I did some digging," the technician says, pecking away on the keyboard until the truck magnifies. "It's a late-model Dodge Ram pickup, dark color — possibly green, blue, gray, or black. Given the years the truck was produced, those were the darker colors available. Of course, it could be a custom paint job. No way to be certain."

"That truck mean something, Finnegan?" asks Captain Beckett.

"Maybe. It could have been what drove Brandon out of there."

"If that's the case, it had to be someone

he knew or at least felt comfortable enough to go with."

"Presuming he went willingly," I say.

"You're thinking abduction?"

"Anything's possible at this point."

Beckett starts with another neck rub. "He was a fit kid. I think there would have been signs of a struggle. The doorman said he didn't hear anything. No shouting or what sounded like a fight," he says. "The owner, bar staff, and dancers that did talk to Walsh's officers said they don't remember seeing Brandon in the club that night."

"Thank you," I say to the technician. She nods and returns to work.

Captain Beckett and I walk into a small conference room serving as a break room with a table, a water cooler, and a machine that makes instant coffee and other hot beverages. "I take it you saw tonight's news?" Beckett asks.

"I did. Any idea who leaked the photos?"

"Forensics is working on it. The website is particularly troubling. All these anti–law enforcement organizations are coming online. Our officers are joining blogs and forums to vent."

"Is that all they're doing — venting?"

"The frustration officers are feeling has to go somewhere, Finnegan. I'm not saying online is the best place for it, but I rather they do it there than on the streets."

"What if it's more than just frustration?"

"Like what?"

"What if these taped altercations are only showing us that we haven't come as far as we'd like to think? These tensions come with deep scars, Captain," I say, working hard not to elevate my voice. "Altercations like NYPD choking Eric Garner to death happen more than we'd all like to admit. Only now it's captured on cell phone cameras for the world to see."

"Don't remind me. I'm not saying the LAPD is perfect, but we've come a long way from Rodney King. This department doesn't even resemble the days when the good ole boys ran things." Beckett mounts his passionate defense. "And just so you know, I never supported that shit. And it wasn't just blacks who weren't wanted — I was subjected to my share of mockery for being Jewish."

These conversations have a way of turning into a contest called Who Had It Worse, and there's never any winner. Maybe Beckett was on the receiving end of harassment, but I know the LAPD, and they didn't put him through the same level of hell most black cops endure.

"I'm just saying, I think we're on the cusp of something," I say. "It's starting to look like the bad days again."

The captain doesn't respond, but I can tell he's wrestling with what I've said. Maybe I sound too much like my father for his liking? Or perhaps I struck a nerve, and deep down, somewhere in his "I only bleed blue" way of thinking, he knows I'm right.

"If it makes you feel any better," he says, "they took the website down. We're working to identify the officers who commented on the crime scene photos."

It should make us both feel better. Those photos should have bothered Beckett and every reasonable person who saw them, but Beckett doesn't see it that way, and that's the problem. "And what will happen to the officers who posted comments?" I ask.

"Varying degrees of disciplinary action."

Beckett's answer is bureaucratic and tells me all I need to know. Gone are the days when white training officers tested their black rookies' sensitivity by using derogatory terms like *boy, nigger, shiner,* and *monkey* to get them to quit. If a rookie could handle the abuse, it meant he wasn't easily bothered, that he wouldn't protest departmental racism. He'd be a good soldier and wouldn't cause any trouble. It put white officers at ease because if a black man didn't object when he heard the word *nigger* on the job, what else was he willing to accept?

Life for blacks and other officers of color in the LAPD might not be as toxic as it once was, but how much has changed if the officers posting to StormWatch aren't fired?

"I should get back to work," I say.

As I head toward the elevator, Captain Beckett shouts: "Make sure you talk to the detectives about the shooting. One of them has already left me two messages. He said you skipped out at the hospital. That true?"

"Duty called, sir. This was more important."

"Give them your statement. It's an order."

"Yes, sir."

"Don't make headaches for me, Finnegan," he says. "I've got enough shit to deal with." It's a stern warning spoken out of caution, but it's more demeaning than he realizes.

"Understood, sir."

I take the elevator up to the lobby, exit the building, and walk back across the bridge toward the parking garage. I get into the Mustang and cruise down the parking levels toward the exit gate.

Captain Beckett doesn't see it. Something is brewing in the department, maybe even with law enforcement all over. Sure, police work is murky — it's rarely black-and-white — but when it takes longer to become a licensed barber than it takes to become a sworn officer, there may lie a much larger problem. How much can an officer learn in six months of training? Is it enough not to fuck up? I'm a walking example of how easy it is for an officer to lose their way. But I know things can change, and something tells me Brandon Soledad understood that better than this department.

I come to a stop. The gate arm rises, and I slowly inch into the street. A man walks in front of the Mustang, trailed by two others wearing hoodies over their heads, concealing their faces. All I can see of the man's face is a shaggy beard. His clothes are fitted — skinny jeans combined with designer sneakers. The group stops in front of the car, and one of the man's hooded companions removes a cell phone from his pocket and shines its light on my face. I duck down in the seat, unsure of what comes next. I quickly pull my Glock from its holster and slowly lift my head to get a visual. When I do, the group is gone.

I take in the darkness, studying it for anything odd, then I hear, "This is for Brandon, you fucking pig!"

The side of the Mustang is showered with . . . maybe rocks, marbles, pennies? I look in the direction of the attack and see three white men. "Black Lives Matter!" one of the men shouts before throwing something that dings the windshield, spawning tiny cracks that extend beyond the dent like a spider's web. The men quickly run across the street, shrieking, "Say his name!"

I consider pursuing them, but from the looks of their modish Westside apparel, I suspect they'd bail out in a few hours anyway, and I don't have time for the paperwork. They're probably thirsty for the political come up and will do anything to make waves on social media. After all, they have the kind of privilege that makes them think it's fine to attack a cop's car outside headquarters.

I take the aspirin bottle from my pocket, flick the cap off, and put two pills in my mouth. I watch the men rove down the sidewalk without worrying I might follow.

I work up enough spit to swallow the pills.

When I can no longer see the men, I slowly cruise away in the opposite direction.

CHAPTER TEN

Day 3, October 18, 2014

I'm exhausted, but there's no time to sleep. It's almost four a.m., and soon Joey Garcia will be getting ready to make his morning commute to the academy. I exit the 110 South freeway and drive through San Pedro, a blue-collar fishing town that sits below Rancho Palos Verdes' sprawling hills. It's easy to see how wealth is distributed in this part of LA. The foothills are dotted with large estates that overlook the Pacific Ocean. The farther north one travels, the cleaner the streets get, the better the schools, the more luxurious the cars, and the more abundant the grocery stores. Joey Garcia lives south of Gaffey Street, the marker that separates those with money from those hustling to get it.

I roll the window down and take in the briny air. The ocean is close; a sign reads a mile to Cabrillo Beach. I make a left down

Second Street. Garcia's neighborhood has older homes, probably passed down through the generations. Having read Garcia's file, I know this is where he grew up and played football for the public high school until he received a scholarship to play for a prep school in Long Beach. I never would have taken Garcia for the prep school type, but strangely, it fits. Garcia moves like a guy who grew up around gangs and everyday hustlers; his body language and vernacular signify street knowledge. Yet when he needs to, he can turn on the all-American charm and dip into his prep school lexicon enough to show people that he's read a book or two.

I drive another couple of blocks and see the Los Angeles harbor in the distance, a radiant cluster of golden and blue lights that reveal fishing boats and barges stacked high with massive containers, goods probably from Asia, Bangladesh, and elsewhere where labor is cheap and in abundance. There's something dismal about this place; it's not like I remember, though I know it hasn't changed much.

Shortly after my mother fell ill, Pop took me to fish off the pier at a crowded beach. I hated fishing, but Pop said he needed to get his mind off my mother's diagnosis, and so we went to San Pedro — charming, old, quaint. I've always equated San Pedro with death. I don't know if it's because of that memory and having to accept my mother was sick and that she might die while we were trying to catch a fish my father could brag to his friends about.

Could it be the ever-present somber vapor of the town? There's a sadness here. People living in San Pedro seem trapped . . . chained to it. Generations upon generations of families of longshoremen, bartenders, cooks, and cleaners — birth and death on repeat.

The streets host vagrants and skateboarding teens who live in strip malls of graffitied liquor stores and 7-Elevens. I pass a small house. Seasoned OGs sit at a card table out front of a minimally lit garage, drinking, smoking, surrounded by younger men who could be mistakes away from their first prison bids. My car isn't known around here, and one of the men, shaved head, a large tattoo on his face, rises from his chair to watch my car pass.

San Pedro is like a faded painting where the colors have washed to white and gray. It puts a bad taste in my mouth, and the sooner I can detain Garcia, the sooner I can leave. If I can connect the black pickup truck to Garcia, it'll be my first real break in the case. But if it is his truck, then it means the tire markings found in the soil where Brandon's body was discovered could be a match, which could mean Garcia is a murderer. It's the type of story that would send shock waves through the department and cause an uproar across the country: a sworn officer — an academy trainer, no less — kills a recruit . . . for what? What could make Garcia do something so terrible, so foolish? What can drive a man to frenzy, enough to kill?

As I close in on his house, I get the answer.

The motion light fixed to his garage comes on and illuminates the driveway. Marlena Sanchez walks out of Garcia's house and gets into the late-model black Dodge Ram pickup truck sitting brazenly in his driveway, like it wasn't used in the commission of two crimes.

Maybe I gave Garcia too much credit. He might be the biggest idiot in the department.

I park a few driveways down from the house but maintain a clear view of the truck and front door.

Things are beginning to make sense. Is this what Brandon discovered? Were Garcia and Sanchez a thing? Did Garcia kill Brandon to keep it hidden? Murder is extreme, but love or even just good sex has a way of making people lose whatever sense they might've had.

Sanchez pulls out of the driveway and makes a left turn in the direction of the 110 freeway. I follow her onto Gaffey Street. The pickup slows and settles at a red light. I turn on my lights and sirens, and when the light turns green, I punch the gas and ride the pickup's tail until Sanchez pulls over into a shopping center and parks in the parking lot. I use the dash-mounted computer to run the vehicle's plates. After a moment, the screen populates with her information: home address, driver's license, the vehicle's VIN . . . it shows her as the registered owner of the pickup.

"Shit," I say, knowing my gut has steered me into something messy. I take my Glock from its holster and disengage the safety. I know it's Garcia who shot me, and there's no telling what Sanchez's involvement is. Maybe she hasn't got a clue, or she conspired with him. Either way, she's been driving around in a vehicle that may still have physical evidence that links it to Brandon's crime scene.

I get out of my car and approach her driver's side with my weapon drawn low. I feel unbalanced with my injury, and I'm more aware of my gun — its heft, the way it's settled in my palm. It feels foreign, and I remember I haven't had to aim my gun in months, let alone fired it while on duty in over a year.

"Turn off the engine," I shout. The engine goes silent as I move alongside the pickup. I have a visual of Sanchez, who has her hands calmly on the wheel and is looking straight ahead. She's following protocol for what she likely believes is a routine traffic stop. "Roll down the window," I say, motioning downward with my left hand. The driver's side window lowers. "Keep your hands on the wheel, and don't move."

"Can I ask what this is about?" says Sanchez.

I look in the cabin for her firearm or anything she could use to hurt me. "Where's your service weapon?"

"Locked in its case . . . on the floor," she says. "Is this a training exercise or something?"

"Are you on academy grounds?"

"No, sir. I just thought —"

"You don't recognize me?"

Sanchez nervously turns her head to get a better look at me. "Detective?" she asks.

"Get out of the car. Slowly."

She unfastens her seat belt, unlocks the

door, and opens it with her left hand while keeping her right where I can see it. She steps out of the truck. She's wearing slacks and a blouse. On the passenger seat is her uniform — navy pants, a light-blue long-sleeved shirt, black clip-on tie, and a chrome name tag with her last name. She leans toward me. "Sir, can I ask what this is about?"

"Cut the act. I followed you from Garcia's house."

She's keeping calm, just like when I interviewed her at the academy. "Detective, it's not what you think."

"And what do I think?"

"I'm not sure, but Officer Garcia didn't do anything wrong. He only wanted to help."

I holster my weapon. "What are you talking about?"

"I needed a place to stay for the night. I'm still living with my parents, and they drink. Sometimes things get out of control. I called Joey — I mean, Officer Garcia — and he said I could crash at his place."

"You're lying." I know from Sanchez's file that she lives in Eagle Rock with an aunt. Her parents have been dead for years.

"I'm not, sir." Her voice begins to crack and bleat. "The DI and some of the staff know things have been hard for me since Brandon died. Officer Garcia was just looking out for me."

The lies seem to roll off her tongue. "Enough!"

I notice the tires on the pickup are new; the small round orange sticker is still on them, and they smell of fresh rubber. "I'm going to ask you a series of questions," I say. "If I get anything other than the truth, you're going to lockup."

"Detective, this is all a big misunderstanding. I have to get to the academy."

"You aren't going to make it."

"What?"

"First question: How long have you been sleeping with Garcia?"

"Please, Detective — this is my career."

"How long?"

"Detective, I'm begging you."

"Are you afraid of him?"

Sanchez bites her lip.

"Are you?" I repeat.

"Joey wouldn't do anything to me. He's a good person."

"You think you're the first recruit to be suckered into Garcia's bed?" I remove my cuffs from my back pocket.

"Please, Detective. I'm cooperating. You can't put those on me. I'm not a criminal."

"Lying to me makes you a criminal."

"I'll tell you everything — just don't cuff me, please." She shrugs. "A month — we've been sleeping together for a month."

"You lend him your truck?"

"Once or twice . . . um, maybe more. I don't remember."

"Did you have any involvement in the death of Brandon Soledad?"

"What? No. Of course not!"

"Did you kill Brandon Soledad?"

"Brandon was my friend. I'd never do anything to harm him."

"But he found out about you and Garcia, didn't he?"

Sanchez looks around as if to be sure Garcia isn't lurking, and then says, "He suspected it."

"Did he tell you he was going to do something about it?"

"Like what?"

"Confront Garcia. Maybe report him?"

"No! Brandon wouldn't do that. All he said was I should break it off, but it was up to me. He wanted to warn me."

"Warn you of what?"

"He told me Joey was dangerous and that I needed to be careful. That was the last time we spoke. I don't know what happened to Brandon. But after they found him, there was talk around the academy."

"Gossip?"

"If that's what you want to call it."

"What were people saying?"

Sanchez looks to the ground to avoid my gaze. "Things about Brandon's father," she says. "There were a lot of stories going around that his father is a junkie that owed some serious people money." Gone is the confident recruit I interviewed at Ahmanson. She's trapped, looking for a way out. "They say Brandon got involved in his dad's dealings. But you have to believe me: I had nothing to do with his death, and neither did Joey."

"I've never been fond of that scent," I say, looking to the fresh black rubber.

"What?"

"Those tires are new. When did you get them?"

"I don't remember. A few days ago . . . I think."

"What was wrong with the old ones?"

"Joey said they were getting worn out. He said I needed good tires for all the driving I do."

"Where's Garcia now?"

"I . . . I don't know."

I flash her the cuffs. "What did I say about lying to me?"

"I swear — he left early this morning. Maybe around two a.m. He might be at the gym or already at the academy."

"What gym?"

"It's a boxing gym on Grand Avenue. That's all I know."

I pull my cell phone from my pocket and dial. When the dispatch operator answers, I say, "Requesting a tow at my location. Also, send a unit." I get confirmation the tow truck and unit are en route and hang up.

"You're impounding my truck?"

"Yes," I say.

"This is crazy! I can't believe you. Joey didn't do anything to Brandon — he'd never."

"You don't know Garcia, and you never took the time to know Soledad."

Sanchez gives me a disgusted look. "I hope you're satisfied. You're ruining people's lives," she says.

"This is just the beginning. As of this moment, your career with the LAPD is finished. I'll be reporting your misconduct to your DI and noting it in my report. You'll be separated from the academy immediately. I'll make sure you'll never work in law enforcement again."

Sanchez leans against her pickup truck — inevitably defeated, but with too much pride to show anything less than contempt for me. I put my cuffs back in my pocket and watch her for fifteen minutes in silence, waiting for the tow truck. When the tow truck arrives, it's followed by a slick top — a patrol cruiser without lights on the roof. The cruiser parks and two officers get out, both young but already squared away, likely P2s. They walk toward me. "What can we do for you, Detective?" an officer asks. His name tag reads MARTINEZ.

"You mind driving her to Pacific Division?"

"She under arrest, sir?" Martinez says, his face a dithery squinch, thumbs tucked into his Sam Browne.

"Hook her up . . . suspicion of murder."

The officers walk over to Sanchez, whose face is red and sweaty. "What?" Sanchez says. "I'm cooperating. I didn't do anything — I'm not a criminal!"

Martinez begins to Mirandize her: "You have the right to remain silent . . ." The other officer, Milton, a white man with an athletic build and boots polished to a glassy finish, applies his cuffs.

Martinez initiates a pat down. "Shit. She's one of ours," he says as he pulls an LAPD ID, a driver's license, and a cell phone from Sanchez's pockets.

"Not anymore," I say.

The officers put Sanchez in the back of their black-and-white and place her belongings in a plastic bag. I retrieve her firearm from the floor of the truck — it's locked in a black case. I hand it to Milton. "Give this to the watch commander," I say.

The tow truck operator, a thin tattooed white man with gray hair down his back, greets me with a head nod and says, looking to the pickup, "Just throw it up?"

"That's right."

"You got it." He moves to secure Sanchez's truck to the flatbed. I take an opportunity to check my phone — there's a text from Captain Beckett asking for a status update. As my ribs start to hurt enough to become more than a nuisance, I take the aspirin bottle from my pocket, pop the cap, and knock two pills into my mouth.

The tow truck driver yanks hard on the straps secured to the pickup's front tires and cranks the Dodge forward with a lever until he's satisfied. Sanchez looks on from the back of the slick top like she knows she'll never see the truck again.

"Take the vehicle downtown to forensics and have them log it under my name," I say to the driver, handing him my business card that includes my name, rank, and badge number — everything he'll need to log the vehicle. The driver nods and slips the card into his chest pocket.

Officer Martinez approaches me with his notepad in hand. "We'll drop her at Pacific Division, but who should we leave her with?" he asks.

"Have the watch commander put her in an interview room until I get there."

"You're not going to follow us?"

"I won't be long. I just have to tend to something."

"Sure, Detective," Martinez says, jotting on the notepad. He walks back to the slick top, and both officers get inside. I watch as they drive away with Sanchez staring me down from the rear window.

I get into the Mustang and exit the shopping center to Grand Avenue. I consider what may occur when I confront Joey Garcia — he may attempt to flee or fight, but I'm not naive enough to think he will come willingly. Somehow, he was involved in Brandon's death, and the moment he sees me with the cuffs poised for his wrists, he's assured to make a move. When it comes to anyone facing prison, especially cops, I never underestimate their will to avoid time behind bars.

As I drive along Grand Avenue, I see a

white building with an old sign that reads BOXING GYM. Most places in San Pedro are unremarkable, and this building is no exception. The windows are covered with posters promoting fights long forgotten, and there is a sliding metal security gate that, when locked, looks to secure the entire front of the building. It's a lot of security for a boxing gym, but it echoes when San Pedro was overrun with MS-13 and Crip factions who kept the historically sleepy town charged with gang violence.

I cut down an alley and park behind the boxing gym. I dial Captain Beckett. After a few rings, he answers: "Finnegan?"

"Captain."

"Where the hell are you?"

"San Pedro. I found the possible vehicle used to dump Brandon's body. I also suspect it's the vehicle that was present at my assault."

"You didn't mention a vehicle at your assault before. What happened to you thinking it was residents in your building?"

"It's complicated, sir, but I believe this vehicle was involved in my attack and the disposal of Brandon's body."

"Who does the vehicle belong to?"

"Recruit Officer Marlena Sanchez."

"A recruit? You telling me a recruit was

involved in Brandon's murder?"

"I'm not sure, but her truck was. It's on the way to the lab, and Sanchez is headed to Pacific Division."

"You arrested her?"

"Yes, sir. On suspicion of murder."

"You know that won't hold. What the hell are you thinking?"

"It'll buy me some time."

"Damn it — you should have let me in on this."

"I wasn't sure, sir, but I am now."

"What else is there?" Beckett asks. I can imagine him on the other end, rubbing his neck, sweat beading down his forehead.

"I believe Officer Joey Garcia, a training officer in the academy, killed Brandon Soledad. He transported Brandon from the strip club in Sanchez's truck and later used the truck to dump his body. Sanchez was leaving Garcia's residence when I detained her."

"So, the black truck from the surveillance camera is registered to Sanchez?"

"Correct, sir."

"Are you implying that Garcia and Sanchez were romantically involved and possibly conspired to kill Brandon?"

"Sanchez admitted to sleeping with Garcia. I believe Brandon confronted Garcia about it, and things escalated. Maybe they argued, and then it got physical, and Brandon ended up dead."

"Maybe it got physical? You need more than that."

"I know it's conjecture, sir, but the truck was in Garcia's possession. It was at his home. He knew the victim, and Sanchez already stated Brandon was suspicious of her and Garcia's relationship. It's motive. Garcia wanted to keep things quiet. Brandon must have met Garcia at Paradise Lost, and he drove him out of there."

"You're going to need overwhelming evidence to make this stick."

"There could be physical evidence in that truck that links to Brandon. But if Garcia gets wind of any of this, he may try to run. I have to bring him in."

"What do you need?"

"I'm putting in a request for a temporary felony warrant for Garcia."

"You realize if this blows back on you, it won't be good. You can't just go after other officers with circumstantial evidence."

"Sir, I've never felt more right about a case than I do now. Garcia is our guy — I know it. I just need to talk to him. If I can get him in the box, I know he'll crack."

"It may be time to loop IAB in."

"I agree. Once I have him in the box."

"If you're wrong, his lawyer, union rep, and half the department will go after you."

"I understand, sir. If this goes wrong, the blame falls solely on me. But if I'm right, I want to see this all the way through. Garcia gets the same treatment as any other perp, and I want a prosecutor who plays hardball."

"Bring him in, and then we'll talk," Beckett says and ends the call.

I know Garcia is the culprit. I can feel it. But there *is* something I can't shake. Something else I don't see — another piece of the puzzle. I can only hope that once he's in the box, Garcia will look out for his best interest, and he'll give me the full story. If Sanchez or someone else is involved, I won't stop until they, too, are implicated and charged.

I was green when I went after Claudio Spirelli. I was too angry. I made mistakes. I should have forced him to confess to Sarada's rape. I should have been relentless, but I won't make that mistake again.

I enter the temporary felony warrant into the computer's application for the National Crime Information Center. NCIC is where a first responder begins to make their case. As I type, I try to keep an eye on the door that leads into the gym from the rear park-

289

ing lot. A few boxers trickle in, but none of them are Garcia. If Garcia is really at this gym, he could still be inside working out his demons.

I finish entering the pertinent information and get out of the car. The sun is beginning to break through the morning gray. As I walk toward the gym's door, I can hear the hard packing sound of gloves against heavy canvas bags. I breathe in the smell of sweat — a salty musk — and I feel the warm air of a swamp fan. I watch men, both average in size and skill, spar in the center ring. Clad in their protective headgear, the men are likely throwing punches around 80 percent, enough force to knock a man down but not out. A few boxers jump rope and work the speed bags. I search the gym for Garcia; I find him standing near a heavy bag in the far rear of the gym. A towel is hanging around his neck as he drinks from a water bottle — he looks like he's ended a good workout. Behind him are five tall lockers, maybe six feet. A duffel bag rests on a faded wooden bench. Garcia finishes drinking from his bottle and starts rummaging inside a locker.

He sees me and smiles slyly. "Long ways from Pacific," he says.

"I heard you might be here. Thought we

could talk."

"And who would have told you that?"

"Marlena Sanchez."

Garcia dabs sweat from his brow with his towel. "I think you've gotten hold of bad information, Detective. You've wasted your time coming here."

"I'll need you to come to the Pacific Division with me."

"Am I under arrest?"

"You're being detained. I have reasonable suspicion you were involved in the murder of Brandon Soledad. I'll also need your beanbag shotgun."

Garcia sniggers. "There you go, treating me like I'm an idiot. You always did think you were so smart."

"It's over, Joey. You need to come with me now."

"I'll go with you under one condition."

"This isn't a negotiation." I take hold of my Glock's grip.

"You won't need that, Finn."

"I don't have time for this. I'm not going to ask you again."

"Then call for backup. I'm a high-risk suspect, according to you. Why are you here alone?"

I watch Garcia for sudden movements. His locker and gym bag are both open. He

291

may have stashed a weapon in either location, and I can't risk him getting the drop on me.

"You want to bring me in on your own, don't you?" he says. "You want all the glory. OK, then, here's your chance. Come and get me." Garcia whips the towel from around his neck, drops it into his duffel bag, then puts his hands up.

"What are you trying to prove, Joey? You're only making things worse for yourself."

"You know what? You never deserved a place in this department. You were a shitty rookie, and you became an even shittier detective." Garcia picks his foot up and rests it on the bench, casually resting his arm on his knee. "You know what you've never understood, Finn? It's that this department is a brotherhood, a family. You care only about yourself. That's why you're here right now. Think of the story: how you collared big bad Joey Garcia all alone."

"I'm giving you the opportunity to come willingly," I say. "Take it."

"Fuck off."

Garcia is baiting me. It's what I expected from him. Even as my training officer, he seemed to revel in chaos, always pushing against the edge of policy and procedure.

But this is his crescendo. Today, he gets to make his statement loud and clear and in front of an audience. Other boxers have stopped working out and are watching from a distance.

"Everyone out," I say as I hold up my badge. Some people begin moving toward the exit, while others continue to gawk. "*Out,* damn it!" I shout loud enough to get the gawkers moving.

Without an audience, Garcia's show lacks luster. But this is his chance to prove that he's better than me. Sure, it's childish and born out of ineptitude, but Garcia is a simple creature governed by emotions. "Tell me, Joey, was there a moment you felt remorse?"

"What are you talking about?"

"You called the sheriff's department, didn't you? You told them where to find Brandon's body. Somewhere inside, you knew you couldn't just leave him there. He was, as you said, part of the brotherhood."

Garcia pauses for a moment, gazing at nothing particular. "You coming for me or not?"

"You don't have to do this."

"You're out of options. I'm not going willingly, and you're not going to call for backup. Besides, I'd take off long before they'd show up." Garcia climbs into the ring. The two boxers, who seconds ago looked too afraid to move, climb out and quickly make their way to the exit. Garcia is wild-eyed and breathing heavy. "Or you can run back to Beckett with your tail between your legs. Tell him you couldn't do it, that you were out of your league. That mother-fucking Joey Garcia put the fear in you, and you turned bitch."

"All right, Joey. If this is what you want, all right." Getting in the ring and mixing it up with a killer has inherent risks. Garcia isn't in his right mind, and my ribs are still sore, but I'm not leaving this gym without him.

Garcia shakes the ropes around the ring and bounces into them like a Saturday morning wrestler on television. "What are you waiting on, Christmas?"

I'll have to strike hard and fast. Once he's malleable, I'll slap the cuffs on him and call for backup. Even with the aspirin, the throbbing in my ribs hasn't gone away since I left the hospital. I know I favor that side, and if Garcia is a halfway decent boxer, he'll read me easily unless I can shield my injury. I'll have to blade my body and maintain a strong guard. Eight years of Krav Maga, kickboxing, and judo have prepared me for fights like this. The odds are never even. If Pop were here, he'd tell me to groin strike, do a hammer fist to the collarbone, and sweep Garcia to the ground.

I climb into the ring and settle into my stance, my left leg forward, my right set back with my heel raised. I keep my abs tight and my knees with a slight bend. I shuffle around the perimeter, keeping my hands up, framed around my face. Even with my injury, I'm agile but with a slight stiffness. I slide across the ring with my chin tucked to my chest and my eyes square on Garcia. His muscles are warm from his early morning workout. His movements are loose; he's far less stiff than me, and his stance is more of a traditional boxer's. I see hints of other martial arts, maybe a few MMA classes, Brazilian jujitsu, but mostly American boxing. He keeps his fists pinned to his chin and moves well, but he's already showing signs of fatigue.

"C'mon, Finn — I know you've got it in you. Let it out," he says, showing his chipped front teeth. Garcia doesn't fully appreciate his challenge. He doesn't want what I've got, this furor that dwells inside, but I'm out of options. Garcia isn't coming freely, so I'll give him what he wants and more. He throws a left jab that I'm able to slip, followed by a series of jabs with no hope of connecting. Garcia is feeling me out. "Not bad," he says, bouncing on his toes.

It's been a while since I've fought anyone. It requires a primal mindset, putting hands on another man. I evade a straight punch and counter, sending a left hook to Garcia's chin. Sweat and spit sprinkle from his mouth onto my fist. He moves in with a combo, and I manage to block two of his punches, but he lands a right hook to my rib cage. I stumble back in pain; it radiates throughout my body. I grind my teeth and send a roundhouse kick to his right leg — his lead leg. The kick causes his leg to buckle, and he begins to lose his balance. I follow with a heel strike to his knee. It's more of a stomp, and I hear a loud pop. His knee shifts out of the socket, and Garcia begins to topple, having to take hold of the ropes to steady himself. He's in pain, but he doesn't want to show it. Garcia gasps like he's trying not to drown in a pool and looks at his knee in disbelief. His lead leg is useless; he shifts his weight to his left leg and tries to remain still.

"It's over, Joey," I say, working to catch my breath. "Stop this before you make it worse." Garcia is an asshole and a killer, but even I don't want to seriously hurt him. I want him to be able to walk into court one day, shackled in an orange jumpsuit, with the judgment of the whole city and the LAPD heavy on him.

"Not so easy, Finn. It's like I always told you — you have to work for it." Garcia composes himself with two gulps of air and shoots his body forward with his arms extended. He grabs hold of my waist and wraps his arms tightly while trying to pull me to the canvas. He's abandoned his fight training and is calling upon his old football days. He tackles me to the ring's floor, and I land on my back. I draw my leg into my chest, cock it, and send my foot into Garcia's face. I can feel his jaw shift under my heel. Bloody teeth dribble to the mat. We both crawl to our respective corners to evaluate the damage.

"This is crazy, Joey. If I have to, I'll end this," I say. My hand moves to my holstered Glock. If I shoot Garcia, it'll be justifiable homicide by a peace officer. He's attacked me, and he poses a deadly risk of serious bodily harm or injury given his fight training. I'd be good in the eyes of the law and within reason, but I would have failed Brandon. Killing Garcia means he doesn't face Brandon's family; he doesn't lie awake in a cell while inmates taunt him with inconceivable threats. Garcia must be sentenced because cops aren't above the law, and killers must be held to account.

"Go to hell," Garcia says before sliding out of the ring and hobbling to the door. A fateful dizzy spell comes on as I try to get to my feet. My ribs feel like they've been broken all over again. I'm coming down from the rush. Adrenaline has a way of numbing pain, if only for a moment. I had heard stories of officers fighting knife-wielding suspects who, after cuffing or killing them, realized they had been stabbed, in some cases, fatally. Adrenaline had gotten them through the fight, but death had the final say.

I roll out of the ring and take to pursuing Garcia, but I trail a pace or two behind him. Even with his dislocated knee, Garcia is managing to stay ahead. Outside, gym-goers have gathered in the parking lot. "Out the fucking way," Garcia says to the crowd, barely managing to stay upright. They stand clear, and I glimpse one of the men from the ring dialing what I hope is 911.

Garcia looms over a motorcycle, Asian-make and sleek. He slams his fist against his knee, trying to pop it back into its socket. Garcia isn't giving up. I've underestimated how far he's willing to go to evade arrest. He strikes his knee again. The knee is held secure by tendons, similar to rubber bands glued to stone. It isn't hard to set back in place if you know what you're doing, and Garcia is initiated. He manages to reset the knee enough to move and reduce the pain, then climbs onto the motorcycle, puts his helmet on, and starts it. He looks to me, and with his middle finger raised high, revs the bike, spitting exhaust before riding off. I move as fast as I can and get into the Mustang. I turn on my emergency equipment — red and blue lights fashioned into the car's grill — and drive off in pursuit.

I accelerate down an alley — the V-8 drags air. The muffler releases a rich cacophony complemented by exhaust that loiters long after the Mustang has passed. I downshift, avoiding a homeless man and two teens on skateboards. San Pedro is riddled with long, narrow alleys that run behind offices and supermarkets. Coming out of the alley, Garcia tries to shake me, taking a sharp turn to Eleventh Street. I'm careful to avoid a moving truck, a semi that's idle in the street.

Garcia starts heading north toward Rancho Palos Verdes. It's a long uphill climb, but I can tell Garcia is used to it. This is where he grew up. He knows San Pedro. He could potentially lose me in the sprawling coastline subdivisions connected to hiking trails and service roads, so I'll need to stay close. I increase my speed as I work to close the distance between us.

Traffic is beginning to thicken as people start their work commutes. Garcia is becoming more reckless, splitting lanes at high speed and narrowly avoiding collisions. I jump in and out of lanes, trying my best to keep up. A few motorists pull over to the shoulder when they see the flashing lights on the Mustang, but most drivers don't notice me until I'm on their tail and sound the siren with the push of the car horn.

I pick up the radio and call: "Requesting backup. I'm in pursuit of Officer Joey Garcia — suspected One Eight Seven. He's riding a yellow motorcycle — Asian-make, late model — traveling northbound on Twenty-Fifth Street. He's considered armed and dangerous. Exercise extreme caution."

Garcia shifts his weight left and right as he navigates the sharp turns. The two lanes have become narrow, rock cliffs bordering the right, fast-moving oncoming traffic to the left. Ahead of us, a series of small hills peppered by slower vehicles: a wide-body luxury car, a minivan, and a hybrid. Garcia slows the motorcycle and then tries to pass the vehicles on the right. It's a risk. He could smash against the cliff's edge, and to the left, there isn't much room to split lanes. He'll need to move quickly, with precision timing.

I see a helicopter pass above, and in my rearview, three sheriff's cruisers are coming fast on my tail. I'm in their jurisdiction now. Protocol says I should surrender my pursuit until I receive clearance, but I can't back off. Garcia is more than some run-of-the-mill suspect, like a car thief looking to make prime-time news; he's got blood on his hands. Where he goes, I go, and I'll deal with the consequences later.

Garcia jumps into the oncoming lane, rides hard and fast, and jumps back into the northbound lane. He successfully passes the minivan and the hybrid, but the luxury car is faster, and he'll need to increase his speed substantially if he intends to pass.

The sun flares white as it rises to prominence on the horizon. I slow down, take my shades from the center console, and put them on. I mash the gas pedal, and the Mustang rumbles up another steep hill. When I reach the top, I see a fast-moving sports car, slick and aerodynamic, likely German, speeding ahead southbound a few miles away. Garcia drifts to his left, probably trying to see if the lane is clear enough to pass the luxury car. He quickly darts back into the lane and slows the motorcycle.

The sports car increases speed. The driver may not be able to see Garcia's motorcycle. He shifts from behind the luxury car again, trying to assess if the lane is clear. Garcia takes a chance and crosses the double yellow line, riding into the oncoming lane.

The motorcycle falls into the base of a small hill, and I lose sight of it.

There's a twinge of dread, and then there's silence. I no longer hear the Mustang's V-8, its sirens, or the sirens of deputy cruisers behind me. It's the absence of what should be sounds of life, and I know it's arrived — death. When the motorcycle reappears, Garcia is facing the sports car head-on. I watch the sports car make impact, cutting into Garcia and sending him and the motorcycle airborne. Garcia's body contorts like a kite whipped in a gusty storm. When the motorcycle and Garcia return to the earth, his body smacks the pavement. The force jets his helmet from his head, and his body rolls to a stop. Parts of the motorcycle litter the road, and there's a long smear of motor oil mixed with blood leading to Garcia.

The luxury car slams on its brakes and

comes to a complete stop half a mile ahead of Garcia's body. The sports car's windshield is shattered from where Garcia struck it, and blood has collected on its hood. White smoke dawdles in the air from the car braking at high speed, and the driver is unable or unwilling to get out.

As the smoke lifts, I can see Garcia, mangled and still. I park the Mustang, so the car blocks both lanes, and I get out. The sheriff's cruisers cluster behind the Mustang, and deputies get out with weapons drawn and trained on Garcia. I slowly move toward Garcia with my gun drawn and aimed at what's left of him.

"Let me see your hands," I say, even though I know Garcia is dead or close to it. "Let me see them!"

I stand over him, then crouch to see his face better. Blood covers his nose and mouth. Slivers of skin and flesh are gone from his face, and what's left resembles the pulp of a citrus fruit after it's been squeezed for juicing. Embedded in the remaining skin are pebbles and shards of concrete. It's no longer the face of a man; instead, it's like the work of a deranged sculptor or a discarded prop from a horror movie. His detached jaw hangs crookedly, chunks of teeth and flesh sprinkled around him.

"You good?" a deputy asks. He's a big white man who looks like he shaves with a dull blade. His skin is coarse with fine raised bumps and pockmarks.

"Code Four. We're all clear," I say.

"RA is on the way," the deputy says, "but he's looking mighty dead from where I'm standing."

"Best to call the coroner."

"You have people coming?" he asks, sizing me up. "Your superiors, I mean."

When one of our own is involved in situations like this, a crisis team needs to be dispatched. The team consists of cross-departmental sergeants, LAPD's most trusted workhorses, and their mandate is to shield the department from exposure and embarrassment. "Yes," I say. "I'll get people here soon. In the meantime, can we set a barrier and get a cover on the body?"

"Sure, Detective. We'll do you the courtesy, but we may need to have a discussion with your supervisors regarding your disregard for jurisdiction," he says before strolling off.

Another deputy, an Asian man, skinny with an I-did-it-myself haircut, is visibly shaken. He stands off to the side, staring at Garcia's body. He looks like he's fresh off probation. "You all right?" I ask.

"Yes, sir," he says, snapping out of his stupor.

"First time seeing a body?"

As part of a deputy's training, they must work the jail circuit before being stationed in the field. The deputy looks like he hasn't seen much action outside of a few jailhouse brawls. "Never one that looked like this," he says.

"You don't want to make a habit of staring at them like that. Why don't you go and walk it off?"

The young deputy nods and heads toward the cruiser he likely came in.

The deputies cover Garcia's body in the customary white sheet and set up a blockade. Angry motorists honk and curse after being told they'll need to find another route to work. Even in death, Garcia is a disruptive prick.

I spent an entire year patrolling with Garcia, praying he didn't do something stupid to get me shot. Every night I went home thankful I didn't die. He was a menace — a madman hiding in plain sight — but it doesn't make seeing him dead any easier.

I look at my watch. Not even eight o'clock. It's going to be a long day. I'll have to stay on the scene until it's processed. Soon the news media will be here. I can see the news headline now: Officer Joey Garcia: Good Cop or Calculated Killer? I don't welcome the media's interest, but in their fight to be first, they always get it wrong, reporting speculation, never waiting for facts. Not that I would give them any until the death investigation is at least midway done, and that takes time. In the wake of an officer's death, especially one like Garcia's, law enforcement cranks through the process. It's a cumbersome machine, slow and methodical, but the job gets done. As for me, a mound of paperwork and endless reports are in my future, which will give the department time to figure out what to do with me. I'll likely be assigned to the department shrink and ride a desk for a few months if I'm lucky. If I'm unlucky, I'll be put on paid administrative leave as they investigate me. They'll try to determine where I went wrong with the case and how Joey Garcia ended up dead. The only question is what price I'll have to pay to keep my job.

I take another look at Garcia's body. "Damn you, Joey," I say to myself. There were plenty of times I wanted to see him hurt, taught a lesson, but not like this, not dead.

Blood is beginning to seep through the white covering. I want to remember this moment, not for any specific reason, but it just feels like I should. Is this how it's supposed to end? With Garcia dead? Is this divine justice? Was Boston right? Are there cases that actually can't be solved and don't want to be solved? Will Brandon's murder be added to the city's lore? Another dead-end investigation — a bona fide whodunit for washed-up PIs, cable news pundits, and unscrupulous news rats hungry for ratings who'll speculate, only to conclude that the LAPD, in its unparalleled corruption, worked to cover it all up. Has there ever been another department with a more enduring legacy of conspiracy?

Maybe I should get out before it's too late. On a long-enough timeline, the LAPD fucks everybody.

I dial Beckett and try to formulate the best way to tell him Garcia is dead. After a couple of rings, he answers. "It's Finnegan," I say. "It's about Joey Garcia . . ."

CHAPTER ELEVEN

I arrive at the Pacific Division around one thirty p.m. When I enter the building, officers avoid me like I'm the carrier of a disease. Word of Joey Garcia's death has spread. I'm the embodiment of misfortune, and a few officers look to me with more pity than disgust. No officer ever wants to be the reason another officer dies. Sure, Garcia fled and became a fugitive, but he was the police. I know what other officers are thinking because it's what I would think if I were them: there had to be another way. Joey Garcia didn't have to die. Why didn't I call for backup?

I approach Javier Perez at the front desk. "Marlena Sanchez, which box?"

"She's in Interview Room One," he says, wiping cream cheese from his mouth with a napkin.

"Did she make any calls?"

"One. I think." Perez takes a moment to

finish chewing his bagel. "You sure you're up for it?"

"Excuse me?"

"You might want to clean yourself up first. Just saying."

I hadn't looked in the mirror, but I can feel dried blood on my face, and my right cheek feels tight and packed with fluid. "Good call," I say, tonguing the bit of dry blood on my lip.

Perez adopts a serious look that breaks from his usual Cheshire Cat grin and jeering. "Look, Finn, I don't know what happened out there today, but we've all been there."

I want to tell him, *Trust me, no one's been where I'm standing,* but I settle on, "Thanks."

"Take a moment. Look yourself over. The girl in the box can wait."

Things must be worse than I thought if Javier is giving me advice. "OK," I say, before leaving Perez's station and entering the bathroom. I look myself over in the mirror: a split lip, and as I suspected, a bruised cheek, but the cuts around my eye are a surprise. I wet a few paper towels and wipe the dried blood from my face.

My work cell rings. Captain Beckett. I don't answer. The call goes to voice mail.

It's the first time I've ignored his call, but I know what he's going to say. He'll want to pull me off the case, but I can't let it go, not yet. Something doesn't feel right. I know Garcia had a hand in Brandon's murder, but he was too stupid to act alone. Did Sanchez help him, and if so, why? I believe she cared about Brandon, but was Garcia able to get her to betray him? Was Garcia's hold on Sanchez that strong?

As I stare at my battered face in the mirror, trying to make sense of the last twenty-four hours, I'm distracted by the buzzing of a fly. Flies are drawn to the shittiest of environments. It's where they breed, and even though they can fly anywhere, they'd rather hang around filthy bathrooms that reek of sullied toilets and urinals. This is what cops and flies have in common. There's no escaping the filth of this job, but some individuals seek out police work because of the filth, where they can wallow in the murk and breed in hate and contempt for the communities they're supposed to protect. Garcia was no exception; he helped perpetuate the narrative that all cops are corrupt and want to rain hell down on people of color, especially poor people who don't fall in line, and for that, I detested him.

Without giving it much thought, I send

my hand against the mirror, smashing the fly with my palm. I wash away the blood and the black-and-green remnants in the sink and dry my hand with a paper towel. I take one last look in the mirror. Having come to terms with my face's condition, I leave for Interview Room One.

I enter the room to find Sanchez sitting in a chair with her face buried in her arms on the table. An empty potato chip bag and unopened cola sit in front of her. I pull a small tape recorder from my pocket and slam it down. "Get up," I say.

She slowly raises her head.

I press the "Record" button and speak into the device: "This interview is conducted by Detective Trevor Finnegan. Time is sixteen hundred on the eighteenth of October, twenty-fourteen. Present is Recruit Officer Marlena Sanchez, the interviewee."

"I told you I don't know anything," she says.

"I also must let you know this interview is being videotaped." I point to the camera mounted in the corner of the room.

"What am I doing here? Where's Joey?"

"Joey is dead."

It must take a moment to register, because Sanchez doesn't say a word. I can see she's bristling with emotion. She wants to cry or maybe scream, hard to tell. But whatever it is, it's fleeting. In a moment, the feeling is swallowed back into the abyss, a gaping pit inside of her, and what remains is a face cold and empty. "How?" she finally asks. "How did Joey die?"

"He was evading arrest after assaulting me."

"You were pursuing him?"

"I was. We fought, and he attempted to flee."

"Looks like he worked you over good," she says, pointing at my face.

"I've had better dance partners. Besides, it could have been worse —"

"How so?"

"I could be dead."

She cuts me a sharp glare.

"You want to talk now?" I ask. "Maybe you can tell me what really happened between the three of you?"

"Yeah, I'll talk. Let's talk about you."

"You'd be wasting time, and that's something you don't have much of."

I'm meeting the real Marlena Sanchez. Her parlance has changed; it's beyond informal. It's brash, how Garcia spoke. "Don't be so sure, Detective," she says. "Joey told me so much about you. I feel like

312

I know you — the real you. Not this sham version you're fronting, this do-gooder bullshit. He said you were the worst kind of cop because you didn't stand for anything. No conviction, no passion for real police work."

"Real police work? Garcia wouldn't know anything about that. He was dirty."

"You think you're better than him? You're an opportunist who would sell out your brother to get ahead, and Joey knew it."

"Did he tell you these things before or after he told you he killed Brandon Soledad?"

"He never said a word about Brandon. Why would he?"

"You're a smart girl, Marlena. The night Joey took your truck, where did he say he was going?"

"I don't remember."

"Don't be a fool! The way I see it, Garcia either set you up to take the fall for Brandon's murder, or he used your truck in the commission of a crime and didn't give a damn about you. So, think hard about what you're going to tell me, because when this interview is over, I can't help you."

"Who said I needed your help?"

"You're going to need somebody. This department isn't going to bat for you. The city's prosecutors are sharks, and they'll want to make an example of you, but it doesn't have to happen. We can work together. We can do it for Brandon."

Sanchez leers with contempt. "That's the best you have? *Do it for Brandon?*"

She makes me more uneasy than Garcia did. Do I have it wrong? Maybe it wasn't Garcia's jealousy or fear of losing his job over Marlena that led to Brandon's murder. It could have been Sanchez who pulled Garcia's strings. Did she coerce Garcia into killing Brandon? But why? What motive would be that compelling? She said Brandon rejected her, so did she kill him out of spite? It's too weak a premise, but the soured relationship angle is all I've got.

"Joey was right — you underestimate people," she says. "You're not the smartest one in the room; you just think you are." She looks to the clock. "Now, get me a fucking lawyer."

I watch as she folds her arms like a pillow and rests her head. I realize the interview was over before it started. She knows we can only hold her for forty-eight hours, and any lawyer worth a nickel knows the evidence we have is thin at best. It isn't enough to bring charges of conspiracy or obstruction of justice. She can easily say Garcia stole her truck or took it without her knowledge and that she had no clue of Garcia's or the truck's whereabouts at the time Brandon was killed. With Garcia in the morgue, there's no one alive to dispute any claim she makes.

The case is dead.

I stop the recorder and put the device back in my pocket. Sanchez keeps her face buried. I leave the room feeling more defeated than when I entered. I need someplace to think, or maybe someplace to mourn the death of Brandon's murder investigation, seconded by the death of my career.

As I stand outside Interview Room One, I might as well be invisible. Most officers pass me without the slightest glance, and those who venture a look in my direction do so with derision. I've become a leper.

"Finnegan!" Captain Beckett makes a beeline toward me from his office. There's fury in his step, and I can't help but notice he isn't blinking. "Damn it, Finnegan. I've been trying to reach you."

"Sorry, sir."

"Save your apology," he says. "They said you had Marlena Sanchez in the box. That right?"

"She won't talk. Asked for a lawyer."

"You already questioned her? Hell, Finnegan, you should have conferred with me first."

I cringe like a grade-school dunce facing down the principal. "I thought she'd break," I say.

"It'll be on the front page now. The whole city is going to be in an uproar." Captain Beckett nudges my shoulder as he struggles to get a look at Sanchez through the door's small observation window.

"What now, sir?"

"We're cutting her loose."

"What — why?"

"The lab said they didn't find anything in her truck that would connect her to Brandon's murder and not a bit of physical evidence that would even suggest Brandon was ever in the truck. And the truck tires weren't a match for the tracks found at the scene."

"Garcia had the tires on the truck changed."

"Even if that were true, it's thin."

I bang my fist against the wall. "There has to be something," I say.

Beckett is caught off guard and looks to me with worry. "Get a hold of yourself, Finnegan."

"Apologies, Captain."

"There is one thing," Beckett says, rubbing his neck. "The lab noted the scratches on Brandon's arm. They think they were from him attempting to record the plate number of the vehicle involved. It's circumstantial, but the markings match the first digits of Sanchez's plate number —"

"I could have used that as leverage."

"Had you answered your phone, you might have known. Besides, it wouldn't have made a difference, anyway."

"Why not? It's something," I say. I can hear the desperation in my voice. "Sanchez might play ball. Sir, let me take another shot at her."

"It only confirms what you've already suspected, which is the truck was involved, but you don't know how. And you can't prove Sanchez took part in Brandon's possible abduction and murder or even knew her truck was missing in the first place."

"Sir, Brandon deserves to have his killers brought to justice — all his killers. If there's a chance someone else is involved . . ."

"It's time we think about minimizing the fallout," Beckett says. "It's time to move on."

My father warned me: the department has only one concern, and that's optics, how the LAPD looks in the press. They want to bury this investigation, maybe even me, too. "Move on? There's more to this case, I know it."

"We have Garcia, and that's good enough."

"But he didn't do it alone. He had an accomplice."

"What makes you so sure? Who's to say it wasn't two men fighting over a woman and things got out of control? You suggested that yourself."

"But the way Brandon died — it doesn't make sense. Garcia would never think to freeze a person to death. He just wasn't wired that way."

Beckett gives a tired sigh and says, "Let's say he did have help. Do you think Little Miss Sunshine in there gave Garcia the idea to freeze Brandon to death and then dump him in the forest? On a popular hiking trail, no less."

"Maybe . . . I don't know."

"I do. Garcia was dumb as a bag of rocks, and it sounds exactly like something he would do. Maybe he read about it on the internet or saw it in a cop show. Who knows? From where I'm standing, Sanchez has no real motive for killing Brandon Soledad."

"She loved Garcia, and she's convinced

he loved her. She would have done anything for him."

"I can't play the what-if game with you. I get it. This thing has put a lump in your throat. We've all been there, but it isn't worth wrapping yourself around in a twist. Garcia is dead. He was our prime suspect, and we don't have another — the case is closed."

"Captain, just give me more time. I know there's more to this."

"No," Beckett says, gesturing his hand as if it were a stop sign. "I'm shutting it down. I want all the paperwork and your report to me by the end of the week. And here's one more thing for you to chew on: the lab traced the crime scene photos posted on StormWatch to an IP address. Guess who it belonged to?"

"Garcia?"

"Bingo." Captain Beckett puts his hand on my shoulder. "You did what you could, Finnegan. You worked the case like a dog, but it's time to put it to rest. You got him — Joey Garcia is our guy. You hear me?"

"Yes, sir," I say reluctantly. "I hear you."

"Go home and rest up. Then get your ass back to the doctor for a full workup. You look like hell."

Beckett is wrong, but if I defy him and

keep digging, following the evidence as my father suggested, I could lose my badge — or worse, continue my career more hated than I already am. I've seen it before: officers make mistakes and get trapped, unable to retire or get promoted. Nobody would work with me. My cases wouldn't get solved, and my track record would cease to exist. After some time, I'd either drink myself to death or retire to some plot of land in Idyllwild or Palm Springs, where I'd take up an obscure craft like making clocks from tree stumps.

As Captain Beckett walks away, I ask, "What do I tell Brandon's parents?"

"Tell them we did our job," he says defensively. "This is a win for us. They get justice, and the city doesn't have to burn." He turns away, certain he's right, and heads to his office. For him, it's simple — a suspect is dead, and a dead suspect is a blank slate.

In death, Garcia becomes whatever the department needs him to be: a rogue officer who sleeps with unwitting recruits, a predator, an outlier — someone who doesn't reflect the mission and values of the LAPD, a cancer that the department is working diligently to cut out. They'll pull all his cases and pick apart each one. They'll demonize him and offer him up to the media as a sacrifice. After Garcia is dubbed public enemy number one, the media will surmise that it isn't so farfetched that a despicable cop like him could have murdered someone.

In time, there will be other crimes, murders more heinous and indelible, and people will forget about Brandon Soledad. Everyone except me. We're bound by something I don't fully understand. Soledad's death holds meaning, and it can't be so easily forgotten. Even in a city shaped by its loss of history, Brandon will be remembered. That I can promise.

I need some air, followed by a strong drink.

Before heading out to my car, I stop by the front desk. Perez is working on a crossword puzzle in the *LA Times*. Eraser residue is smeared across the newspaper.

"She talk?" he asks.

"No."

"I'm not surprised. She looked like a hard-ass. Did she ask for a lawyer yet?"

"She did."

"Has some brains, then. Might have made a decent officer, you think?"

"Maybe, if she wasn't nuts."

"You know what they say," Perez eases his voice, so he's not to be overheard by officers passing. "The only thing that separates a cop and a convict is getting caught."

"Shit, man."

Perez cackles. "What's a four-letter word for a shade of green?"

"Jade," I say.

"Smart guy," Perez says, writing the word down. "That works."

"Do me a favor and process her release in about an hour? I figure she can stew a little longer."

"I'll handle it, Detective. Take it easy."

After years on the job, any bit of joy left in a cop's face is shown in a flinty smile. There's something catastrophic in the curve a cop's lips make when it's clearly forced. It's in their laughter, pushed up with desperation — loud, sustained howls over frosty beers and shots of liquor. Gestures are proclamations, heralding that they belong, that they're just like everyone else, but that isn't the truth. Cops aren't like everyone else, and most aren't sustained by admiration or honor but by guttural rage.

A sergeant once told me a cop's greatest tool was anger, and right now, I'm in Jester's, a downtown bar, with the angriest men in the city. They watch me feverishly and hold their beers tightly. They want to hurt me. I know it. Garcia's death and his possible involvement in Brandon Soledad's murder have permeated the department. Garcia had friends; some might be in this bar, holding steadfast to the belief that Garcia was a good man and a good officer. However misguided that idea is, I understand it. Even when facing compelling evidence, people will break from rational thought if it reassures their worldview. Some officers in the department still believe the first black president wasn't born an American citizen and others avidly listen to radio jockeys who argue mass shootings are theater put on by the government in a plot to abolish gun rights. LAPD — and any police department in the country, for that matter — is a slice of society: the good, the bad, and the batshit crazy. The only difference is that these people have guns, badges, and the power to take away citizens' freedom or end their lives.

Early in my career, I came to bars like this to learn how to look and sound more like the officers I saw storm around the division. The hardnosed cops — the rugged and spent with dead-eyed stares and shaved leathery faces that twitched. I suppose the bar will always hold significance for me. It's the first and only cop bar my father took me to. After I graduated from the academy, he told me Jester's was a sanctuary, a place I could go to decompress after a hard day of working the beat, and there would be many hard days.

Since then, the bar and the officers who drink here have changed. It's still a dive, but now, a large Blue Lives Matter flag — black and white with a single blue stripe where red should be — hangs draped from the ceiling. More of the flags have been appearing around the city — like the one outside the police union's building, until the mayor ordered its removal. A few officers even had shirts made with the insignia and put decals on their cars, and my first thought was, *How is this any different from a street gang repping their colors, throwing up a set?*

Gone are officers who prefer to be left to their beers and cigarettes and the sounds of the dusty jukebox. Cops today have become tribal and splintered into their respective corners — the conservative whites and Latinos, one or two Asians, and the nearing-retirement group in expensive suits, puffing cigars. Occasionally, I'll hear a mumbled racial slur or a derogatory term for women or homosexuals, but when I turn to face where it came from, the party quiets down, cops shifting in their seats and dropping their heads like schoolchildren who got caught cheating on a test.

It used to be that drinking at Jester's with other officers felt less isolating. But today's LAPD is a department fragmented and infected by political ideology, and I couldn't be more alone. It's sacrilegious to suggest some of my fellow officers are shitty and can't perform their jobs without bias and unnecessary use of force. Yet we all know who they are — the bad cops, the walking lawsuits like Garcia. And no one dares to spotlight them for fear of being labeled a Judas, spineless, a snowflake . . . but there are worst fates that can befall a member of this police department.

"Another beer?" the bartender asks before I finish the glass I'm sipping.

"Sure," I say, watching as he pours the frothy brew into a smudged glass.

I'm on my third beer . . . no, fourth, and I feel like Jester's is the last place I should be. The bar is a relic paying homage to the LAPD's past, what many call the golden days. A large brass-framed photo of Chief Daryl Gates addressing a massive crowd gathered around torched rubble is displayed on a shelf behind the bar, next to bottles of gin and bourbon and trophies for police-sponsored marathons like LA to Baker.

"Getting late, don't you think?" the bartender asks. It's code that translates to, *Maybe you've had enough?*

I check my watch. Almost eight. I've been drinking since three, and getting drunk isn't really on the itinerary for the night. I need all my faculties for the drive home, and catching a DUI would be the nail in my coffin.

"I'll close out."

The bartender nods and walks over to the register. He returns with my bill. It's fifteen dollars; I pay with a twenty. "Thanks," the bartender says, "but you need to know something."

"What's that?"

"I like you. I always have, but I'm not so sure you can drink here anymore. No hard feelings; just the way it is. You understand, don't you?"

"Figured as much."

"It's a hell of a thing, that Garcia business. It's just going to make life tougher for us."

"Us?"

"That's right — us," he says.

"You were on the job?"

"Eighteen years," the burly white man with a bald head says. "And I miss it every day." I'm betting it's been years since he's fit into a uniform. His belly laps over his waistline like bread baked with too much yeast. I bet he would make a great mall Santa when Christmas comes around, though his deadpan glare would frighten the children.

"When did you retire?" I ask.

"1996. The zoo was real wild then. The whole city was rappers, gangbangers, and cops, and I'll tell you, sometimes you couldn't tell them apart."

It's around the time my father retired. Normally, when I meet an old-timer, I'd drop Pop's name and ask them if they knew him. If the conversation goes well, I ask their academy class and make small talk about the job, but I don't care that much to know in this instance. All this guy has ever done is serve me warm beers and flip TV channels, but today, he knows me. Today, we're supposed to be brothers.

"The zoo? Not really something cops say anymore."

"That right?" the bartender says, wiping his hands on a terry towel. "Everything is so damn PC these days."

"Did you even know Joey Garcia?"

"No, I didn't, but quite a few good men in here did."

"It appears that way."

"Sad thing. I guess we'll never know what happened between him and that kid?"

"Brandon Soledad."

"What was that?"

"His name was Recruit Officer Brandon Soledad . . . not kid."

The bartender drops my money into the register and gathers my change. He lays the money down on the bar in front of me. I leave him three singles as a tip.

"We're not all good, you know."

"Excuse me?" the bartender asks.

I'm sure he heard me, but I elaborate. "Sometimes, we deserve what we get."

The bartender sucks his teeth and looks over my shoulder at the group of men playing pool behind me. I know what comes next. I slide off the barstool and prepare for drunk cops' favorite recreation activity — a brawl. And just as I'm loosening up my shoulders and beginning to think how infantile, how self-destructive it is to throw blows with my broken ribs, a slick white man wearing an ill-fitting brown suit enters the bar. A pair of rimless readers is tucked in his Oxford pocket, and on closer inspection, the suit's fabric is spotted with stains. The pool-playing cops return to their game as the man takes a seat next to me.

"You sure you want to sit there? I think

I've got the plague."

"I'll take my chances," he says. "You're a hard man to get a hold of."

"I know you?"

"Your father sent me. He thought you might be here. The name is David Bergman."

"Ah, yes," I say, taking a sip of my beer. "Shantelle's lawyer friend. The man we're all supposed to hate."

"An unfortunate side effect of my vocation."

"How does it feel to hold the record for the most lawsuits against the LAPD?"

"I don't think much about it, honestly."

"You sure it's safe for you to be in here? I think these guys hate you more than me."

"If I scared that easy, I couldn't live in LA, could I?"

"How did my father know I was here?"

"He wasn't sure, but he said it's where he'd be if he had the day you had."

"What's he know about it?"

"I think he still has some friendly relationships left on the force. I'm sure it isn't hard for him to keep tabs on you. And given the recent developments surrounding your investigation, I think he thought you could use a little legal advice."

"What developments?" I ask, taking another sip of beer.

"You haven't heard? Brandon Soledad's mother is filing suit against the LAPD. She also has a coplaintiff, a woman alleging the department was involved in her son's disappearance."

I feel like I've lost more than a few hours. Things have transpired around me as I've been in a timeless void. I look at my work cell. I've got eight missed calls with three voice mails.

"I thought I told you to get out of here, and you can take your friend with you," the bartender says.

"Give me a second," I say. "There are more important things than your feelings right now."

"We can speak outside. It's not a problem," Bergman says to me. There's a worry in his voice, and he's already gotten up from his barstool.

"Fine — we're leaving," I say as I snatch the three singles from the bar and drink the last of a warm beer, leaving the fresher one on the counter.

The bartender shoos me away as if I were a stray dog that wandered onto his lawn. "Go sleep it off, dick," he says. As much as I want to take a swing at him, I'm not one for putting innocent people in harm's way.

If a fight were to break out, I'm sure Bergman would find himself on the business end of a pool stick.

We walk out of the bar and into the night's quiet coolness. Broadway is barren, except for a young couple dressed like models from a print ad arguing a few feet away. Bergman looks to the bar's entrance as if the men inside will spill out at any moment; then he looks relieved when they don't.

"Give me a second, here," I say, taking out my cell phone. "It's work."

"Yes, of course. Go ahead."

I take a moment to listen to my voice mails. The first is from my father, asking if Joey Garcia's death is related to my case. The next is from Captain Beckett. I'm reminded that I ignored his call in the Pacific Division restroom. The third is from Brandon Soledad's mother, who simply says: "This is Mrs. Graves. Please call me when you can. It's important that we speak."

I put my work cell phone back in my jacket pocket and turn to Bergman. "What's the real reason you're here?"

"It's like I told you —"

"I know what you told me, but that's not why you came. It has something to do with Soledad's mother's lawsuit. She tried to retain you, didn't she?"

"Yes, but out of respect to your father, I turned her away."

"That's noble of you. I assumed you would have been foaming at the mouth for that kind of press."

"You don't think much of me, do you, Detective?"

"It's that obvious?"

"Contrary to what you've heard about me, I'm not an ambulance chaser. The work I do is crucial, necessary. It's about holding those with power accountable."

"And what power is that?"

"The power you and your fellow officers have."

"Get with it, Bergman. I'm a garbage man, a tiller in the field. The power I have has limits," I say, shrugging my shoulders. "I'm a chameleon in this department. My job is to blend in. People like me have to toe the line and try to keep our heads above water."

"Forgive me if I don't sympathize, Detective. Maybe I've seen too many of your fellow officers get away with the most violent, lurid offenses."

"Do you think I like to hear cops brag how they made some black or Latino ten-year-old boy cry walking back home from a corner store? All because the kid's pants hung a little low, and he walked with some confidence, it means he's a gangbanger, right? How dare a kid living below the poverty line have some confidence about him — unless he's affiliated, packing, and slanging."

"Those are the types of officers who don't belong patrolling our communities."

"Yeah, you tell them that. They're right inside that bar."

Bergman looks to the bar's entrance again, still on edge. He's passionate — I'll give him that — but he's glib. He doesn't fully understand the department he's at war with. Just him being in the bar tonight is courting disaster.

"Mr. Soledad's mother seems to think the LAPD doesn't want people to know what happened to her son," Bergman says, aggravated. "She feels something is terribly wrong, and she's not alone. So, tell me, Detective, what's going on?"

"I don't know what you're talking about, but if she's suing, why the hell did she call me?"

"She called you?"

I give an affirming nod. "Maybe to curse me out and tell me how terrible a detective I am."

"Why would she presume that?"

"Because maybe I am. I got Garcia killed, didn't I?" It must be the alcohol. The words are forming in my head, and before I know it, I'm speaking them against my better judgment.

"The news report indicated Garcia tried to avoid apprehension."

"It should never have happened. I should have had backup ready before engaging him. I was reckless. Stupid."

"What are you saying?"

"I fucked it up. Garcia baited me to get into the ring with him. After we mixed it up, he got away, and a chase followed. He ended up a pavement smear, and I'll be lucky to keep my job."

"So, you *do* need my help."

"I don't know — don't you sue cops instead of defending them?"

"I've been known to make exceptions. Are you going to call Mrs. Graves back?"

"And say what? The woman wants to sue the department. I can't talk to her."

"Set the badge aside for a moment. How would you feel if the man who possibly killed your son died? Maybe she's looking for closure, and hearing what happened from you might help her achieve that."

"It's getting late. She . . . she probably won't answer."

"Leave a voice mail."

I take my work phone from my pocket, scroll through the missed calls, and then after a moment, dial Mrs. Graves. After six rings on what I figure is a landline, she answers: "Hello?"

I clear my throat that's gone raspy from drinking. "It's Detective Finnegan, returning your call."

"I didn't think I would be hearing from you, especially not at this hour."

"I apologize. We can speak another time."

"No. Since I've got you, let's talk."

"You said it was urgent?"

"Yes. There's information about my son. Information I think you should know. It's time you know the truth."

"The truth?"

"A woman came to see me," she says and then pauses. "We really should speak in person."

"OK. When?"

"Tomorrow morning. Call me then, and we can arrange to meet somewhere."

"All right, Mrs. Graves. Tomorrow."

I end the call.

"So, what did she want?" Bergman asks.

"We're meeting tomorrow. I need to get home. Can I drop you somewhere?"

"I can walk."

"You sure? It isn't the safest neighborhood this hour."

"I live just three blocks west of here," he says, "but take my card." Bergman hands me a forgettable business card — white stock and black ink. I put the card in my jacket pocket and watch Bergman walk down the shadowy sidewalk. He passes the young couple who've ended their tiff and are now in a tight embrace.

I walk to the Mustang and get in. I catch myself in the rearview mirror. I look more worn out than drunk. I shove a piece of chewing gum in my mouth and start the engine. I slowly make my way down Broadway toward my loft, driving well under the speed limit.

In an instant, I see the red and blue lights of a patrol car flash in the rearview mirror, followed by the wail of the siren, and I think, *Way to top off the night, Finn.*

Black-and-whites are forever tucked in alleys, concealed in the darkness waiting for screw-ups like me to roll through a stop sign, but I haven't broken any traffic laws.

I slow down, looking for a place to pull over. The patrol car then cuts off its siren and lights and accelerates until it's cruising next to the Mustang. I park the car in front of a Korean supermarket, and the patrol car stops next to me. The window goes down, and I see two officers, both black women.

Given the tint on the car, there's no seeing my face at night. I'm tentative, but I lower my window anyway. "Evening," I say, the window lowered just below my chin. "Is there a problem?"

"Are you Detective Finnegan?" the woman behind the wheel asks.

"I am," I say, working to silence a belch and sound upstanding.

"Told you," the officer says to her partner, a short-haired woman with crimson-brown skin. "I knew it was him."

"Everything cool, Officers?"

"Just wanted you to know we're out here," she says. "And we got your back."

I smile, remembering the feeling I had as a boy, watching the black officers congregate at the Barbecue Church. I feel at home again. "That's reassuring," I say. "I very much appreciate it, Officers."

"But we're going to need you to solve this thing," the driver says.

I'm not the only cop who doesn't believe Garcia acted alone. "I'm working on it."

"Uh-huh, bet you are," says the short-haired partner, gum wedged in her teeth. She eyeballs me as if to doubt my resolve. "You look tired, Detective. Probably should head home, don't you think?" She points two fingers forward, signaling for me to move along.

I roll up the window, then start driving. Once I'm a block away, I look in the rear-view to see the patrol car make a U-turn and head in the opposite direction. When I arrive at my building, I park and scan the lot for anything suspicious. I get out of the car and look into the black pools where the streetlight doesn't penetrate. Nothing stirs. I keep walking until I reach the entrance to the building. I unlock the security door and enter the lobby. I take the lift to my floor.

As the lift doors open, I see a woman standing in the hallway, leaning against the wall. She's wearing a long camel overcoat and black high-heeled leather boots that end below her knee.

She brushes her hair away from her face and looks at me.

"Sarada? How'd you get in?"

"One of your neighbors let me in. He thinks you're a graphic designer."

"That's what I tell them."

"He also thinks the ambulance and police were here because you were mugged or something."

I'm tipsy, but Sarada is talking slower than usual. Her words drawn-out, wispy. "Sarada, what's going on? Are you all right?" As I walk closer, I can see she's been crying. "Did something happen?"

"I just needed to see you," she says. "Your father told me about today and about that cop you were chasing. Is it true what they're saying? Did he kill that recruit?"

"Yes, I believe he did."

"I couldn't stop thinking about it, that recruit and what his poor family must be going through."

"It's like you say, people heal in time." I'm mindful not to slur when I speak. "Are you sure you're OK?"

"I was wrong, Trevor. I wasn't honest with you at the hospital, and I should have been. It could have been the last time we spoke, and I would have regretted not being truthful. I don't want to pretend anymore. I can't —"

Maybe it's the belly of alcohol or the fading adrenaline rush of the morning's pursuit, but without much thought, I take Sarada by the waist and pull her close. I kiss her hard, and she pushes me against the wall. I flinch when she brushes against my ribs. "Shit. I'm so sorry," she says.

"I'm OK," I say, pulling my key from my pocket to unlock the door. The door swings open, and Sarada pushes me inside. I kick the door shut behind us and reach around her body to turn the deadbolt. I drop my holstered gun to the floor. She slips out of her coat and pulls off her boots — we fall onto the bed. Sarada works her sleeveless shawl-collared dress along her body and pulls it over her head. It falls to the floor. With my bum ribs, I can barely get my shirt off without her help. She works my arms through the sleeves, all while looking at me the way she did when we were younger.

"You sure?" I ask.

"I am," Sarada says, then kisses me. Everything feels new, a burgeoning landscape we're discovering together. Tonight, we defy the monsters that hissed in our ears that we couldn't be happy, that we were too broken and unworthy of love. Whatever love I'm capable of giving, Sarada can have it. She can have it all.

I kick off my shoes. Sarada tugs at my pants, working them to my ankles, and then she tosses them aside. I kiss below her navel and breathe in; I'm drowning in her. Something I thought had died in me grows stronger with each kiss, and I'm reminded of what I felt that night in Culver City, when all I wanted to do was take her away from Los Angeles, to someplace nice where grief couldn't follow.

I look into Sarada's eyes, and I know there's no going back for us. Tonight we're relinquishing our fears and letting go of the past, and while our lovemaking is the most honest thing I've felt in years, I can't help but feel damned.

CHAPTER TWELVE

Day 4, October 19, 2014

It's four a.m. I'm lying awake as the light from my alarm clock adds a blue hue to Sarada's face. She's sound asleep, naked under the sheet. My entire body is sore — chest, ribs, legs, and places I didn't realize that Garcia had struck me in our fight. I recall the past twelve hours, all that's happened, and then I look to Sarada. If there's one good thing to come out of this investigation, it's us. We've found our way back to each other.

Sarada and I made love so many times that I lost count. The first few times, my heart was beating hard and fast, and with the bump of a tender bruise, the pain sent me reeling. Each time I hissed, and Sarada gently stroked and kissed me where my hand braced against the wound. Then, as the night progressed, we found a kind of rhythm. We held each other for hours afterward, listening to each other's breathing. We didn't have any use for words. With every look and caress, I knew what Sarada was thinking. Sometimes it was an unbridled joy, her smile bursting with hope and possibility. Other times, she retreated to a place I couldn't reach. Distant, solemn, tucking her knees tightly into her stomach and curling her body into a ball. In those moments, she looked afraid, and I felt it, too.

Love is a frightening notion, even for someone who's been threatened with a knife, shot at, and had his ribs caved in by a beanbag, but I'd be a fool to think love can fix all that ails us. Like church folk say, "You need Jesus for that." And maybe they're right? I've never been much for religion, but I prayed for my mother, for God to take her cancer away. It took her life anyway, on an early December morning before the sun burned away the crystalline dew.

Even when facing certain death, my mother was unwavering in her faith and loved the church with zeal. Growing up, I dreaded Sunday mornings, when my mother would wake me before sunrise and drag me to Sunday service with her. My father usually slept in or did odd jobs around the house, like changing light bulbs and pulling weeds in the yard, but my mother never hounded him about his lack of attendance. Maybe she thought with all the horrible things he saw as a police officer that it was best to leave him alone to manage his soul. But it didn't keep her from placing a bible on his nightstand, and even if it collected dust and the spine never split, she wouldn't forsake him.

In her last week of life, she told me she prayed for my father and me every day that we would find happiness without her and that I would grow to be a good man. I know she never doubted her prayers weren't enough. After her death, my father didn't require church attendance, and we spent our Sundays on the couch watching sports and rooting for the home teams.

It's hard to see God in my line of work. Where is God when a child starves to death after his parents lock him in a bathroom for days? Or when a man is carjacked and murdered after leaving a dentist appointment? Does God watch as a woman is thrown to her death from an apartment window by a drug-addled ex-boyfriend? Where was God when Sarada was being raped? And what about Brandon Soledad? Where was God when he died, alone and cold, left to rot in the dirt? It's enough to make me doubt God's very existence. If he were all-powerful, he couldn't be benevolent. A good-natured deity wouldn't let human beings tear each other apart for sport. But if God is in the horrors, then he's in the splendor, too, and maybe this night with Sarada is a glimpse of the splendor that's awaiting me. Maybe God is showing me what's possible? Perhaps Sarada and I can carve out a little light amid the misery. Maybe we can be happy?

I kiss Sarada on her forehead, take her by the hand, and close my eyes to sleep.

I awake to my phone ringing on my nightstand. It's after seven, and the sunlight is beginning to peek through the blinds. I don't want to wake Sarada. I quickly reach for the phone, fumble, and then finally take hold and answer. It's Mrs. Graves.

"Detective?" she asks.

"Yes," I say, wiping the crust from my eye.

"Are you still available to meet me?"

I've got a splitting headache, and all I want to do is lie in bed with Sarada all day, but that's a fantasy. "I am."

"Good. I'll be at the corner of Colorado and Roosevelt in Pasadena. It's a little coffee shop. I forget the name, but you shouldn't have trouble spotting it. I'll be there at nine o'clock."

"Yes. OK." I end the call. Sarada begins to stir, slowly opening her eyes.

"What time is it?" she asks as she looks at the alarm clock. "Seven thirty? It feels earlier."

"You're probably still tired. You can stay here as long as you'd like."

"Where are you going?"

"I have a meeting."

"The shop opens soon. I should get going."

"OK."

Sarada climbs out of bed and starts to perform yoga stretches: downward-facing dog, and two other positions I've seen but can't name. "So, is it business as usual?" she asks.

"What's that?"

Sarada stops stretching and looks at me with sincerity. "I just need to know what last night was," she says. "I mean, I just showed up at your door and —"

"If you're asking if I want to go back to our uncomfortable existence, no, I don't."

"So, you don't think it was a mistake?"

"I know it wasn't a mistake. Is that what you think?"

"I know what a mistake feels like, the shame, the guilt." She brings her hand to her chest, makes a fist, and positions it over her heart. "But I don't feel any of that. I feel good."

"I do, too."

"But there is something else."

"Are you worried?" I ask.

"I'm terrified," she says, breathing deeply, and exhaling. "At first, I wasn't sure of what, but now I know for sure. I can't lose you, Trevor. And I hope last night isn't sending us on a collision course."

"I've given it a lot of thought, and I know how you feel about me being a police officer. If you want me to do something else, I'm OK with that," I say, sitting on the edge of the bed watching Sarada as if under a spell. "If it means I get to come home to you and you look at me the way you did last night, I'll lay the badge down."

Sarada lowers her head and brings her hand to her chin to consider what I've said. "Are you sure?"

"I am."

"You would be giving up your career. It's something you've worked so hard for."

"It would be for us and whatever future we're trying to have. I just want us to have a shot at this — I mean, a real shot, without anything standing in our way. Besides, things have changed now that Garcia is dead." I walk over to Sarada at the opposite bedside. "It's going to be hard for me to define my future in this department. Garcia's death will follow me forever. It may be time for me to move on."

"But there are other departments. I know you're a good detective. I know what you do matters. You help people, victims like Brandon. I don't want to be the cause for you giving up something you love."

"Maybe I can still help but in a different way."

"I don't know, Trevor. That's a big change," she says. "It's who you are."

I take her by the hand. She smells of cocoa butter, and her skin, shimmering, feels warm in the morning light. "I've done things I'm not proud of. I've stood on the sidelines and let people get hurt. There's a price I pay for these things, and most days, I feel like I'm paying it. But with you, it doesn't hurt so much. I've dreamed of this moment, and of last night, many times over, and I told myself if the dream were ever to come true, I would seize it."

"And what if we don't live up to each other's expectations?" she asks. "What if I let you down?"

"We've known each other for so long that I can't imagine giving up on each other now or ever."

Sarada touches my cheek lovingly. "My goodness, when did your ass get so sappy?"

"I don't know. Guess I'm softening up."

"You should get going," she says, slapping my naked backside.

"There's a spare key in my nightstand," I say. "Are you going to be all right locking up?"

"Of course."

"OK. See you later tonight?"

"Yes."

I shower, get dressed, and leave Sarada scrolling the Spinners social media accounts, drinking a cup of green tea brewed from a tea bag I find in a rarely opened cabinet.

The smog is heavy over downtown. I climb into the Mustang; it's low on fuel, but I have enough to get to Pasadena. I start the car and drive toward the 110 on-ramps on San Fernando Road. I merge onto the 110 North toward Pasadena. The traffic is moderate as I pass Arroyo Parkway and then the exit ramp to Dodger Stadium. The freeway bottlenecks at the 5 North interchange. I cross a few lanes to avoid slow-moving vehicles, and I accelerate, putting distance between the Mustang and the other cars. I ride the winding expressway until it ends and becomes North Arroyo Parkway. I keep heading north until I reach Colorado Boulevard, where I make a right turn and drive east.

When I reach Roosevelt Boulevard, I see a small coffee shop that looks like it's been operating since the 1950s. It's a cream-colored building with a bright-red door. A large antique sign in the window reads:

OPEN
SERVING BREAKFAST & LUNCH

I park in front of the building and grab a few coins from the center console to feed the meter. I can park my vehicle anywhere while in law enforcement capacity except in red or yellow zones, but parking enforcement outside LA jurisdiction often can't run plates and confirm I'm police. Tickets issued by other cities are challenging to have voided. They require paperwork and time I don't have.

I doubt I'll be meeting with Brandon's mother long. She'll likely ask about Joey Garcia, and with the lawsuit filed, I won't be able to tell her much. After I duck most of her questions, she'll relent and accept the lawsuit as a stonewall tactic. Maybe she'll get upset with me, curse at me, call me everything under the sun. I anticipate that because my mother would have done the same if I were in Brandon's shoes. Even though she was a woman of faith, grief and anger have a way of stripping people down to raw nerves, and there's nothing rawer than the agony of the mother of a murdered child.

I enter the coffee shop and look around. It's a small place with a few stools under a Formica counter, wooden booths, and circular tables covered in red-and-white checkered cloths. The menu is simple, offering refillable coffee and a blue-plate special of bacon, eggs, toast, and shredded potatoes. Old license plates from around the United States are nailed to the wood-paneled walls. Tennessee, Kansas, Utah, Kentucky — places I've never considered visiting, let alone living. I wouldn't know what to do with myself outside LA, but I imagine life to be quieter in those places, safer maybe, where time is measured in seasons rather than long summers and occasional bouts of rain.

The coffee shop looks to have existed before specialty coffee chains flourished and boutique eateries started serving sliced avocado on toast. It's what my father would call a greasy spoon, and it's the type of place

I liked going to as a child. Something about the ordinariness, the cozy charm, made me feel safe.

Toward the rear of the shop, I see Mrs. Graves drinking from a mug. She's sitting in a booth across from a plump, brown-skinned woman who's stirring sugar packets into a tall glass of iced tea. They remind me of my mother and aunt, her sister, who liked to sit at our kitchen table drinking coffee and playing Spades while talking about the latest episode of a soap opera and the exploits of her ex-husband who went to prison for tax evasion. The plump woman is wearing casual clothes — jeans, a black T-shirt, a denim jacket, a pair of white thick-soled sneakers. I can't see how she fits into the story. She may be an attorney, but that would be foolish. Any respectable attorney would know no police officer would speak about an open case when the department is facing a lawsuit.

Mrs. Graves notices me standing and beckons me with a wave. "Over here, Detective."

I start walking over, still unsure of the plump woman. Could she be a representative of an organization? The type of group fighting to end gun violence and work to improve relations between the police and

352

the community. While I support such an endeavor, she still won't get more than blanket statements from me. I've already formed one in my head: "This case is ongoing, and I'm unable to comment at this time." It's cold, but it's supposed to be.

Of course, I could be way off, and the woman is just a family member or close friend here to lend her support.

I approach their table. "Good morning, Mrs. Graves."

"Good morning, Detective."

She looks ten years older than when I last saw her. There are bags under her eyes, and her skin has developed a pallid coloring, like it's in desperate need of sunlight and nutrients. Around her mouth and between her eyes, deep wrinkles have settled. More curly gray hairs have grown, sporadic pops of lighter strands that look striking against her black hair. To say she looks tired is an understatement; she's ill with grief.

"Sit down," she says.

Typically, I would never sit with my back to the door, but to ask the women to move to another table on my behalf would be insensitive, given the circumstances. I pull a chair from an empty table and push it between the two booth ends.

"This is Clara Montgomery," Mrs. Graves

says. "I asked her to join us today. I hope that's all right."

"Well —"

"People call me Ms. Sugar," the woman chimes in abruptly. "Gon' have a seat, dear. You standing like that makes me nervous."

I take a seat. "Mrs. Graves, I understand you've filed a lawsuit against the department. Is that correct?"

"Yes, I did," she says.

"That lawsuit will preclude me from answering any questions regarding the handling of Brandon's case or its current status. Do you understand?"

"Detective, I didn't call you here to talk about my son's case. I already know enough about that. Maybe that dirty cop Garcia killed him, but he didn't do it alone. And whatever reason the LAPD is giving for not finding out what happened to my Brandon is a lie."

I want to tell her she's right, that the department is closing the case before it's solved, but I can't. "What are you saying, Mrs. Graves?"

"Maybe you should hear it from me," Ms. Sugar says. "I was willing to let the past remain in the past. See, I told myself there wasn't anything good that would come out of me getting involved in this. After all the pain I've been through over my Ruben, it just made no sense for me to get mixed up in this." Ms. Sugar slides her iced tea near the napkin dispenser so as not to spill it as she plops her thick arms on the table. "But I couldn't in good conscience just sit by while they ran Brandon's name through the mud. I couldn't do it. Once I saw the news that he was dead and then that website with those pictures and all those ugly things people wrote about him, I knew what I had to do."

"Ms. Montgomery, with all due respect, I don't understand what you're doing here."

"Brandon came to me months before he started at the police academy. He told me I was the forty-fifth Montgomery he'd contacted. Then, he asked if I had a son named Ruben. I told him I did, but he'd been taken from me a few years ago."

"Ma'am, what do you mean? Brandon tracked you down?"

"He came to my home, Detective. Knocked on my door, and I almost didn't let him in until he showed me my son's ID from the community college where he was taking masonry classes."

Mrs. Graves takes a long sip of coffee, reaches across the table, and holds Ms. Sugar's hand as if to help calm her nerves.

"How did Brandon get your son's ID?" I ask.

"He told me he found it where my son was last seen — in an alley in Westchester."

I feel a tightening in my chest, and my throat grows dry.

Ms. Sugar continues: "Brandon told me he watched two LAPD officers beat my son until he was limp and bleeding from his eyes. Then he said they picked him up and put him in the trunk of their patrol car. That same week, I called the police to report my son missing because he never came home that night." Ms. Sugar begins to choke up. "LAPD tells me my son fled the scene on foot, and they never caught him. A month later, after calling and calling, a detective says they think he ran off to Louisiana. It was a bald-faced lie. I just couldn't prove anything because I wasn't there. Then one day, here comes Brandon with this story. It was almost four years to the day my Ruben went missing, and I just knew God had sent Brandon to me."

"Mrs. Graves, I don't understand. Why didn't Brandon go to the police if he witnessed this?"

"Have you forgotten what it's like for black boys, Detective?" she asks, gripping the coffee mug. "It was too dangerous. And

I know my son. He didn't say anything because of me."

"Because of you?"

"Things were rough back then. A lot was going on with me and Brandon's father, Ishmael. Brandon wouldn't have wanted to bring on more stress. He knew I needed a son more than anything. I needed him to be there."

I'm reminded of Ishmael and his penance, his eyes blinded in the sun, and I think how truly decimated Brandon's family has become.

"That night, Brandon had football practice at the park, and he stayed after to work some drills with his friends. He liked to cut through the alley, said it saved him exactly six minutes. He had a thing about time. He was mindful not to leave me somewhere worrying about him. Black boys are taught to avoid the police, the same as they would gangs and troublemakers on the street," Mrs. Graves says, taking a moment to sip her coffee. "If Brandon had reported what he saw, it would have been like bringing hell on himself. Boys like Brandon don't matter to anyone but their mamas. They can be erased, just like that. And just like Ms. Sugar's son, Brandon would have disappeared. And as much as it pains me, at least I have his body, and I can bury him. I can lay him to rest the proper way."

"This is a serious allegation, Mrs. Graves —"

Ms. Sugar pats my hand. She's geeked and can't tell the story fast enough. "There were four officers there that night. And two left once my son was down on the ground, but it was clear my son needed medical attention." She leans in closer, her voice shy of a whisper. "Do you know what it means when a person bleeds from their eyes?"

"No, ma'am, I don't."

"It happens when a man gets hit in the head by a nightstick — over and over again. It's a sign that something done popped . . . a blood vessel, an artery . . . something gives out in their head, and blood flows like a busted valve."

My palms are growing clammy, and the tightness in my chest isn't going away. That pain in my side starts to pulse again. I don't think I've ever been this afraid before, but it isn't the type of fear that comes from being threatened with death. This fear is something buried deep inside; it's fragile like an egg, and with enough pressure, it will crack and out will spill every truth about that night. And these women deserve the truth. They deserve to know what happened to their sons.

I always knew that night would bring hell on me, and here I am, sitting between two women who could very well be my family. To offer them the truth would mean sealing my fate. My career would be over, and maybe I'd even see prison time. But looking at Mrs. Graves and Ms. Sugar, I can feel their suffering. It taints the very blood that pumps through their veins, and no matter how hard they try, they will never recover. They are forever changed down to their cells and the minutiae that makes up those cells because that's what grief does. It changes you. It sentences you to sleepless nights and longing, trying to satisfy an unappeasable need to see that person again and to make wrong right. I know these women. I've seen them countless times before, crying at funerals for dead sons, black men who were taken too soon for trivialities and perceived transgressions. Generations upon generations of men gone, but this time, I could have stopped it.

My body is slowly lowering in the seat. I want to slip away. It's an involuntary reaction, a need to escape. The night I found Sarada in the gallery's back room, I felt the same way. My body rebelled against my mind, and I wanted to run, but what kept me there was love. I don't know what's keeping me at the table now except needing to know why Brandon died.

"Detective, you OK?" Mrs. Graves asks.

I reclaim my body and sit up in the chair. "Just a moment," I say, my elbows on the table, leaning forward with my head down. "I just need to catch my breath."

"I can get you some water," she says.

I nod. The room starts to spin.

The thought of leaving Ruben alone — that's his name? Ruben. I don't think I remembered it until today. I left that brother to die at the hands of Boston and Garcia. I can still see him looking at me with blood in his eyes, mouthing the words *"Help me, please."* And what did I do? I straightened up and walked away, justified, hiding behind a badge that I thought meant I was beyond reproach. I tried to rationalize Ruben's assault. It was the sufficiency of fear, what recruits are taught the first month in the academy. If an officer fears for his or her life, that fear informs their actions. I told myself it was why Boston and Garcia had been so aggressive. Ruben was a large man, strong and agile. He could have gotten the better of them. Sure, he was unarmed, but Penal Code 834a states a subject must submit to arrest. Ruben Montgomery failed to do that. He escalated the situation, and Boston and Garcia were reasonable under color of law. It was legal, it was by the book, and it was bullshit. Ruben should have received medical attention, but instead he was given what Garcia used to call the NHI — No Humans Involved — treatment.

The waiter places a water glass on the table, and I take a sip, then another, until the glass is empty.

The women look at each other, confounded but accepting. "I'm OK. Please, continue," I say.

"Brandon said his voice was too small . . . and you know what happens to small voices. Unless . . ."

I'm not sure I want to know what comes next. Mrs. Graves needed a son, not a damn martyr. "Unless what?" I ask.

"That voice comes from inside the beast. Loud and clear. Brandon believed he was put on earth to make that department better. Like a warrant from God. Becoming an officer, getting those cops for what they did to my Ruben, became his obsession," Ms. Sugar says, taking hold of the silver cross around her neck. "Them cops threw Ruben in the back of that patrol car like he was garbage. Hell, less than garbage," she says, looking to Mrs. Graves as if to read the emotion in her face. "But Brandon had a plan, and that's what got him killed. See, I think he found those cops, and they tried to make sure he didn't let their secret out."

"But this is hearsay. Where's the proof?"

"Brandon always had a backup plan, Detective. The first thing he did when he walked into a room was note all the exits," Mrs. Graves says. "It's just part of who he was."

"He recorded what they did to my son on his camera phone, and he made me a copy," says Ms. Sugar.

"A video recording?" I ask.

"That's right," she says. "Brandon told me to keep it safe in case . . . well, in case something happened to him, and now, here we are."

I try to mask the concern in my voice. "Did you watch this video?"

"I did."

"And what exactly do you intend to do with it?"

"That's why you're here, Detective. It's not what I'm going to do. It's what you're going to do." Ms. Sugar removes a disc in a white sleeve from her purse and slides it toward me on the table. "It's best you watch for yourself. I trust you will make the right decision."

"The right decision for whom?"

Ms. Sugar looks to me with pity. "Oh, Detective," she says, "you are far from the peaceful shore."

The waiter drops the bill on the table, and Mrs. Graves pays with ten dollars, which seems generous for coffee and tea. Then they both slide out of the booth.

"I almost forgot," Mrs. Graves says, pushing a pair of dark shades onto her face. "Last night, I received a call from your superior — I believe he's your captain. He told me I could have my son's body since the case was officially closed."

"What about the video? If what you say is true, this has implications for the case."

"Detective, my son wanted to become a police officer more than anything. He wanted to right a wrong he witnessed and to help end the corruption that plagues your department. No matter how naive you may think my son was, I believe in what he was trying to do. Your department has shown my son nothing but disrespect. You have treated his murder like an inconvenience, and the LAPD is only interested in protecting itself from lawsuits. I don't trust your department as far as I can throw it. So, I intend to rectify the very soul of the LAPD. I will work to make it into what my son hoped it could be. The change will come, Detective. You can be an advocate of that change, or you can be its obstacle. The choice is yours."

"I don't understand. What do you want from me?"

"Watch the video, and you'll know what to do," Mrs. Graves says.

"I'll be praying for you, Detective," Ms. Sugar adds.

The two women leave me at the table in anguish.

For a moment, I ponder ways to destroy the disc, but Ms. Sugar likely made copies. Besides, no matter how much I wish I could outrun this mess, I can't. I've failed as a police officer, as a human being. Ruben is dead; he died that night. I sensed death at the scene, and I did nothing. If only I had acted, called for the medic . . . did *something,* Ruben Montgomery might be alive today.

That brother's blood is on my hands, and there's no washing it away. I will carry this forever.

I was willing to lay the badge down for Sarada, but I should never have put it on. What will they say, Sarada and my father? How will they see me once they learn the truth? I can only imagine what the video shows: Boston's partner and I walking away while Ruben begs for the beating to stop.

The waiter returns to pick up the bill and the cash. "Sir, is there anything I can get you?" he asks.

I didn't notice him before, but he's a young Asian man, thin and short, with a kind face. I look to him begrudgingly — a bad day at his job would be bliss for me. Maybe I should consider serving flapjacks as a profession. It might be the only job I'm fit for once the truth about Ruben and Brandon comes to light.

"I'm fine. Thank you."

The waiter nods and walks away. I slip the disc into my jacket pocket and leave the coffee shop.

CHAPTER THIRTEEN

When I return to my loft, I quickly enter and take a seat at my desk. My computer is old and barely gets used, except to answer emails or shop online. I open the disc drive, remove an old rock CD — Soundgarden's *Down on the Upside* — and then insert Ms. Sugar's disc. It takes a moment to load. The computer cranks and grinds while blowing hot air from the back of the tower.

Then an image appears on the monitor. Brandon's sitting at his desk in his room. He's a teenager, maybe seventeen or eighteen.

He can't stop shaking.

"Tonight, I saw something," he says. "I mean, I know these things happen. I know the police aren't all good. But tonight, I saw what they could do — and they did it like it was nothing, like he was nothing." Watching Brandon speak is haunting, a ghost making proclamations from the grave. His voice isn't what I expected. It's deep, strong, commanding. "There were three officers . . . no, four. Yes, four officers, and there was a black man on the ground. They were hitting him with batons and kicking him. It was like Rodney King or something. At first, I thought it wasn't real, like they were actors shooting a movie. But there were no cameras, no crew, just the officers and the man on the ground . . . ."

The video of Brandon cuts to black. The next image is that of my fellow officers and me standing over Ruben Montgomery. Garcia shouts obscenities while Boston circles him the way coyotes survey their wounded.

"Get up! Get up!" Boston shouts.

Ruben attempts to rise, and she pushes him back to the ground with her boot heel. Then, Garcia takes a swing, sending his side-handle baton across Ruben's legs. Ruben curses and attempts to defend himself from the strikes, kicking his legs and using his forearms to deflect each advance, but Garcia continues his assault.

The beating is worse than I remember. It's like my mind had removed the most brutal moments. Things are said in ways I don't recall. In the video, I stand watching as if I were in a trance.

"Get the rookie out of here," Garcia says to Castillo. She takes me by the arm and leads me away from the scene. I disappear from the frame, but not before turning to look at Ruben one last time.

"What the hell are you watching?" Sarada asks.

I didn't hear her come in, but when I turn around, she's standing in the doorway, holding grocery bags and staring at the computer's screen. I turn off the monitor. "I didn't know you were here."

"I went to the grocery store. Your refrigerator was empty. I thought you could benefit from some essentials."

"Who's running your shop?"

"My assistant manager opened," Sarada says, placing the grocery bags on the counter. "I thought I'd hang here until traffic dies down, but I can go now if you'd like."

"No, it's fine."

"I don't want to impose."

"Sarada, really, it's fine," I say emphatically.

"Did something happen? You seem upset."

I sigh. I'm not sure where to begin. To tell Sarada any of what has transpired could mean the end of us, and I'm not ready to lose her.

"Are you in trouble, Trevor?"

"I don't know. God . . . I might be."

Sarada walks over to me; she rests her hand on my shoulder. "Whatever it is, Trevor, it will be OK." I take her hand and press her palm against my forehead. Her presence is comforting, a lifeline for a drowning man.

"I hope so, but I think this time I messed up, and I can't fix it."

Sarada is quiet. I'm afraid to look up at her, thinking the delicate world we're building might dissolve before my eyes. I feel her breath against my skin, deep, steady breaths. If this is how we end, then I'm thankful for the night we shared, our passing euphoria.

Is this how I fall? Not with a shudder or a bang, but with Sarada's silent discontent.

"Please, say something," I say.

I look up as Sarada strokes my forehead. "I'm sure there's a way to make it right," she says.

"I can try, but it'll cost me."

"Like what?"

"Everything. Maybe even us."

"We decide what becomes of us."

"I wish it were that easy. I think Baldwin was right," I say. "There are unseen laws that govern this world. Laws of reciprocity."

"Baldwin?" Sarada says. "I thought you said he was too highbrow for you?"

"Doesn't mean he wasn't right. People truly pay for what they do, don't they? One way or another."

"He wasn't talking about you, Trevor. You're a good person. Misguided at times, but good. Whatever this thing is you're involved in, I know it will work out."

"I hope you're right."

"No matter what, I'm not going anywhere." Sarada leans in and kisses me. I think back to our time at Pershing. Conversations under the pergola about our futures, where we would be in ten years, twenty years. Casting out our hopes like fishing lines into the sea. We were so sure about life, convinced everything would fall into place.

It would be so easy to pack a bag and run away with Sarada to some island where nothing could touch us — our little paradise. We could live a life far from Los Angeles and its painful reminders of our frailty. We could start anew; it could be beautiful.

But who am I kidding? I can't run from this, and if I did, I wouldn't be the man Sarada deserves.

I compose myself and rise from the chair. "I have to leave."

"We still on for dinner?"

"Yes. I'll call you later with the time and place."

"OK. By the way, your dad called me. He sounded concerned about you. You should call him."

I kiss Sarada like it's the last time. When I pull my lips from hers, she exhales and opens her eyes, a bit flustered. She stammers out, "Be careful."

I remove the DVD from my computer's disc drive and head out the door.

The gray sky gives way to a downpour that grows heavier by the minute. I pull into a gas station and get out of the car to pump. I'll need to fill up the tank; it's a long drive to Sherman Oaks. I put in forty dollars' worth of premium fuel and get back into the car. I look at my work phone to see missed calls from Captain Beckett. A missed call notification is displayed on my personal cell as well. Tori. I almost forgot I owe her coffee. I hate to keep brushing her off, especially now that Sarada and I have something going, but she'll have to wait. As for the captain, if I'm right about what happened to Brandon and who helped Garcia kill him, then the captain will have more significant concerns than where the reports are that I owe him.

The department will be facing the greatest shitstorm since Rampart.

I start the engine and drive. The rain beats against the windshield as I merge onto the 110 North and then drive northbound on the 101 toward Ventura. Traffic is what I expected. The early morning rush has subsided, and there are mostly truckers and late-morning commuters. I show Code 3 and use my emergency lights and sirens to force vehicles from the fast lane. Once the lane is clear, I accelerate and send the speedometer from 60 mph to 90 mph, where it holds steady.

I exit onto Sepulveda and drive south. The streets are busy despite the rain. I pass a man arguing with a traffic officer over a ticket. Paparazzi are clustered outside a restaurant trying to get photos and footage of a celebrity eating inside. People sit outside a café, conversing while their dogs lie next to them. If I didn't know it was real life, I'd presume it was a staged scene. Like other parts of the city, Sherman Oaks resembles a movie set starring familiar actors and extras with bit roles plucked from central casting.

I'm two blocks from my destination when I stop at a red light. In the distance, I can see a few empty parking meters. When the light turns green, I pull into an empty spot. Since I'm within the department's jurisdiction, I don't bother feeding the meter. I get out of the car and head into Fitopia, the gym owned by Boston and her wife. Inside, celestial music plays through speakers installed in the ceiling, and I smell burning incense. The space is vast; it looks less like a gym and more like a wellness center where they charge $200 for an hour's back massage. Centralized in the middle of the gym are weights and cardio machines. To the left of the reception area is a staircase that leads to a second floor.

As I walk toward the reception desk, a woman appears from a small makeshift office that resembles a large cubicle. She's middle-aged with long blonde hair and tan skin, a bronze color that looks unnatural but is endemic for white women throughout Los Angeles. She's dressed the part of a trainer: leggings, a workout bra that reveals her ab definition, and posh sneakers.

"Good morning," she says. "Let me guess — LAPD?"

"That obvious?"

"I've been around enough cops to recognize the signs. Plus, I'm married to one."

"You must be Cynthia?"

"That's right. Cynthia Hale. And you are?"

"Detective Trevor Finnegan."

Cynthia extends her hand, and we shake. "It's my pleasure," she says. "Do you work with Mandy?"

"Mandy?"

"I mean, Boston. Not the most original nickname, I might add."

"Officers can lack imagination."

"What do they call you?"

"Finn, short for Finnegan."

"You're right. Not very imaginative. I have some time before my next client. I can give you the grand tour, if you'd like?"

"Is Boston available?"

"She'll be in later. But between you and me, she's a terrible tour guide. You're welcome to wait for her, though."

I give a genial chuckle. "It's fine. Lead the way."

I play the prospective member's role and follow Cynthia around the gym, enthused by the prospect of working out surrounded by enormous throw pillows.

"I wanted to make a place where working out was comfortable, and afterward, you don't race home but hang out and talk with friends," she says. "We even have a juice bar, but if that's not your thing, there's coffee and an assortment of teas."

Cynthia is pleasant and knowledgeable about exercise routines. There are photos of her and Boston framed on the walls. One picture shows Cynthia participating in a long jump event; she flies over the sandpit wearing a USA unitard, her legs stretched, her face pensive.

"You were an Olympian?" I ask.

"I competed twice in the Games, even snagged a silver in the long jump. That picture was my record-breaking jump," she says, pointing to the photo.

"Impressive."

"It was for a time. Then your body tells you it's the end of the road."

"What happened?"

"Injuries. First my hamstring and then Achilles."

I follow Cynthia upstairs. There are two rooms, one with three tanning beds and another with two colossal machines that resemble refrigerators. "If it weren't for this, my recovery would have been much longer and more painful."

"What are they?"

"Cryotherapy. It's a service we offer to exclusive members, but if you decide to join, you'll get three free sessions a year."

"How much does one of these machines

run you?"

"About two hundred thousand each. I could have bought a condo in Reseda."

"Or a Bentley. You mind if I check it out?"

"Sure, go right ahead."

I survey the chamber. It smells of disinfectant; it could be ammonia.

"How does it work?" I ask.

"Liquid nitrogen cools the air around your body. Your skin drops in temperature but not to a critical level, so your body temperature shouldn't fluctuate. You're also never unsupervised in the machine. Mandy or I would be monitoring you, and you can end the session whenever you like by opening the door and walking out. It's completely safe."

"How cold can it get?"

"Around negative two hundred forty degrees."

"Cold enough to freeze to death."

"Sure, but no one sets it that cold. There would be no medical benefits at that point, just frostbite and a headache."

"But if for some reason it were lower than the recommended setting, it could be fatal, correct?"

"At the lowest setting, sure. If you were in there long enough. But it's like I said, we monitor everyone's sessions." Cynthia turns on the cryo chamber with a push of a button. "I assure you, it's safe."

"What exactly are the medical benefits?" I ask.

"It helps resolve inflammation in muscles and joints, and promotes fast healing."

"How long would someone have to stay in this thing to see any benefit?"

"Everyone is different. We recommend two minutes. Some people prefer five to seven. It varies depending on the customer. Do you think cryotherapy might be helpful for you?" Cynthia presses buttons to adjust the machine's temperature; degrees shift on what looks like a microwave display. "We can do a quick intake form and get you started."

"Does it mend broken ribs and cure insomnia?"

"That's what whiskey is for, Finn," Boston says as she comes up the stairs.

"Detective Walsh," I say. "I was just enjoying the tour of your digs."

"What do you think?"

"I think early retirement will suit you."

Boston throws her arm around Cynthia's shoulders and pulls her close. "Yeah, I'm pretty blessed."

"You're soaking wet," Cynthia says, laughing and then prodding Boston away.

"Got caught in the downpour earlier. You mind putting some coffee on for our guest? I'm sure he could use some. How do you take it, Finn?"

"One cream. Two sugars."

"Coming right up," Cynthia says as she heads downstairs.

"She's lovely," I say.

"That she is, but I know you didn't come down here to gawk at my wife, or if you did, we've got a problem," she says, followed by a banal laugh and snort. "What's on your mind?"

"Joey Garcia."

"Jesus, Garcia. A real shame, but he was never too bright, was he? Sleeping with a recruit like that. What was it, some fucked-up lover's triangle?"

"Brandon wasn't killed over a woman." I lower my voice. "He was killed because of what he saw and who he saw doing it."

"What did he see?" Boston asks, feigning surprise.

"Ruben Montgomery."

Boston frowns. "Doesn't ring a bell."

"So, that's how you're going to play this," I say. "I'm talking about the man you and Garcia beat to a pulp and threw in your shop. I'm guessing he died in your trunk, and you disposed of the body."

Boston laughs, loud enough for Cynthia to hear. "Shit, Finn, you are losing it," she says, whispering. "I don't know any Ruben Montgomery, unless you're talking about a member of the PGs who jetted on us that night and fled to Louisiana. What was his name? Double Stuff? OG Madcap?"

"Cut the shit. I know Ruben didn't run that night."

"You weren't even there. Garcia sent you with Castillo back to Division. What the hell do you know?"

I pull the disc from my jacket pocket. "It's on video, Boston. Brandon Soledad recorded it that night. He witnessed everything."

Boston puts her hands to her hips. "You expect me to believe that?" she asks, relinquishing her whisper, her voice metered.

"Try me."

"OK, I'll play along. Let's say you do have some video. What's it going to show? A couple of cops using necessary force to arrest a known felon."

"It'll prove you lied, and he didn't flee."

"It doesn't mean I killed him."

"You and Garcia were afraid of Brandon Soledad."

"Afraid? I didn't even know the kid."

"You didn't have to know him. Brandon

379

realized who Garcia was, and that was enough. Maybe he threatened Garcia, told him if he didn't leave Marlena Sanchez alone that he'd tell what he saw that night. But no one threatens Garcia, right? He decided to talk it out with Brandon, maybe come to an agreement. He had Brandon meet him at Paradise Lost in Downey. Things didn't go well; they argued. It got physical. Garcia hit him, maybe knocked him out, and that's when Garcia called you for help."

Boston's applause is faint. She softly taps her fingers against her palm like a debutante in an opera house. "Seriously, Finn. You need medication . . . ," she says. "It's a hell of a show, though. What else you got?"

"You had him meet you here, at the gym, and you put Brandon in the cryo chamber. Such an odd way to kill someone. Maybe you hoped it would be so baffling that the case would stall, but Garcia got nervous. So, he popped me with the beanbag to slow me down. It was stupid and desperate, but that's who Garcia was. Not the best coconspirator, was he? He was going to get you pinched. So, you decided to pin it all on him."

"Shit, Finn. Talk about detective skills. Fuck what they say about you . . . you're the real thing. A regular Sherlockian."

"You knew how to access his computer's IP address. You made it look like Garcia posted those photos of Brandon's body to StormWatch. You played him."

Boston grins and pushes her wet hair back behind her ears. "I think your crackpot father is rubbing off on you. You're fucking certifiable if you think I murdered that kid."

"You walked Garcia through it every step of the way. He was your lackey. And who knows? Maybe Castillo grew a conscience since that night, and she'll back me up."

"I wouldn't bet on it. She's dead."

"You kill her, too?"

"Cancer, shithead."

Cynthia comes up the stairs with the coffee in hand. "Sorry, it's a new machine, still learning it. I hope it's still hot."

"That's quite all right, babe. Finn was just leaving," Boston says.

"What about your coffee?"

Boston watches me the way I would a suspect that I couldn't read. "He'll take it to go. Won't you, Finn?"

I take a moment and consider my next move. I don't have Boston on the ropes, but she's thinking hard and heavy, thinking maybe the disc is a bluff — but what if it isn't? I can see it in her eyes — the fear.

"Sure. That'll be fine," I say with as much pleasantness I can muster.

"OK, I'll fix it up for you. We just got these great biodegradable to-go cups. You'll be the first customer to use them. You'll have to let me know how you like it."

"Sounds excellent. Thank you."

Cynthia slowly maneuvers the stairs, trying to avoid spilling the coffee.

"She has no idea who you are," I say. "And I feel for her when she finds out. It's the people we love who we hurt the most, right?"

Boston's patience looks to be wearing thin. She takes hold of my shirt and pulls me close. "Speak for yourself, Mr. High-and-Mighty. How long were you watching Ruben get the shit beat out of him, huh? What? Is your memory not so good? You saw it going too far, but you did nothing —"

"Take your hands off me, or I tell Cynthia everything."

"Oh, fuck you, Finnegan," she says, letting go of my shirt and shoving me back.

"I'll be naming myself in my report," I say, smoothing out the shirt's wrinkles. "Along with you and Garcia."

"Your report is a bullshit formality. The

case is closed. Garcia killed the kid. End of story."

"How do you know that?"

"Everyone knows it. The entire department, for Chrissake. Garcia is dead, and so is your investigation."

"Sure, but he didn't act alone. People need to know that."

"You've got no evidence. It's conjecture. You can't implicate me in anything. Even with your video, the only thing you can prove is a false report. My retirement papers have already been signed and processed. My pension's safe."

"You broke the law. It's prosecutable."

"Please, they wouldn't waste time and money. Face it, Finn, the department will wipe its ass with that report and flush it down the shitter. Then they'll take your badge."

"Maybe, but at least I can sleep at night knowing the department knows the full story."

"How virtuous of you. But something tells me that video is garbage — old camera footage? The lighting is probably shit, too. You're not a complete idiot. No prosecutor would move on that, and you know it."

"Who said I was giving it to a prosecutor?"

Boston puffs up aggressively and wags her fist in my face. "Get out of here, Finn. And do yourself a favor: mind your six because next time, it might not be a beanbag."

"Threats, Boston? That's weak, even for you."

"If you don't get out of my gym, it'll be a reality faster than you know."

I smile. "You're going to get what you deserve," I say. "I promise you that. Maybe not today or tomorrow, but you're going to rot in prison, Boston."

Cynthia returns with the coffee in a to-go cup. "Everything all right?" she asks, looking to Boston, who's glowing red.

"Sure, honey. We're fine."

"Here you are," she says, handing me the cup.

"How much do I owe you?"

"On the house," Boston says, forcing a smile. "From one cop to another. We have to look out for each other. Isn't that right, Finn?"

Cynthia beams. "Got to love the camaraderie."

"Best of luck with the gym, ladies."

I head downstairs as Boston watches me with disdain. I feel sorry for Cynthia. Cops are good at keeping secrets; Boston is no exception. Cynthia may never truly know what her wife is capable of, nor what she's done. And if Boston is right, and my report does get sidelined by the department, I'll have to escalate things. There's only one person I know who can do that.

David Bergman.

Chapter Fourteen

Back at Pacific Division, a large crowd of citizens and reporters has formed outside the building. People hold protest signs that read No Justice, No Peace; Say His Name; and Justice For Brandon. I enter the parking lot, and after scanning my badge at the kiosk, I park the Mustang in the usual spot.

My work cell phone rings. Captain Beckett. Again. I ignore the call and enter the building.

Inside, the silent treatment prevails, and officers continue to avoid me. I go to my modular and take a seat at my desk and start working on the report. I'm thirty minutes into writing when Captain Beckett enters my office.

"Something wrong with your phone?" he asks.

"No, sir."

"What makes you think you can ignore

my calls like this? Step into my office. Now."

I follow the captain into his lair and shut the door behind me. He takes a seat in his high-back chair and rests his elbows on the large executive desk.

I continue to stand.

"I've tried to be patient with you. I even let you keep working after your injury, when I should have benched you. But now I hear you met with Mrs. Graves."

Word travels fast through the department, especially when Boston is the one spreading it.

"Yes, I did," I say.

"What the hell for?"

"She said she had new information."

"The case is closed, Finnegan. The department will be releasing a statement this evening in a press conference, and I want everything you have on this case on my desk before you leave today."

"There's something you should know, sir. It could change everything about this case."

Beckett scowls. "What did I just say? I'm not interested, Finnegan."

"It's about protecting this department, sir, and avoiding a public relations crisis."

"Well, if it's that dire, I expect it to be in your report."

"Yes, Captain."

"Then I want you to take some time off."

"Time off?"

"It will do you some good."

"How long, sir?"

"A month. You've got the time."

"Am I being suspended?"

"Did I say that? It's just time off. You can reflect on your career choices."

Maybe he's doing me a favor by keeping me away from the job until things cool off? Or is this the first step to being terminated? "I understand, sir. Am I dismissed?"

"Get out of my office," the captain says before directing his attention to his computer screen. I return to my desk and continue working on the report. After an hour of pounding keys, I receive a text message from Tori asking if I'm free to talk later. I text: Sure, I'll call you.

I write for another two hours, completing the report just before five o'clock. It's exhaustive, and at times, it reads more like a confessional with me assuming the role of witness, perpetrator, and contemptible police officer, but every word is accurate. I print the report. Then, I compile statements from Brandon's parents, interviews with his classmates, a transcript of Marlena Sanchez's interrogation, photos of Brandon's autopsy and the ME's report, photos of the crime scene and the tire tracks found near the body, forensic reports (including what I deem questionable evidence gleaned from Joey Garcia's computer by Boston's team), a summary of my meeting with Mrs. Graves and Clara "Sugar" Montgomery (including the existence of the video disc), photos of Brandon's abandoned car and notes on the Paradise Lost's parking lot and exterior surveillance cameras, summaries of the interviews with the club owner and patrons, photos of Joey Garcia's crash along with a summary of events, and anything else germane to the case into the LAPD's standardized format known as the murder book.

Before I take the murder book to the captain's office, I scan all the documents and save them onto a flash drive. Beckett's office door is open, but he isn't there. I set the large binder on his desk and start heading down the hallway toward the exit when I hear a commotion coming from the lobby. Two patrol officers rush past me with their hands on their pistols.

"It's a Ten Thirty-Two, Detective, in the lobby," an officer says as he runs past.

It's one of the greatest fears for any division. A gunman on the premises. I follow the officers to the lobby, where I see Ishmael Soledad brandishing a long-barrel revolver and pointing it at Javier Perez.

Officers have taken cover behind the check-in desk and in the hallway. There are at least twenty guns trained on Ishmael.

"You killed him," Ishmael says. "You killed my boy!"

Perez is frozen with his hands high above his head.

"Put it down!" Captain Beckett shouts. "We will not hesitate to shoot you."

"Kill me?" Ishmael says. "Just like you killed my boy? Fuck you. Fuck all of you!"

"Put the gun down!" the captain repeats. "I will not tell you again."

I draw my gun and move toward Beckett, who's crouched in the hallway. "Sir, let me try and talk him down. I'm the lead detective. If he's here for answers, it's best they come from me."

"Not going to happen, Finnegan. Fall back."

"Sir, please? He'll listen to me — I know it."

"You're out of your depth."

"Please, sir. Let me try." Captain Beckett mulls over my request. "The last thing we need is for Brandon's father to die by our hands, too."

Beckett's nostrils flare. I know he's still angry with me, but I'm our one tactical advantage. As the only person here who knows Ishmael, I stand the best chance of talking him into surrender. "Sir?"

Beckett nods reluctantly. "Don't be a hero."

"Copy, sir."

Beckett follows with, "Any sudden moves, and he's dead."

I leave Beckett hunkered in the hallway. I move toward Ishmael but maintain a good distance, slightly off-line, so if he is to fire on me, he'll need to turn his body to face me. "Mr. Soledad?"

Ishmael keeps his gun on Perez, whose face is coated in sweat, and whips his head around to face me. "You the one," he says, his eyes pink and flushed, possibly still healing from the sun's hellacious effects.

"Let's talk about this."

"What's there to talk about? My boy is dead because of you devils. You all killed him, and for what?"

"I know you're angry. You have every reason to be."

"You have to face judgment!"

"You're right, Ishmael. We do," I say, slowly lowering my gun. I look toward Perez, whose shirt is soaked through with sweat.

"What the hell are you doing, Finnegan?"

Captain Beckett shouts from the hallway.

"I got this," I say to Beckett, holstering my Glock. "You want justice. I get that, but this is only going to end one way."

"It isn't right," Ishmael says. "I wasn't there when he needed me. I failed him."

"No. We all failed him."

Ishmael begins to sob. "I just want to hear it," he says. "I want to hear the words."

"Hear what words?"

"Say it. Say you killed Brandon."

"Bullshit," Captain Beckett mumbles, loud enough for me to hear. Ishmael extends the gun closer to Perez's face. No amount of training accurately prepares you for a gun pointed inches from your nose. Perez is losing his footing, wobbling like a palm tree caught in a Santa Ana wind.

I turn and give Beckett a harsh glare and then return my attention to Ishmael. "OK, Ishmael. OK, just focus on me. Forget about them."

"The words, damn you," Ishmael bemoans. "Say the words."

"All right, we killed him. We killed Brandon," I say. "Now, put the gun down."

"No — not you. I want to hear it from him," Ishmael says, looking to Captain Beckett.

"What?" I ask.

"He's the boss, ain't he? He's giving the orders, so I want to hear him admit it. I want someone to take some fucking responsibility."

"Captain?" I say, looking back at him. He's stone-faced, mouth sealed, not budging.

"No one has to die," I repeat, looking to Ishmael. "We can end this."

"Tell him to lose the gun first," Captain Beckett says, keeping his eyes on Ishmael like he's weighing his life against speaking a sentence.

"Captain, please?"

It's as if time has stopped or slowed to such an incremental pace that we might as well be moving in slow motion. "Fine," the captain says. "We killed him. We killed Brandon Soledad."

"Again," Ishmael demands, stepping closer to Perez with the revolver still aimed between his eyes. "Say it again. Say you killed my boy."

"Drop the fucking gun," Beckett snaps back.

"We killed Brandon Soledad," I say, repeating it another five times.

Officer Ahn stands behind me and begins repeating the words, and soon, other officers join in, chanting: "We killed Brandon

393

Soledad."

From the window, I can see protestors congregating around the station, screaming for justice, demanding a reckoning, and it's all being captured on camera phones for the world to see.

A SWAT unit, a large armored truck, pulls into the parking lot, and officers empty from the vehicle in full tactical gear. Other officers returning from patrol take to directing the crowd away from the building.

I advance toward Ishmael with my hands positioned in front of my chest, palms open. "No more death, Ishmael. It isn't what Brandon would want. That much I know."

"He was my son, a child of God. Flesh and blood. Can't you people see that?"

He slowly lowers his gun. I keep between him and the dozen officers with their fingers on the triggers of pistols and shotguns.

"I know, Ishmael. I know what he meant to you," I say. "I know he mattered."

I breathe in, exhale slowly, and grab hold of the revolver's barrel and pull it away from Ishmael. Perez quickly moves away from the front desk, seeking refuge in the hallway. Officers pounce on Ishmael, manipulating his arms behind his back to cuff him. I open the revolver's chamber. "Empty," I say, looking to Captain Beckett.

Officer Ahn kindly takes the gun from my hand. "I've got it, Detective," she says.

"Check him for other weapons, Finnegan," Beckett orders.

I search Ishmael, running my hands across his pockets and waistband, along his legs, and down to his ankles. "Got anything sharp in your pockets?"

Ishmael shakes his head, and I reach into his pockets, pulling out a few coins and my business card. Captain Beckett snatches the card from my hand. He looks at it. Disappointment turns to fury. "Get the hell out of here, Finnegan," he says.

"But, sir —"

"Go now! Get out of my fucking sight."

I can feel the hard glares of my fellow officers; when I look at Ahn, in her face, an ardent declaration of forgiveness, but both of us know there may be no salvation for me.

I turn and leave out the rear entrance. I can hear the roar of the protestors growing more agitated. In the parking lot, I get into the Mustang. My heart is beating out of my chest. Is it a heart attack this time? Or the panic that's becoming commonplace? I try to get a handle on the feeling, gripping the steering wheel tightly, jerking it with force.

Then, without much thought, I release a

primal scream loud enough to be heard blocks away. It's a strident cry; my throat burns raw.

I collapse over the steering wheel, emptied, fearing I'm going mad.

My phone rings. Tori. "Hi," she says. "Can we meet?"

I catch my breath and steady my voice, but I can't subdue the tremble. I look at my watch, then I say, "Six thirty."

"That works. What's the place?"

"Doyle's Pub. Downtown."

"OK. Finn, you sound strange. Is everything all right?"

"I'll see you later."

I end the call.

CHAPTER FIFTEEN

"Is it weird I prefer LA when it rains?" Tori asks, looking out the window at the wet streets. She's dressed for the weather, a beige trench coat over a navy-blue sweater dress and brown heeled boots, more fashion than function.

"No," I say.

"This city — dry for months, and then it pours rain. All I want to do is watch it fall." She speaks with an uneasiness, and I find myself trying to think of ways to break the ice; then I realize it's the first time we've eaten at a restaurant together. It's a deviation from our usual evenings of wine and sex in my loft, and I have a feeling Tori has come to this realization as well. "How's work, Finn? I've been watching the news. It's getting crazy out there with the protests."

"The department is prepared," I say, speaking with the authority of a loyal

397

disciple. Though my faith in the department is waning.

"So, do you think things will calm down?"

"I don't know. The department will be making a statement later. Maybe it'll make a difference. Maybe it won't. People are angry, and that anger needs someplace to go."

"But if they're making a statement, it means you solved it, right? You caught the killer?"

Tori's question makes my job sound trivial, like a plot in a police procedural show on television. "We have a suspect, and formal charges will be filed."

"You don't sound pleased," she says. "I thought you wanted to come here to celebrate. It's pretty fancy."

The pub is high-end, not the type of place frequented by college students from nearby USC; instead, the patrons are lawyers and bankers.

"A celebration might be premature. I just thought we could use a change."

Tori looks at me suspiciously. She's no fool. Taking a woman to a nice restaurant to break up with her is trite and predictable. Had I given it more thought, I would have picked a diner or stuck with a coffee shop, but I wasn't thinking clearly. My thoughts were on Ishmael and his dead son. Still are.

A woman wearing all black — a buttoned-up shirt, slacks, and casual shoes — places two water glasses on our table. "I'm Melody. I'll be serving you this evening. Can I start you off with something to drink?"

"Water is fine," Tori says.

"I'll have an old-fashioned."

"Particular whiskey?"

"Doesn't matter."

"I'll give you some time to look over the menu," Melody says before walking away.

I open the menu and gloss over the sandwiches and burgers. "The house burger is pretty good."

"You've eaten here before?"

"Sometimes, after work," I say. "It stays open late."

"I'm not particularly hungry."

"Me, either."

"Are you OK, Finn?"

"No, Tori. I'm not OK."

"Want to talk about it?"

"Why?"

"Because I'd like to know what's bothering you."

"Tori, I don't think you could even fathom the type of day I've had or the type of life I've lived, for that matter."

"How do you know if you don't open up?"

"Why bother? So you can offer me some Pollyanna bullshit about how if I just think positive thoughts, shit will get better? Well, I live in the real fucking world, and in the real world, people die. Good people. It's going to take more than happy thoughts and mantras to fix this broken place."

"What the hell, Finn?" Tori is taken aback. "That was uncalled for."

For the next few seconds, we're silent. I'm coming undone, slipping into darkness. The precursor to something ugly. "I didn't mean that," I say. "It just came out . . ."

"What's up with you?"

"It's been a horrible day. Maybe the fourth-worst day of my life, and I'm sorry."

By the time this sit-down is over, I know Tori is going to hate me. I can't blame her. I've been careless with her feelings, and if she makes a scene and dumps the water glass over my head or simply storms out, it would be warranted.

"I've been thinking about what you said in the hospital about how you want to change. Do you think that's possible?" she asks.

"I'm trying, Tori. And I know change means being honest with you. There's something you need to know —"

"You love her, don't you? The woman who came to the hospital with your father. Sarada. I saw the way you looked at her. It's a way you've never looked at me."

"Tori . . ."

"I get it. I do. This thing with us was about convenience, and neither one of us wanting to be lonely." Tori brushes a strand of hair from her face. "Do me a favor, Finn."

"OK. Like what?"

"Tell me something about you that's true. One fact."

"What do you mean?"

"Fine," Tori says, frustrated. "Do you even know when my birthday is?"

"No."

"You were born on May 19, 1984. You're wondering how I know that?"

"I am."

"I had to look at your driver's license because you refuse to tell me anything about yourself. I'm snooping around trying to find something, anything, to hold on to, so I don't feel like I'm wasting time with a stranger."

"I'm sorry —"

"Don't be sorry. Be honest." Tori taps her finger against the table. I liken it to a flickering flame moving down a wick set to an explosive that's primed to detonate. "I've got another one for you. Easy question," she says. "What did you like about me?"

"C'mon, Tori. You really want to do this right now? Here?"

"Yes," Tori says, joining her hands together on the table like a judge ready to hand down a sentence. "I drove here for an hour in the rain so you can end this thing with me, so yes, damn it. We're doing this."

"Fair enough."

"Tell me one thing you liked about me that doesn't have to do with the way I look or what we did in bed. Give me one honest thing I can hold on to."

I think a moment, knowing nothing I say will be received well and will only reveal my shortcomings as a man. I knew Tori wanted more than I could give, and I should have told her the truth: there wasn't any room for her in my world, and there never would be.

Tori stops tapping and says, "It's not that hard of a question, Finn —"

"I envy your life." I blurt out the words, and I know my honesty has either defused the bomb or guaranteed it to explode.

"What are you talking about?"

"It's like you don't have a care in the world. Nothing's holding you down. You do what you want. You go where you want."

My voice is spiked with resentment. "And no one will ever question if you're supposed to be there."

Tori relaxes her hands and brings them to her lap. "So, you envy me?" she asks in wild disbelief. "You think my life is perfect? Some crystal stair?"

"I know it's wrong, but I never truly saw you — not all of you, anyway, the complicated, complex parts. But you never saw me, either. I was a name, a face, a flimsy bio . . . an uncompelling profile on a hookup app."

"It wasn't that for me," she says.

"Are you sure?"

Tori bites her bottom lip, ruining her perfect lipstick. "Maybe at first, but things changed between us."

"When we're together, I get to pretend I'm like you," I say. "I get to test-drive that freedom. And it feels good. I crave it. And sometimes I like it so much that I confuse it for intimacy. I listen to you speak and I try to imagine what it's like . . . to live without worry."

"That's how you see me. Another privileged white girl?"

"You wanted something true. I gave it to you."

"No, you're right," she says, her voice choked with pain. "I guess it's my turn."

Tori draws in a deep breath and exhales slowly. The moment feels familiar, like when my mother told me she was dying. The long stillness, and when she finally spoke, the words *I have cancer* were deafening, instantly changing everything.

"Finn," Tori says, "I'm pregnant."

The sensation of suffocating comes over me. It's like all the oxygen in the room is being sucked out. I have to remind myself to breathe.

"Finn, are you going to pass out or something?" Tori waves her hand in my face trying to get me to snap out of it. "Say something."

"I need a moment to process this."

Tori takes a tissue from her purse and dabs her watering eyes. Even when she cries, her face is flawless.

"I guess I thought you were taking contraceptives."

Tori squeezes the bridge of her nose and closes her eyes. "I might have missed a day or two."

And I was too drunk on passion and wine to think about using protection — a perfect storm. How could we have been so stupid?

"In case you're wondering but too afraid to ask," she says, "you're the first man I've been with in over a year."

"I didn't know that."

"Of course you didn't," she says, dabbing her cheek. "How could you?"

I take Tori's hand. "I know this isn't easy for either of us, but —" I lean in closer and lower my voice. "What should we do?"

She pulls her hand into her lap. "We?" she asks. "Is there even a *we* in this situation?"

"Yes," I say. "I'd like to be a part of your decision. Whatever it is."

Tori pulls a pocket mirror from her purse and looks at herself, clearing the mascara smudges from under her eyes. "I don't know what I'm going to do, Finn. I just thought you should know."

"I know I don't have much of a say in this, but if you decide to have the baby, I want to help."

"Are you just saying that because you think that's what I want to hear?"

"No. I mean it."

"Because I know you better than you think, and I don't see you as a father."

"I'm telling you, I can provide."

"It's more than just giving financially. Will you be there when we need you? I don't know the first thing about raising a child, especially with a man who doesn't love me, and it terrifies me. I'm not even sure I'd want him or her to grow up in this country.

It's, like, black children face so much trauma here. I worry I couldn't protect our baby from the ugliness and the hate. Maybe that isn't new for you, but it's another world for me."

Tori might be right. I may not be father material for countless reasons. Children are a parent's hopes incarnate, and the thought of being a father is a new sensation — genuine and warm. I know, without question, I'd be a better father than Pop was to me. There would be no other way.

"Finn?" Tori says, looking at me wide-eyed. "Are you listening to me?"

"Yes. You're right. There is nothing about me that says I'd be a good father. For you to let me be a part of our child's life would mean putting complete faith in me. The only thing I have going for me is that I've never lied to you. So, when I say I'll be there and that I'd love our child no matter what, please know I'm telling the truth. Maybe our child wasn't conceived the way either of us would have liked, but it doesn't mean it's a mistake."

There's a clamor at the bar, and I turn to see people huddled together, watching a news broadcast on a flat-screen mounted on the wall. The chief of police and district attorney each stand in front of LAPD headquarters behind a podium filled with microphones.

The lower-third banner reads: LAPD Recruit Murder Suspect Identified, Charges Filed.

"What is it?" Tori asks, sounding concerned.

The chief says: "Today is not the finest hour for the Los Angeles Police Department. As police officers, our job is to serve this city with honor and integrity, and we failed to do that. Citizens should be proud of their police department, not afraid of or embarrassed by it. We have worked hard to build better relationships with the communities we serve. But it is disheartening to know that we have overlooked our own house. Brandon Soledad was one of ours, and he would have made a fine officer. This is why the following is difficult. The district attorney's office will be filing charges of first-degree murder against Officer Joey Garcia of the Los Angeles Police Academy's Physical Training Division. Since Officer Garcia is deceased, these charges will be filed posthumously. We urge the citizens of this city not to give up on our department. We are not your enemy. We are your neighbors, friends, family, and you mustn't lose faith in us . . . ."

There's a collective gasp in the restaurant, voices overtaking voices. Some people are visibly angry, banging their beer glasses against the marble counter. Others are apathetic, resigned to ordering more drinks and carrying on muted conversations. But anyone who remembers August 11, 1965, or April 29, 1992, knows how quickly life in the city can change.

"Finn, something's going on out there," Tori says, looking out the window.

I see a group of people dressed in black clothing and bandannas, carrying signs, pleas for justice, marching in the center of Flower Street. But behind those peaceful protestors is a smaller group without signs, faces covered in Halloween masks: crude depictions of Barack Obama, Ronald Reagan, Guy Fawkes, and Pennywise the clown. I'm reminded of the boys outside of headquarters who hurled rocks at my car. "Shit," I say, watching as Ronald Reagan takes a baseball bat to the windshield of a parked minivan. I watch two of the peaceful marchers plead with the masked disrupters to cease the destruction, but the vandalism continues.

A barrage of horns erupts as vehicles slow down and park against the curb to avoid the protesters and the group intent on detracting from their message. The procession passes the pub. Signs read BLACK LIVES MATTER and END THE POLICE STATE, and there are poster-size pictures of Brandon, likely downloaded from his social media accounts. Many protesters appear to be young. Though bandannas cover their mouths and sunglasses shield their eyes, they move like people disenfranchised and determined. People who have years ahead of them and want better. I know their anger — I live it. But if burning and looting commence, death and sorrow will surely fill the streets.

One person, hidden behind a Guy Fawkes mask, kicks over a garbage can, empties its contents, and with the help of the other culprit wearing a Barack Obama mask, throws it into the windshield of a parked car. It's beginning. Predation.

"You should get home," I say. "You don't want to get caught in this."

"I don't understand. Why is this happening — isn't the Garcia guy dead?"

"Garcia's death means nothing," I say. "This is about principles and the erosion of trust. The city may be veering to the point of no return, and if so, it's because its failures are what got us here." I help Tori out of her chair. "Where'd you park?"

"The lot in the back," she says.

"Let's go."

We leave the pub and walk around to the rear of the building. There's a break in the rain, and the rioters are taking advantage. A few have mounted car roofs and hunker down in truck beds. They spray-paint symbols and phrases like No POLICE STATE; NO JUSTICE, NO PEACE; and LAPD = MURDERERS. I can hear sirens in the distance. The officers will soon arrive in full riot gear: helmets with face guards, ballistic shields, tear gas, and OC spray.

When we reach Tori's car, the parking attendant's booth is vacant. Thankfully, Tori's Beetle isn't parked in tandem. She gets in, starts the engine, and lowers her window. "Be careful," she says.

"I will."

"Finn . . . I have a lot to think about . . . I want to believe you're a good man, but —"

"I understand, Tori."

Tori nods and then pulls out of the parking lot. I watch as she drives down Flower Street and makes a left turn, pushing into traffic.

I go back into the pub, where Melody has placed the old-fashioned on our table. I take the drink down fast — no use in wasting a thirteen-dollar cocktail. I put twenty dollars on the table and leave the restaurant.

By the time I get to my car, which is parked a block away, I'm soaked through with rain. I quickly get in the Mustang and head toward David Bergman's office. I now understand why Ms. Sugar gave me the recording. Justice for Brandon and Ruben will come only one way. It's the time for daylight; the citizens of Los Angeles deserve the truth.

Many people join the department not knowing its legacy. They join because it's one of the only jobs that pays over $50,000 a year without a college degree. And most recruits have no idea what they've acceded to. Some will never learn of the department's insidious truths — like how the first officers to patrol the city were Rebel soldiers, disaffected after the Confederates lost to the Union. Or of the tenure of Chief Jim "Two-Gun" Davis, who violated citizens' constitutional rights and civil liberties when he formed a fifty-man gun squad that killed suspected criminals in the streets. You won't find this history in the LAPD's museum. It would mean a police force acknowledging where it came from for the public to know these things. And to do that would mean admitting that its role in such brutalities as the Zoot Suit Riots and the bulldozing of

Chavez Ravine weren't just missteps but calculated measures to inflict harm on Angelenos. The time of department puff pieces in the local newspapers is over. It's time for attrition, time for the department to bare its soul and let the citizens decide its fate.

I drive down Broadway. People walk in front of the Mustang, ignoring the traffic signals. The sidewalks are crowded with people rushing to the train access and bus stops; they push and bump each other — anything to get home.

Bergman's office is in a tall building on West Seventh Street. I pull into an alley and park illegally. There's no point in worrying about the Mustang being towed. By now, parking enforcement has been called in for their safety, and soon armored trucks and SUVs carrying LAPD officers in riot gear will arrive to set a grid around the epicenter of the unrest. The department trains for days like this, and once the smoke clears, I'm certain there will be injuries and, possibly, fatalities.

I enter the lobby of the building and approach the security desk. The lobby is large, with two hallways that lead to elevators and a café that smells of fried food.

"Detective Finnegan to see David Bergman," I say, showing my police ID to the security guard.

"Is he expecting you?" the security guard asks. He's well-built with a buzzed head and diamond stud earrings in both ears.

"It was more of an open invitation."

"Mr. Bergman requires people to have appointments. I'll need to call for approval."

"Fine."

The security guard picks up a phone and dials a number on a large keypad. He waits while I stand dripping water on the marble floor.

"No answer. He could be busy," he says, nonchalant. "I can try again in a few minutes."

"There's no time for that. You see what's happening out there?"

"Is this like a police thing?"

"Son, you're trying my patience. You're hindering my investigation."

"I'm sorry, Officer. If I knew it was police business, I would have let you up. I'm all about the Blue. I'm trying to join up. Just took my written exam last week."

"It's 'detective.'"

"My bad, Detective," he says as he hits a button on a switchboard. "Elevator Three is all set for you. It'll take you right up."

"OK."

"The name's Manny. I mean, Manuel Lopez. Maybe I'll see you around a division one day?"

I take the elevator up to the thirty-fourth floor. When it opens, I'm met by two double doors with a plaque that reads DAVID BERGMAN, ESQ. When I enter Bergman's lobby, I'm greeted by a woman in her early twenties with an olive complexion wearing a striped, loose-fitting blouse and sitting behind a reception desk. "Can I help you?" she asks.

"I'm here to see David Bergman."

"Mr. Bergman is on a call. Did you have an appointment?"

"Not exactly."

"The security guard let you up?"

I show her my police ID.

"That's great, but you still need an appointment. And *clearly,* this isn't a criminal matter."

"Excuse me?"

"If it were, you would have shown me your badge. You can tell me what you want, and I can leave a message for Mr. Bergman."

"I can wait until he's free," I say.

"That isn't an option, Detective. I can take a message, but then you'll need to leave and come back when you have an appointment."

"It's not what you think. I'm a friend."

"You know how many cops try to get up here with the same line? Do you think you're the first?" she asks, putting on a headset connected to her phone. "Mr. Bergman has restraining orders on quite a few of you, and he has no problem adding to the list. I suggest you leave if you have any intention of keeping your job."

"Give me a break. Bergman knows me." I speak with assertion, but it can spell aggression for a black man. I soften my voice. "I'm just asking for you to call him so we can settle this."

"I'm calling security." Her hand moves to dial when she's interrupted by a man's voice.

"What's going on?" Bergman asks, entering from an office in a spotted suit, deeply wrinkled. I question if all his suits share the same affliction.

"This man doesn't have an appointment," the receptionist says. "I was just about to call Manny."

"No, that won't be necessary, Kimber." Bergman motions for her to cease making the call. "I know this man."

"Are you sure —"

"Yes, hold my calls."

"OK, Mr. Bergman," Kimber says, deliver-

415

ing a spiteful look in my direction.

I follow Bergman into a large conference room with panel windows that offer the city's spanning view. The Harbor Freeway below is congested with traffic, and police cars have blocked off the Seventh Street overpass.

"Have a seat," he says. "Can I get you water, tea, coffee?"

"No, thank you," I say, sitting down in a faux-leather office chair.

Bergman pulls a water bottle from a small refrigerator sitting on a table in the room's corner. You can tell a lot about a firm's revenue stream based on the brand of water they purchase. Bergman's water is decent — it's something that can be purchased in bulk from a discount warehouse. Fancier firms buy mineral water, and they serve it in glasses with lemon wedges and would charge me $500 to breathe their office's air.

"What can I do for you, Finn?"

"It's about the Brandon Soledad case. I need your help."

Bergman sits down in one of the faux-leather chairs, twists the cap off the water bottle, and takes a sip. "If you're asking for my help, things must be bad."

"LAPD is going to fire me."

"What grounds do they have to fire you?"

"As I told you before, my investigation hasn't been stellar. The department will find something to justify my removal. The reason won't matter. The real purpose will be to silence me."

"And why would they want to do that?"

"Because I know the real motive behind Brandon Soledad's murder and that Joey Garcia didn't act alone."

"I never bought the lover's triangle, but what evidence do you have to support your theory?"

I remove the disc from my jacket pocket, along with the flash drive containing all my evidentiary material, setting both on the table. "Brandon Soledad witnessed the murder of Ruben Montgomery, and he recorded it on his cell phone. He then downloaded it to this DVD."

Bergman sits up in his chair. I've got his full attention. "Go on."

"The video shows Officers Joey Garcia and Amanda Walsh kicking and beating the suspect beyond submission. Montgomery is later handcuffed and thrown into the patrol car. Brandon Soledad recognized Joey Garcia — one of his training officers. And I believe he confronted him. Together, Walsh and Garcia conspired to murder Brandon and dumped his remains in the Angeles

National Forest."

Bergman brings his fingers together to form a triangle and leans back in his chair. "Why didn't you go to your superiors with this?"

"It's in my report, but who knows where that will end up."

Bergman's brow furrows. He sighs. "And where's the body of this Montgomery?"

"I don't know, disposed of . . . I doubt we'd find any remains."

"And you're suggesting the department is willing to let a murderer in their ranks go free because it's an inconvenience to look deeper?"

"To go after Walsh would expose the department as inept, at best, and orchestrating a cover-up at worst."

"And IAB? You could have tipped them. I know detectives there who would have made careers off this. Hell, you could have blown the whistle yourself. There's more to this, isn't there?"

Bergman is no slouch. He's sharper than I expected, and that's a good thing. I'm going to need his wits. "I appear in the video," I say.

"You were present during Montgomery's assault?"

"For part of the assault, yes. Then I was

directed to leave with Walsh's partner, Castillo."

"Why was that?"

"I was a liability. Once Garcia realized Ruben was near death, he wanted me gone from the scene."

"So, why kill Ruben in the first place? Why not bring him in like any other collar?"

"I remember mostly everything about that night. The way charcoal smoke hung in the air. I can see Garcia, Boston, Castillo — and Ruben so clearly. Garcia's baton whistling with each blow and that wailing. It was a sound that petitioned death, called it out of the shadows. A hustler, a dealer, a killer — whatever type of person Garcia thought Ruben was, that night he and Boston beat him like he was trivial, a common insect. Maybe they didn't set out to kill him, but Garcia had more than just an anger management problem. Beating Ruben was an impulse, and Garcia knew no one would give a damn because people like Ruben don't matter, and I'm starting to believe they never will."

"You believe that's why Walsh didn't stop it?"

I rub my head with the same frustration and anger I felt that night. "I don't know. I've played that night over in my mind, and

I couldn't tell you why she did what she did. But shortly after that incident, she made detective and transferred to Forensics. I think she let the streets burn her out. That night she gave in to something that officers fight to keep suppressed — that yearning to do irreparable harm," I say, remembering my father and those nights he came home from patrol, seething, ready to pounce. "Some officers leave it on the streets; others drink until that feeling is gone. But then some bring it home to their spouses and kids. That night, Walsh worked it out on Ruben Montgomery. He was a suspected car thief. Who would miss him, right? But that's the thing. He had a mother who loved him, and he mattered to her."

Bergman nods, but I'm unsure if it's in agreement or if he's confirming his skepticism. "Are you familiar with antisocial personality disorder?"

Speaking the whole story aloud sounds like bad fiction, some mad delusion, but if Bergman doesn't believe me, maybe others won't, either. "Not really," I say.

"Well, that's the clinical term. You officers like to call those with the condition sociopaths. Law enforcement tends to attract those with this predisposition. However, some mental health professionals would say sociopathic officers come into their careers primed for corruption and abuses of power. And others suggest it's the environment that makes them that way. These officers see abuses of power that go unpunished, and in some cases, abuses are rewarded. They determine their best course of action is to behave in the same fashion."

"Are you suggesting I'm a sociopath?"

"No, I don't believe you are. Still, if Garcia and Walsh exhibited sociopathic, violent tendencies, they successfully managed to hide their mental conditions from detection during the psychological exam at hiring."

"You serious? It's two hundred multiple-choice questions and thirty minutes with the department shrink. As long as you don't say you like to torture animals or admit to any prejudices, you're good to go."

"I guess the question is, were Garcia and Walsh just bad apples, or is the whole barrel rotten?"

"Maybe it's a bit of both?"

Bergman gets up from his chair and begins to pace. "You aren't here out of completely altruistic reasons, are you? You want me to keep you from being prosecuted."

"I want justice for Brandon. I'll deal with

421

whatever comes of it."

"You do realize I don't practice criminal law anymore?"

"You were a prosecutor for ten years. I'm sure it's like riding a bike."

"For this to work, we have to trust each other. While you gave me the broad strokes of this *mishigas,* you omitted one thing: Do you want to tell me how you leveraged all this into making detective?"

"What?"

"Talk gets around; my ear stays pinned. Some have questioned your rather rapid promotion without having to cut your teeth in tougher divisions."

"If I answer, does this mean you'll represent me?"

Bergman stops pacing and looks at me. "Yes, I'm your attorney," he says without a second of reluctance.

"So, from this moment, the attorney-client privilege applies?"

"It does."

"All right, then. I affirmed Garcia's and Walsh's report. I kept my mouth shut about what I saw and validated that Ruben Montgomery eluded arrest by running away."

"Even though you never saw him flee, and by your account, he was immobilized and possibly near death?"

"Correct."

"And you told your superiors this?"

"I told them the last time I saw Ruben Montgomery, he was lying on the ground bleeding from his eyes. They said I needed to get my eyes checked and that two veteran officers said he fled, so that's what they believed. In exchange for my cooperation, I was fast-tracked to detective and assigned to the Robbery-Homicide Division."

"You do realize you could be prosecuted?"

"I understand."

"I'll seek immunity for your cooperation, but we're talking federal involvement. The Justice Department. The fallout could be monumental."

"I know."

"And you're prepared for that?"

"I am."

"OK, then."

"You aren't going to ask me why I didn't report Garcia and Walsh?"

"Detective Finnegan, as your attorney, I don't need to know your reasons, only the facts."

I rub an index finger against my temple. "Have you ever been so lost, but you just knew if you kept going, you'd find your way?"

"Once or twice."

"I thought cosigning that report would mean getting a seat at the table, that the sooner I joined the brass, the sooner I could work to make real change. Along the way, I lost sight of that, but I kept going, thinking I could find my way back. That was, until Brandon Soledad."

Bergman listens, seemingly without judgment or sympathy. Then, as if recognizing the commonness of my folly, he says, "Good intentions can often lead to disillusionment."

"I think you should hang on to the disc and flash drive," I say, pushing the items across the table to Bergman. "They'll be safer with you."

"I have a security safe, and only I have the key."

"And you may want to call it an early evening. Things aren't looking good out there."

"What's going on? Another broken water main?" Bergman looks out the window to see the commotion below. "My goodness."

"The department announced charges against Garcia today. You and your receptionist might want to leave before the officers set the grid and you have trouble getting out."

"I think that's a good idea."

"Thank you," I say, getting up and extending my hand for Bergman to shake. His grip is snug, and while his outward appearance may be in disarray, he knows the law and exudes confidence.

That puts me at ease.

I leave Bergman's office, and I take the elevator down to the lobby. Manny is on his cell phone. He seems worried, like bad news is on the other end. I walk past him and exit the building.

The rain has stopped, and officers are setting up blockades and ordering pedestrians off the streets. I round the building and head down the alley toward the Mustang. When I reach the end of the alley, I see a young man — possibly black or Latino — dressed in a ball cap, gloves, and sweatshirt. A black-and-white bandanna covers his mouth. He holds a crowbar high above his head and slams it against an ATM located outside a shuttered nightclub. At best, there are a few thousand dollars in it, and if the boy can get it open, it's a lucrative score.

I take my shield from my pocket and unholster my firearm and advance slowly. "LAPD. Drop the crowbar!"

The young man, startled, turns to face me and freezes.

425

"Put it down and step away from the ATM!"

He slowly lowers the crowbar to the ground.

"Keep your hands where I can see them and walk toward me, slowly."

He's small and slender, maybe in his late teens. His clothes are filthy and torn like he's been living on the streets. The closer he moves toward me, the better I can see his face — I confirm he's black, and there's terror in his eyes.

"You a real cop?" he asks.

"LAPD. Put your hands behind your back and interlace your fingers."

"Shit — please don't kill me, man," he says, looking afraid to move. "I'll never do it again."

"Do what I'm telling you," I say sternly. "Hands behind your back and interlace your fingers."

"I'm begging you, don't kill me." He reluctantly follows my command. "It wasn't my idea," he says. "Dee told me to do it."

"Turn around and walk backward toward my voice."

"Dee said I owed him. He said if I didn't get him the money, I'd have to work it off some other way."

"We can talk about that, but right now,

you need to do what I'm telling you."

He turns and begins to walk backward. I put my badge in my pocket and holster my weapon. I remove my handcuffs from their holder that's attached to my belt. As I reach for his wrists with my left hand, I feel a sharpness and then burning in my lower back.

I shout and nearly topple over from the pain. Then, I feel the sharpness again, but more profound than before. The discomfort of my broken ribs pales in comparison — this pain has eclipsed it. I struggle to keep my wits when I'm yanked backward and driven to the ground by my assailant. My head smacks against the concrete, and things go black.

When I open my eyes, standing over me are the young man and a larger, much older white man holding a long makeshift blade resembling an ice pick. A teardrop is tattooed under his right eye; a scar is drawn down the side of his face from temple to cheek.

"Dee, stop!" the slender teen shouts. "What the hell are you doing? He's a cop."

Dee isn't obscuring his face, and a prideful smile has settled across it. He readies the blade for another attack. "I don't give a fuck."

The young man gets between Dee and me. "You didn't say nothing about killing no cops. A dead cop — we don't need this shit."

Dee pushes the teen. The teen pushes back. "Slim, you crazy muthu-fucker!" Dee says, turning the blade on him. "Don't ever run up on me when I got a blade in my hand."

Slim stands firm. "I am not going to prison for no cop-killing!"

I can't think straight. Everything is a blur. I need my weapon. There's numbness below my waist. My hand moves to my hip, and I slowly take hold of the pistol's grip. Slim spins to face me and takes hold of Dee's shoulder. "C'mon!" he says. "Before he shoots both of us." To pull my weapon feels like a herculean act. Have I lost coordination? Is it nerve damage? Before I can unscramble my thoughts, Dee and Slim flee down the alleyway.

The wound in my back feels like a deep puncture. I'm losing a lot of blood.

After two tries, I manage to pull my cell phone from my pocket and dial 911.

"Nine-One-One operator. What is your emergency?" the voice is female and clinical.

"Officer down. I'm requesting an RA at

428

the south end of an alleyway adjacent to 1022 West Seventh Street. Be advised, suspects possibly in the vicinity. Two males: one black, late teens or early twenties, the other white, mid to late forties with facial tattoos. They fled on foot."

The phone, slick from water and blood, slips from my hand and topples to the ground.

There is tingling, followed by more numbness, isolated in my left leg. Things are happening in my body that I don't understand. Dee's blade has done significant harm. Blood steadily flows from my wound, my body cooling.

It's hard to stay awake.

I hear sirens closing in and the footsteps of the officers running over from the Seventh Street overpass. It won't be long now. An ambulance will be here soon, and I'll be treated and back on my feet in no time. I know everything will be fine. It has to be . . .

And maybe in a few weeks, after I've recovered, I'll take Sarada away to New York, Paris, or the French countryside. We can spend our days in galleries and evenings making love in a chateau. I'll tell Sarada about the baby, and she'll understand. Maybe she'll be mad for some time, but she'll understand. And Tori will design a nursery for our baby, and I'll help her paint, and we'll assemble the crib and rocking chair. And I'll sit with my father as he tells stories of old LA, and we can look through the family photo albums over beers, remembering Mom and pining over her excellent cooking and conversation.

Mom? I swear I can hear my mother's voice, faint and distant, calling. Everything around me darkens. The air tastes like copper.

Is this it? Is this death? Has it finally come? It's always been circling, a buzzard soaring high above me as if I were a wounded critter soon to expire on a highway sizzling in the sun.

No — it can't be. I can't die like this. Not in this godforsaken alley.

This can't be how my story ends.

Please, God, this can't be how my story ends.

CHAPTER SIXTEEN

December 2014

On days like this, when my self-loathing is heaviest, a blanket of despair I can't get out from under, Sarada drops me off at my father's place before she goes to work at the bakery. She doesn't like to leave me alone, even though I tell her I'm fine. She worries I haven't healed completely, and she's right, despite what the doctors have said. Only, it isn't my body that still needs mending. My mind is shot. I can't seem to focus on anything for longer than five minutes. I don't sleep much, and when I do, I often awake from nightmares and reach for an imaginary pistol. Sometimes Brandon comes to me in my dreams, standing under the light of an empty street, looking at me with tortured eyes, white pupils sunken in black. He doesn't speak; he just watches me with those eyes like he can read my thoughts. And those thoughts are always on

431

my failures and how I let him down.

When I think of the Soledad investigation and my life before Dee's blade, it feels like scenes from a life that isn't mine. My father doesn't talk about the LAPD, my investigation or stabbing, or his Black Lives Matter involvement, so there isn't much we say to each other. I know he's disappointed in me, maybe even ashamed. He stopped watching the news cycle after Ruben Montgomery's assault footage seemed to play on an endless loop. It's strange, but I miss our philosophical disagreements. Now my father treats me delicately, which only expands the distance between us. Shantelle stopped cleaning his house and spending time with him. She told him that I disgusted her and that she couldn't be with a man who raised such a despicable human being. I had humiliated and shamed our people — black people, that is.

Shortly after their breakup, he stopped going to rallies. The most he's said to me in months was, "You see the news? They caught the asshole who stabbed you." He turned on the TV, flipped to the news, and dropped the remote on the coffee table. The news anchor said Daniel "Dee" Cunningham and Martin "Slim" Jones were apprehended and charged with second-degree attempted murder of a peace officer. "Hope they rot," Pop said before taking a beer from the fridge and walking back into his bedroom, leaving me on the couch alone.

Pop resents me, of this I'm certain, but my therapist, Dr. Angell, suggested he also blames himself for my becoming a police officer. The department was a gateway to suffering, sacrificing my mind and body . . . and for what? The LAPD has been silent. No flowers. No fruit baskets or "get well" cards. All I have to show for my years of service are a suspension and a union rep who doesn't return my phone calls.

Sarada picks me up from my father's condo in the evening, around six o'clock. Even though it's a long drive from her shop and traffic can be taxing, she never complains. I know Sarada's love is real, which I'm thankful for. We share a quaint two-bedroom town house in Hancock Park that overflows with natural light throughout the day. Sarada has a love for bright colors and classical artwork — watercolors and oiled landscapes are strategically placed in each room, and her furniture is upholstered in warm yellows and blues. My favorite piece of furniture is a chair of modern design — turquoise with a high back. When I was walking with a cane, I thought I would never be able to stand on my own, walk over to the chair, and sit down on its plush cushion like I could have done months before. Some days, I couldn't imagine life without a cane. I hobbled around the town house, looking for anything to keep my mind off my plight.

I worked hard in physical therapy, which was twice a week and every Saturday. It incorporated walking with assistance, massages, and ice baths when I refused to use the cryo chamber. When I finally was able to walk on my own, I paced around the town house studying Sarada's artwork and photographs as if I were in a gallery, noting the use of color and perspective. I was reconnecting with a passion I had long forgotten. Sarada bought me a small acrylic paint set and brushes. "I think it'll help take your mind off things," she said, setting the tubes of paint and brushes on the table and pulling a pack of canvas boards from the shopping bag.

On days I can't endure my father's silent treatment, I remain at home and pass the time painting still lifes of items I find around the house. Bold renderings of teacups, apples, grapes, Sarada's sunglasses, loaves of bread, jars of peanut butter.

Most evenings, I join Sarada for walks

after dinner. However, I tire easily because of my hip buckle, which tends to be sore after thirty minutes, a side effect of the surgery needed to repair the muscle tissue in my back. The surgeon said I was lucky: a few centimeters to the right, and the blade would have penetrated my spinal column. I could have lost feeling permanently in my legs. I don't know what lucky is supposed to feel like, but I take comfort in knowing it could have been much worse. That doesn't stop me from feeling what Dr. Angell calls malaise, a fancy word for the sense of drowning that keeps me in bed for days or affixed in the turquoise chair, staring at Sarada's painting of a flowering desert cactus. On those days, I sink into depression, remembering my assault in the alley. Pills help elevate my mood and keep me somewhat pleasant, but I refuse to take the painkillers for my hip, opting for three ibuprofen tablets an hour instead.

I haven't heard from Tori for some time. She stopped taking my calls when footage of Ruben's beating aired on television. Shortly after, her number stopped working. I'm confident I could find her. Maybe she's in LA, in Orange County with her family, or living out of state. But I know she doesn't want anything to do with me.

I've considered telling Sarada about Tori being pregnant, but I talk myself out of it each time. Could it put undue strain on our relationship? I can't keep piling more drama on Sarada and expect her to stay by my side. Besides, I don't know Tori's intentions. She could have already ended the pregnancy, or maybe she wants me to stay away, never to lay eyes on my child. When I think about not meeting my child and the other unfortunate happenings in my life, I find myself back in the turquoise chair, trying to determine when things went so wrong. Was it when I hurt Claudio Spirelli? Or the day I entered the academy?

Would life have been different if I'd graduated from CalArts and pursued art? Would Sarada and I still fall in love? Would we be living in New York or Paris? Would we be happy? I know there's no use in wishing for things to be different. Nothing can be undone. The department stripped me of my badge and weapon. One early morning, Sarada and I were awakened by a tow truck that came to reclaim the Mustang from the driveway. The car that had been my shop, my office, was taken away on a flatbed.

My career was over.

CHAPTER SEVENTEEN

January 2015

It's early morning, and there's a chill in the air. Winters in Los Angeles are mild compared to the majority of the country, but the recent weather has had an unusual bite.

I've been standing outside Sarada's town house for fifteen minutes, waiting on a stranger to pick me up. The app on my cell phone says the driver's name is Mark, and he'll be arriving in a black hybrid. The idea of getting into a car with a person I've never met and trusting them to take me where I need to go is unsettling. If it weren't for my hip spasms, I would drive myself. My cell phone chimes, alerting me that Mark will arrive soon.

In Hancock Park, the sanctity of my personal space is never compromised. Joggers, walkers, and mothers pushing strollers would rather cross the street than pass me on the sidewalk. On two occasions, a black-

and-white slowed down so the officers inside could size me up, only driving past once they were satisfied that I didn't pose a danger. I suppose I had forgotten that feeling of vulnerability. I had put so much stock in the badge, believing it granted me liberties and protection. I convinced myself I was different, that being a police officer inoculated me against the tribulations of blackness.

The hybrid pulls along the curb. The window lowers, and Mark, a young black man, says, "Are you Trevor?"

"Yes."

"Hop in."

I open the rear passenger-side door and climb into the back seat.

"Going downtown, right?" Mark asks.

"Yes, Seventh Street."

"We may have to take a few side streets. Parts of Seventh are still being cleaned up."

"Cleaned up?" I ask.

"The rioters spray-painted everywhere, and the city has just about removed it all, but they tagged some areas pretty bad, and it's taken a while. I don't notice it much anymore. Downtown has always been kind of a shithole."

The car eases forward, accelerating slowly. It's my first time riding in a hybrid; not hearing the engine hum makes me anxious.

I miss the rumble of the Mustang.

I don't speak for most of the ride. Mark talks about how bad LA traffic has gotten and that he's considering returning to Washington State, but of course, the rain is a "bummer," as he puts it. I nod a few times, so Mark thinks I'm listening, but after ten minutes of traffic on the 405, I decide to rest my eyes, not because I trust Mark's driving but because the drone of his voice is like a clicking metronome. I can just focus on the sound and not have to think too hard.

When I open my eyes, we're traveling on Grand Avenue, near Seventh Street. Mark wasn't exaggerating. Buildings have been sprayed in yellow and red paint. I recognize the anarchist symbol but nothing else. Most of it looks like gang graffiti and odd glyphs that incorporate arrows and numbers.

Mark notices me looking. "Pretty wild, huh? They say the rioters marked businesses they said were contributing to the economic inequalities in the city."

"They spray-painted gas station pumps."

"I'm just saying what I heard."

"I thought they were protesting the death of Brandon Soledad?"

"The rookie?"

"He wasn't sworn, but yeah, him."

"Maybe it started that way, but it went zero to one hundred real quick. I'm talking torched cars. Cops were getting bottles and rocks thrown at them. I even heard a cop got stabbed. Shit was insane."

"You can pull up on the right," I say. Mark parks alongside the curb in front of Bergman's building. He was right about the street; it's been recently paved, and the sidewalk is freshly power washed. The concrete varies in shading; some sidewalks are still tarnished with dirt, grime, and paint while other sections are bleached white.

"You good?" Mark asks.

"Thanks," I say, getting out of the car and closing the door behind me. Mark flashes a peace sign in the rearview mirror and drives away.

I was worried that returning to Bergman's office might be triggering, but I have no choice. Bergman is likely the only one who knows what the hell is going on. I'm tired of being in the dark. Sarada and my father handle me like glass and evade my questions. I need to know things: Did the department suspend me because of the Soledad case or something else? Why didn't my union rep advocate on my behalf, and why doesn't she return my calls after I've left messages? And the question that I most want to be answered is: Where is Amanda "Boston" Walsh, and why isn't she rotting in a prison cell?

I enter the lobby, and Manny greets me. He does a double take and then asks, "That you, Detective?"

"Reports of my death were greatly exaggerated."

"Damn," he says. "I saw them load you into the ambulance. You weren't looking too good. Some punk really stab you?"

"Yes."

"Damn junkies. You should have shot their asses."

Manny isn't the first to suggest that not shooting Slim and Dee seemed a departure from my police training. "I guess I couldn't get the shot off," I say. "It happens."

"Hopefully never to me," he says.

"You think I can go up to see Bergman?"

"Appointment?"

"No."

Manny pauses and then shrugs. "Yeah, fuck it. I'm out of here in a few weeks, anyway."

"You got a new job?"

"I'm entering the academy next month."

"Well, shit," I say, extending my hand for Manny to shake. "Congratulations."

Manny has a strong grip and large hands that should make holding a pistol a breeze. "Thanks. Any tips you can give me?"

I hesitate, debating how forthcoming to be. "Remember," I say, "it's just a job."

Manny nods. I feel like some old-timer with twenty years under his belt and wisdom to spare. He calls the elevator. "It'll be the first one on the left," he says.

I ride the elevator to Bergman's floor and enter the office's lobby, where Kimber sits looking at a computer screen. I'm still unsure if she's his receptionist, assistant, or paralegal, but she knows the law and seems to be a true believer in Bergman's cause.

Kimber looks at me; her face doesn't hide her disappointment. "You," she says, accusatory as if my presence constitutes a crime.

"I don't have an appointment. We can skip the perfunctory dance. I'd like to speak to my attorney."

"I'll see if he's free." She picks up a phone that must be a direct line to Bergman's office. "Mr. Finnegan is here to see you," she says. She listens for a moment and hangs up. "You can have a seat."

I opt to stand. My hip is tight from sitting in Mark's car for an hour, and standing is good for the tendons.

Bergman appears from his office and

walks with zeal, greeting me warmly. "Mr. Finnegan, so good to see you," he says, extending his hand and drawing me in for a hug. It's odd since I don't recall us being so close, but it beats Kimber's contempt. "It's nice to see you back on your feet. I came to see you in the hospital a few times. You probably don't remember."

"I was pretty out of it," I say.

"I was glad when your father told me you would be released. How is he?"

"You haven't spoken to him?"

"Not in a month or more."

"He seems all right, but I was hoping you could help me make sense out of a few things."

"Let's take this to my office." I follow him down a hallway lined with bland corporate art and into a large room with a desk, a circular table, and chairs. Bergman leans against the front of his desk and crosses his arms, shifting nervously. "So, what brings you by?" he asks.

"Are you still my attorney?"

"I am."

"Good. So that hasn't changed."

"No."

"Because I'm beginning to think I hit my head on that concrete a lot harder than I remember. No one is telling me anything about anything."

"Your family didn't want me speaking to you until you healed," he says. "They're concerned about your well-being, that's all."

"I need to know what happened while I was in the hospital. Where's the disc I gave you? Did you give it to the Department of Justice?"

"I did —"

"So, where's Walsh? There's no mention of her in the news or anything. Please tell me she's sitting in a cell somewhere."

"No. Walsh was tipped off. Law enforcement isn't sure where she is. She may be on the East Coast — Boston or Philadelphia. Your family was worried she might even go after you."

"She isn't that stupid."

"Maybe, but she's proven to be dangerous. She's currently sitting at the top of the FBI's Most Wanted. Agents are surveilling her wife, in case she tries to make contact."

"Waste of time. Walsh knows better than that. Tell me, did any good come out of this? I can't walk normal or keep my thoughts straight half the time, and I just need to know it was for something."

"Brandon's recording made quite an impact. The Justice Department is investigating the LAPD, and there's talk about another consent decree. There were terminations and resignations of captains, deputy chiefs, and commanders. Everyone who helped cover up Ruben Montgomery's disappearance." Bergman relaxes his arms and takes a seat at his desk. "It was a purge."

"What about all the cases Walsh worked? She could have been planting evidence this whole time."

"The FBI put together a task force that's reviewing her entire case log, going back years. People she helped send to prison have filed appeals to seek new trials. Brandon Soledad's mother has filed the largest civil suit in the city's history, along with suits filed by Ms. Montgomery and other plaintiffs who claim Walsh violated their civil rights."

"And what does all this mean for me?"

"We were unable to prevent your suspension. As you suggested, there were numerous failures in departmental procedure on your part, specifically, the arrest of Jocy Garcia. Due to the altercation in the alley with the two assailants, your physical condition would likely prohibit you from working in a law enforcement capacity. They will move to terminate you, and when they do, I will file a wrongful termination suit."

"So, it's what I thought. I can't be a police

officer again."

"No."

"Give it to me straight, Bergman," I say. "I falsified my report. I need to know if I'm looking at time."

"Not likely. Your investigation started something. New legislation is being written. And I let all parties know you will fully co-operate pending immunity. So far, they've shown no interest in going after you. It seems the LAPD wants you forgotten. You came out of this clean, considering."

"I don't feel clean," I say, pounding my fist on the table. "What am I supposed to do for money? I've got nothing."

"You have skills, Mr. Finnegan. That means you can be useful."

"To whom?"

"Have you considered there are others like Walsh and Garcia?"

"Sure. Of course," I say, taking a seat in an armchair when I feel an impending hip spasm. "There's a decent number of shitty cops."

"In the wake of these revelations brought about by your investigation, my office set up a tip line — it's more of an email on a server with very tight security. People don't trust the police are taking their officer complaints seriously, so they're turning to us."

"You really have it out for us, don't you?"

"Us?" Bergman poses the question with a slight air of cynicism. "The department is going to fire you for doing your job and telling the truth. I have no desire to see good cops punished, but if the LAPD isn't going to police themselves, then who will?"

"OK. So, what do you need from me?"

"Your expertise. We receive nearly one hundred complaints a day about officer misconduct. Many reports are anonymous, but some aren't. Things like sexual assault, battery, stalking, kidnapping. I could use insight. You know how officers think, how they operate."

"You're offering me a job?"

"Just a few hours a day reading emails. You would be determining which allegations we should look into."

"Bergman, I'm not sure I could do it if I wanted to. Something happened to me in that alley. I'm not the same. Things get fuzzy for me now. I can't always focus."

"I'm asking for your instincts, that's all. You read through the emails, and if something piques your interest, you let me know."

"I don't know . . ."

"I'll pay you seven hundred dollars a

week, cash."

"For reading emails? That's it?"

"That's it."

I can't expect Sarada to carry me when my savings run out. I need to work and pull my weight. Maybe the job will do my head some good. I can treat it like rehab for my brain. If physical therapy worked for my back and legs, reading a few emails might boost my recovery, and I can get back to my old self.

"OK," I say. "I'll do it."

"Good. You can start next week. I'll have Kimber provide you with a laptop and cell phone. Care for a drink?"

"Depends what you're pouring."

Bergman removes a bottle of top-shelf brandy from a cabinet, along with two tumblers. "This is cause for celebration," he says, pouring the liquor. He slides a half-full glass over. "Cheers." He simpers as he knocks his glass into mine.

I take a sip. I can't remember the last time I had a drink. The doctor had advised against it — something about mixing mood pills with alcohol could be dangerous for my heart. But the way I feel, I don't think the mood pills will be necessary much longer. I'm employed again, but I didn't take the job solely because of my dwindling cash flow.

"I'll have Kimber get you what you need," Bergman says before leaving the room.

I take another sip and look out the window over the city, watching as traffic drones along for nearly ten minutes, when Kimber enters the room and places a laptop bag and cell phone on the desk. "Here you go," she says. "I guess you're working with us now?"

"That's right."

Kimber's face is sour like she's sucked on a lemon. "David is very trusting. He can't help it," she says, "but I know about you — the vile things you've done. I don't trust you."

I don't respond to her, and after a few seconds of silence, she leaves. Bergman's crusade has its acolyte.

"So, it's settled," Bergman says, sailing into the office with folders tucked under his arm. "You've got everything you need?"

"I do."

"Good."

We shake hands, and I wonder what price I'll pay for working with Bergman. If word gets out that I'm helping him, it means I'm out in the cold. Even if I recover enough to be cleared for full duty as a cop, what department would have me? I'm damaged goods, and now, I'll be working to take offi-

cers off the job — albeit suspected dirty officers, but officers nonetheless.

"I believe we're going to do great things
together," Bergman says. "I've always
thought out of life's many stages, it's the
second act that's the most thrilling."

"There is one thing I'd like you to help
me with."

"Name it."

"I want to find Walsh."

"I think the feds have it handled," Bergman says, maintaining his nicety. "No offense, but it is the FBI we're talking about.
What makes you think you have a better
shot at finding her?"

I finish the glass of brandy. "I know her.
Boston will reveal herself."

"And what will you do?"

"I don't know yet. It might not be by the
book."

"You mean legal?"

"That's what I have you for. You'll be sure
all the t's are crossed."

I arrive at the town house in Hancock Park
in the evening with the laptop bag hung over
my shoulder and mild soreness in my hip;
it's bearable but annoying. The traffic leaving Bergman's office was stagnant due to an
accident on the 101 freeway, and unlike

Mark, the driver the app sent me was new to Los Angeles and drove like a tourist.

As I walk toward the entryway, Sarada meets me at the door. She's dressed like she's come from work, her clothes dusted with flour and her hair wrapped in a scarf. "I didn't know you were going out today," she says, intrigued.

"I went to see Bergman."

"Really?"

"I needed answers."

"This has to do with LAPD?"

"Yes."

Sarada sighs. "I was going to tell you about Walsh once you got better."

"It's fine, Sarada."

"Did you get what you needed from Bergman?"

"I think so. I got enough, anyway."

"So, what's with the laptop?"

"I got a job today. And it pays cash."

"Are you serious? Doing what?"

"Consulting on cases for Bergman."

"And he just offered you the job out of the blue?"

"He said he could use someone like me, a person with my expertise."

"Wow. OK."

"I think it'll be good for me."

"It's great, Trevor . . . it is. But just ease

451

into it, you know? Pace yourself."

I'll be wise to heed Sarada's warning, but I'm eager to get busy — back in the thick of things. "I will, I promise," I say.

"Let's go inside," she says, turning to the door.

"Wait," I say, taking her by the hand.

"Yes?"

"Sarada, how are you so sure about me?"

"What do you mean?"

"There are things you should know . . . things I've done."

"You're talking about Ruben Montgomery? Trevor, I don't blame you, and you have to stop beating yourself up about it."

"There's more to the story. It's how I became a detective."

Sarada slips her hand from my palm, looks me in the eyes, and cups her hands around my face. "I'll promise you this — there is nothing you can say that will make me love you any less. You understand me?"

"I do."

Sarada takes me by the hand, and we go inside. We sit at the dining table eating mini loaves of sweet pound cakes — chocolate, red velvet, lemon crème — and drink coffee. I tell her about the deal I made with the brass, corroborating Garcia's and Boston's reports in exchange for a detective spot. I tell her how I loved her before I knew what love was. How in my household love died with my mother, and Pop didn't know how to fill the hole she left. I explain how hurting Claudio Spirelli didn't make all the pain from that night go away but sent me down a swarthy path. She listens as I pour out more truths than I knew I had in me. We finish a half dozen mini cakes and an entire pot of coffee, and then we sit in silence. All I told Sarada seems to ruminate behind her eyes, and for a moment, I'm convinced I made a mistake in unburdening myself.

Sarada stands up from her chair and walks over to me, placing her hand on my shoulder. I close my eyes and imagine what comes next.

Unable to stand the silence any longer, I say, "So?"

There's a long pause, then she says, "You coming?"

I open my eyes to see Sarada heading upstairs with a sway I can only describe as a walk in verse. I feel tender, vulnerable as boyhood, as I watch her float up the stairs.

Pop once told me, after we had committed my mother's remains to the ground, that a man's life is measured in pain, and that if I were to live well, I should do all I can to keep from having to feel the pain he felt that day. He was an awful husband, but I understand his sorrow if he felt half of what I feel for Sarada Joi Rao.

I rise from the chair and turn off the dining room light. A soft glow cascades down the staircase, leading to our bedroom. I head toward the stairs in mourning, stripped of purpose and frightened of the unknown. As I stand at the foot of the stairs, a tear grows in the corner of my eye. I wipe it clean, knowing that Detective Trevor "Finn" Finnegan is gone.

The early-morning air is brisk — a cold, dry wind blows, feels like needles pricking my cheeks. These days, it's a sin to be up before sunrise. I get into Sarada's Mercedes. She starts the engine, switches on the defroster. Warm air steams the frosty windshield.

"It's Saturday," I say, fastening my seat belt. "What happened to sleeping in?"

"I told you, it's for a good cause," she says, tuning the radio to R & B. "Sit back and relax."

Sarada is wearing faded jeans, a hooded USC sweatshirt, and sneakers. She didn't bother with makeup or styling her hair this morning, which is typical if she's going to exercise or participate in a beach cleanup with her bakery staff. She told me to dress comfortably, which means track pants, a sweatshirt, and a pair of old running shoes that I probably should throw away.

"You really won't tell me where we're going?"

"Nope." She pulls out of her parking spot and exits the gated complex onto Wilshire.

The clock on the dash reads 5:15 a.m. The last time I was up at this hour and expected to be alert, I was a police detective. Working for Bergman means I get to the office around nine o'clock. Most mornings, Kimber brings bagels. When I arrive, they're usually cold, boxed on a table in the break room. She's hawkish about the food, making a point to tell me it's intended for clients before staff.

We drive from Hancock Park into the Wilshire district. Traffic is light. The city's slow, quiet before the midmorning rush. When I'm not distracted by the reflection of the streetlamps bouncing across the windshield, I notice the carefree joggers and bikers confidently moving down the boulevard.

Sarada hums along to a song I've never heard and looks at me, my head resting against the window. She smiles like a child with a secret she's ready to spill. "How far we headed?" I ask.

"Not far. Twenty minutes, probably."

We merge onto the 10 East from Hauser Boulevard. Sarada accelerates, the gears shift, and we drive the fast lane to the 110 South freeway. The lanes are open. The Mercedes whispers at 80 mph.

"Almost there," she says, exiting onto El Segundo.

Unlike in Hancock Park, people rarely jog in South LA. The sidewalks are too chaotic. For blocks, people peddle goods — art, clothes, bean pies — while the homeless camp in tents, keeping watch over shopping carts full of belongings.

We stop at a red light at El Segundo and Broadway. I watch a police officer, a young white man on a foot beat, weave between the tents and clutter. He takes his baton and taps the foot of a man who looks to be asleep on the sidewalk. When the man doesn't move, he taps his foot again and seems to shout at him. I can't hear what he says, but it doesn't matter. The man isn't moving. The officer pulls his radio from his belt and calls, then summons his partner, who's a few feet away.

Sarada drives another two blocks before pulling into the Holy Assembly Church of

God — the Barbecue Church. She parks in a spot along an iron fence. "What are we doing here, Sarada?"

"Look," she says, pointing to a group of people gathered around scaffolding. I can see the outline of a large mural on the church's wall behind them.

"I don't understand," I say.

"A group of artists and LAPD officers organized this with the church. Brandon wasn't a member, but apparently black officers treat this place as hallowed ground. They thought it was where they should remember him, and the pastor agreed."

"They're painting a mural of Brandon?"

"More of a memorial, but yes, a mural. I thought you could help."

There's a fluttering in my chest. I haven't set foot here in some time or painted anything larger than an eight-by-eleven-inch canvas. I watch people young and old of all shades eating from paper plates, gathered around a table of food — pancakes, biscuits, sausage, bacon. Gospel music plays from a boom box.

"So?" she says. "You want to get out and at least look at it?"

I'm hesitant, but Sarada's taken the time to drive me down here, and I'll feel guilty if I don't have a look at the progress. "All right," I say. We get out of the car, and I gaze at the wall. It looks over ten feet. Brandon's likeness is sketched in yellow and brown paint over a white background. He's standing proudly, wearing a uniform he was never given, along with a badge.

"What do you think so far?" she asks.

It's a beautiful dream. The closest thing to immortality. "How many artists are working on this?"

"Five, maybe six," she says. "And a few officers are here to lend a hand."

I notice off-duty officers, some I've come to know over the years, watching artists mix large vats of paint. "I don't know about this," I say. "What if they don't want me here?"

"You're fine," Sarada says, taking me by the hand. "It's where you belong."

We begin walking toward the group. I hold my breath. A black officer, a petite woman with long, flowing braids, hands me a paintbrush and greets me like kinfolk. Sarada smiles knowingly.

I exhale, smitten by a forgotten feeling. One I haven't known since childhood with my mother . . .

Mercy.

ACKNOWLEDGMENTS

There have been many people who have helped get me to this point in my writing career. I suppose I should begin with my parents, who encouraged my creativity at an early age. My father helped fuel it with weekend trips to the comic-book store, and my mother bought me art supplies and stored many of my writings, paintings, and drawings in a memory box for safekeeping. Their love has always been a safety net. Even in difficult times, when I was unsure which path to take, I knew I had their love and support.

I want to thank my agent, Gina Panettieri, for her unshakable confidence in *Under Color of Law* and me as a writer. And thank you to the editorial team at Thomas & Mercer for listening and working to preserve my vision throughout the publishing process.

Writers and publishers along the way gave me guidance, support, and a home for my novels: Gar Anthony Haywood, Gary Phillips, the late Lewis MacAdams, Jon Bassoff, Ron Earl Phillips, Eric Beetner, and James Sallis.

I want to thank my wife for her patience and understanding. I couldn't have gotten this far without her being in my corner. A hearty thanks to my sister, aunts, uncles, and cousins who are unwavering in their support and never hesitate to spread the word when a book is released into the world.

Lastly, a very special thanks to my late uncle, Stephen T. Clark (retired LAPD), whom I learned to understand better by and by. And respect and admiration to the countless black law enforcement officers who are striving to make their communities better. Wearing the badge doesn't mean you don't stand with us . . .

READING GROUP DISCUSSION QUESTIONS

1. Los Angeles isn't just the setting for *Under Color of Law;* it's a pivotal character. How does the city of LA play a role in the narrative and contribute to its social and cultural context?
2. How does Trevor's relationship with his father influence his professional and personal life throughout the novel?
3. Trevor and Sarada have a complicated relationship born from a tragedy. How has their relationship evolved since Sarada's assault?
4. The novel depicts the LAPD police academy as paramilitary. Do you believe paramilitary training aligns with or contradicts community policing strategies?
5. How do police killings of unarmed black men such as Eric Garner inform the narrative? In what ways do these killings influence characters' decisions and worldviews throughout the novel?

6. Trevor faces many conflicts within his department. Do you think Trevor's actions and attitude contribute to his negative standing in the LAPD?

7. What significance does the Barbecue Church hold in Trevor's life? How does the church reflect Trevor's view of the black community?

8. Trevor often wrestles with morality and doing the right thing. How do his views of integrity and justice evolve throughout the story?

9. In chapter 15, after Dee stabs Trevor in the alley, Trevor doesn't pull his gun but manages to pull his cell phone from his pocket to call for help. Are there other factors besides his physical injuries that contribute to Trevor being unable to shoot his attackers?

10. In the epigraphs that open the book, what function do the quoted LAPD mission statement and the Department of Justice's definition of "under color of law" serve?

11. Trevor struggles with his identity from a young age. How do Trevor's feelings of alienation shape him from youth into adulthood?

12. How does Trevor view the badge? What privileges does he believe it allows him?

How does his view of the badge differ from Beckett's and Pop's?

13. Race is often at the forefront of police encounters. What scenes in the novel support this idea?

14. Trevor comes from an art world. How does his training as an artist assist him in his detective role?

15. Compare and contrast Trevor and Brandon. What are some of their similarities and differences?

16. Pop expresses that his Black Lives Matter involvement is rooted in his desire to atone for actions he carried out as a police officer. What other characters in the novel long for atonement?

17. In the school locker room, Trevor strikes Chasen, and he later assaults Claudio Spirelli with a metal pipe. How does Trevor justify these actions? What might these altercations reveal about his character and sense of justice?

18. Do you believe Trevor's view of law enforcement has changed by the end of the novel?

19. Does the novel suggest a hopeful future for Trevor and Sarada?

20. Trevor says he'd be a better father to his and Tori's baby than Pop was to him.

Considering what you know about Trevor, do you agree or disagree?

ABOUT THE AUTHOR

Aaron Philip Clark is a novelist and screenwriter from Los Angeles. In addition to his writing career, he has worked in the film industry, in higher education, and in law enforcement. For more information, visit www.aaronphilipclark.com.

The employees of Thorndike Press hope you have enjoyed this Large Print book. All our Thorndike, Wheeler, and Kennebec Large Print titles are designed for easy reading, and all our books are made to last. Other Thorndike Press Large Print books are available at your library, through selected bookstores, or directly from us.

For information about titles, please call:
(800) 223-1244

or visit our website at:
gale.com/thorndike

To share your comments, please write:
Publisher
Thorndike Press
10 Water St., Suite 310
Waterville, ME 04901